It's Different This Time

DELL
NEW YORK

It's Different This Time

JOSS RICHARD

Dell
An imprint of Random House
A division of Penguin Random House LLC
1745 Broadway, New York, NY 10019
randomhousebooks.com
penguinrandomhouse.com

A Dell Trade Paperback Original

ISBN 979-8-217-09365-6
Ebook ISBN 979-8-217-09366-3

Printed in the United States of America on acid-free paper

4th Printing

BOOK TEAM: Production editor: Annette Szlachta-McGinn • Managing editor: Saige Francis • Production manager: Meghan O'Leary • Copy editors: Tom Cherwin, Beth Pearson • Proofreaders: Caitlin Van Dusen, Jennifer Abella, Nicole Ramirez

Book design by Kim Henze Walker
Title-spread art: Mykola Syvak/Adobe Stock

The authorized representative in the EU for product safety and compliance is Penguin Random House Ireland, Morrison Chambers, 32 Nassau Street, Dublin D02 YH68, Ireland. https://eu-contact.penguin.ie

Jack and Janet, this one's for you

It's Different This Time

Chapter 1

"THE SHOW'S NOT GETTING RENEWED." THEO'S VOICE INTERrupts my thoughts.

My eyes cut to the time on the car dashboard, which reads 8:27 A.M., and two things cross my mind. The first being how I no longer have time to pick up a coffee before getting to the studio. The second being that there should be a general rule of thumb for bad news. Specifically, that your agent shouldn't tell you you're out of a job before 9 A.M.

"Oh," I respond, trying to sound cool. "Well, that . . . fucking sucks."

Swindlers is . . . or I guess *was* a half-hour comedy following the lives of TV executives in the seventies. Was it my defining role as an actor? No. Did it pay the bills? I mean, it was starting to.

"I know, but it happens all the time," Theo assures me. There's a painful stench of optimism filling my car through the Bluetooth speaker. I crack a window open and breathe in what one would normally call fresh air, but let's be honest, it's smog. Right now, LA's eighty-degree weather in September is more suffocating than anything. "And, June, I know it's shitty," she continues. "But the industry is suffering right now. They're barely making more than one season of anything."

My brain goes on autopilot as I drive down Melrose, which is, no surprise, congested. These things *do* happen, especially on streaming networks. Shows have been getting canceled all year, leaving most of my actor friends out of work for months. While I can more than empathize, landing a recurring role on a show felt like a new chapter of security, a steady career.

I'm a *working* actor. That means I've had a few lines in almost everything, yet am known for nothing, and ironically, never know *when* I'll be working again. People definitely don't stop me on the street when I go out, which I prefer, and I'm lucky if my monthly residual checks are enough to pay the rent.

My knuckles turn white, gripping the wheel as I try not to feel overly defeated.

"Okay, so what's next?" I try to pump myself up. "What about the self-tapes?"

"Well, that's actually one of the things I want to talk to you about," Theo says. "Film and TV are *great*, and I can get you the auditions . . . but let's chat about theater again."

"Is there a production in the city?"

"No, New York."

"Theo . . ." I shoot an exhausted look at her name on the car's display screen.

"I know it's a stretch, but there are some amazing revivals happening, and with your background, you have a good shot. June, theater is steady, and you're good at it."

Theo's been my agent for the past five years. She holds a level of authority most people work decades to attain, and she's the most honest person I know, whether I like it or not. At thirty-two, it doesn't get easier hearing *she's not white enough, she's not Asian enough, she's not ethnic enough, she's too pretty to be the friend but she doesn't have leading lady potential.* So, when Theo says that I should go back to theater . . . she's probably right.

"What are the revivals?" I ask.

"A few Off, but there's two for spring that are on Broadway. They're shopping around some big names."

Almost missing my turn, I pull into the studio entrance. I tap my key card and nod toward the older man in the security booth.

"Morning, Gus! So, did we win the Powerball?"

"Morning, June." He playfully tips his hat. "I'm still here, aren't I?"

"There's always next time." I give an encouraging smile.

"Ain't that the truth," he laughs. "Have a good one!"

"You too!" The gate rises and I drive onto the lot for what might now be the last time in a while. "Theo, I just got to set. . . . Can I think about it?"

"Of course. Happy last day." She lets out a weak laugh.

"Thanks." I realize the irony.

"Okay, how about you give me a call next week and we can see how you're feeling?"

"Sure, sounds good. Thanks."

I jerk my key out of the ignition and close my eyes. There's a pulsation around my temple that could be from the news or the lack of caffeine in my system. I rub the side of my head with my index and middle fingers, trying to ease the pain.

Lately, my career has been less dependent on how well I can deliver an emotional monologue and more on my ability to be socially relevant behind my phone screen. Which I hardly am. It's not that I *don't* want to do theater. I'm in no position to turn down a role on a Broadway or even an Off-Broadway play. I just can't relocate to New York.

New York is not an option.

BEFORE LANDING THE part on *Swindlers,* I went almost a full eight months without booking any jobs. That meant giving up my studio apartment and moving in with my friends Shivani and Zach until I found something stable. Yes, I'm bummed about the show getting canceled, but I'm more bummed about losing a steady paycheck. A paycheck that, if I was guaranteed another year of work, could get me a place of my own.

"Okay . . ." Shivani initiates a *cheers* motion once all of our happy-hour drinks arrive. A week after wrapping, they managed to drag me to a bar in Silver Lake to "celebrate" my last day of filming. "How are we all doing?"

It's a toss-up what to celebrate first, my health care ending or my next job being nowhere in sight.

"You know." I nod sarcastically. "I've been better."

"This just means that the universe has something else planned for you." Shivani reaches across the table to squeeze my hand.

We met when I was still new to LA, almost five years ago. We went to the same Pilates class and she's now an instructor and has managed to become a pretty successful influencer at the same time. It's not surprising—Shivani is absolutely stunning, and since she started to date a shortstop on the Colorado Rockies, she's someone the internet likes to pay attention to.

"I really thought *Swindlers* was what was planned for me," I say.

"Don't feel bad—the show was trash anyway," Zach says with a shrug. Zach has been roommates with Shivani for the past couple of years, and he's someone I immediately hit it off with.

"You literally said last week that it was the best show you've watched in a while and it was going to be a game changer for my career." I laugh.

"I was hyping you up! Being a good friend."

"Why do you think it wasn't renewed?" Shivani cuts a piece of her wedge salad.

"Nobody's getting picked up for a second season," I say, scooping more guacamole onto my nacho chip.

"What about soap operas?" Zach says.

"Zach, please . . ." Shivani rolls her eyes.

"What? That actor on *The Young and the Restless* has played Victor Newman for like fifty years."

Shivani squints. "But do we *want* that?"

"I mean, I'd want that paycheck every week." He shrugs. If it were anyone else, I'd be slightly offended, but Zach's a videographer who very much understands the ups and downs of freelance work.

Shivani turns to me. "June, what's your agent saying?"

"I don't know," I sigh. "She wants me to go back to theater."

"Okay, you *have* to do it." Zach sits up. "If I could sing and dance, it would be over for everyone."

"No, he's right," Shivani says, nodding. "All these celebrities are doing theater now! Do you have anything lined up?"

"She said there are some auditions she could get me . . . but I don't know how I feel about going back to New York."

"Mmm, I get that." Zach nods. "I can't do the subway."

"First off, New York is amazing," Shivani dismisses him. "Besides, it's not forever. If you get a part, aren't runs only like a year, tops? Just come back after."

Despite my career trajectory, I never fantasized about my face being on the big screen. Performing on stage and the thrill I get from a live audience was always my first love. When I was growing up, you would find me burning through my *Music Man* VHS tape or reciting all the parts of *My Fair Lady.* My grandparents pretty much raised me, and when they passed away, I left home to study theater. The one place I could be anyone but myself. And I did it. I made it to Broadway. I had the career. I had the life I wanted. But I can't go back.

"Okay, okay, I'll think about it." I take a sip of my margarita. "Happy?"

"Yes! Now seriously." Zach straightens his posture. "What's wrong with soap operas?"

"Hey, if I get offered a role on a soap opera, I will take it." I sigh. "It's tough out there."

"Speaking of tough out there." Zach grabs another nacho. "What the hell is going on with men?"

"Just like in general?" I ask.

"Yes." Zach points a finger. "But specifically when it comes to dating me."

"Oh no, what happened with Andy?" The last time Zach told us about his dating life, he and Andy were going to take a trip to Vegas.

"Apparently things are *going too fast* for him," he says, using air quotes. "He wants to take it slow."

"Isn't he like sixty?" Shivani asks.

"Sixty-four."

"Oh my—no, see, this is why you have to wait for the universe to bring someone to you . . . like the way I'm trying to set up June with Ben." Shivani flashes me a wicked smile.

"*No.*" I shake my head. Ever since Shivani got a boyfriend, she has been determined to get all of her single friends in relationships. Her main project is setting me up with one of her clients who takes private Pilates classes.

My other friends in their thirties are either married, in committed relationships, having children, or buying homes. I can confidently say I'm none of those things. It's impossible to buy property on a single income, and the LA dating scene is quite depressing. On the bright side, if I ever have to pivot career paths to stand-up comedy, which at this point doesn't sound unrealistic, I'll at least have good material.

"Come on! Why not?" Shivani urges. "It's been like a year since you've been on a date. Probably two since you've had sex."

"That is not true!" I defend myself, but Shivani and Zach look at each other without saying a word. "Okay, fine! Maybe it's true." I think about the last time I was intimate with someone . . . all I can remember is the awful one-night stand I had with another actor from *Swindlers.* "I'm just not interested in dating right now. You end up with guys like Andy. Sixty-four-year-olds who cancel Vegas trips just as you're getting serious."

"She's not wrong." Zach takes a sip of his margarita.

"Fine," Shivani says. "But just so you know, Ben's objectively attractive, and funny, and he runs this all-natural supplement and protein powder company."

"Like a pyramid scheme?" I blink.

"*No,* he owns it."

"Is that supposed to be a *good* thing?" Zach scrunches his face.

"He's an entrepreneur!" Shivani says.

"I'm curious how you described me to him," I say with a laugh.

"You're like Michelle Pfeiffer in *Grease 2*," Zach interjects, and I appreciate the inside baseball reference. "You're a Cool Rider, ya know? Mellow, sarcastic, but fun."

"Michelle Pfeiffer wasn't a Cool Rider, she was *looking* for a Cool Rider," I correct him.

"What the fuck are you both talking about?" Shivani shakes her head.

"*Grease 2*," Zach repeats.

"You two are literally the only people who have seen that movie . . . We just want to see you happy, June."

"Well, a relationship isn't going to make me happy. You know what'll make me happy? A job."

Shivani laughs and then holds up her glass. "Touché."

AFTER A NIGHT of three too many half-off cocktails, I wake up the next morning in a slight panic and with a mild headache when I realize I have no job, no upcoming paycheck, and no plans. While this fear isn't uncommon for someone in my line of work, I've come to learn it only gets worse with age.

Because of the inconsistency of roles I book, it's hard to keep a full-time job with flexibility. Every few months I'm back where I started: either at the end of a project or on the receiving end of another rejection, wondering if this is the right career for me. And I'm tired.

It's far too early in the morning to be self-inflicting this kind of pain, but I grab my phone and open my mobile banking account. All the muscles in my face tense as I stare at the numbers. I have much less than I thought in my combined checking and savings accounts. I don't even count the lump sum I received from *Swindlers,* since that will be going straight to our friend the tax collector.

My mind does some quick math and subtracts my share of next month's rent. It's safe to say that unless I book my next job *today,* I'm most likely going to have to ask Shivani and Zach for an IOU.

Groggy-eyed, I make my way to the bathroom and catch a glimpse of my reflection in the mirror. My eyes and bone structure are inherited from my mother's Filipino side. Despite her vacancy in my life, I can admit she's a beautiful woman. My nose and head of thick curly hair are a gift from my father, whatever he may look like. My curls look more out of control than usual, so I grab the closest silk scrunchie and tie it up in a bun, wincing at the few grays over my dark hair.

Our apartment sits on the edge of Eagle Rock and South Arroyo. We don't live anywhere close to the ocean, and I prefer it this way. There's something upsettingly commercial about the Westside, and this is a part of LA that feels like its own tiny town and not a performative social club.

My last place had no washer and dryer, no AC, and the shower tiles had a permanent black stain that I was told by my landlord multiple times was *definitely not mold.* While this three-bedroom apartment is the complete opposite of my old studio, I was looking forward to having a place of my own again. It looks like that won't be in the cards for a while.

With the natural sunlight feeling a bit too much for my eyes, I draw the curtains and make myself a pot of coffee. My saving grace this morning is that both Zach and Shivani are at work, so I have the place to myself. As the pot makes a soothing sound of brewing the grounds, I pull out my phone, and am deflated. It's been one week since we spoke, and there are no updates from Theo.

It's then that I notice an email from an unknown sender appear.

Subject: 74 Perry Street

I jerk up and move the phone closer to my face. There's no way. This must be spam, or better yet . . . a mistake.

Cracking the tops of my knuckles, a bad habit since high school, I click on the unread message. When I see that it's in fact *not spam,* I move to the couch and pull it up on my laptop.

Hello Ms. Wood,

My name is Mara Davis. I am reaching out on behalf of Bower & Robbins Accounting. We have a matter of legal documents that require your immediate attention as they pertain to your residency at 74 Perry Street, New York. We kindly ask that you email us back with your availability for an in-person meeting with one of our representatives before September 24.

Best,
Mara Davis
CPA, Bower & Robbins

"What the fuck?" I mutter to myself.

My eyes scan the email, two, three, then four times over, and I'm thoroughly confused. The only people on this email are myself and this Mara woman, which is even more puzzling. Pulling up a new tab, I google "Bower & Robbins Accounting." All right, so they're legitimate, but the name doesn't ring a bell. What legal documents would require my attention? Specifically, legal documents for a place I lived in five years ago?

My hands run through my hair, pulling out my bun. The beeping in the background lets me know my coffee is ready, but I draft a response before getting up.

Hi Mara,

It's very nice to e-meet you. I am no longer based in New York. Would it be possible to sort out these details through a phone call or video chat? I'm available at any time.

Thanks,
June

Squeezing my eyes shut, I hit the send button and immediately close my laptop as if it was on fire. It's not often that I drink black coffee, but this morning I'm dismissing the milk. I down the thin, watery liquid in an impressive amount of time and immediately pour myself another cup. Not even five minutes later, my phone vibrates across the kitchen counter.

"Ugh, come on . . ." I aggressively strum the side of my mug. "It's just an email, June."

June,

I appreciate your quick response. We cannot disclose specific details at this time, but please consider that there are potential monetary benefits involved and it is in your best interest to meet in person. I understand that this is a tight turnaround, but it is unfortunately nonnegotiable. I have shared our address below. Please let us know if you have any further questions.

Mara

"Are you kidding me?!" I throw my head back in disbelief. Yeah, I have a few questions. The main one being what the actual fuck is going on?

I quickly grab my laptop and search flights from Los Angeles to New York and wince at the prices for the rest of the week. Opening a new tab, I audibly groan at the list of available hotels.

If I ignore this, I'm positive I won't be able to concentrate on much else today—or ever again, for that matter. Plus, it's not like I have any other commitments right now. But more than anything, I *need* to know what this is about. Even if I'm terrified for reasons I have never allowed myself to fully process. I can't ignore this.

My stomach begins to feel queasy and my heart beats at an alarming rate, which is not a direct effect of the caffeine on an empty stomach. This trip is going to cost me practically my entire savings, leaving me just enough to make it through next month.

"Shit," I say under my breath, mentally preparing myself to lose the last $1,000 in my bank account. This better be worth it.

I reach for my phone and call Theo. As it rings, I scan Mara's email over and over again like I'm memorizing lines. Not a single detail or punctuation mark missed. Legal documents that require my immediate attention? Best interest to meet in person? I can't make sense of any of it.

"June, hi!" she answers.

"Hey, it's not too early, is it?"

"No, you're good, I just finished a yoga class." In addition to being one of *The Hollywood Reporter*'s and *Variety*'s Top Film and TV Executives Under 40, Theo is a mom of two and the type of mother who attends all her kids' soccer games and gymnastics competitions. I don't know how she does it.

"Hypothetically," I start. "If I were to be in New York next week . . . would I be able to book an audition?"

A fun fact about being an actor is that, like most freelance jobs, it allows you to write things off for taxes. An audition, if you're lucky enough to land one, is one of those things. The only way I can justify spending my savings to go to New York is if I technically don't spend them at all.

"Why are you asking me like this isn't the only thing I've been trying to book you for years?"

"Theo, seriously!" I stifle a laugh.

"Yes," Theo says. "Just tell me the days."

"Thank God." I let out a sigh of relief. "Are you sure?"

"I am sure," she says slowly.

"Okay, I'll text you once everything is booked."

"I'm assuming you're going to tell me what's going on at some point?"

"Hopefully nothing," I say.

"You know what, I'm not even going to ask," Theo says. "Let me make some calls. I'll talk to you soon."

"Okay, thank you!"

After a heavy pause, I click reply.

Hi Mara,

Tuesday, September 24, works best for me.

June

Well, I guess I *am* going to New York.

Chapter 2

IN LESS THAN FORTY-EIGHT HOURS, I'M ON THE FIRST FLIGHT to JFK. The book I brought sits untouched in my purse and I don't bother to look at the selection of films "curated for my viewing pleasure." If ever there's a slight hint of turbulence, my fingernails dig into the armrests on either side of me. Not because I'm a fearful flier, but because I don't know what the hell I'm doing here. It's been five years since I've been in New York and as each minute goes by, this starts to feel more and more like a bad idea.

My first instinct was to reach out to Chloe, who lives in the city—well, Connecticut; don't tell her I said they're the same thing—but my trip is for only forty-eight hours and socializing is not on my agenda. Not even with my best friend. Not because I don't want to. I want nothing more than to see Chloe and hang out like we used to. Not to mention it would be actually much more economical to stay with her, take the train in, and save hundreds of dollars in hotel costs. Believe me, I thought about it. But what comes with that is an explanation. An explanation for why I'm out of a job . . . again. An explanation for why I'm back in the city, and a real explanation for why I left.

My goal is to go in and out. Easy peasy, painless, like it never happened.

"We'll begin our descent into JFK in twenty minutes," I hear a muffled voice say on the intercom. "The local time is 1:13 P.M. For your safety and the safety of those around you, please remain seated with your seat belt fastened and keep the aisles clear until we are landed."

My chest stings when the plane gently leans to our left and I catch a brief glimpse of the Manhattan skyline. It's just a mere moment, but it feels like I never left. I'm that bright-eyed girl who left Toronto to study theater. My days consisted of rehearsals and drama classes, my nights were filled with shifts at the local bookshop. That girl was hungry, and I miss her.

It's not possible, but I swear I can hear whispers of the city's rhythm beneath me. The buskers, the sound of subway tracks, the sirens wailing in harmony with the bustling traffic. As predicted, in no time the plane's wheels touch the ground, and I'm back.

I'm back in New York.

I haven't used public transportation in ages, and I'm not sure if I love or hate how naturally getting on the E train comes to me. Like muscle memory. Though driving is something I had to get used to once I moved to Los Angeles, the alone time in bumper-to-bumper traffic slowly became second nature. But sitting on the subway, I remember the way people are so exposed to one another here, how you can feel a sense of community.

My instinct is to get off at West Fourth Street and pick up a slice at Joe's Pizza, one of my favorite spots on this side of town. But I fight the urge, remembering I'm here for business, not pleasure. Once I get to the hotel in Tribeca, comparable to your typical Hilton or Marriott, I'm assaulted by the clear snapshot of Manhattan from my room.

It's a beautiful, sunny, late-September afternoon, and seeing the city from this high up, I find it's easy to remember what the appeal is. Forcing myself to look away, I pull out a wool sweater from my carry-on and find the address Mara shared in her email.

IT'S A MODERN building, clean, and with a mostly white interior. Very sterile. The elevator takes me up to the eighteenth floor, where I see the plaque on the wall that reads *Bower & Robbins.*

"Hi, how can I help you?" a man with a head of thick brown hair and a black dress shirt asks from behind the receptionist desk.

"Yes, hi, I have an appointment with Mara Davis at four," I say. "It's under 'June Wood.'"

His eyes scan his computer screen. "Perfect. If you could just take a seat. Mara will be out soon."

"Great, thank you." I take a step but then stop in my tracks. "Actually, do you happen to know what this meeting is regarding?"

"Mara will be giving you all of the details," he says.

"Right, of course." I nod. "But it doesn't happen to say anything in your notes or—"

"If you could take a seat, please, Mara will be out shortly."

I take a deep inhale through my nostrils and power a smile. "Fine."

There's nobody else in the waiting area, so I make my way to the opposite side and choose a corner spot to maintain a view of the space. Down the hall, there's a *ding* from the elevator and someone emerges, heading to a different office unit. Every movement or sound makes me more anxious than I already am. This anticipation is far worse than any callback I've ever experienced.

"Ms. Wood?" A woman who looks to be in her early fifties turns the corner. She has a chic blond bob and thick-rimmed glasses. They're the kind of glasses that are begging for you to say *nice glasses.* I stand up and before I can answer, she shakes my hand. "I'm Mara. It's so nice to officially meet you."

"Likewise." I force a smile.

Mara leads me down the hallway, passing six or seven offices, and we turn into the last door on the right. She steps behind her desk and gestures to the seat across from her, which I take. Behind her is a floor-to-ceiling window, with once again a breathtaking view of the city. Okay, I get it. New York, you're beautiful.

"Thank you for coming all the way here, Ms. Wood. I know this wasn't exactly a cab ride away."

"Oh, no problem at all," I lie, trying not to think of how much of a dent this trip could put in my savings account. "And please, you can call me June."

"June," she says, nodding. "So, to introduce myself, I've been a CPA for over twenty years. I've been with Bower & Robbins for the past twelve years. We offer services for businesses, individuals, real estate companies, estates, trusts, nonprofits, and more," she says, and I don't tell her I already know this due to my extensive research over the past forty-eight hours. "And I specifically focus on individuals and families, as well as real estate."

"Oh, okay."

My brain continues to sweep through all the possible reasons I could be here. There had never been an issue when I lived on Perry. Could this be about the rent? Maybe the checks never went through, and I somehow owe a small fortune in rent money?

"Okay." She adjusts her computer monitor. "Before we get started, there are a few details I need to gather from you that I didn't have a chance to ask in our emails."

"Of course." I nod and tuck my hair behind my ear.

"So, I have here on file that you resided at 74 Perry for . . ." I watch her eyes dart back and forth across her screen. "Six years?"

"Correct." I clear my throat and prepare myself for the rest of the questions.

"Perfect." She hands me an iPad with a form full of details: legal name, occupation, current address, number, etc. "If you don't mind taking a few minutes to fill this out, please."

"Sure." I take the device from her and fill out the necessary details and return it.

"Thank you." She glances over my answers and then smiles. "Actually, it's probably best if we wait for everyone before we continue."

I move my head as if it will help me hear better. "Everyone?"

"Yes, he should be here any—" Then, as if on cue, her office phone rings, and she answers it. "Yes? Mhm. You can go ahead and send him in."

She's talking about someone else. She *must* be talking about someone else. Perhaps another CPA. There's no way . . .

My palms start to get clammy and I can't shake my heart palpitations. For the love of God, it can't be. I remember specifically rereading my email exchanges with Mara and making a note that I was the *only* one in the chain.

There are some muffled sounds through the wall. I can't make out any words being said, but I know I hear a man's voice.

I know that man's voice.

Typically, I'm not a huge planner. While I do have a calendar for any meetings or appointments, I'm usually a go-with-the-flow type of gal. However, there are things I like to mentally prepare for: auditions, going to a concert and knowing I won't be home until 1 A.M., and possible encounters with people I've told myself I would never see again.

My hands squeeze so hard into a fist that my nails dig into the center of my palms. This is probably the closest thing I've ever had to a panic attack. Maybe I'm actually having a fucking panic attack, I don't know. What does a panic attack entail? Does it feel like not being able to breathe and wanting to shit your pants at the same time?

My eyes go to the window behind Mara, and I wonder how many people have survived an eighteen-story jump. I clutch my purse, ready to make a run for it, but it's too late. The sound of footsteps is getting closer, and I hear the man's voice more clearly. I can quite literally feel my ass sweating. I didn't even know that was physically possible.

He's getting closer and closer, and the door finally opens. I refuse to turn around, but I see Mara's face light up at whoever is behind me.

"I'm sorry I'm late," a deep voice says. A voice that you can feel throughout your veins. A voice that you never forget.

Maybe it's the adrenaline; I couldn't tell you, because everything that's happening is a blur, but somehow, I manage to stand up and turn around.

For the first time in five years, I'm face-to-face—well, face-to-chest—with Adam Harper.

The realization dawns on him, except the blood isn't rushing to *his* face the way it is to mine.

He looks older, but not old. There are a few more lines around his eyes, slight facial hair that he would never have let grow before, and, although Adam Harper was always one to keep in shape, he looks somehow more fit, bigger, than I remember. He's wearing an army green denim shirt and black pants with leather boots. He looks *handsome.* I guess he always was. His sleeves are rolled up a little and I notice a watch. He never used to wear watches.

"Hey," Adam says.

My lips slightly part. Hey? *Hey*?! He is not supposed to be here.

"Hi," I say, although it comes out a little shakier than I'd like.

I force myself to look into his eyes. The same hazel eyes I used to look at every day, eyes that apparently still make me go weak in the knees, for reasons that are unclear right now. Memories tower over me like a huge wave about to cascade.

I remember the way his fingers would run through my hair.

I remember how satisfying it felt to earn one of his laughs.

I remember the last time I saw him and our final words to each other.

"How are you?" he asks, keeping his focus on me.

I'm not imagining it: Adam looks calm and composed, like he's asking his fucking barber what's been going on since his last haircut. Instead of panic, I now feel slight *anger.* I'm angry that he's . . . okay.

"Good." I smile, only slightly concerned that my heart rate is not slowing down.

It's not supposed to be like this. This is not how we should be reuniting.

"All right, let's all take a seat." Mara's voice snaps me back to reality and Adam puts his arm out, gesturing for me to sit first.

Okay, well, I guess we're doing this.

Mara begins talking but it's hard for me to process what she's saying, because Adam and I are sitting next to each other. We are really in the same room right now. I'm going to be sick.

At some point she passes him the same iPad that was in my hands a few minutes ago and he starts filling out the form. She then begins to scan our IDs and says something trivial about the weather. I have no idea. We are less than four feet away from each other and, yeah, I'm definitely going to be sick. The worst part is that Adam looks *fine.* Tall, strong, handsome, and fine with this situation.

He hands her back the iPad and looks at me. The moment we make eye contact my eyes dart back to Mara, like he's the male counterpart of Medusa. Too late—I already feel like stone that's crumbled.

"Mr. Harper, I have here on file that you *also* resided at 74 Perry for six years?"

"Correct." Adam keeps his focus on Mara.

Six years. Six years we lived together. But Adam wasn't just my roommate—you can't reduce someone you shared a life with to a label like *roommate.* A roommate is someone who is strictly a percentage of the rent, a ship passing in the night that happens to dock at the same port as you. A roommate doesn't know your deepest, darkest secrets, or your most intimate hopes and dreams. They certainly don't know what spot on your collarbone makes you moan in pleasure.

There's an urge in me to pull Adam's arm and say *hey, let's get out of here . . . separately,* but that would require talking to him.

"Great." Mara continues to focus on her screen. What's the point of those gigantic glasses if she can't see that someone is about to throw up all over herself? "Okay, so thank you both for taking the time to come here in person." Mara pulls out a brown folder containing a pile of paperwork.

I shift uncomfortably, because the last thing I need right now is to be looking at any form of documentation. I can barely concentrate. Had I known he would be here, I wouldn't have flown across the country. I would've demanded this be a Zoom call with cameras *off.*

"As I was saying, I've been a certified public accountant for over twenty years and for fifteen of those years, I've worked with Stanley Hill."

I sit up straighter. Stanley Hill is a name that I haven't heard since I left New York. My mind travels to the few but lovely memories I have from when he was our landlord. The stories he would tell us of growing up in Brooklyn, how he'd always let it slide if we were a week or two late on rent, the comforting feeling I had knowing we could go to him if a pipe was leaky or the furnace needed repair.

"How is Stanley?" Adam asks.

Mara's smile becomes somber. "It saddens me to let you know that Mr. Hill passed away earlier this month."

"What?" My face falls, and I instinctively look at Adam. His arms are crossed with a fist to his mouth, telling me he had no idea either. My words come out gentle and slow. "M-May I ask how?"

"Alzheimer's," Mara says, and my throat becomes tight. I know he didn't have a family or kids and that he must have battled his illness alone. "At Mr. Hill's request, there was no funeral. But I want you both to know he didn't suffer long and had a peaceful passing. I saw him a week before . . . and he was happy."

Despite my regrets about not having stayed in touch and the utter shock of this news, those details are a silver lining.

"Thank goodness," Adam says softly.

"That being said, as the granted executor of Mr. Hill's assets . . ." Mara tentatively guides our conversation to a pivot. "There are some matters that need to be attended to regarding 74 Perry Street."

Between Adam's showing up and the news of Stanley's passing, I'd almost forgotten that there was a reason we were summoned here. The past five minutes have already been far too much to process and I don't think I can handle anything else.

Adam shifts and takes a breath in. "Yes, of course."

Mara licks her index finger and flips to a specific page. She adjusts her glasses and scans what's in front of her. Pulling out a single sheet, she places it on her marble desk. "Based on the estate plan"—Mara spins the paper in our direction, then pushes it forward—"74 Perry Street is now under the ownership of Adam Harper and June Wood."

Chapter 3

Say something, I tell myself. *Say anything.*

Mara is staring at Adam and me, and we're staring back, speechless. This is quite literally the longest anyone has ever gone without talking. Ever.

"Excuse me?" I hear my voice after what I imagine was fourteen minutes of silence. *How is this possible? Adam and I haven't lived in that house or spoken to Stanley in years. Why would we own it?!*

"I'm sure there's a mistake . . ." Adam says, his eyes shifting from Mara to me. Even the brief eye contact feels overwhelming.

"No mistake, Mr. Harper. It's stated right here." She pushes a paper in our direction.

Adam snatches the paper in question off the desk, and I see his eyes dart back and forth. After a moment he passes it to me and I get a whiff of Adam, and he smells like cedar or pine, some sort of tree.

The room starts to spin as I process the fact that both of our names are indeed printed under "Property Owners." This flimsy sheet of paper is telling me that I own a house with a man I don't have the stomach to even look at? Being sued for a small fortune in rent money sounds like the ideal scenario right now.

"I'm a little confused." Adam leans back and pinches the bridge of his nose. "Who lives there now?"

"So, it's a vacant residence. It's been used as an Airbnb under a property management company. Hence the slight renovations." Mara moves her monitor to face us, and there are photos of the house—well, a completely new house if I knew any better. "Nobody has actually *lived* there since the two of you."

From the outside, the brownstone looks identical to the last time I saw it, and my heart starts to feel heavy; 74 Perry holds so many memories, both wonderful and painful. The interior, on the other hand, easily looks like something that would be featured on the cover of *Architectural Digest.* There's a gallery wall with a variety of artwork leading up the stairs and a giant textured rug in the living room, which now holds a vintage-looking piano, floor-to-ceiling bookshelves, and a couch you could fall into and disappear in. It's a significant portion of my life, and the cosmetic makeover stirs up a pang of emotion. This is not the same house Adam and I lived in all those years ago.

"All assets within the home are also included in the overall value," Mara adds.

My brain is processing everything in slow motion. "Overall value?" I ask.

"Yes." Mara licks her finger again and pulls up another sheet of paper from the pile. "So, as of three weeks ago, when the appraisal was conducted, the thirty-two hundred square feet with the included assets result in a total property value equaling approximately six-point-two million dollars."

I nearly fall out of my chair while a sharp inhale comes from Adam. Is this a joke? Are we on a reboot of *Punk'd*?

"I just . . ." I choose my words carefully. "I'm just confused how this happened. Why us?"

"Ah." Mara nods. "Mr. Hill's estate plans clearly outline that homeownership is to be absorbed by whoever resided there last. In this case, the last people were the two of you." Mara adjusts her glasses again. "Look, like I said, I've known Mr. Hill for many years. As I'm sure the two of you know, there wasn't anyone in his life to leave this property to. The options were either the State of New York or the bank takes over, and he opted for this."

Adam and I look at each other, completely dumbstruck and speechless. What she's saying *sounds* logical, but I'm still unable to make any sense of it.

"Is there any mortgage to absorb or—" Adam leans in toward the desk and studies the paperwork. In most cases I would too, but it's still a little difficult to think. I also can't help but be bothered that Adam is acting like this is a casual business deal.

"No outstanding mortgage, Mr. Harper," Mara says. "Of course, there will be logistics such as property taxes that come with owning a home . . . all of which will be detailed in the terms. It's really just a matter of signing the proper paperwork to hand it over."

"This is . . ." Adam says softly, and I'm still not used to hearing him talk. It's a mix of not wanting to hear his voice but hanging on his every word. "A lot, as I'm sure you can imagine, but we're very grateful." He looks over at me, and I wince at the word *we.* There is no we.

"Of course, it's a lot to take in. And if you decide to go the route of selling the property, I'm always happy to recommend some people."

Sell the property! I feel a sudden release. *Yes! Okay, now we're talking. Let's make this a quick and easy transaction. We'll sell the house and split everything fifty-fifty.* It then dawns on me that this house is a game changer. Selling it could mean security in between jobs, a decent savings account, a place of my own . . . not having to see Adam again.

This house, whether I like it or not, is the answer to everything.

"I'd like to have a lawyer look over everything first," Adam says, not giving me a chance to oppose.

"Yes, absolutely. I will email everything over by the end of the day and we can regroup."

"Thank you, Mara." Adam shakes her hand, and whether intentional or not, his attitude feels like a response to me.

"It's my pleasure. Now, a few housekeeping items," Mara says. "We'll set a follow-up meeting at the end of the month to sign and process all paperwork."

"Sounds good," Adam says, nodding.

"As part of the inheritance clause, we'll need a deposit equivalent to one month's mortgage." She flips to another sheet of paper and highlights in yellow a sum value.

"What?" I let out an uncontrollable scoff. There's no way in hell I can afford to pay that amount right now.

"Legally, we cannot make the ownership transition until these terms are met," Mara says regretfully. "You will get the full deposit back after the paperwork is processed."

I sit speechless, because the number staring at me is more than my entire savings.

"No problem." Adam turns to Mara, pulling out his wallet. "Is credit okay?"

"Yes, that's fine," she says, taking the card from his fingers.

Everything is happening far too quickly. Adam is signing something, and before I can say anything, the transaction is done. Mara opens one of the desk drawers and pulls out a white envelope.

"There are two sets of keys. Feel free to take a look at the house, make your plans, and stay there if you wish."

I stare at the envelope, confused. "So that's it? We own the home?"

"Well, yes and no." Mara lets out a laugh. "Your deposit allows you to have access to 74 Perry, but you can't legally change your address or begin the selling process until our next meeting. Does that make sense?"

"Yes, thank you." Adam takes the envelope from her, since I clearly can't move.

"Does October twenty-third at ten work for you both?" Mara asks.

"I'm sorry . . . *October*?!" I say. "That's a month from now."

"I know it's not ideal, but similar to being in escrow, we need at least twenty days to go through the vetting process."

"But you said that we own the home?" I say.

"Technically, yes," she says, clearly now annoyed. "But all the paperwork still needs to be signed."

"Look, Mara." I stand up and say her name as if we're old friends, and like I haven't forgotten her last name. "I have a life back home that I can't put on hold. Responsibilities. Surely in this day and age, there has to be a *virtual* option here . . ."

Adam flips through the paperwork when Mara shakes her head.

"These terms were made a little before the kids were using Zoom." She uses air quotes, and I'm sure I'm doing a bad job at hiding the look on my face. Mara awkwardly laughs and puts her hands down. "Anyway, I apologize to you both for any inconvenience, but this is a nonnegotiable."

"October twenty-third is fine," Adam interjects, and my face whips to his. "This is *a lot* of money we're talking about here, and of course, a sensitive time for all of us . . . We definitely don't want to make things more complicated than they already are."

It sounds like he's talking more to me than Mara.

"Hypothetically," I say, "what would happen if we couldn't go through with this?"

"Then the bank owns it." Mara stands up and guides us out of her office, causing Adam and me to follow her like puppies. "And if I could share my two cents, that would be an awful loss. Especially considering the increasing value." She shakes both of our hands once we're back at the front desk. "Someone at the firm will be in touch with an appointment confirmation to finalize everything."

"Mara—"

"Congratulations," she says, and turns her attention to an older man waiting in the same seat I was in twenty minutes ago. He nods at us, then follows her down the hallway.

Before I know it, she's gone. It's not until Adam and I are awkwardly standing in the empty waiting room that I realize the only thing that was keeping me calm was Mara's presence, knowing I couldn't make a scene or burst into tears in front of a stranger.

It's near impossible to not think of the history between us. Memories that took years to bury continue rushing back like a river bursting its banks. Adam's standing there with one hand in his pocket, another one going through his hair, and he gives a little shrug.

I can't do this.

"I have to go," I say, pushing through the glass doors. The elevator is down the hallway, and I'm determined to be inside of it before I hear another word that comes out of Adam's mouth.

"June," I hear him calling out behind me. Saying my name in a way that only *he* can. "Can we talk about this?"

That's a loaded question. Does he want to talk about what happened five years ago? Or the fact that we now own a multimillion-dollar home together?

My thumb jabs the elevator button over and over again, aware that he's coming down the hallway. I consider taking the emergency stairs but then the elevator opens up and I jump in. He's a few feet away and I hit the close button as many times as possible. Just as the doors start moving, he swoops in and *of course* I'm here alone with Adam Harper for eighteen floors.

Chapter 4

APRIL, 11 YEARS AGO

THIS MUST BE THE WRONG PLACE. THIS IS A BROWNSTONE. IN the West Village. I pull my phone out, scrolling to Chloe's name because she gave me the address in the first place.

I hear her voice on the other end. "Hello?"

I met Chloe in freshman year of college, in line for orientation, and even though we never had a class together, we hit it off and were inseparable. Everything about Chloe demands your attention: She's tall, dark, beautiful, loud, eccentric, and somehow the funniest and smartest person in every room. In the time I've known her she's always looked out for herself—maybe that's why we relate to each other. She rarely shows her emotions, and when she does, it's genuine.

"Hey, are you sure it's *74* Perry?" I ask, looking around me in case there's a more realistic 74 Perry in view.

"Let me check," she says, and I can hear her shuffling around. "Yeah, that's it."

My gaze travels from the reddish brown hue of the exterior

to the tree-lined street on either side of me. There's a woman in a white sundress listening to music through her headphones across the street, and coming up on my left is a man jogging alongside his gray and white pit bull. This is by far one of the nicest neighborhoods in the city, so much so that I don't even feel worthy of knocking on the door.

"How did Ethan find out about this place again?" I lift my head, subtly trying to catch a glimpse inside one of the windows.

"I think his aunt knows the person renting out the apartment."

"Okay, yeah, *apartment*. Chloe, this is a *brownstone* in the West Village."

"What? Really?"

"Yeah, it's like very nice." I continue to scan the street.

"Then what are you waiting for? Go!"

When you're a recent graduate paying off student loans with a part-time job at a bookstore, and your current roommates have little to no respect for personal space, you will do *anything* to move. In this case, showing up at a random address because your best friend tells you the guy she's sleeping with heard it's for rent.

"Okay, well, if I get murdered or something you know where I am."

"You won't get murdered in a brownstone," Chloe says.

I sigh, turn off my phone, and put it in my back pocket. If this is really the right place, then it's a steal.

I make my way up the stairs and knock on the front door, and about twenty seconds later an older man with white hair, khakis, and a cardigan over his dress shirt is in front of me.

"Hello there," he says.

"Hi." I wave politely, hoping that I didn't interrupt this man's morning tea. "It's nice to meet you. I'm June Wood. I heard that this unit is for rent?"

"Oh yes!" He opens the door wider and gestures for me to come inside. "I'm Stanley, the owner. Nice to meet you."

The house is empty, but it's not difficult to imagine what furniture and a touch of home decor could achieve. Although it has a cozy charm, it's *big*. I've never been inside of a brownstone before, and I now understand why it's the New York dream. The stair banisters are a dark oak and there's a breathtaking fireplace in the living room and the crown molding along the ceiling has been well preserved. The lighting fixtures are deep brass surrounded by antique herbarium wallpaper. This is the Plaza compared with the one-bedroom apartment I share with two other people.

I quickly take out my phone and text Chloe.

It's stunning . . .

"We're not posting the listing until tomorrow, but I guess word got around." Stanley guides me into the living room. "So, June, as you can see, it's pretty straightforward. Two bedrooms, two baths, and the square footage is a decent size and the neighborhood is safe compared to these other areas around the city."

Chloe texts back.

Get it!

"It looks great," I say as I peek around the corners and catch a glimpse of a kitchen with all the necessary appliances. There's even a radiator, which will come in handy for the winter. Stanley gives me a tour of the place: It's clean, spacious, and no comparison to the studio apartments I've been looking at within my budget.

"I'm just looking for someone who will take care of it. It's been passed down for two generations, but far too big for me to stay here by myself," Stanley says. "No pets, no loud parties or orgies or anything like that, and I'll stay out of your hair." He laughs as we make our way back to the living room.

"Oh, I promise there would be none of that!" I brace myself for the deciding factor. "Um, how much is the rent?" I say as coolly as possible, like no number can scare me off.

"Seventeen hundred a month with an eighteen-month lease."

Holy shit. Anything in this neighborhood for less than $2,500 a month is unheard of. My only concern is that I'm still paying off my student loans, and it's a hair over my budget. I also technically don't need two bedrooms.

Stanley's phone starts ringing, and he waves a hand to me. "Sorry, I'll be right back. Feel free to keep looking around."

Getting this place is a no-brainer, but I shouldn't commit, knowing I can't afford it. I pull my phone out of my back pocket and call Chloe.

"Pick up, pick up, pick up," I mutter to myself.

"How'd it go?!"

"It's *perfect,*" I whisper, mindful that Stanley's in the next room. "I want it, I need it, but it's a little over budget."

"By how much?"

"Like four hundred dollars?"

"That's not bad. Just pick up a few extra shifts at work."

"I would, but I can't with my rehearsals and class . . . Move in with me," I beg.

"June, I literally just signed a twelve-month lease."

"Nooo," I cry. "I need this place."

"Is there anyone else you could ask? At school?"

I've already tried asking everyone I could see myself living with if they'd go in on a new place with me. For some reason, everyone lives with their partners or just *loves* their current apartment and can't imagine giving it up.

"I don't think so . . . Chloe, I don't want to lose this place."

"Okay, okay," she says in a voice that calms me a little. She's always been good at that. "It's only ten o'clock. Ask for an application and tell them you'll fill it out tonight and get it back to them first thing tomorrow morning. We will figure this out."

I hang up and pace around the empty living room. There's a bay window where I could sit and read my books and a wall opposite the fireplace where I could install the floor-to-ceiling bookshelf I've always dreamed of. There's a small outdoor space by the kitchen and an oak tree that would provide shade on hot summer days. I have already fallen in love with this house and I can't lose it.

"June, I'm sorry about that," Stanley says as he makes his way back to the living room.

"Oh, no worries at all."

"So, what do you think?" he says.

"I love it! I really do. I was wondering if I'd be able to take an application and bring it back tomorrow morning?"

"Yes, yes, of course." He walks over to the staircase and grabs an application from a stack of papers. "How about you come by tomorrow at eleven?"

"That's perfect, thank you! And here's . . ." I reach into my purse and pull out my wallet. I'm a little deflated about the lack of cash I have with me. "Five dollars . . ." I nervously laugh. "And my number and address. Can this be considered a deposit?"

"You know what, you keep the five. I'll take your word that you'll be back."

"Sounds great—thank you, Stanley!" I head out the door and try to figure out how the hell I'm going to afford this home.

"WHAT ABOUT ALEXA? Wasn't she looking for a place?" Chloe lies on my bed playing with a Rubik's Cube.

"She went to Boston for postgrad."

"Taylor?"

"Already asked her. She's moving in with her boyfriend." I flip through our old yearbook and scan each photo. "My shift starts in an hour. I need to figure this out before tomorrow."

"I'll ask around, don't worry." Chloe sits up. "But, June, if it doesn't work out, maybe we just start from square one. There are a lot of studio apartments in Jersey you can live in."

"Yeah, I know. It's just that Perry is so perfect," I whine.

"Jesus Christ!" Chloe practically screams, looking over my shoulder. "How long have you been standing there?"

Peeking his head into my room is Mason, one of my roommates. Not my roommate by choice—it was a last resort for trying to lower the rent. Katie in my theater class asked if I wanted to sublet a place with her last year and thought it would be smart to bring in someone else and split everything three ways. Now that Katie has a new girlfriend, she rarely comes home, so it's pretty much just Mason and me.

"The door was open," he deadpans at Chloe, reeking of weed

and cat piss. "June, can you wash this for me?" He holds up a sweater with a beige stain.

"Ew, what is that?" I squint.

"Suki threw up on it. She keeps eating walnuts."

"I don't think cats should eat walnuts," Chloe says.

"Well, no shit, that's why she keeps throwing up," Mason bites back, and Chloe widens her eyes at me.

"I'm not washing that for you." I say with a shrug. How I got roped into doing his laundry on a regular basis is beyond me. "Besides, I'm moving out."

"Just wash it with your next load then." He throws the sweater on my desk and walks away.

I need to get out of here.

I'M ONE HOUR into work and trying my best to not think about the house. On most days, setting up book displays for a children's author event would be the perfect way to spend my afternoon, compensated or not. Today, it feels difficult to concentrate on anything.

The Arcade Bookshop is one of the few independent bookstores in the West Village, and one of the more popular ones. I got the job in my sophomore year of college and always thought if I could no longer pursue theater, I would find a career in publishing.

There are only a few people in the store right now: a woman intently studying the titles in the historical fiction section and two men in deep conversation about a book for their thesis. It's not hard to notice the shop doorbell signaling a new customer.

I set aside the stack of books I'm arranging and see a guy around my age, maybe a few years older, looking at our curated staff-picks table.

He's attractive, and not in a "Is he hot or is he just tall?" way. His hair is dark, a little shaggy, and he's wearing a jean jacket with a gray sweatshirt underneath. I subtly smooth my hair and adjust my cardigan. His eyes lift to mine, and he smiles.

"Can I help you with anything?" I ask, walking toward him.

"Yeah." He smiles. "I'm looking for a book."

"Well, you've come to the right place." I lift my arms to my side and look around.

"You know, there was a fifty-fifty chance," he says, looking over to the giant *Arcade Bookshop* sign painted on the window.

"You'd be surprised how many people come in here looking for video games," I say, and he lets out a morale-boosting laugh. "Is there a book in particular you're looking for?"

He puts a hand on the back of his neck and looks around, overwhelmed. "A good one?"

"Well." I nod. "This *good one* is always a hit if you're looking for a thriller." I show him one of my favorite Stephen King novels. "This *good one* is The Lord of the Rings meets *Eyes Wide Shut.*"

"Whoa," he says.

"It's crazy." I walk over to a shelf on our right. "And I haven't read this one yet, but the staff says it's a *good one* if you're into historical fiction." I continue to scan the books in my view in case there's anything else that pops out.

"What's your favorite?" he asks.

"Mine?" I turn, and he's pretty good at the eye contact thing. He nods. I'm not sure why his interest in my preference catches me off guard; after all, I *do* work at a bookstore. "Oh, I mean I like them all, but I'm a sucker for romance." I walk over to the table he was originally looking at and point to a book under my *staff pick* sign. "It's from a debut author in Chelsea, actually."

"June," he says, looking at the name card I drew myself with a small sunflower on the top right instead of at the book. "Is that short for anything?"

"Just June." I humbly shrug.

"It's my favorite month."

"No it's not," I say, a laugh escaping me.

"It is," he says, giving a single nod. "The end of school, the start of summer. What's not to love?"

"No, see, this is why October is the best month." I shake my head. "Nothing beats the autumn weather, and from October on, you have Halloween, Thanksgiving, and Christmas to look forward to. It's like the Friday of months."

"Damn, okay, I might have to rethink a few things."

"As you should."

He smiles and then takes a breath. "As tempting as the erotic Harry Potter sounds, I'll go with this one." He picks up the book under my name and I bat away thoughts of this meaning anything more than a customer choosing a staff recommendation.

"Great choice," I say, and hurry behind the cash register. I can feel his eyes on me as I ring him up, but I try my best to not look.

"I'm Adam," he says.

I conceal a smile, like we're in on an inside joke together. "Nice to meet you, Adam." I place his book and receipt in a paper bag. "I expect a full review once you're finished."

"Oh, it's not for me."

Right. Of course. Unless it's from the queer section, it's not often that men buy romance novels for themselves. It's usually for their girlfriends.

"Sorry." I shake my head. "I hope whoever reads it enjoys it."

"My mom," he says, and a surprising wave of relief fills me. "And probably my sister once she's done with it."

"Oh, I'm happy to wrap—"

"That's all right, no special occasion. I just always try to get her a book when I go home. She's a big reader."

There's a wide range of clientele that comes through these doors, but an attractive guy who buys books for his mom and sister? I'm only human. It's not until I see his gaze drop from my eyes to my hands that I realize I'm still holding his book. I cough and pass him the paper bag.

"Um, so where's home?" I ask.

"Long Island," he says.

"Oh, cool, I've never been. Do you like it?"

"Parts of it," he says, nodding. "It's looking like I might actually be moving back unless I can find a place in the city, so I kind of *have* to start liking it."

"I know what that's like," I say, mildly triggered. "What kind of place are you looking for?"

"God, anything right now." He sighs like I've hit a nerve. A nerve I know all too well. "A couch will do," he says with a laugh. "I'm in a shoebox on the East Side and they just raised the rent. It's tough with culinary school and— Sorry, you don't care about any of this."

"No, *I do,* actually. There's this amazing brownstone on Perry, only a couple blocks away from here that I saw today, and the rent is crazy cheap . . ." I look at the time on the computer screen to my right. It's almost four, which means there's no way I'm finding a roommate before tomorrow morning. "But I don't think I'll be getting it, so it's back to looking at studios in Hoboken."

My coworker John emerges from the storage room behind me to start his shift. "Hey, June." He gives me a nod and steps to my side, pulling out some inventory papers we both need to finish by the end of the day.

"Well, it was great meeting you, June." Adam smiles and holds up his paper bag with his newest purchase.

For a brief moment, I wonder if I should ask for his number. I've never been good at reading those cues, especially when it comes to the opposite sex, but it feels almost like a missed opportunity to never see him again.

"You too, Adam" is all I end up saying.

He keeps his eyes locked on mine for a second, and then he's gone.

AT 10:53 A.M. I'm waiting outside of 74 Perry. In the same spot I was almost twenty-four hours ago. I pull out my phone and text Chloe.

I feel sick.

10:54 A.M. Only six more minutes until I have to give up my dream home and tell the nice man inside that I wasted his time.

There will be other places. I promise!

10:55 A.M. I put my phone back in my purse, close my eyes, and take a few deep breaths as if preparing for a scene in class. When I open them, what I see fifty feet ahead of me causes my skin to prickle.

Shaking hands with Stanley is *Adam.* Hot guy from the bookstore. It looks like they're saying their goodbyes. Stanley pats Adam's upper arm and then closes the door behind him. Adam casually puts his hands in his pockets and heads down the stairs of the front stoop. He's almost too far away at this point, but my vocal cords are more developed than the average person's.

"Hey!" I run across the street.

He turns around, brows grooved, but then looks genuinely happy to see me. "Oh, hey, June!"

I meet him on his end of the sidewalk and cock my head. "What are you doing here?"

While I'm still genuinely confused, I notice how effortlessly attractive and confident he is. He's the type of guy you can't help but do a double take at. He surely has an equally attractive partner waiting at home for him who believes in helping a non-profit when she's not working her full-time job.

"I checked out the place." He points behind him. "You're right, it's incredible."

"Yeah, I know . . ." I squint and repeat myself. "What are you doing here?"

"Checking out the place." Now he's the one who looks confused. "You told me to."

"No I didn't."

"Yes you did." He lets out an incredulous laugh.

I try to think back to our conversation. I'm quite positive I didn't tell him to look at the place I intended to get for myself.

"Are you going to get it?" I don't mean for it to sound accusatory, but this is kind of psychotic behavior on his end.

"Oh yeah," he says. "I mean, it's such a steal."

"But I was going to get it!" I say almost too loudly.

"I thought you said yesterday you were giving it up?"

"What, did you transcribe our conversation or something? *I* found this place." I fold my arms. "The fact that you came here to check it out is kind of fucked up, don't you think?"

"Whoa." He holds up his hands. "It's not uncommon for multiple people to apply for the same unit."

"You don't think I know that?"

"So, we'll let Stanley decide who he wants," he says in the most nonaggressive way possible, which only riles me up more.

My face drops. "You already submitted an application?"

"Didn't you?" he asks.

"I mean . . . not *technically.*" I roll my eyes. "I'm not positive if I'm getting the place or not."

"Wait a minute," he says, shaking his head. "You just made me feel shitty about seeing this place after *you* told me about it and then you say it's yours when it actually isn't? *That's* kind of fucked up."

I swallow from being intimidated and *maybe* being turned on. "Well, when you put it like that, I sound crazy."

"Maybe you are crazy." He shrugs. "I don't know."

I ignore him. "Are you actually going to get this place?"

"Would you have a problem with that?"

"Yes," I say. "It's a *brownstone.*" Saying it out loud and knowing it's slipping through my fingers makes me want to cry.

"Well, you can come over anytime you want." He smiles, and I shoot him an irritated look. He takes a breath and puts his hands in his pockets. "June," he says, and I just want to hear him say my name again. "I get your position, I really do, but I've been looking for a roommate for weeks and I finally found someone who—" Then a light bulb goes off. It must be obvious in my face, because Adam frowns. "What?"

"You're not getting this place on your own?" I clarify.

"I wish. I've been on roommate finder websites all month and there's a guy in Queens who's ready to move in tomorrow."

"I have a proposition," I say. My stomach churns but my words are coming out faster than my sense of judgment. I just *need* this house. "What if we live together?"

His head tilts, confusion creased across his brows. "I'm sorry—*live* together?"

"I know it sounds ridiculous, but it's perfect! *You* need a place. *I* need a place. And think of how much we'd save!" I grab his forearm, surprised how the physical contact makes the hairs on the back of my neck stand up. "You already know me and where I work. I'm twenty-one, from Toronto, and I just graduated as a theater major from Columbia. I'm sort of a neat freak and I don't have a criminal record. Do you even know this guy from Queens? At least you know me—I'm normal! I mean, aside from yelling at you two minutes ago . . . which . . . sorry, by the way." I smile.

He blinks and has no immediate reaction. If he doesn't say anything in about thirty seconds, I have a feeling one of us is going to be halfway down the street and it's a toss-up at this point as to who would be running away.

He continues to look at me, stunned, the jaw in his muscle working overtime. I'm waiting for him to laugh in my face, humiliating the stranger from the bookshop who scolded him and then suggested they be roommates. Except he does this thing and looks up and takes a deep inhale.

"I'm twenty-three, currently studying at the Culinary Institute of New York and I work at Galaxy's Diner on 46th on nights and weekends. I also don't have a criminal record. I'm kind of messy, but I cook a mean veal parmigiana."

I chew the inside of my cheek. Somehow, this doesn't feel like the craziest idea.

"Dogs or cats?" I ask, and he cocks his head.

"Dogs," he says slowly, and then ping-pongs back to me. "Any weird habits?"

"I sometimes sing in the shower . . . but I can control myself."

"Don't," he says intently, and I bite my lip. "Favorite holiday?"

"Christmas." I roll my eyes, and he nods toward me as if to say *obviously.* "Early riser or night owl?"

"Night owl, but not partying. I'll be in the living room watching movies until two in the morning." He pauses. "Pet peeve?"

"People who burp in public." I make a face. "You?"

"Slow walkers."

Oh, that's a good one.

"Favorite month?" I raise my eyebrow.

He stops the fast pacing of our back-and-forth and looks at me. He's *been* looking at me, but now it feels different.

"Still June," he says, and I realize I'm holding my breath.

"If we do this . . ." I clear my throat. "A few ground rules," I say confidently. "We *always* pay our rent on time and split bills fifty-fifty." He nods and I continue. "No drugs, outside of weed, and if we bring any significant others home, we give the other twenty-four hours' notice."

He takes a step closer, and I see the corner of his mouth curl into a little smile that makes me feel certain things deep in my belly.

"Anything else?"

My brain juggles all of the possible reasons we shouldn't do this, but then I think of all the better reasons that tell me we should. The main one being *that house.* I push aside the fact that he's the most attractive guy I've ever met in real life or that him being mere inches away from me makes me feel my blood rushing through my body. This dynamic could easily get messy, and there's only one way to make sure things *don't* get messy.

"Nothing ever happens between us," I say. He tightens his lips, and I see his jaw twitch. I don't know Adam well enough—I barely know him at all—but the look on his face tells me he's no longer in. "I mean, just because we live together doesn't mean we can hook up randomly or make out, or whatever else you might be into."

"I'm curious what you think I could be into that isn't hooking up or making out."

I roll my eyes. "So, are you in or not?"

Our eyes lock and I put out my hand. He looks at it and then back up at me and I put on my best smile and flutter my eyelashes.

He laughs and shakes his head. "You got a deal, roomie."

Chapter 5

30 DAYS UNTIL THE MEETING

Being stuck in an elevator with Adam Harper does warrant a fit of hysteria, but I'm saved when three men in business suits step in between us on the seventeenth floor.

As if they're burning a hole through the side of my skull, I can feel Adam's eyes on me. But my attention stays focused on the numbers above the elevator doors, slowly decreasing by each second. Once we reach ground level, I adjust my stance and prepare to make a run for it. The doors open and I push through everybody, heading for the exit.

"June," Adam calls, but I ignore the sound of his voice and keep moving. The smell of fresh air, or at least open air, fills my lungs and I'm able to think a little more clearly. Adam's voice pleads over the sounds of traffic and I stop and turn around, unintentionally allowing him to catch up. Once he gets within two feet of me, he takes a step back, mindful of my personal space.

"I didn't know you were going to be here, June," he says, and

I believe him. I don't know the person standing in front of me, at least not anymore, but I do know Adam wouldn't want our reunion to be like this.

"Me either," I say, swiping my hair out of my face.

We stand awkwardly in the middle of the sidewalk while people walk around us, yet neither he nor I move. I do my best to not make eye contact, but I keep looking back at the details on his face. The way his clothes hang on his body and how he's taller than I remember. It's like meeting someone who's on TV—you know more than you want to admit about their physical appearance, but it's hard to believe they're really in front of you.

"I had no idea about Stanley," he says with regret in his voice.

There's a knot in my chest but I push myself to respond.

"What are we going to do? This is *insane,* Adam." My voice shakes a little, not used to saying his name out loud. He wipes a hand over his face like he's thinking, contemplating. I'm positive he wants the money as much as I do—how could he not?

"I mean, we sell it. Right?" he says.

"I-I guess," I say. I've had just enough time to think about this as he has. I close my eyes for a moment, collecting myself, attempting to process everything. There is no way I can be expected to make a rational decision right now. While getting rid of this problem as fast as possible sounds more than appealing, it also means security for a long time. We have to be strategic. The alternative is we don't sell it, but that would mean owning property together. "If we keep it . . ." I start. "What would that even look like?"

"It wouldn't be a permanent solution," he says. "I just don't want to make any rash decisions."

"Who's making rash decisions?" I say defensively.

"Nothing, never mind." He runs his hand through his hair, the way he always used to when he was stressed, and it's frustratingly distracting.

"What are you trying to say?"

"Nothing," he says firmly, and then scratches above his eyebrow. "Look, I don't want to argue. Can we just take a night before we decide what to do?"

My head shakes. "I can't."

I don't even know exactly *what* I can't. Simply talking about this is painful enough. I can't bear the thought of what happens after today, after the next ten minutes. Adam Harper is the one person who can make me feel like everything is going to be okay and at the same time the only person who can thoroughly crush my entire world.

"June, please," he presses.

Adam's eyes are deep and darker than I remember, desperately searching for an answer, but there's pain behind them that's making me consider what he's asking. He's not just asking me to come to a solution about the house with him, he's asking me to put our history aside, to forget everything that's happened. To pretend like I haven't been trying to bury my feelings and push through the pain and heartbreak for five years. So if he's asking me to do all of that, I don't think I can.

"June?" he repeats, and it brings me back to reality.

"O-Okay," I hear myself say for some reason.

"Okay?" His eyes lighten with relief.

I'm not on board with this and almost every part of me is screaming to run away, except the part of me that's Adam's. A part that has always been Adam's, and I'm learning, no matter how much I resist, maybe always will be.

"Let's take the night," I nod, mostly telling myself. "And I'm going to pay you back that deposit. It just happened so fast and—"

"It's fine," he says.

"I'm paying you back," I press. "Half of that house is mine too."

"Okay. No rush."

"You're not doing me any favors, Adam."

"Of course not." He shakes his head. My instinct is to say something clever, to banter, because that's what comes naturally when I'm with him. Adam brings out a side of me I have to otherwise force with anyone else. But we're not doing this, so I don't say anything. He takes a look at his phone and puts it back in his pocket, "I, uh, I've got to head to work, but are you busy tomorrow? Maybe we can meet at Perry and take a look at everything."

Oh right. I didn't even think of actually going back to the house. I feel sick again.

"Sure," I say, remembering that my flight is tomorrow evening. That should give me enough time to figure out what the hell I'm going to do. "Eleven?"

"That works," he says. "And if we need to bring anyone else into this conversation, that's fine too."

I give him a blank stare. "You mean lawyers?"

"Yeah, or . . ." He looks down and scratches the side of his nose. "Anyone else this might invol—"

"I think this should be a conversation between us for right now," I say curtly.

"Right," he says, nodding. "Okay, I'll see you tomorrow."

He starts walking in the other direction, and once he's out of sight I remember to breathe again.

WHEN I GET back to the hotel I open an unread email from Theo.

Hey June,

How's New York? Still waiting to hear an update on an audition. Regardless, there might be another guest spot on NCIS, they have your self-tape. Will let you know what they say.

Theo

A guest spot is always good news—it usually holds me over for a couple of months until the next job. But as I read this, there's nothing I'm excited about. I'm grateful, and always will be, to continue working, but is it selfish to *not* be excited?

I mark the email as unread to remind myself to call her in the morning.

The shower water runs so hot that I can hardly feel my own skin anymore. The steam fills the bathroom until I can barely see anything but fog in front of me, similar to my mind.

My thoughts wander as my fingertips begin to prune. I'm well aware that I live a fortunate life, but this house could be the means to a *different* life. How can I turn that down?

And then there's Adam. How can he possibly be okay with this? What does *his* life look like? Where does he live? What does he do? Is he with anyone? Is he with *her*? *Stop it.* I lift my face up to the showerhead and let my mind become a blank slate.

When I wake the next morning, although it's debatable if you could call last night a legitimate night of sleep, I go for a walk to clear my head. I wind up at the Elk, one of the coffee shops I used to go to almost every day once I had enough expendable income. When I step through the doors, my senses take over and it feels like visiting an old friend. A few minor differences through the years, but there's something familiar, comforting, about reuniting. In a way, that's how the whole city feels.

As I sip my pecan latte, I gradually become more alert and acknowledge how alive New York is before eight o'clock. There's something gratifying about how life on the West Coast is slower, but the electricity that flows through Manhattan is unmatched. There's no final destination on my morning stroll, yet I feel like I have purpose, like everyone around me has purpose. These are people who choose to wake up and do something with their day, even if it is just walking, and that's admirable. I didn't realize I was homesick for a place that I refused to think of as home.

MEETING ADAM IN a couple of hours has nothing to do with me buying a new sweater. It also has nothing to do with me spending a few extra minutes on my hair and makeup. While taking a final look at myself in the mirror, I catch an incoming call from Theo.

"Hey!" I answer, hoping that there's good news on the other end.

"So, update . . ." she says, and her tone gives me an uneasy feeling. *One* audition is all I need to write off this trip. Just one. "The *NCIS* thing isn't going to happen, unfortunately. I'm sorry."

"Oh . . ." I sit on the edge of the bed, not upset about *NCIS* in the slightest. "All good."

"But on the bright side, it looks like we're on track to set up a meeting with the producers of *Les Mis*. They haven't even started auditions but—"

"Wait." I stand up. "*Les Mis*?!" I search my brain, because she never mentioned anything about *Les Misérables*.

"I told you about this last week," she says in a *you weren't listening* tone. "It's a huge deal too—it's been fourteen years since they've been on Broadway."

Although I'm not as in touch with the theater scene as I used to be, I know that a revival of *Les Misérables* is a *huge* deal.

"You never mentioned anything specific, Theo!"

"I didn't?" She sounds genuinely confused. "Oh well, sorry. But yes, it's for *Les Mis*. There— *Stella! I gave you an avocado this morning and you didn't want it. DON'T TAKE BECKHAM'S.*" Theo's voice switches into mommy-mode and then switches right back, something I've learned to get used to. "There isn't a specific role in mind, but let me try and set something up ASAP and I'll email you this week. June, please tell me you can stay a few extra days."

My stomach does a little flip, and for the first time in a *very* long time I'm excited about a role. My hand instinctively touches my throat. It's been a year or two since I sang in front of an audience, but Theo has been adamant that I keep that skill polished so I've continued consistent voice lessons. Maybe being here, at least right now, isn't such a bad thing.

"I can stay." I try not to sound too excited. "Just let me know what I need to do. I'll be here."

"Amazing. Okay, let me— *Stella! There is a banana on the counter—you can have the banana. Leave Beckham's avocado alone*—let me make some phone calls and then I'll be in touch," she says, and then hangs up.

MY MEMORY IS sharp. It's a gift and a curse. I can remember a face from anywhere, I always know where I left my keys, I remember not just how people made me feel, but what they said. And even though it was five years ago, I remember clearly the last time I stood in front of 74 Perry Street. Even though I wish I could forget.

The yellow leaves on the oak tree to my right are in the early stage of metamorphosis, on the cusp of turning orange, reminding me how I miss seasons. How I miss change. I have an urge to touch its bark but control myself. More nostalgia is the last thing I want, but being here feels exactly as it did before. It's funny how the world turns, changes through the years, yet a structure surrounded by brick will stand still in time.

At the top of the block, there's an older couple walking their dog. A few doors down, a father follows his child dressed up for ballet. The street is as undeniably charming as it always was, and I'm lucky I was able to call it home for years.

My lips press together as I brace myself for the emotions I

know I won't be able to control once I walk through that door. It's already unlocked and on one hand, entering feels natural. On the other, it feels like I'm trespassing.

Cautiously, I turn the knob, and hold my breath at the sight. It's home. Except it's not. I've failed to remember that this is an active Airbnb listing. Who knows how many people have gone through this door in the past five years? It's redecorated, just as Mara showed us in the pictures, but it feels like there has been a whole other lifetime within these walls. I guess there was.

The interior design really is impeccable. A maximalist's dream and at the same time, still cozy. It's a delicate balance between turn-of-the-century details and a modern style, timeless, almost. I cross the mosaic tiling in the foyer, toward the bookshelf filled with colorful novels, leather-bound books, and plants. I hang my purse on the stair banister and take the same steps I used to take countless times down the hallway into the kitchen.

It's then that I catch Adam in the backyard on the phone, which brings an all-too-familiar feeling of comfort. The saying "Absence makes the heart grow fonder" is proving to be true, because he's pacing, wearing a dark green sweater and jeans, looking like a goddamn Ralph Lauren model. He catches my eye and nods at me, holding up a finger, signaling he'll be inside in a moment. I take a seat at the kitchen island, which has always been the heart of the home, as Adam enters through the back door.

"Hey, sorry about that," he says.

I shrug. "No worries."

He starts opening the cupboards, and he looks comfortable. This *feels* comfortable, as if we do this all the time.

"It looks like everything's mostly stocked still. Do you want a coffee or tea or something?"

But we're not here to have tea and catch up, we're here to figure out this arrangement.

"I'm fine."

His eyes tentatively catch mine and he leans back against the counter. He pulls up his sleeves, and I look away when he reveals his forearms.

"This kitchen will take some getting used to," he says as he looks around.

I've wanted to fawn over the kitchen since seeing the photos. The marble and the green backsplash with the gold hardware? It's beautiful. But I stop myself. It's unsettling how effortless this all feels, how it's almost too easy to pick up where we left off.

"It's nice."

He crosses his arms, a dead giveaway that he's just as uncomfortable as I am. "So, how have you been?"

"Good." I nod, purposely keeping my answers as short as possible. "Mostly just working."

"I saw you in the trailer for that new show," he says, and I wonder what that must be like. For my face to not now be an old painting he was once familiar with, the details slowly having faded as each year went by. "*Swindlers.*"

"Oh." I give a weak smile. "Well, don't get excited. It's already canceled." I realize it's the first time I'm not embarrassed to tell someone.

"Sorry." His voice is so smooth and deep. Almost like velvet.

"It's all good," I say. "On to the next one."

"It seems like you're doing good out there," he says.

"How have *you* been?" I say, changing the subject. "Where are you working now?"

He takes a beat before answering me. "Alden. It's a resta—"

"Oh, I've heard of that place." I straighten. "I feel like everyone's been talking about it. It's like the hottest restaurant right now."

I think of the endless number of odd jobs Adam took working at diners and hole-in-the-wall food joints. Now he's a chef at one of the most popular restaurants in the city. It's a strange feeling, being happy for someone and at the same time knowing they got all they wanted the minute you left their life.

He just smiles and runs a hand behind his neck. Which makes his sweater rise a bit, revealing some skin and a trail of hair above his pants. Dear God, it's just as distracting as his forearms.

"So." Adam clears his throat. "I went through everything that Mara sent. Had my lawyer look at it too. It's all legitimate." He reaches for a folder on the counter and passes it to me. "Printed you a copy too, just in case."

The sudden switch to business throws me off. Upset that for thirty seconds I allowed myself to forget what we're doing here. Like this is just another Wednesday when we're hanging out in the kitchen talking about nothing.

I'm not sure why I thought going through everything was something we'd do together, but I take the folder and bring it closer.

"Thanks."

"I think it's a really great investment property. I don't see any reason why we shouldn't rent this and keep it for as long as we can."

He doesn't see any reason why us owning joint property is a

problem? Things didn't end in a great place with us, and while I'm not ready to dive into our past, it's clear that he's already pushed everything aside.

"Well," I start. "That requires *being here,* making sure everything is okay, meeting with agents. It'd be a lot of work to get it set up. Not sure how that would work with me in LA . . ."

"For the amount of money, we can try to make it work."

"That's easy for you to say—you live here."

"Right." His jaw clenches. "Okay, well, we can do as much as we can before our meeting on the twenty-third. You're going to stay here until then, right?"

"No . . ." I say slowly. Although I told Theo I would stay in the city a little longer, that certainly doesn't mean until the twenty-third.

"Couldn't you just stay here for the month? Is that a problem?"

"Yeah, *a little.*" I almost laugh.

"Are you filming?" he asks.

It feels like he's just rubbed salt in a very fresh wound. "No," I say bitterly. "I just wrapped."

"Then what's the problem?"

"I have other responsibilities, Adam," I say, slightly offended, even though I actually have *nothing* waiting for me back in LA. "I can't stay here for a whole month."

"Well, not with that attitude" is the only thing that comes out of his mouth.

"Excuse me?"

"June." He narrows his eyes. "You're telling me you don't want six million dollars?"

"Well, it's technically three if we're splitting it." I shrug, aware of how difficult I'm being, but he cannot be serious right now.

"I know this isn't the ideal situation—"

"You think?" I scoff.

"—but it's only a month. We figure out what we want to do, use this as an investment property or sell it, whatever we want. And then I promise, you'll never have to see me again."

I look away, because as much as I hate to admit it, Adam's right. This house means financial stability. It means focusing on my film and TV career and finding a place of my own. I already canceled my flight for tonight and if I'm staying a few extra days, I guess I can manage to extend my entire trip.

"All right," I say with defeat. "I'll stay."

"Great," Adam says, looking quite pleased with himself. He reaches into his back pocket and slides a gold key across the counter. "I'd show you the place, but I think you know your way around."

I shake my head. "I'm not staying here." Being within these walls for merely ten minutes has brought up too many emotions.

"Oh right," he says, nodding. "I'm sure a hotel for the next month is more ideal."

"Ugh, fine." I roll my eyes knowing he has a point. Considering how much is in my bank account, staying in a hotel isn't even an option.

Adam gathers up his papers and grabs his coat. "All right, well, I'll be back around seven," he says, heading toward the front door.

"What?" I stand up and follow him. "Why?"

"Because I'm done with work at six . . . and I like to be in bed by ten."

"Oh no, no, no *no!*" I shake my head, crossing my arms across my chest. "Don't you have a place of your own?"

"Yeah, I have an apartment . . ." he says. "But *now* I have a brownstone."

"You're joking . . ." I say incredulously. There is *no* way Adam and I are staying under the same roof for four weeks.

"Why would I be joking?" he asks.

"We can't both stay here!" I spit out.

"Then do you want to pay me your share of the deposit now, or . . . ?"

A sound of shock escapes from me, but I'm speechless. I stand in front of him in pure rage, and he merely raises an eyebrow. I think he's actually enjoying my discomfort.

"You're doing this to spite me," I say, realizing what's happening.

"Actually, no. But nice to know how highly you think of me." He nods to himself.

I let out an exasperated sigh. "Then why would you want to stay here?"

"Alden is in SoHo," he says calmly. "It would be nice to walk to work every day instead of taking the subway."

"Okay, so you get a shorter commute." I shrug. "That's it? That's why you're so adamant on living together?"

Adam crosses his arms and leans against the stair banister. "June, why don't you tell me why you're so adamant on *not* living together?"

Adam and I continue to glare at each other. The tension is

palpable, but it's teetering between vengeful and, dare I say, sexual. I don't know whether I want to leave and slam the door in his face or have him slam me against the door and let him have his way.

This is bigger than the money. Being here, I know what I need.

What I need is closure.

"Fine." I straighten my shoulders. "We do this and then we never see each other again."

Chapter 6

28 DAYS UNTIL THE MEETING

"ARE YOU SURE IT'S OKAY?" I ASK.

"Oh my God, obviously," Shivani says. "Take as long as you need!"

"I just feel bad with the short notice and all." I switch the phone to my other ear. "But I wasn't expecting this job to come up."

"June, you *do* know Zach and I were living together for years before we asked you to move in, right? We are not dependent on your share of the rent." She laughs. "We'll be fine."

"Okay, okay," I sigh. "I'll see you in a month."

"All right, babe. And, June . . ." Shivani says. "Enjoy New York. You deserve to have fun."

"Yeah," I say with a nod. "I'll try."

WHEN I ARRIVE at Perry, it's empty. While hauling my luggage up the stairs I notice Adam's bedroom door is open, with two suitcases sitting by the dresser. We haven't spoken since yesterday. I don't know what his schedule looks like, nor do I know much else about his personal life. The less I know and the less we see each other, the better.

Out of habit, I make a right and head to my old bedroom, now decorated with olive green floral wallpaper, warm overhead lighting, and a flax linen duvet that I can't wait to climb underneath. Although it looks different, my hand gently grazes the wooden doorframe, allowing memories to flow through my mind like a river all over again.

"It's only four weeks, June," I say, falling onto the bed and staring at the ceiling. "It's only four weeks."

Bringing myself up to a seated position, I reach for my phone and start typing in my contact list.

DO NOT TEXT

A number appears, and I take a deep breath. My thumb hovers and I finally press *Unblock Number.* I click on the name *DO NOT TEXT* and change it back to its original name: *Adam Harper.*

I make my peace with the fact that this will be home again for the next month and start to hang my clothes in the closet. Being an over-packer has its perks, and I thankfully have enough clothing to last me at least a few more days.

About twenty minutes later, I hear the front door open and then close. My initial reaction is to call out *Hey,* but I don't.

I throw a sweater onto the bed and walk to the hallway.

"I'm sure it's a given, but I'm taking this roo— *Jesus Christ*!"

Holding the back of my hand to my face, I look over my shoulder as if my vision's been compromised.

"What?! What?" Adam puts his hands up and instinctively backs away.

"Why are you naked?!"

"I'm not *naked.*"

Okay, fine, he's not naked, but he may as well be. A sheen of sweat shines on his bare chest, staring back at me like a billboard. His hair is messy, and he's wearing black joggers that reveal a V-line that goes down to where his pants hit. When the hell did he get that? He looks more muscular than I remember. Like he's been training to be in a fucking fight or something.

"I don't care, put some clothes on." I manage to look at his face, but his abundance of torso is still in my peripheral view. Adam walking around shirtless has never been an issue, but now I'm triggered. Not because I have a problem with the view, but because I quite *enjoy* the view. *God, June, get it together!* "I think we need some boundaries," I huff.

"Like what?" he says, unimpressed, a pec muscle twitching as he wipes his forehead with his shirt in hand.

"Like what we wear and *don't* wear," I say, gesturing to him. "You won't find me walking around half naked."

"My loss," he says sarcastically, and I feel my cheeks tinge pink.

"I'm serious, Adam. This is a business deal. This is not what it used to be."

"June, I'm well aware things aren't what they used to be," he says, and we hold our gaze for several seconds.

"Good," I barely get out.

"Great," he says.

He inches toward me, but I jerk away. "What are you doing?"

"I'm going to take a shower." He nods behind me to the bathroom. "Is that within your boundaries?"

"Oh." I move sideways to let him pass. He throws the shirt in his hand over his shoulder and continues past me. I open my mouth to say something, anything, but my eyes shut when I hear the impact of the door closing behind me.

TYING MY HAIR, taking out my contacts, and throwing on my overworn Columbia sweatshirt makes it feel like the weight of today is off my shoulders . . . for now. There's a leather-bound copy of *To Kill a Mockingbird* that I pull off the shelf, and as I fall onto the couch I make a mental note to find out where it's from. This is truly the comfiest piece of furniture I've ever sat in.

The urgency to return to Los Angeles has slightly dissipated. It feels oddly nice being here, and it's not just the couch. I think of my call with Theo and allow myself to imagine what life could be like being back on Broadway.

The possibility of entering a new chapter of my career is the motivation I needed. The past few years feel somewhat like a fever dream, jumping from job to job, from man to man, chasing something I couldn't see. Now there's a painting of a future in front of me once the month is over. I could return to the theater, have enough money for a place to call my own. Maybe I'll even consider going on a date now and then.

"Look at you." The sound of Adam's voice intrudes on my thoughts. He makes his way down the stairs, hair damp, now in gray sweatpants. He's wearing a shirt that's hugging him in a way that reminds me of exactly what's underneath. "You look right at home."

I try not to roll my eyes at the irony.

"And look at you," I say without glancing up from my book. "You found clothes."

He plops down on the opposite side from me, and I pull my feet in closer. Sitting on the couch together feels almost too intimate. I continue to remind myself that I have nothing in common with this new Adam. That this is in fact *very* different from all the mundane nights we spent together. But it's hard to think that way when I remember vividly the last time we were on a couch together: his fingertips pressing into my hips, his breath on my neck, and the taste of his tongue inside my mouth.

"I was looking into it, and we can't even start the process for listing the house until we sign the paperwork," he says.

"Oh," I say, feeling suddenly very warm at the thought of doing *nothing* for the next four weeks. "I guess that makes sense."

"So, we're kind of just in limbo this month until then."

Limbo. That seems to be the theme of my life currently. It's not like I can afford a flight to LA and then come back here for the meeting with Mara. Even if I could, I don't have enough money to pay Shivani and Zach for rent. The silver lining is the potential audition, and I will do whatever it takes to get that audition. Even if it means staying in this house.

"Do you think it's going to be easy?" I ask. "The selling process."

"I have no idea." He shakes his head. "I still find it hard to believe this is even happening."

"Tell me about it," I say under my breath.

"Are you sure you're okay with this?" he asks.

"Do I have a choice?" I say, and he gives me a look that says *you always have a choice.*

Adam stands up and then looks down at me. "Are you hungry? I went grocery shopping."

It's not until he asks that I realize I ate hardly anything today. But that's going to be a big no to Adam making me dinner.

"I'm fine."

"So, if I go in there"—he looks at the kitchen—"and make shrimp scampi, you're not going to have any." He says it more like a statement than a question.

"Nope." I keep my eyes on the book, reading the same line over and over again until he's out of the room.

The sound of pots and pans and the smell of sizzling garlic and butter make my stomach grumble. Adam is by far the best chef I've ever met; not that I've met a lot of chefs, but I've met a lot of people who know how to cook. *A chef is someone who makes a recipe, a cook is someone who follows it,* I remember him telling me when I asked the difference.

When Adam reenters the living room, he's holding two hearty bowls of pasta. Thick linguine with shrimp and a dusting of seasoning taunts me. He places one bowl on the coffee table in front of me and proceeds to eat his without saying a word. I'm actually offended that he was able to pull this together in less than thirty minutes.

I close my book a little too hard. "Why are you doing this?"

"We have to eat" is all he says. "Or do they not do that in LA?"

I glare at him, but he's not giving me the satisfaction of looking back. Instead, he takes the remote and turns on the television, not asking if I want to watch anything. He chooses the first movie queued on Netflix and hits play.

I'm aware I'm being difficult and yet I can't stop. Adam's acting like we can pick up from where we left off, like everything is normal. I can't pretend it didn't take me weeks to stop crying every night, months to try to move on, and years to forget about him. I'd almost rather him yell, give me the cold shoulder, show some sign of emotion. Him being *okay* is more hurtful than I could have imagined.

Abruptly, I get off the couch and head up the stairs. I don't bother to look back. I slam the door shut and open a window to kill the smell of garlic.

Chapter 7

MAY, 11 YEARS AGO

"I STILL CAN'T BELIEVE YOU'RE MOVING IN WITH A TOTAL stranger." Chloe holds down the flaps of the cardboard box as I tape up my books.

"Can you stop saying he's a stranger? He literally knows Ethan." After finding out about Adam, Chloe went on an investigating spree, as most friends do, and made it her mission to find out if we had any mutual friends. To our surprise, the guy I'm moving in with and the guy she's casually sleeping with are from the same town on Long Island. "He's also genuinely nice and he'll be good protection."

"And it doesn't hurt that he's hot." She nudges me with her elbow.

"He's not hot," I say to her, but really to myself, because being attracted to my future roommate is not an option.

"You're joking, right . . . ?" Chloe says seriously. "There's no way you can't think he's attractive. He's six five and has that dark wavy hair and probably an eight-pack."

"He's only like six three . . ." I say.

"You guys are going to hook up," she tells me.

I choke on nothing. "What? No we're not!"

"Oh my God, of course you are!" Chloe rolls her eyes. "Two attractive, single people living under the same roof?!"

"That's where you're wrong." I shrug. "We have a deal."

"What? Your stupid deal that *nothing is ever going to happen*?" Chloe says, using air quotes. "Do you know how many times I tell myself I'm not going to hook up on a first date? And then before I know it, I'm faking an orgasm."

"That's . . ." I make a face. "Did you ever think I have more willpower than you?"

"Yeah, but does Adam?" She raises an eyebrow. "All it takes is him seeing you wrapped in a teeny tiny towel coming out of the shower for his testosterone to go wild. He's going to say *June, forget the deal,*" she says, putting on a deep voice that kind of sounds like Antonio Banderas. "And you're going to say *okay*!" she says in a high-pitched voice that sounds like my IQ is much lower than it is. "Because no matter how much you try to deny it . . . you're attracted to Adam."

"Okay, I just want to make it clear neither of us sounds like that," I say. "And besides, even if I do decide to walk around half naked after a shower—which I won't—it doesn't matter, because I'm not Adam's type."

"You're like one of the prettiest people I know . . ." Chloe frowns. "What's his type?"

Fine, I actually don't know Adam's type. I just know that guys like Adam who are tall, good-looking, athletic, and charismatic are the types of guys who go for people just like them. There are certain women who are just out of the average man's league, and those are the women who people like Adam date.

"Not me," I say. My phone vibrates in my back pocket and when I reach for it, I see a text from Adam flash across the screen. "Speak of the devil." I hold it up to Chloe and she simply raises an eyebrow.

I'm going to Ikea, need anything?

We exchanged numbers and all those important details you should probably know about someone you're moving in with. But this is the first time we're actually texting.

A lot actually . . . but I don't want to hijack your trip.

I set my phone down and go back to taping another box.

"Okay, I've got to head to class." Chloe picks up her bag from my bed. "Let me know if you need any more help tonight."

"If I need you to sit and watch me pack, I'll let you know," I say, but the irony is she's one of the hardest workers I've ever met. And the only person I know who got into law school, specializing in criminal law, of all things.

My phone buzzes again.

I'll be there at 2.

AT 1:59 P.M. Adam pulls up to the front of my apartment in a black sedan with the passenger window rolled down. He leans across the seat, ducking his head. "Hey."

"I didn't know you had a car." I open the door and slide onto the seat. It's surprisingly clean, and there's something about being in a mode of transportation that's not the subway that feels more personal than it is.

"Did you think I was going to make you ride the handlebars of my bike?" He turns to me with an amused look on his face.

"I assumed we were going to take the subway." I tap the air freshener in the shape of a New York Yankees logo. "But now I know we're living the life of luxury . . ."

"Don't get used to it—it's my parents'." He pulls the parking brake and starts driving. "So, what do you need to get?"

"Um." I pull open the list I made on my phone. "Mostly kitchen items, and stuff for my bedroom, but I wanted to ask what your thoughts were on furniture?"

"We should have some." He nods.

"Cool, agreed. But are you bringing anything, or should we go in on some new stuff?"

"I have a couch," he says. "It's a good couch."

"Great." I delete the word *couch* from my list.

"But I don't have a dining table."

"The one in my apartment is technically mine, but it's so old I'd rather get a new one."

"We can split it." He looks at his blind spot and switches lanes. "We should actually split everything we get today. I'll be using the kitchen stuff as much as you are."

"Perfect, because I can't cook."

His grin widens and it's a nice feeling, knowing I'm the cause of it. "Don't worry, I'll teach you some stuff."

"What's culinary school like?" I turn to him, genuinely curious.

"I love it. Really." He turns his head to me, and his eyes flash in a way I haven't seen before. "A lot of it's technical, which is necessary, but still fun. It's cool when we can create our own dishes and menus and stuff."

"Okay, that sounds pretty cool."

"I'll make you something once we're settled in," he says.

"Oh, you don't have to do that." I adjust my seat belt, suddenly self-conscious.

"I want to, it'll be fun."

I feel a smile fill out across my face, and I sit back. "Nobody's ever cooked me anything before."

He frowns. "What do you mean?"

"I mean, when I was a kid my grandparents would make me food, obviously. But never as an adult."

His gaze falls on me, a moment longer than feels natural, then he turns his head back to the road.

"Well, it's my pleasure."

I turn away and look out the window because for some reason I'm blushing. "So, what made you want to be a chef?"

He rolls the sleeve up on his driving arm, and for the first time in my life, forearms are attractive.

"I'd always follow my mom around the kitchen as a kid. She let me make the pasta sauce for dinner with my grandma's recipe. She was watching, but she like *really* let me make it. Cooking together sort of became our thing . . . and I just fell in love with it."

"Wow," I say under my breath.

"It's stupid, I kn—"

"No!" I sit up. "Not at all—that's actually beautiful."

"You don't have to say that." Now he's the one blushing.

"I'm not," I say, shaking my head. "I wish I had childhood memories like that."

It's silent for a moment, but he looks over and gives me an assuring look. It's nice. Almost like he's telling me I can share more with him at my own pace.

"Why did you move to New York?" he asks.

"Probably the same reason you did," I say, and he nods. "I fell in love with the city. When I lived in Toronto, we had to come here for a choir competition and it was truly the best forty-eight hours of my life, to this day. And then after high school, I gathered my savings, took the first bus here, and never looked back." I smile at him, and he lets out a breathless laugh.

"What made you want to study theater?"

"Oh God." I look out the window. "I don't know, it's the only thing that really brought me joy as a kid. Pretending to be someone else, escaping from whatever was happening. Plus, I'm a sucker for a musical number."

I see a hint of a smile. "What's your favorite musical?"

"*Les Misérables,*" I say. "Have you heard of it?"

"Yeah, but I don't know what it's about."

"Well." I let out a chuckle, because anyone who knows *Les Mis* knows it can't really be tied down to a logline. "It takes place in nineteenth-century France and follows the main character, Jean Valjean, an ex-convict who's released from jail after nineteen years."

"What did he go to jail for?" he asks.

"Stealing a loaf of bread for his sister's starving kid." I look at him.

"Damn," he says.

"There are other storylines too, though," I say. "Love triangles, prostitutes, broken dreams, abandonment—all those good things."

"Holy shit . . ." He reaches for the middle console. He pulls out an auxiliary cord and hands it to me. "Let's listen to it."

"Really?" I turn to him, a little too excited, and he nods. I plug the cable into my phone, and we make it through half of the album before reaching IKEA.

THREE HOURS AND an embarrassing amount of money later, which I justify as my first investment as an adult, we're parked back in front of my building. The engine sputters, and I reach for my bag of belongings in the backseat.

"It's a good thing we're getting everything delivered," I say, not knowing where we would've stored our furniture otherwise.

"You know you have an amazing voice, right?" he says like he didn't hear anything I just said.

"What?"

"Your voice," he repeats. "It's incredible."

"Stop!" I throw my hands over my face, embarrassed. I'd made a conscious effort to control myself when listening to the soundtrack but, apparently, I didn't succeed. "I wasn't even really singing."

His eyes widen. "You weren't even trying?"

"I'm done here." I cover my ears and step out of the car. "If you want to keep listening, I can send you the second half."

"I'd rather listen to it with you. Let's do it next week when we're home," he says.

"Okay, drive safe." I close the door and adjust my bag over my shoulder.

"Night, June."

When we're home. That sounds nice.

A FEW WEEKS into us living together, I rarely see Adam. Between shifts at the bookshop, my acting classes, his school schedule, and working on weekends, he's usually out the door when I come home and vice versa. It doesn't take long for me to learn a small detail. Adam Harper will *always* have a date planned on his night off, and rarely with the same person. Our twenty-four-hour rule? It has yet to be in effect, because something else I learn is that Adam *never* brings a woman home.

My first night off in weeks I spend doing what I love best, reading a book with a cup of tea. As someone who's the type to read multiple books simultaneously, tonight I decide to finish my thriller. It's not the brightest idea, because by the time I finish, it's almost eleven and I know I won't be able to fall asleep.

Naturally, my plan of action is to turn on a rom-com. So, I curl up on the couch, make a bowl of extra-butter microwave popcorn, and play *My Best Friend's Wedding.* About thirty minutes into the movie, Adam carefully walks through the front door, making sure to keep quiet until he realizes I'm awake.

"What are you doing up?" He sits on the couch beside me

and grabs my bowl of popcorn. There's a faint smell of beer on him, and I can tell he's exhausted, but the way his hair is pushed back and his denim shirt is open, he still looks attractive.

"Couldn't fall asleep." I stretch out like a cat and then curl my legs back into my body. He watches me, smiling. "What?"

The sides of his mouth turn down as he shrugs. "You look cute."

I laugh. "Is it the stained sweatshirt or the messy bun?"

"I think the flannel pajama pants and the glasses, honestly."

"How was your date?" I adjust myself.

"Good."

"And are we seeing her again?" I smile, anticipating the answer.

"Probably not," he says as he puts a kernel into his mouth.

"Why not?" I turn onto my back and look at him.

"I don't know." He shrugs. "Wasn't feeling it."

"But I thought it was *good.*"

"*Maybe* I'll see her again."

"Are you a fuckboy?" I put an arm behind my head to get a better view of him.

He starts coughing. "What?"

"Hey, I only know the version of Adam that lives here. I don't know what you're like on dates. I don't know whose texts you're not responding to and what girls you're making cry."

"What about the girls making *me* cry?"

"I *thought* I heard a noise coming from your room the other night."

He laughs and then puts his feet up on the coffee table. "I assure you, you are not getting a certain version of me." He burps. "You're getting the whole package, June."

"Lucky me." I turn onto my side to face the TV.

"So, what are we watching?" he asks.

"*My Best Friend's Wedding.* One of the best rom-coms of all time."

"What's happening?" His eyes stay focused on the screen.

"Well, Julia Roberts is in love with her best friend, Dermot Mulroney, but he's engaged to Cameron Diaz, so she's trying to break them up."

"What the fuck, that's messed up."

I laugh. "Yeah, I guess it is."

"What's wrong with your ankle?" He looks down, and I'm unaware that I've been moving it in circular motions.

"Oh, I don't know. It's been hurting the past few days. I think it's from dance class."

"Here." He puts the popcorn back on the coffee table and pulls my leg on his lap and starts massaging.

For a moment, I feel the urge to pull away because his skin is touching my skin. Even though it's just the skin between my socks and pajama pants, it's enough to distract me from the movie. One of his hands is wrapped around my calf while the other kneads my ankle. My mind becomes a blank slate, pulsing, yet I can focus only on where exactly his hands are.

Glancing at Adam, I see that he's still focused on the movie. His eyes are dark, illuminating only when the light from the screen hits them.

I inhale and continue to watch Julia Roberts' attempts to win the affection of her best friend.

Chapter 8

27 DAYS UNTIL THE MEETING

IT'S DIFFICULT TO SAY WHO'S KEEPING THEIR DISTANCE FROM whom, but for the next two days, Adam and I barely cross paths. Our interactions continue to be minimal. Cordial, but minimal. Adam stays out of my way, and I stay out of his. On occasion we'll see each other in the kitchen, but if one of us is in the living room, the other goes straight to their bedroom. It's how *normal* roommates interact, two people cohabitating. What Adam and I used to be wasn't that.

I stay in bed until I can hear Adam leave for work. Once I hear the front door close, I head to the bathroom to brush my teeth.

I'm in New York.

I send the text and place my phone on the bathroom counter. Not even thirty seconds later, the name *Chloe Patel* flashes on my screen. I spit my toothpaste out and answer it.

"June . . ." Chloe's whisper sounds threatening. She's clearly at work; otherwise, I'm positive I would be hearing a much louder reaction. "Since when?!"

"I know, I know." I nod, feeling guilty. I haven't seen Chloe in two years. The last time we were together was when she came to LA for a case she was working on. We text each other as often as friends with full-time jobs and kids do, time permitting, but between living across the country and life naturally happening, it's surprising how quickly two years can go by. "I would've told you sooner, but it was only supposed to be forty-eight hours and . . . things changed. Besides, you're like two hours away!"

"Okay, Connecticut is only an hour and a half away." A few years after law school, Chloe got a job at one of the top law firms in Stamford. She still likes to say that she lives in New York since it's only a train ride away, and I'll never pass up an opportunity to tease her about it. "How long are you in town for? I'm seeing you, obviously," she says.

"Obviously."

"Are you filming something?"

"No, just taking care of some things," I say.

"Where are you staying?"

"Would you believe me if I told you my place?"

"Your place?" she says. "What place?"

"Perry—"

"I don't get it." She sounds not amused in the slightest and I suck my lips in, not saying anything. "You're at Perry? How?!"

"It's a long story."

"Tell me what the fuck is happening right now, I swear to God—"

"In person." I fall onto the bed. "When are you free? I can come to you."

"Ugh, I'm in back-to-backs all day," she groans. "Sunday after lunch?"

"Perfect. Where should I meet you?"

"No, I'm coming to you," Chloe says, and it's crazy to think that the two of us will be back in the city together again. But then, a lot of what's happening this week is crazy. "Shit, I have a meeting right now. I guess I'll see you . . . at Perry?" she says, and I can picture exactly the puzzled look on her face.

"Yeah, I guess so." I throw my hand up because this entire situation is laughable. "See you tomorrow."

WHEN TAKING MY morning stroll, I find myself walking the same route I used to. Slowly, I become one with the flow of bodies around me, as if I never left. Once, I read an article in *The New York Times* describing the West Village as low-key with a small-scale charm, which is spot-on. Sprinkled on every corner are mom-and-pop coffee shops, and in Washington Square Park you're guaranteed to find regulars playing chess. The streets are narrow, with curved corners full of undeniably charming architecture, making it a true village within a concrete jungle. Between the dogs, big and small, being walked along Bleecker and the crisp September air combating steam rising from the construction chimneys, it's difficult to not romanticize my life while being here.

On a stretch well populated with small independent shops

sits a stationery store full of bright-colored pens, pencils, and cards that catch my eye. I'm about to enter when Theo's name appears on my phone screen.

"Hello?" I answer, and hold my breath.

"Hey! You're still in New York, right?"

"I am."

"Perfect. Dan Sackler wants to have lunch with you tomorrow," Theo says matter-of-factly. I search my brain because the name doesn't sound familiar. Then again, I haven't been plugged into the theater world lately. "He's kind of an up-and-coming director. Done a few things Off-Broadway, but he's *really* talented. I saw his production of *Belfast Girls* last year."

"That's amazing." I make a mental note to do some research. "I'm excited to meet him! Do you know how far along they are in everything?"

"Girl, I'm getting to it!" She laughs. "So, he's currently casting. I just know they have their Valjean, and no, I don't know who it is. But— *Beckham, please leave Mommy for two minutes. I'm on the phone . . . With a friend . . . Yes, we'll do yoga after*—he's not looking for huge names."

Not a huge name is something I hear quite often when I get put up for roles. It's never easy hearing you're not as well established as you could be. I've been consistently working for the past ten years, wondering when my résumé is finally going to pay off, but I'll take not being big enough if that's what they want.

"But, they came to me directly asking for you, so . . ." Theo's voice trails off.

"Seriously?" I perk up.

"June, I told you, this is going to be a really great pivot. I—*Stella, I told Beckham Mommy's on the phone. Start the yoga video without me*—I'll send you the details in a bit."

"Perfect. Thanks, Theo."

"Of course." She takes a beat. "So, are you going to tell me what you're doing in New York? The hellmouth of all things?"

I laugh at her using my own words against me. "Okay, I know I talk shit, but it's not that bad . . . I actually like it."

"Yeah, welcome to the eightieth percentile. So, what are you doing there?"

"Just visiting a friend," I say.

"Got it. Well, have fun. I'll text you in like an hour."

There's a stupid grin on my face the rest of the morning. I take my time during the remainder of my walk and treat myself to a colorful greeting card that reads *YOU'VE GOT THIS* at the stationery store. As I turn onto Perry and the house is within view, my phone vibrates.

> Saturday, 1:30pm at Alden in SoHo. I've been dying to go so let me know how it is.

I CONSIDERED ASKING Theo to change the reservation, but I left it. Being difficult before meeting Dan probably isn't the best first impression, and I selfishly want to see what Alden is all about. Adam works in the kitchen, which means the chances of running into him are slim to none. So, what I don't do is tell him I'm having lunch at the place where he works.

My outfit consists of an oversized houndstooth blazer on top of my white shirt and jeans. I stack my gold rings on my fingers, layer on a thin necklace, and gently run my fingers through my curls. As I take a final look in the mirror, it hits me that it's been too long since I've done this. I'm used to self-tapes and lengthy auditions with a group of people who look almost identical to me.

Despite what people think, being an actor in LA is not all that it's cut out to be. What I do is quite depressing actually—it's a *service industry,* as Theo would say: catering to what people need and giving them what they want. But today, thinking about a live audience instead of a boom operator on their phone reminds me exactly why I do this.

THE COBBLED STREETS of SoHo lead to a brick-covered establishment with a small gold plaque that reads *Alden* by the door. Aside from the discreet signage, there's no indication of a restaurant being here.

Inside, it's loud. The sound of chatter from deep conversations over appetizers and wine blends with the clatter of pots and pans from the kitchen, mixed with a subtle undertone of upbeat jazz to tie it all together. It's no surprise why this place is impossible to get a reservation at. There's an impressive lunch rush, maybe a few empty tables here and there with a *Reserved* sign on top, but there's no doubt it's full.

There's a wall covered with a variety of wine bottles of all colors that travels from the floor to the ceiling, while on another wall is a collection of black-and-white photographs in frames.

It's beautiful, with the natural light seeping through the windows, but I'm already curious to see what the restaurant looks like at night. The mismatched chairs and tableware complement one another, and it's almost shocking how this place *is* Adam. If he were a restaurant, this would be it. His being able to land a job at a place like this is, for lack of a better word, perfect.

Behind the hostess stand is a young redhead wearing high-waisted black pants and a matching vest.

"Hi," I say, looking around to see if I can spot Dan. "Reservation under 'Sackler.' "

Her eyes trail the sheet below her and she smiles and grabs two menus.

"You're the first one here. You can follow me." She leads me over blue-and-burnt-orange checkered tiling and past a giant olive tree in the middle of the restaurant. We walk by tables filled with dishes that tempt me to ask *excuse me, that looks delicious. What did you order?* I'm guided to a spot deep in the restaurant across from an elaborate glass window granting me a view of the kitchen. My eyes widen and I quickly scan the faces through the pane. Thankfully, it looks like Adam isn't working today. Regardless, I'd rather be safe than sorry, and choose the seat facing away from the kitchen and any chance of him seeing me.

I hadn't thought to search Alden's menu beforehand, since I'd already heard all the chatter about it back in Los Angeles. But scanning the menu now, I realize I had *no idea* how expensive it is. My eyes fall to something called a Wagyu porterhouse and I see the number $255 beside it when I hear a voice above me.

"June?"

I know the man looking down at me is Dan Sackler. He carries himself like a college professor—mousy brown hair and sneakers and an overworn jacket. I did some extensive Google searching over the past twenty-four hours and Theo was right, he's incredibly talented. From what I've learned, he's only in his early forties and he and his husband are a director/producer powerhouse on the path to taking over Broadway.

"Dan, hi!" I stand to shake his hand and wait for him to take a seat before I do. "It's so nice to meet you!"

"Oh my God, please, I should be saying the exact same thing." He takes off his jacket and places it on the seat beside him. "I know you're based out of LA, so when I heard you were in the city, I had to make the time."

It's not often I hear of anyone taking time out of their day to see me—it's usually the other way around.

"The pleasure is all mine," I say. "Really."

Our waiter comes by and Dan orders us both a glass of Pinot and the king crab risotto.

"You're going to love it. It's their specialty," he says to me, and then hands the waiter our menus. "Okay, so, June, let's cut to the chase. I'm a big fan of your work."

I raise my eyebrows. "My work?"

"Yes! The revival of *Rent* was legendary," he says, and my hands start to clam up. He's not talking about my onscreen work; he's talking about theater. "I saw you *twice* that year. You were incredible."

"Oh." I look down to hide my discomfort, but I don't think Dan notices. "Thank you. *Rent* was really fun."

"If you don't mind my asking, what happened?"

I'm unprepared for his candidness. Of course this would

come up, why wouldn't it? He knows this industry—it's his industry.

"Well." I clear my throat. "I moved to Los Angeles to pursue film and TV," I answer, knowing that's not what he's asking.

"Yeah." He nods along like I've just said *the sky's blue*. "And Becca Kirke took over and the Tony would have been hers, but she was disqualified because she didn't originate the role that year. I know . . . but *what happened*?"

Well, he's also clearly done his research. I'm looking at him like I'm a kid in the principal's office, walking on eggshells with every answer. He already knows my career, whether he read it on BroadwayWorld.com or asked Theo. He knows, and there's no pretending.

"I was just going through a hard time in my life," I answer truthfully, hoping that's enough.

"I'm sorry, June." His eyebrows groove together. "I'm sorry I brought it up." He relaxes into his seat. "Is coming back to Broadway the right move for you?"

"Yes, absolutely," I say a little too quickly. "I was young and stupid back then. More emotional than logical." I swallow through a swell in my throat. "*Les Mis* is the reason I got into theater. I don't even know what you had in mind for me, but I know this is an opportunity of a lifetime. I will work my ass off," I ramble, not even realizing how much I want it now that the opportunity may be slipping through my fingers.

"June," he laughs. "I'm not worried about you working your ass off. I saw what you're capable of, and if I can be honest, your leaving the theater was a huge mistake—" Our waiter suddenly appears and sets out our wine, and Dan waits until he's gone. "Also, if this all works out, promise me you won't give me that emotional-versus-logical bullshit. That's why we're in theater. We all think with our hearts."

"Noted." I let out a laugh and we clink our wineglasses.

The rest of lunch goes well and we hit it off. Dan is open, honest, funny, and someone I want to be around. As the next hour goes by, it becomes clearer that being a part of this revival is what I *want.* There's a current throughout my body that I've been longing for, for years. I feel as if a small part of me that was gone is slowly being restored to life.

As I'm fawning over the fresh taste of garlic butter wine sauce and king crab, a tall figure in my peripheral view walks through the front door. A figure that my subconscious seems trained to spot, that for months after I moved to Los Angeles I would see wherever I went, taunting and teasing me.

My fork stays raised in midair while my head turns to see Adam walking by, holding his phone to the side of his face. He's wearing black slacks and dress shoes with a navy blue button-down shirt. His sleeves are rolled down and he's wearing that watch again. He *looks* important, making his way through the restaurant in a way only someone with authority would, which puzzles me. We make eye contact for a second and he does a double take, and I instinctively look down at my food as if that will hide me.

"That's the owner," Dan says as he leans in.

I look past Adam. "Where?"

"There." He nods. "Tall guy, dark hair. He's a really great guy too. Big supporter of the arts," Dan says as he waves him over.

If my head had whipped any faster my neck might have snapped.

"*He's* the owner? Of *this* restaurant?" My thumb points to

Adam, and when I turn back, he's quickly approaching our table. I cough, then take a sip of my wine.

"Dan, how's it going?" Adam puts his hand out and Dan stands to shake it, patting him on the back. My eyes are wider than I'm sure they've ever been in my entire life, but I don't say anything.

"Good, good—you know how it is," Dan says, still standing. "Working on a revival for the winter."

"I heard. It's the only thing anyone is talking about." Adam smiles. "How does it feel?"

"Oh boy, I don't know, a lot of pressure but— Oh, I'm so sorry, how rude of me." Dan sits back down and turns to me. "This is—"

"June Wood," Adam says, his gaze fixed on me, my heart quite literally skipping a beat. His mouth curls into a slight smile, and it's a look I haven't seen in the past few days. I haven't seen it in years.

"You know each other?" Dan looks back and forth between us.

"Oh, I, um—" I hesitate, apparently losing the ability to talk.

"I'm a big fan of hers," Adam says calmly.

Dan looks over at me, impressed. "Right. I mean, same. We were actually just talking about her time in *Rent.*"

"You should hear her belt out 'On My Own,'" Adam says, casually dropping my favorite *Les Misérables* song, and it makes my stomach flip.

"I think I may have to." Dan smiles.

"Anyway, if you'll excuse me, I have to get back to a few things." Adam nods to both of us. "Dan, hope to see you again here soon. June . . . how's the food?"

For a brief moment, it's only me and Adam. It's eleven years ago and he's showing me a dish he created on a random Thursday night. We're young and hopeful and the whole world is ahead of us and our fate depends on me nailing my audition song and him impressing his culinary teacher.

"It's delicious, Adam," I say sincerely, and he smiles. He smiles like every critic's praise in *The New York Times* doesn't mean anything and like his restaurant hasn't been booked solid since the day it opened. He smiles like my uneducated palate is the only opinion he cares about.

"I'm glad to hear. And please, don't worry about anything. It's on the house. So nice to see you both." He puts a hand to his chest and walks toward the kitchen.

Adam Harper owns New York's hottest restaurant.

Holy fucking shit.

Chapter 9

NOVEMBER, 10 YEARS AGO

IT'S A NO-BRAINER. EIGHTEEN MONTHS INTO LIVING TOgether, Adam and I sign for another year on the lease.

While we don't see Stanley very often, he's been the perfect landlord. He'll stop in occasionally to check in on any maintenance needs, and when he does, it feels like an older uncle coming to say hi. Since he lives alone, Adam's gotten into the habit of preparing a lasagna for him, while I always grab a new science fiction novel from work as a treat. The small gestures unintentionally must have paid off, since he let us renew our lease at the same price.

A month after graduating from culinary school, Adam lands a gig as line cook for High Rise, a gastropub in Brooklyn. It's a significant step up from his job at the diner, and I can't complain when he brings home their short rib grilled cheese.

While I'm more than thrilled for Adam's trajectory, for me the next three months feel immobile. After acting class, I continue to work shifts at the Arcade Bookshop, and while I'm getting auditions, I have yet to land any roles. Auditioning in a room with your competition is not only laborious but trying for your self-esteem. There's always someone who's a better dancer, who can belt it out louder, or who chooses a better monologue.

Things start looking brighter when I get a callback for a theater troupe touring North America, but I don't get the part. It's the first time I doubt doing any of this and consider giving up and pursuing something more steady like my mom always told me to. She refused to enroll me in dance classes, so my grandparents paid for it, and she never understood why I would stay after school for choir practice.

Since moving to New York for college, I haven't returned home, and she's never bothered to come visit me. It's a jarring feeling when your own mother becomes spiteful about your aspirations, when she thinks her not being able to pursue her dreams warrants me not pursuing mine. From a young age I've noticed the way my mom looks at me, like her life would have been different if I wasn't in it.

Through the years, I've noticed the looks of sympathy when people find out I don't have a relationship with my parents. Maybe it's worth holding room for disappointment, but to me, it's normal. Having what most consider a *healthy* relationship with your parents feels fabricated, something that you would see only in a movie. Chloe and her mom are *friends,* and it's never made sense to me. A parent isn't someone you laugh with and talk about your life with; a parent is someone who yells at you and asks for money to go gambling or buy alcohol.

On some level, I've always pushed harder to prove my mother wrong, for her to open up the morning paper and see my name in the Arts and Entertainment section, for my dad to think that maybe it was a mistake to leave. But wishing things were different is no use—people leave and people disappoint you. It's those who have yet to realize that whom I feel bad for.

So now I'm sitting on the foot of my bed crying. I'm sobbing into my hands like a teenage girl who's gotten her heart broken for the first time. It feels good. I let myself feel all the things I've been suppressing.

There's a knock on my door and before I can wipe my eyes or say *just a minute,* Adam's head pops in.

"Hey, sorry, I'm going to the grocer—" His face drops when he sees my red eyes and snot running down my nose and he opens the door wider. "What happened?"

"Nothing." I sniff and wipe my face with my sleeve.

He nods thoughtfully and squints. "I'm not usually this intuitive, but I have a feeling you're upset."

I let out a laugh that then turns into more crying, and say, "I didn't get the part." My eyes are shut and it's not until I feel his touch that I see Adam kneeling in front of me, pulling me in for a hug. I don't resist, and bury my face into his shoulder. "I don't even know why I do this. I shouldn't have wasted my degree." I let out another cry.

"Hey, hey." He rubs my back. "There's going to be more auditions."

I know that Adam's trying to be helpful, but it's hard to listen to someone who hasn't worn your shoes. Being an actor isn't like applying for a normal job. It's dependent on your looks, your ability to hit a high C, how strong your pirouettes are, if you can make a director cry during a monologue—if you're good enough. I'm starting to realize that maybe I'm just not good enough.

"Thanks." I force a smile. "But this was a small troupe . . . it was low-hanging fruit. My drama teacher told me I was a shoo-in and if I can't even get this then I don't know, Adam . . ."

"It's their loss," he says.

"Oh yeah. I'm sure they're just going to be kicking themselves in six months and realize they made a mistake," I say over his shoulder.

"They will," he says confidently. "Maybe not in six months, maybe not in six years, but one day you'll get to where you need to go, and they'll wish they could say they started your career."

"Okay." I let out an unimpressed exhale through my nose.

"No, I'm serious." He pulls away so that way we're face-to-face, but he keeps both hands on my arms. Despite him crouching, his eyeline is parallel to mine. "A theater group like that—Off-Broadway, Broadway, whatever—they're a business. They need money, they need talent. You do this because you love the art. You don't need them, they need you."

He wipes a tear from my cheek. It's intimate, but not in a romantic way—in a way that says *you will always have someone who supports you.* He squeezes my hand, and I have a feeling this is one of those moments, the ones where no matter how much time passes, I'll never forget.

"You don't have to be so nice," I say. I don't know when it happened, this shift in our dynamic. We went from being roommates to genuine friends.

"*Nice* would imply that I'm going to ignore the snot all over my shoulder," he says, and there is in fact a large damp spot where my face was. "You *will* be buying me a new shirt."

It takes less than three seconds for me to start crying again. Except this time, it's laced with laughter. "Deal."

IF ANYTHING, THAT night only pushes me harder. I spend a few extra hours after every dance class practicing my pirouettes and take the time to do my vocal warm-ups every morning, even if I'm not planning on singing. My acting teacher tells me that there's an eight-week run of an Agatha Christie play Off-Broadway and that he'd like to set me up for an audition. I graciously accept and wait for details. In the meantime, I pick up *Murder on the Orient Express* from the library to get myself in the mood.

When Adam comes home from High Rise that night, he closes the door a little louder than usual.

"Adam?" I call from the kitchen, where I'm making a sandwich.

"I'm going to quit," he spits out, and throws his jacket onto one of the kitchen chairs.

"What happened?"

"Michael. I hate him," he says as he paces around the kitchen.

"What did he do this time?" I lean on the counter, worried to hear yet another horror story about Adam's new boss.

"I was supposed to switch stations before he became GM," he says, continuing to pace. "Today, he gave the job to Chris."

"Oh no . . ." I know he's been working his ass off for the past few months. While Adam's career trajectory is on par with those of other students in his graduating class, he's always held himself to the highest standard when it comes to his job. "Why don't you talk to him?" I suggest.

"To who?" He frowns.

"Michael," I say. "Maybe there's a reason you didn't get it."

"Forget it," he sighs.

"Opportunities aren't going to be handed to you unless you ask for them, Adam."

He raises an eyebrow. "Is that what your morning horoscope told you?"

"Fine, don't ask for my help." I roll my eyes and go back to making my sandwich. He's clearly fine enough to be making jokes.

"All right, I'll think about it," he says with a sigh. "And let me make that for you. I can already smell you burnt the toast."

"I did not!" I move away as he hijacks my sandwich-making station. He ignores me and begins creating a masterpiece with my mess.

Adam doesn't simply toast bread, he butters the sides and pan-fries it with some salt. He crumbles goat cheese and pesto on top with sautéed mushrooms and onions. Although the two of us don't have an overflowing amount of expendable income, we always make sure our fridge and pantries are full of ingredients. Denying ourselves a real meal is never an option for Adam.

"Okay, I could have done that," I defend myself, and lean against the counter.

"Not with the stove on high."

"That was *one time*!" I say defensively. "I was just in a hurry."

"I don't know how many times I have to say it, but setting it on high doesn't cook food any faster. It just burns it," he says, his focus still on the sandwich, which has now turned into a panini that could easily make the Eater NY list.

I shrug and reach for my phone vibrating on the other side of the counter. It's not a familiar number, but it's in our 212 area code.

"Hello?" I answer skeptically.

"Hi, is this June Wood?" the voice on the other end asks.

"This is she." I stand straight.

"Great! This is Caitlin from The York Theatre Company. I have some good news. I wanted to let you know that we'd love to offer you a chorus role in *The Mousetrap*."

I whip my head over to Adam, who's already watching me with anticipation. He raises his eyebrows, and I aggressively nod and smile. He fists the air, and I try my best not to squeal.

"Oh my goodness, thank you *so* much!" I attempt to sound as normal as possible but can't contain my excitement. "I can't wait!"

"We can't either," she laughs. "Rehearsals start November seventeenth. We'll be emailing everyone details by the end of the week but wanted to personally say welcome and congratulations."

"Amazing," I say. "Thank you again!"

"Have a wonderful evening, June," she says.

"You too!" I hang up the phone and run over to Adam. *I did it. I got my first paying role.* "I did it! I did it! I got *Mousetrap*!" He meets me halfway and I jump into his arms, and it takes little to no effort on his end before I'm lifted and seeing him eye to eye.

"Hell yeah you did," he says, and when the adrenaline wears off, it's abundantly clear my legs are wrapped around his waist and his hands are on my ass.

Adam's face drops and I loosen my grip on his shoulders.

This physical contact is a first for us, and I'm surprised that I *want* to narrow the space between us. Being close to him feels as natural as breathing. Except he clears his throat and slowly eases me back down to the floor, my crotch rubbing against his torso through my yoga pants, but that's fine.

My mouth opens, yet no words come, my mind still lingering on ten seconds ago and the fire in my core that needs to be smothered.

"Congratulations," he says, giving me an awkward smile, then walks out of the kitchen.

I'm left alone, feeling cold without his warmth. Even though I just got the best news, that feeling of not being enough still prickles at my skin.

Chapter 10

When adam walks through the front door he's dressed differently from when I saw him at Alden. He has on these army green pants with sneakers and a gray sweatshirt. There's a large pumpkin under his arm with two smaller ones between his fingers. The fact that a *casual outfit* is piquing my interest is mildly concerning.

"Oh, you're home," I say out of habit. This is not our *home.*

"That's always a nice thing to hear when you walk through the door," he says as he sets down the pumpkins on the bench by the entryway.

"What are those for?" I ask, ignoring him.

"We're the only house on the block without any decorations."

"Oh," I say, and pick one up and analyze it. "It's kind of a waste, though."

"A waste?" He frowns.

"Yeah, I mean we won't even be here on Halloween."

"I was just going to set them out," he sighs. "I wasn't going to carve a jack-o'-lantern."

I shift from one leg to the other. "Are you doing this on purpose or something?"

"Am I . . . decorating the house? Yes, June."

"Making me feel like an asshole," I correct him.

"I'm not doing anything," he says as he takes the pumpkin out of my hands. "I wonder why you feel that way," he says flatly.

I snort.

He tilts his head.

We're now caught in this duel that consists of squinting and head-shaking and I'm pretty sure I'm losing.

"Were you going to tell me?" I say, and his eyebrows raise in response. "About Alden?"

"I told you." He kicks off his shoes and heads to the kitchen.

"You said you *worked* there." I follow him. "As a chef."

"You *assumed* I was a chef," he says, not looking back.

"You didn't say you *own* it."

"I would've," he says.

My brain searches for something to say. What do you say to someone who has accomplished everything they've ever wanted?

"Congratulations," I say. It's probably the first nice thing I've said this whole week, but I mean it.

His lips twitch.

"Thanks, June," he says sincerely.

"And how do you know Dan?" I ask.

"I don't really *know him.*" He sets his phone down and pours himself a glass of water. "He's come in a few times, and we were once invited to the same dinner party. But I'm familiar with him through his work."

"Because you *support the arts*?" I ask, remembering the words Dan used.

He nods and doesn't seem surprised that I know. "Yeah."

"What does that even mean?"

"Alden usually sponsors any theater-aligned missions."

"Like, investing in Broadway shows?" I ask.

"Just donating," he says, and takes a sip from his glass.

"Oh . . ." I'm not sure why this information bothers me. "Since when?"

"Since I could afford to," he says.

"Why did you hide that from me?" I genuinely ask.

He frowns. "I didn't *hide* it from you, June."

"Well, you never told me . . ."

"You never asked," he says, and I know he's playing my game. "Are you mad that I support the arts?"

"I'm not mad!" I say a little too loudly, negating my point. I lower my voice. "I just think it's weird. Wouldn't you want to know if I was, I don't know . . . giving money to restaurants or something?"

"I would know if you were," he says as if my scenario is unheard of. "And I think that's why you're so bothered."

"What are you talking about?" I shake my head.

"That you're so far removed from this world that you didn't know."

My throat squeezes and I look away. "You don't know what you're talking about."

"I wasn't trying to hide anything from you," he says calmly.

"You still should have told me," I insist. Of all the things that have happened this week, this current topic is the least of my problems. Yet I can't stop pressing Adam.

"And when would I have done that?" He turns to me, a sharp edge to his voice. "You haven't bothered to talk to me, or so much as *look* at me, since we've been here. Excuse me if I didn't feel it was appropriate to tell you, unsolicited, about my life," he says, and my neck becomes hot. Not because I'm mad, but because he's right. "You know, you're not the only one this is difficult for, June," he says in response to my silence, and I know we're no longer talking about business.

I've been so focused on *me* that I've failed to acknowledge that maybe Adam doesn't *want* to be doing this . . . and that I'm not making it any easier.

"Can we just forget it?" I say when he turns to place his glass in the sink.

"What part?"

"All of it," I say, so quietly I can barely hear myself.

"You don't think I've tried?" he says, and then walks past me.

Defeated, I put the kettle on to make myself a cup of tea. I'm sitting at the kitchen island when Adam walks back in, swiftly opens a drawer, and pulls out a butcher's knife.

"Really?" I squint. "You're *that* mad?"

"It's for the pumpkins . . ." Adam deadpans.

"I thought you weren't going to *carve a jack-o'-lantern*," I say, mimicking him.

"Yeah, well, I changed my mind." Adam's nostrils flare as he walks out.

The kettle whistles and when I turn it off, I notice my phone light up on the counter. Leaning over, I tap the screen to view the message.

Kelsey

Adam I'm soaked

My stomach drops. This is not my phone.

My cheeks suddenly become flush and I whip my head around to see if Adam's behind me. Suddenly another notification appears.

Kelsey

Get over here

This is fine. This is totally normal. This is just a harmless text that I wasn't supposed to see. It's also typical Adam to have his messages show a preview when his phone is locked. I quickly tap the screen again and reread the words.

Adam I'm soaked

Get over here

This is simply a message from a female acquaintance of Adam's. It's just a message from someone who needs him to get over there. Someone who clearly isn't opposed to sexting. Someone who's apparently—

"SOAKED?!" I say out loud. "Really?"

A very explicit image comes to mind of whoever Kelsey is—probably a standard influencer type—standing, hair disheveled, underwear pushed down to her ankles, and holding up two vibrators, just waiting to get railed.

Of course Adam's seeing someone . . . at the very least, hooking up with someone. I don't know why I thought he wouldn't be. This is Adam. The same Adam who at some point in our lives always had a date on his night off. Whenever we went out, there would be at least one person doing a double take because his presence is just that magnetic. Even middle-aged women at the grocery store seemed flustered when he made small talk at the checkout line.

It stings to find out this way, but I'm not surprised Adam didn't tell me about his personal life. It's not like I've been the best conversationalist this past week. Besides, Adam can do whatever he wants, with whomever he wants.

"Did I leave my phone here?" Adam's voice says behind me, and it causes me to jump.

"W-What? I-I don't know," I stammer.

He checks his phone on the counter and I swear I forget how to breathe. I intently watch his face as he reads his messages. I notice his throat bob and the sharp inhale he takes. Kelsey probably sent another text of her soaked sheets, begging for him to do something about it.

"I, uh, I have to go," he says as he puts his phone in his back pocket.

"Everything okay?" My voice cracks as I look anywhere but at him.

"Yeah, it's, uh, a work thing," he says. "I'm not sure how long I'll be."

"All good," I say, still avoiding eye contact.

Before I know it, he's gone.

So what if Adam's involved with someone else? These texts don't change anything. Why would they?

THE NEXT DAY I hear a knock and rush to the door. I swing it open and Chloe and I simultaneously scream and collide on the front stoop into an uncomfortable hug, but neither one of us lets go. An uncontrollable sob comes out of me, and I wipe a tear from my eye. I've missed her, but it's not until I can feel and see her in front of me, in this house of all places, that I realize just how much.

It's not that I haven't made friends in LA. Considering how hard it is to make friends as an adult, I'm grateful for Shivani and Zach. But the bond that Chloe and I have is unmatched.

"I can't believe you're actually here!" She grips my arms, staring at me to make sure I'm real.

"*You* can't believe it?" I say.

"You look amazing." She gently touches my hair. "I told you your natural hair looks *so good.*"

"Thanks, it's more laziness than anything. Glad it's working to my advantage," I say with a laugh. "But look at *you*—what are you, a partner or something?"

Chloe places the top of her hand under her chin and flashes me a shit-eating grin. The girl who used to work part-time at Forever 21 is now a law firm partner who holds a level of authority I couldn't even imagine being responsible for. I eye her perfectly fitted denim jumpsuit. Her dark skin is looking clear as glass with not an ounce of makeup on except a deep red lip oil, and her thick hair has been filled with blond highlights since I saw her last.

I push the door open behind me, and when she steps inside her eyes go wide.

"Wait . . . what happened to this place? It's gorgeous!"

"It got renovated after we left," I say as I follow her.

"Yeah, no shit." She walks around the foyer, peeking her head into the different rooms. In typical Chloe fashion, she kicks off her heels and makes herself at home by sitting on the couch. "Okay, so tell me everything."

"Well . . ." I take a seat next to her, unsure how to start. "I own this house." The sides of my mouth curl up into a fake smile.

Her neck stretches out to me, confused. "Girl . . ."

"I'm serious."

"What do you mean you *own* this house?"

"I guess technically *not yet,*" I say. "But in twenty-five days, I will."

"Did you win the lottery?"

"Chloe." I stifle a laugh.

"I'm serious!" she says. "Because there's no way in hell you're telling me you own this house right now."

"Mr. Hill passed away." I look down and explain the situation. "His will stated that whoever lived in the house last inherits it."

"Oh shit." Chloe breathes out. "So you literally *own* this house?"

"Well . . ." I let out a nervous laugh. "Me and Adam."

"Is this a joke?" she deadpans, looking very unimpressed.

"Chloe, I wish I was joking." I cover my face and roll back onto the couch. "We found out on Tuesday."

"June, this is insane!" Her eyes widen. "Do you realize how crazy this is? And when was the last time you two even saw each other?"

"I don't know. Before I moved?" I shrug, acting like I don't know exactly when the last time I saw Adam Harper was. As if it's not burned into my memory, where we were standing, what we were wearing, the look on his face.

Chloe moved to Connecticut a year before I left New York, so I never told her the full story. I haven't told anyone the full story. I'm not proud of hiding what happened from Chloe, but I've done a good job of keeping Adam a topic that was off-limits, someone I always shrugged off if he ever came up in conversation. Being in a new city with people who knew nothing about my history, I found it was pretty easy to erase him from my past.

As far as Chloe's concerned, I moved to Los Angeles to pursue my acting career, and Adam and I went our separate ways.

"Damn, I mean, I guess it makes sense why it would be under both of your names . . . Do you need help or—"

"*Yes!*" I grab her arm. "I mean, if you don't mind reading everything over. I just don't know anything about all that, and I can't afford anyone right now."

"I got you," she says, and squeezes my hand. There are perks to your best friend being a lawyer. Her posture changes, and she smiles. "Does this mean you're moving back?"

"No." I shake my head. "*No.* This is temporary. We're selling it the minute we can."

"Right, fair." She nods. I know she wants to ask me a million more questions, and I don't doubt she'll get to all of them. "So . . . how is Adam? I think it's been literally years since he's posted anything."

Considering I don't follow Adam anywhere, I wouldn't know. But I'm not surprised at his lack of a social media footprint. He was always quite private. High level, I know Adam's doing well for himself. He looks great, he has a dream job and a woman to warm his bed at the very least. The funny thing is, while we've been living under the same roof for five days, I don't actually *know* how Adam Harper is doing.

"Well," I say. "He owns his own restaurant."

"Which one?"

"Alden," I say.

"He *owns* Alden?" Chloe rubs her temples. I don't blame her. It's a lot of information to process in sixty seconds. "Lucia and I went there for our anniversary. It was *really* good."

"And I think he's seeing someone," I say as casually as I can. Because that text I saw last night is totally *not* a big deal.

"I see," Chloe says, trying to gauge my temperature, but I'm fine. "Well, good for Adam. I miss him."

"When . . . uh," I say slowly. "When was the last time you saw him?" I know that even after I moved, Chloe and Adam stayed in touch. I never expected them not to, and I would never want them to put their friendship on hold on my account.

"God, I mean, I don't know. A while." She rolls her head back like she's thinking. "It was probably only like a year after you moved. I was in the city and we grabbed lunch."

"Oh," I say as casually as I can. I remember her mentioning she saw Adam, but I hadn't asked any questions.

"I'm obviously to blame too for not making more of an effort, but he really fell off the map after that," she says. "Makes sense, though—he was probably focusing on opening a whole-ass restaurant."

"I'm sure you'll see him at some point. I don't know what time he comes home but—"

"Home?" She raises an eyebrow. "Is he staying here too?"

My lips turn into an awkward smile. "Maybe . . ."

"I give up." She throws her hands up in an exaggerated motion. "Girl, you need a newsletter."

"It's just for three more weeks," I say.

"Are the two of you . . . good?" Chloe's voice is now as serious as it ever gets.

"Yeah, we're great," I lie, but I'm met with another raised eyebrow. "You know, life happens, and we lost touch." I shrug, casually trying to backpedal. "The same way you did."

"Okay . . ." she says skeptically. She's never pushed me on the topic. Me moving across the country was too much of a distraction, her becoming a partner at the firm, me getting my first role in a movie, her getting married, her new baby—life *did* happen. It was easy to move forward, at least on the outside.

"Anyway." I smack her leg, trying to change the subject. "We're in the city, you have a night away from Lucia and Teddy—I say we go out."

"Absolutely! I need a glass of wine." She stands up and grabs her purse. "I'm going to freshen up first."

"Bathroom's in the same place," I say, pointing my chin past the stairs.

As she disappears, the front door opens to Adam, who's wearing a plaid peacoat with a pair of Converses and a navy blue beanie.

"Hi," he says softly.

"Hi." I stand up. "I didn't hear you come back last night."

"Oh." He takes off his hat. "I, uh, was held up and just ended up going back to my place."

"Right . . . at work," I say, wondering why he isn't telling me the truth.

"Right." He nods. "Anyway, I should—"

"Adam Harper?!" Chloe's voice causes us both to jump back as if we're two kids who got caught in a closet.

"Chloe Patel?!" Adam's face breaks out into a smile that I have not seen in these past few days. She's already running toward him and, in one fell swoop, he effortlessly picks her up into a hug and twirls her around. Their enthusiasm almost makes me feel left out, like somehow I'm the one who doesn't belong in this picture.

"Look at you," she says, stepping back and taking an exaggerated look at him from head to toe. "You look fine as hell—what have you been doing?"

He tries to conceal a laugh. "What about *you*? What are you doing now? Are you still in Connecticut?"

"Yes, sir, and married." She flashes her wedding band. "You have to meet her."

"*And* you're a mom," I say.

"Oh my God, congratulations, Chloe!" Adam gives her another hug, and this is the most alive I've seen him all week.

"I mean, I'm the one who should be saying congratulations to two new *homeowners*." Her eyes widen. Adam huffs out a laugh and looks at me, but he doesn't say anything. "You have to come out and celebrate with us." Chloe grabs his arm.

"Oh, Chloe, I don't think—" I step toward her. As nice as this little reunion is, I'm not ready to pick up from where we all left off.

"It's okay," Adam says, putting a hand up to Chloe, sensing my hesitation. "I'm sure the two of you have a lot to catch up on. Besides, I have some things I need to do."

"Okay, well, you both have to come over to my place then,"

Chloe says like it's the most obvious thing in the world. "You'll get to meet Lucia and Teddy! Tomorrow?"

"Oh," Adam says, reaching for the back of his neck, and even through the layers of clothing he's wearing, my eyes instinctively go to the line of skin exposed. He needs to stop doing that. "I'm working tomorrow."

"Tuesday?" Chloe offers.

Adam looks at me, and for the first time all week, it feels like we're in something *together.* There are things like body language, looks, inflections that a person will carry with them no matter how much time passes. In this moment, I know that Adam is looking to me for approval. He and Chloe haven't seen each other in years, and I'd be a monster to stop this from happening. I give him a nod and he does a thing with his eyes. Something that nobody would notice, but *I* notice, because I know him. He's grateful.

"Tuesday's perfect," he says, looking back at Chloe.

"Yay!" Chloe quite literally squeals, which doesn't happen often, and pulls us both into a hug. Adam's and my arms hit each other, and the impact goes straight to my chest. This is the first time we've touched in years, and I wonder if he reads into this mundane contact the same way I do. She lets go and then grabs her coat. "Okay, well, Adam, you'll be missed tonight. June, you ready?"

I nod and give Adam an awkward smile. In return, he gives me a tight-lipped one. Chloe leads the way out of the house and I make it a point to try not to talk about Adam for the rest of the night.

THE WHOLE "NOT talking about Adam" thing lasts a good forty minutes. We end up walking to our favorite speakeasy behind a coffee shop in Chelsea and ask for two cocktails. From what we remember, their fried chicken sliders were to die for, so we get an order and sit at the bar.

"June." Chloe takes a sip of her martini, which has some crazy coconut-oil-popcorn taste, contrasting with my Moscow mule. "Can we be real for a second?"

"Aren't we always?"

"What does this mean for you and Adam?" she asks.

"*Nothing*, Chlo." Chloe has always been Adam's and my number one fan. She's wanted us to be together ever since I can remember. "He has his life and I'm going back to LA in a few weeks."

"You are aware he looks fine as hell, right?"

"Oh, thanks, I didn't notice."

"Like he somehow got *more* hot since I last saw him," she says.

"Okay, I know, Chloe," I sigh. "But it doesn't matter. He's seeing someone, remember?"

"I don't think it's anything serious," she says, shaking her head confidently.

"What makes you say that?" I ask.

"Trust me—if he was with someone, he wouldn't agree to live with you for a month," she says. "There's too much history there."

"Well, whatever. It wouldn't matter, because nothing's going to happen," I say, and she lets out a scoff. "What?"

"You can't sit there and tell me being back here with him hasn't rekindled any feelings." She waves her hands around like she's referring to a fairy tale.

"It hasn't," I say.

"You're such a bad liar," she says, laughing.

"Okay, *maybe* I thought about it—*maybe*," I say. "But that's beside the point."

"Why?!" She sits straighter.

"It's just complicated," I sigh, feeling defeated once the words come out.

"That's a bad rebuttal." Chloe puts her drink down, and there's a flicker in her eye. "You two are like lightning in a bottle."

Chloe's right. What Adam and I shared was few and far between. It's a bond that happens once in a lifetime, if you're so lucky. Friendships like that take time and effort to build. Relationships like that require trust, openness, and honesty. They're like beautiful trees with deep roots. You don't cut them and expect them to keep growing. It's impossible.

"I guess you're right." I look at Chloe.

"Of course I am," she agrees. "About what?"

I let out a breathless laugh and twirl my straw around my drink. My gaze stays fixed on the ice cubes slowly disappearing into the barely touched liquid. "I guess we were lightning in a bottle," I say.

"Cheers to that." Chloe holds up her glass and I give it a clink.

The thing about lightning in a bottle is that it's a fleeting moment in time, a spark that's rare and special . . . but it's also impossible to re-create.

Chapter 11

DECEMBER, 10 YEARS AGO

"I'M NOT INVITING THEM." I PULL MY COLUMBIA SWEATSHIRT over my head and grab my bag off the floor. I'm already late for rehearsal and not in the mood to have this conversation.

"You don't think you'll regret it if they're not there?" Adam follows me around the living room with a coffee mug in hand.

"I really don't."

This conversation started when I told Adam I was reserving tickets for him and Chloe for opening night of *The Mousetrap,* and he asked *what about your parents?*

"I know you don't have the best relationship with them," he continues. "But I'm sure they'll want to know."

"You don't get it." I dismiss him and slip my running shoes on.

How could he? Adam goes home to Long Island almost every other weekend to have Sunday dinner with his family. Whereas I've never had a meal with both of my parents. Adam always invites me, but I'm usually working or in rehearsal, and I've kept the tradition of spending holiday dinners with Chloe and her family. There's something about going home with him that feels daunting. Maybe I'm afraid I'll enjoy myself too much.

"I don't get it, because you don't talk about it," he says. "How am I supposed to understand if you won't tell me?"

"What do you want me to tell you?" I turn to face him, and he flinches. "That my mom got pregnant at nineteen and blames me for her mediocre life? Or that my dad left when I was two?"

"June, I didn't—"

"You know, sometimes I think it would be better if he just got my mom knocked up and left . . . instead of him getting to know me for two years and realizing he didn't want me." I move my bag to my other shoulder and continue talking like a faucet whose spout won't shut off. "One time in high school, I had a speaking part in our spring play. I remember being *so* happy because my mom was able to attend one of the shows. On the car ride home, I told her I wanted to study theater in college, and she told me to do something I would actually be successful in. She told me to focus on getting a higher-paying job to pay off our debts. *Our* debts." I let out a pathetic laugh, but I have no tears, no lump in my throat to swallow. I'm past the point of being sad or disappointed. "I don't want them to come."

Adam stands there looking at me speechless, the groove between his brows deepening. "I'm sorry."

"I don't want you to be sorry," I say firmly. "I just want you to leave it."

"I will," he says.

We're doing this awkward thing where if I didn't have to leave for rehearsal or if I wasn't so worked up, we'd probably hug. But neither one of us is moving so I head out the door.

Two blocks away from the subway, I give in to the tick in the back of my brain and let out an audible groan. I take my phone out of my pocket and scroll through a significant number of chats in my queue until I get to the last text exchange between my mom and me. Merry Christmas. This is what she wrote in response to my greeting. Who types *Merry Christmas* with a period?

Instead of typing, my finger hovers over the call button—one ring, two, three, then four. My mother's voice brings on a flare of PTSD as it tells me to leave a voicemail.

"Um." I swallow. "Hi, it's me, June. I wanted to let you know that I'm going to be in a new Agatha Christie play. It's here in the city but . . . I can get you a ticket if you want. Let me know. Bye."

I shove my phone back into my pocket and continue to walk.

SHAWN, OUR DIRECTOR, calls a ten-minute break, so I sit against the wall in our rehearsal room and take a swig from my water bottle. The rest of the cast disperses and pulls out their scripts to run over lines or break into casual conversation, but I don't feel like joining in on the usual chatter.

"Penny for your thoughts," Caleb, another chorus member, says as he sits next to me. He's British, with pale skin and green eyes. I remember those eyes catching my attention at our first table read. This isn't the first time we're chatting, but any interaction between us has always been in a group setting.

"Just one of those days." I smile, trying to forget about earlier.

It doesn't take much time, but before the ten minutes are up, he asks me if I want to grab dinner with him this week and I say yes. As we exchange numbers, a text message appears from my mom.

Can't make it.

Instead of disappointment, I kick myself for having had an ounce of hope.

"SO, WHO'S THE guy?" Adam leans against my doorframe.

It's been a while since I've been on a date with anyone. Unlike Adam's, my love life has become obsolete in the past year.

"He's in the play with me," I say, comparing two different outfits laid across my bed. "What are you doing tonight?"

"I'm finishing up a baked ziti for Stanley, then going to Robby's to watch the game."

Robby's my favorite friend of Adam's. They went to culinary school together and he's the one who got Adam his job at High Rise. I've met him only once, but he's the epitome of Williamsburg cool, from how he dresses to the collection of tattoos on his arms. Whenever I hang out with them it feels effortless, almost like I'm one of the guys.

"Nice—who's playing?" I ask.

"San Antonio and Miami," he says. "Where's he taking you?"

"Estella." I hold up a black dress in front of the mirror and he watches me switch between that and jeans with a silk blouse. I notice his jaw twitch when I choose the dress.

"Let me know how their whipped eggplant dip is," he says.

I pull out another dress from my closet and hold it against my chest. "God, I don't know why I'm overthinking this."

He stares back, straight-faced. I expect a joke, but he just puts his hands in his pockets. "Been a while?"

"Can I tell you something?" My eyes are still on his in the mirror and he nods. Turning around, I toss the outfits back onto my bed. "I've only been with one guy before."

His eyebrows rise; this was clearly not what he was expecting me to say.

"Oh."

Now, to clarify, while I've had sex with only one person, that doesn't mean I've had sex only once. I have zero qualms when it comes to casual sex, but it's never been something I've had a desire for. My ex-boyfriend and I met in freshman year of college, we dated for two years, and after we broke up, the opportunity never presented itself again.

While Chloe always supports my decisions, she can't necessarily . . . relate, and for some reason Adam's the first person I've ever felt comfortable enough to talk about this with. He's someone I completely trust, whom I can let my guard down in front of, and who's, well, of the opposite sex.

"I know it's stupid but—"

"It's not stupid," he says firmly, and my train of thought is lost for a brief moment.

"Have you . . . also . . . ?"

"Oh," he says, and rubs the back of his neck. "No, but I understand."

Right. Of course. I pull the sleeves of my sweatshirt over my knuckles. Now I'm actively wondering how many women he's been with.

"Well, I'm a little nervous," I say. "Lucas, my ex, was really . . . vanilla."

"Vanilla," he repeats, making a face.

"You know . . ." I say, realizing Adam and I are entering a new threshold in our relationship that most roommates, and even friends, don't cross. "Pretty much missionary the whole time, with him on top."

Adam frowns. "How long were you two together?"

"Just under two years."

He pushes himself off the doorframe and takes a step toward me. "And in those two years, you *only* did missionary?"

"I mean, we did it sideways once."

"So, you've never been—" His brows furrow, correcting himself. "You've never tried doggy style?" he asks, and I shake my head. "Or been on top?" he continues, and I shrug. "Oral?"

"Well, I've given oral," I say. "But I've never received it."

His face drops. "You've never . . . *Jesus Christ, June.*" He runs his hand through his hair in frustration, and if I didn't know any better, I would say he's *mad.* "This idiot was with you for two years and he never—" He stops and wipes his palm over his mouth. "Sorry."

"It's not because I didn't want to," I emphasize. "I *want* to now, but I'm nervous." I laugh, knowing how embarrassing this conversation is. "What if I'm bad?"

He gives me an incredulous look. "June, trust me, you're not bad."

"How would you know?"

"*Because,*" he says, and shrugs. "There's no way anyone could have sex with you and not enjoy themselves. It would be a fucking privilege for any guy to be with you."

My cheeks become flush, my mouth opens and then closes. Before he can say anything else, the doorbell rings and my head whips to the clock on my bedside table. "Oh my God, he's early! Adam, you have to keep him busy." I push him into the hallway.

"What? For how long?"

"Just ten minutes, please," I beg.

"That's about nine minutes more than I want to talk to this guy."

"You'll live." I slam the door in his face.

To spare Adam, I finish getting ready in seven minutes. I land on the first dress with sheer black tights and heels, surprised at how sexy I feel. As I make my way down the stairs, I see the back of Caleb's head, and on the armchair across from him, Adam with his foot over his knee, looking like he'd rather be anywhere else. He does a double take when he sees me, his eyes widening in the process, but he quickly recovers, looking away.

Caleb turns around and then stands up at the sight of me. "Wow, June, you look incredible."

"Thank you." I blush, meeting him at the bottom of the stairs. He takes the leather jacket I have in my hand and drapes it over my shoulders.

"Ready?" he asks, and I nod. "Nice meeting you, man." He holds a hand up to Adam.

"Likewise." Adam tips his head.

I follow Caleb out the door and for a brief second turn back to Adam, who's still in the living room.

"Thank you," I mouth, hoping he knows everything I'm thanking him for.

"Have fun." His shoulders move slightly in a way that says *that's what I'm here for.*

"You too." I smile and then close the door behind me.

Estella is all the way in Murray Hill, which is an interesting choice, but I'm never in this part of town so it feels like an adventure. It's dimly lit and if not for the candlelight directly in front of Caleb's face, I wouldn't be able to see him. But the night feels romantic, and I don't remember the last time I've been on a proper date.

We end up going back to his place after dinner, which is conveniently two blocks down from the restaurant. While we're sitting on the couch watching an episode of *Grey's Anatomy,* he reaches his hand under my dress, and pulls my tights down to my knees. I'm not *not* enjoying it when he fingers me, but I close my eyes and imagine someone a little taller, whose arms are slightly bigger, and who has a deeper voice. When we have sex, it's *fine.* I can pretty much now check off all the positions I've been curious about. Caleb's the type of guy who likes to say *cock* and finishes on my boobs. While it doesn't do anything for me, it's nice being intimate with someone.

A few weeks go by, and Caleb and I continue to see each other. We're on the subway back to his place after one of our rehearsals when he casually says, "Have you and Adam ever slept together?"

A laugh escapes me, but I realize he's not joking.

"What? No, of course not."

"I don't care if you have," he says.

"We *haven't,*" I say, a little annoyed that he doesn't believe me.

"All right," he says with a shrug.

"Why're you asking?"

"Just curious."

I frown at how vague he's being. "That's a weird thing to be thinking about."

"I just find it hard to believe a straight man and woman can live together platonically."

"Well, I feel like that says a lot about you." The subway doors open, and I move a little closer to him, allowing people to enter. "You don't think men and women can be just friends?"

"I think that unless there's zero attraction to one another, then no. Heterosexual men and women can't be just friends."

"So, if you're slightly attracted to a friend of the opposite sex, you're telling me that you're going to end up sleeping with them?" I say loud enough that everyone within our vicinity can definitely hear our conversation. I don't care.

"No," he says. "But if I was *living* with said friend and they were single, then probably."

"Are you joking?"

"I'm just saying it's inevitable. If it hasn't happened with the two of you yet, it most likely will soon," he says matter-of-factly.

I scrunch my face. "And you'd be *okay* with that?"

"Sexuality is not linear, June. I also don't believe in monogamy," he says. "I just assumed the two of you were already fucking."

If anyone is wondering, it *is* possible to break up with someone in eight subway stops.

EVEN THOUGH I'M not emotionally attached to Caleb, I'm still allowed a night in my room to eat my feelings and watch old movies. I hear a knock on the door and ignore it. Another knock.

"Go away," I call out.

I hear Adam's voice on the other side of the door. "June."

"She's not here."

"I'm coming in." Adam opens my door and stops, taking in the sight in front of him. Me with my hair a mess, half-empty cartons of lo mein and kung pao chicken on my bed, and *It's a Wonderful Life* on my laptop. "Jesus, what happened?"

"Men." I glare at him.

"Caleb?" he asks, and I catch his hand slightly folding into a fist. I nod and roll my eyes, hearing his name. "What did he do?"

"Nothing, he's just a piece of shit. I'm fine," I say, too embarrassed to bring up our conversation on the subway.

"You don't look fine," he says with a wince.

"Thanks."

He inches closer and slams my laptop shut. "Come on, get up." He offers me his hand, but I don't take it. "*June.*"

"No! Leave me and Jimmy Stewart alone!" I throw my blanket over myself. Before I know it, he's pulling the covers off and reaching around my waist. I start yelping but with little to no effort he throws me over his shoulder.

"What are you doing?!"

"God, you smell," he says, and carries me down the hall, placing me in the bathroom. "Take a shower, then we're going out."

"You can't tell me what to do," I scoff as if he's not thirteen inches taller and seventy pounds heavier.

"You'll know when I'm telling you what to do."

Oh. My mouth opens and I quickly close it. "Fine," I say. He gives a satisfied smile and then closes the door.

I HAVEN'T A clue where we're going. It's not until we reach the Fifth Avenue stop and Adam says we're getting off that I have a hunch of what's to come. The December air bites my face when we emerge from the subway stairs and I fist the front of my jacket, moving a little closer to him.

"It's freezing! Do we have to be outside? I'm sure there were ways you could've taken my mind off Caleb at home." I catch the way it sounds, and Adam huffs out a laugh.

"We're almost there," he says.

As we walk through Midtown, I hear the faint sound of Christmas music in the distance. The iconic Radio City Music Hall wears a soft white blanket as snowflakes fall from the sky.

"Wait a minute, are we going to—" Once we turn the corner, it's clear where Adam's taking me.

For two years, I've begged him to go to Rockefeller Plaza during the holidays with me, but he always said it was *too touristy.* Up ahead I see a local's nightmare, but exactly what one would picture when you say *Christmastime in New York City.* The sound of Bing Crosby echoes and the famous seventy-five-foot tree laced with an unbelievable display of lights glows beneath the night sky. The crowd is unbearable, filled with people holding festive cups of hot drinks and a skating rink smack dab in the middle of the chaos.

Adam's right: It's absolutely packed with tourists, but it's beautiful.

"Adam . . ." I stand there speechless, feeling a rush of serotonin and pure joy course through my veins. The essence of the city lifts my spirits higher with each passing moment and whatever I was upset about is entirely nonexistent.

"Okay, this is *much* worse than what I was anticipating," he says.

"It's perfect," I say, and look up at him. "Are we really doing this?"

"Oh, we're doing this. The whole thing, because I'm never coming back here ever again."

Adam and I walk around Rockefeller Plaza and then down to the Bryant Park holiday market, which is a few blocks away. He nods toward a pop-up vendor that's decked out with garlands and fairy lights. We find a place in line in between a family of four and a group of teenage girls eating mouthwatering Nutella-filled doughnuts. As I read the menu above the vendor, drink flavors like chocolate tahini or matcha white chocolate catch my eye. One girl walks away holding a drink with a pretzel in the shape of a candy cane sticking out of the top.

"Hi, what can I get you?" the girl behind the counter asks.

I lean in. "I'll have a regular hot chocolate, please."

"And I'll have the dark chocolate. Thanks." Adam passes her a twenty and throws the coins she returns into the tip jar.

To our surprise, we find a bench in the middle of the holiday market and people-watch with our drinks.

"We are literally in the middle of a scene from a Hallmark movie," I say.

Adam takes a sip of his hot chocolate. "Remind me never to watch a Hallmark movie."

I bump his knee, and he bumps mine back, but once we make contact he doesn't move it, and I don't want him to.

"I can't believe it's taken us this long to do this."

"It's my fault." He keeps his eyes on the skaters in the distance. "This is nice, though."

"You know, when I was a kid, I would see this in the movies and always thought *that's what I'm going to do when I grow up*."

"Sit in the middle of Bryant Park drinking hot chocolate?"

"All of it." I wave my arms around. "Just being and doing whatever I want . . . What is it about this city?"

"I know what you mean. It's like anything is possible," he says.

"Would you ever leave?" I look at him. We've never talked about it before, what the next few years would look like.

"Maybe," he answers honestly. "It would have to be for a good reason, though. Like what could I get anywhere else that I can't get here?"

"A house with a yard."

"Right," he laughs. "Imagine."

"You know." I nudge my thigh against his. "You didn't have to do all this. I know how much you hate crowds."

He shrugs. "Are you feeling better?"

"I am, thank you."

"Good," he says, and his gaze shifts to our knees, still touching. "I don't like seeing you sad."

I look down at my almost empty drink and play with the lid. "He thinks men and women can't be just friends."

Adam squints but then nods, understanding whom I'm talking about. "I used to think that too."

"What changed?" I lift my head up and look at him.

"I met you," he says, and I don't know why that doesn't make me feel better. My thoughts shift to when I got the news about *The Mousetrap.* It almost feels like a foggy dream at this point. It was the first time I *wanted* him. "I've never had this," he says, gesturing to what little space is between us.

"The ultimate holiday date?"

"Exactly," he says, smirking. "With anyone else, the night

would have to end in a proposal, but with you . . . I don't know, there are no expectations, no ulterior motives."

For the past year and a half I've spent almost every day with Adam, and life hasn't been the same since. The reminder of our closeness, our bodies molding into each other, sticks to my memory like nicotine, but I try to overcome my withdrawal. Whatever level of friendship we've reached is far too precious to be tainted by that night.

"We're lucky," I say.

He nods, and then scans the ice rink with far too many people. "Want to go skating?"

"Yeah." I smile and down my drink.

"You know, despite being *just friends*"—he pulls me up from the bench and we walk over to the skate rental booth—"this is still the best date."

"Why?"

"Because I know that whatever happens tonight, you're still coming home with me." He winks.

Chapter 12

23 DAYS UNTIL THE MEETING

I've been in New York for one whole week. There isn't a view of palm trees lining the street, it's far from eighty-degree weather, and instead of salt water, you're more likely to get a whiff of a Nuts 4 Nuts cart. Los Angeles is infinitely different from Manhattan, and I don't know if I miss it.

I'm sitting in front of the bay window with my coffee when my phone buzzes. There's an unread email from Theo with the subject: *NBC Pilot.*

> Submitted you for a new NBC pilot. It's a book adaptation of this YA fantasy series–I attached the notes.
>
> Are you still in New York? Should hear next steps about Les Mis next week!
>
> Theo

When I open the attachment, I can safely say I've never heard of this book. It's about a young group of witches who time-travel to solve their teacher's murder. I'm not sure how I feel about my career leading me to roles like "murdered teacher" in a young adult witch series.

When I was doing theater, I used to be *somebody.* I had a career trajectory everyone in my drama class could only dream about. Something I quickly learned when pursuing film and TV is that my past life on Broadway doesn't matter. Hollywood made sure to remind me that I was in a different playing field and that I didn't even know the rules of the game.

The theater used to be who I was, and since leaving it, I'm not sure I know who I am.

I set my phone down and decide to not think about work for the rest of the day. Adam is at Alden until this afternoon, so I'm free as a bird until we go to Chloe's for dinner.

I prepare a cup of warm lemon water and instinctively make my way to a corner of the living room. Can you still call it a habit if you haven't done it in five years? After taking a sip, I start my vocal warm-ups. It's been a few weeks since I've done them, but my voice comes out clearer and stronger than I expected. Perhaps it's a testament to the environment; the oak wood in this home has always lent itself to excellent acoustics.

As I sing the beginning of "On My Own" from *Les Misérables,* my voice quavers. Out of the corner of my eye, I catch a glimpse of myself in the mirror by the entryway. I wonder why we never had a mirror in that spot before—it's fitting. My gaze focuses on my reflection, and I push down the lump in my throat. It's not from sadness, but from an overwhelming feeling of joy for the girl who used to stand in this spot, who fought and prayed so hard for all the things that are now within reach.

I'm not one to be overly sentimental, but I swipe the back of my hand along my cheeks and look out to the space in front of me. I do love it here. The coziness of the home, the familiar balmy scent that somehow never went away. All of the details I refused to let myself take in, at least not while Adam was here, I'm now welcoming like a warm hug. It's like I had blinders on until this very moment.

My fingertips gently graze the fireplace mantel beside me. A slight breath of laughter comes out when I notice a chip on the underside of the wood. Adam, Chloe, Ethan, and I were playing charades one evening and Adam was in the middle of acting out *Titanic* and saw a spider out of the corner of his eye. He grabbed the fire poker and in one swift motion hit the mantel instead of the spider.

I inhale deeply, parting myself from the memory, and start singing.

FOR LUNCH, I walk to Chelsea Market and eat at a new—well, new to *me*—place that serves Japanese-inspired Mexican food. I won't argue with anyone who says no place does tacos like LA, but this is a *very* close second. Before picking up a pie to bring for dinner tonight, I take a final stroll along the High Line, embracing the autumn view of the Hudson. On my way back to the house, I purchase a wool camel-colored coat—which is a need, not a want in this East Coast weather. The past week, I managed to get away with wearing sweaters, but now the air is much too crisp.

Three pumpkins, a large orange and two smaller white ones, greet me at the front of the brownstone. The orange one has a standard carving of a jack-o'-lantern. It's not the best, but the sentiment makes me smile.

When I open the door, I hear a mellow jazz mix playing and get a whiff of something delicious. I imagine this is what a home feels like, with people waiting for you inside, wondering how your day went. A place that feels permanent. A place you can't wait to come back to. My heart feels full, but I tell myself it's just the excitement of seeing Chloe later.

"Hey." I enter the kitchen and see Adam folding together phyllo dough, which I'm proud of myself for recognizing.

Meanwhile, there are two pots on the stove and something in the oven. He's wearing a burnt orange Henley with the sleeves rolled up and a dish towel over his shoulder. I don't know why I expected anything less than Adam preparing a feast for tonight.

"Hey," he says, still focusing on his dough with precision. Once he folds over a final piece, he gives me a second glance. "Is this new?" He points his chin toward my outfit.

"It was getting chilly." I look down at my new coat and take off my hat.

"I like it" is all he says, and then he turns around to stir whatever is in his pot. *I like it* is something someone's grandparent would say to them, but somehow, it sounds sexually explicit coming from him.

After putting my stuff in the closet, I place the pie on the kitchen island and nudge it toward him. "Caramel apple."

"Oh my God," he says as he looks at the box. "I haven't been to Amy's in *years*."

"When I moved, I was always craving it. I considered flying back and buying a dozen and just freezing them."

He gives me a half smile and goes back to concentrating on his dough. While I haven't necessarily been the friendliest this past week, it doesn't feel great to get a taste of my own medicine. But after my conversation with Chloe the other night, I'm feeling better about our arrangement. Like maybe this doesn't have to be as hard as we're making it.

You can do this, June.

"Do you . . . need help?" It comes off a little disingenuous, but I'm trying here.

He looks up, surprised. "You want to help?" I simply nod. "You still remember how to julienne?" he asks.

"Pfft." I wave my hand. "Does one simply forget how to julienne?"

"We'll see," he says, passing me a cutting board and a few parsnips. After washing my hands, I begin to peel and trim a parsnip, then cut it into flat planks. I feel Adam watching me from behind and continue to the next step. Stacking the pieces on top of one another, I then begin cutting long, thin strips.

"Well?" I look back, awaiting the final verdict.

Adam takes a step toward me and leans his head over my shoulder. It's the closest we've been all week and I get that whiff of cedar again. My heart begins to beat faster as he reaches and pulls out one slice from the bunch and analyzes it.

"Not bad, Wood," he says, his voice low enough I can *feel* it. When he moves back to the stove my body feels cold. Like a blanket I needed that's now disappeared.

"What are you making?" I ask.

"*We*," he corrects, and it comes out more intimate than I'm sure he intends, "are making butternut squash congee with chili oil, harissa roasted sweet potatoes, and a mushroom kale bread pudding."

Jesus.

"What, no macaroni and cheese?" I squint at him. He gives me an unimpressed look and then reaches over the island, grabbing a deep mustard-colored dish that I didn't notice was there. He removes the lid and reveals macaroni and cheese with some sort of crust on top.

"What do you think this is, amateur hour?" He puts the lid back on.

"I stand corrected." I mindlessly arrange the parsnips and watch him go back to folding the dough. "You know you don't have to do this, right?" I look at him. "I'm sure Chloe would have been okay with takeout."

"I want to," he says while opening and closing the kitchen cupboards. "Shit," he says under his breath.

"What?"

"I need another pot," he says, and reaches for the top shelf, which is too high, even for him. "I can't reach it. Can you help, June?"

"If you can't reach it, there's no way I can," I scoff.

"I'll lift you," he says like that's obviously our only choice here, and a fire rushes to my core.

Yeah, I don't think so.

"Let me get a chair—"

"It'll take two seconds—just come here," he says impatiently.

I hesitate for a moment, but he's staring at me like *I'm* wasting time. "Fine," I sigh.

When I stand next to him, he takes a step behind me and

places both of his hands on my hips. It takes all of .02 seconds for the smell of cedar or santal to penetrate my senses and his body warmth to transfer onto me. There is not enough space in this kitchen. His hands feel like they're covering my entire body, and that's all it takes for me to remember what it's like to be touched by Adam Harper. It feels like a lifetime ago but right now, I remember it like it was yesterday.

"You ready?" he asks.

No.

"Yeah." I nod. In one swift motion his fingers grip my waist and I'm lifted into the air as if I weigh nothing, and then he wraps an arm around my thighs, hoisting me higher. I try desperately to not focus on how my ass is practically being held up by his chest, or how much my heart rate has increased. "Um, which one do you want?"

"The smallest one," he says. I choose a pot I think will work and he slowly slides me down his body until my feet are back on the floor. "Thanks," he says, and then turns to the stove as if we just did the most simple act.

I try to shake what just happened and turn up the volume on the Bluetooth speaker. When I situate myself back on the barstool, the smell of home cooking and the sound of music fill the house. That feeling of being *home* is back, but I don't allow myself to forget that this is all temporary. In three weeks, I'm never seeing Adam or this house again.

THE DRIVE UP to Connecticut will take over an hour. Approximately one hour and twenty-six minutes, according to Google, and that's quite a long time for two people to be in the same car. Especially when they haven't really spoken more than sixty words to each other over the span of the past week.

I don't know a lot about cars except the basics, but I know that when Adam pulls up in front of the house in a black SUV, it's not a necessity, it's a luxury.

"Where have you been hiding this?" I walk toward him holding the dish of mac and cheese.

"There's a lot on Bleecker." He takes the dish out of my hands and places it on the backseat.

I open the door and get in on the passenger side. "I can't believe you're *that guy* now."

"What guy?"

"The guy who owns a *BMW* in Manhattan."

"It has an eco-mode," he says defensively.

While he puts the rest of the food in the trunk, I take in the tanned leather interior and the cleanliness of the vehicle. This is nicer than what most people I know in LA drive. When he opens the driver's door, I brace myself. We're going to be sitting together for almost an hour and a half and there's no escape. Adam's close enough that I can smell him again. It's definitely fresh sage or cedarwood. He needs to take fewer showers.

"Okay," he sighs, and puts his seat belt on. I hold my breath as he moves his hand toward me, only for it to land on the gearshift. "You ready?"

I nod, and before I know it, we're off. The first five minutes or so are completely quiet. There's no radio, music, or anything. Just the sound of the tires against the road, the smell of the food behind us, and the traffic of Eleventh Street ahead. Even though we spent the afternoon passing each other in the kitchen, this feels different. There's nothing to distract us, or to use as a crutch for conversation.

Once we hit the FDR, I get lost in the view of the city. As the sun begins its descent over the East River, vibrant hues paint the horizon an autumnal crimson and gold. To our left, the streets of Manhattan pulse with life.

Adam's voice cuts through the silence. "When's the last time you've been back?"

"I haven't . . ." I shake my head. "Been back."

He keeps his eyes ahead of him, and nods. Almost like I just confirmed something he already knew the answer to. "Do you miss it?"

I look out the window again, watching the city pass by. "I don't know. I miss parts of it. The energy, the seasons . . . Amy's." I look at him and catch a smile. "But there's a lot of things I love about LA too. I think you'd like it."

"Yeah, I've been," he says, and I don't know why that feels like a punch in my gut. *When?* I want to ask, but don't.

"What did you think?"

"Weather's nice, obviously, and I did like seeing things like palm trees, or the ocean. But I don't know, everything felt a little too spread out."

"I will say, you get used to being in your car a lot," I note. "It's my audiobook time."

"I do like a good audiobook," he agrees.

"Well, then you're halfway there," I say.

"Are you excited to go back home?" He looks at me, and for a split second I think he means back to the house.

"I think so," I answer truthfully. He doesn't say anything, and I don't bother to look at him to see his reaction. "So . . ." I take a deep breath in, feeling the hardened exterior I've built around myself start to crack. "I've been meaning to tell you . . . I'm happy for you."

Adam briefly turns his gaze to me, long enough that I can see the genuine warmth in his eyes. "Thanks, June," he says, then looks ahead as the corner of his mouth curls up.

There's always been a deep connection between the two of us, the ability to have a conversation with a mere look across the room. Sometimes the most intimate things we've said were in silence. For the rest of the drive, things feel a lot easier. Like a weight has been lifted from both of our shoulders. In the comfort of our silence, Adam carefully taps his phone a few times.

"For old times' sake." He smiles, and the beginning notes of *Les Misérables* fill the car.

Chapter 13

AUGUST, 9 YEARS AGO

WE'RE GRABBING COFFEE IN COBBLE HILL WHEN CHLOE CASUally tells me she landed an associate attorney role.

"Oh my God!" I say through a mouthful of oatmeal chocolate chip cookie. "Chloe! Congratulations!" I stand up and give her a hug across the table.

"Thank you!" She squeezes me back. "It's a midsize firm but it has an incredible reputation."

"It could be a tiny-sized firm, and you'd still be the most impressive person I know." We sit back down. "We have to celebrate. Should we do drinks tonight?"

"I can't tonight. Ethan's taking me out for dinner."

"Ethan? Davis?" I cough. "Since when have you been seeing him?"

"I'm not *seeing* him," Chloe says. "I actually hadn't seen him in almost a year. But I ran into him at this party. One thing led to another . . ."

"That's exactly what you'll be saying nine months from now."

"June!"

"I'm kidding!" I laugh. "But seriously, I didn't know he was your type."

"I don't have a type. Unless you count narcissistic assholes?"

"Well then, maybe he fits perfectly."

"Shut up. Isn't this what your twenties is all about? Doing stupid shit so you have stories to tell in your thirties?"

"You sound like Adam," I say with a snort.

"How is Harper? It's been a minute since I've seen him."

"Good." I take another bite of my cookie. "His shifts at the restaurant are so crazy, *I* barely see him."

"Relationships are so hard." Chloe takes a sip of her iced coffee.

"We're not in a *relationship,*" I say, getting tired of hearing myself constantly telling her.

"Oh?" Chloe raises her eyebrow. "Then what would you call it?"

"Roommates," I say slowly as if she's never heard the term.

"Uh-huh. Okay, well, if you're currently single, why don't you go ask that guy out over there?" I look behind me and see a man a few tables down looking in our direction over his laptop.

"Why would I do that?"

"Because he clearly can't stop staring," she says.

"Chloe, he's looking at *you* . . ."

"Oh." She sees him wave. "Okay, well, never mind. I'm just saying you deserve to have fun, June!"

It's not that I'm not open to dating. I just don't usually put myself in situations where anyone can approach me, or I can approach them. The only relationship I'm interested in having is the one with my career.

"You're making it sound like I'm this homely woman who never leaves her house."

"Well, I guess if Adam's there you have no reason to leave," she shrugs.

I roll my eyes, because she has yet to accept what I already have. My friendship with Adam is too important for me to be thinking of him any other way.

"SHOULD WE HAVE gotten a more expensive bottle?" I look over at Adam as the grocery store clerk rings us up.

Since I'm starting to book paid productions while still keeping shifts at the bookstore, and Adam's working more at the restaurant, it feels like we're in a position to splurge if we need to. Two and a half years into us being roommates, we've quickly transitioned into thinking of any extra money as *our* expendable income, which only makes sense when we do literally everything together.

"Forty-five dollars for a bottle of wine is more than enough," Adam says.

"I guess, but celebrating your best friend getting her first job at a law firm is a big deal."

"Which is why we're getting the bottle that's forty-five dollars, instead of the one that's seventeen," he says.

"I guess . . ." I say, still debating our choice.

We walk outside into the sticky August heat, the stench of garbage being taken across the Hudson doing no favors for the city. Chloe's apartment is only another twelve blocks, so we figure we'll save ourselves a subway ride. I can feel my hair on the verge of frizzing, so I tie it up in a loose bun on top of my head, too tired to smooth out the tendrils falling around my face. Adam's eyes focus on me, his gaze settling above my eyeline.

"I know it looks stupid, but I'm taking it down once we get to Chloe's."

"No, you look cute."

I look down at my yellow sundress with thin spaghetti straps and a hem that comes mid-thigh. I've been waiting to wear this outfit, and it did cross my mind that there would be many lawyers, hopefully single, at Chloe's tonight.

"How cute?" I lift my shoulder to my cheek, giving him a smile.

"The cutest," he says.

When we get to Chloe's, there are more people than I expect. Easily thirty people in her seven-hundred-square-foot apartment. We could hear the music and chatter from the hallway, so it's no surprise how loud it is once we're inside.

The crowd is mostly Chloe's friends from law school whom I haven't met but know from photos. Similar to how I have my theater friends, she has her own circle of people separate from me, and I'm always fascinated to see this side of her world.

"Hey!" Chloe spots Adam and me from across the room and runs over to pull us inside. She grabs the wine from my hands without looking at it and passes it to someone in the kitchen. Adam gives me an *I told you so* look, and I roll my eyes. "How goes it, Harper?"

"It goes," he says, and gives her a hug. "Congratulations, Chlo."

"Thank you," she says, then squeezes my arm. "How's the music?"

"Loud," I say.

"About time you showed up." Ethan comes over and pats Adam on the back and then gives me a hug. I still find it a little weird that the guy Chloe is casually sleeping with knows Adam.

As Adam and Ethan head to the kitchen, Chloe brings me over to meet some of her classmates from law school.

"Adina, Michelle, this is June. June, Adina and Michelle." She gestures to the two girls looking at me. The name Adina sounds familiar, but I don't recall ever hearing about Michelle. "I'll be right back," Chloe says, then pulls a disappearing act to greet more people.

"Hi," I say, and take a sip of the beer Chloe managed to put in my hands somewhere between the door and here.

"Chloe's told us so much about you," Adina says. "I can't believe we're only meeting now."

"Good things, I hope?" I laugh.

"All terrible." Adina shakes her head. I like her.

"So, are you both working now too?" I ask.

Adina nods. "I'm actually at the same firm as Chloe, and Michelle is at Martin and Harding."

"Oh wow, that's awesome. How are you liking it?"

"This quarter's been tough. One of the cases—"

"Okay, sorry—" Michelle says to both of us. "Who is that?"

"Who?" Adina asks as we both look over our shoulders.

"Don't be so obvious," Michelle says, and we both turn back. "Behind you. The tall guy, dark hair."

In a sea of people, it's pretty obvious whom she's talking about. Adam sticks out not because he's one of the tallest people here, but because there's something about him that catches your attention. It's the same reason I was drawn to him the day we met at the bookstore.

Adina subtly looks over her shoulder again. "I have no idea, but he's hot."

As if he can hear our conversation, Adam runs a hand through his hair. He's listening intently to something Ethan is saying, and takes a sip of his beer, nodding. I've grown used to his looks but I'll admit, seeing him in this light, and hearing girls swoon over him, they're not wrong.

Adam turns his head and our eyes lock for a brief moment. His beer bottle pauses against his parted lips, and he gives me a wink from across the room.

"That's Adam," I say. "My roommate."

Both of their eyes get wider, and I feel like I'm on an episode of *The Bachelor* or something. The visceral reaction they're having is making me uncomfortable.

"Is he gay?" Michelle asks.

"No," I laugh.

"Is he single?" Michelle moves in closer. Even though Adam is usually involved with someone in one way or another, he's never referred to anyone as his *girlfriend.*

"He is," I say.

She gives Adina and me a *here I go* look, and I have to hand it to her for being so forward. It's something I definitely couldn't do.

We stay where we are and watch Michelle politely tap Adam on the shoulder. She tucks her short black hair behind her ear and laughs at the first thing he says. More than anything, I'm amused by how Adam manages to wrap any woman he meets around his finger. I've seen it up close; women at the supermarket, bank tellers, coffee shop baristas. Adam just has this effortless charm about him.

They look good together; she's probably five ten and one of the only people I know who still wears a crop top and low-rise jeans. I'm hoping she dresses more professionally in the office. As I observe their interaction, I notice something different about Adam. There's a way he's looking at her that looks unfamiliar, reserved for women who look like Michelle. I caught a glimpse of it that night in the kitchen. The night that he so suddenly decided he would rather be anywhere else than touching me. The way Adam looks at me isn't like how he is right now. I haven't seen him look at anyone the way he looks at me. It's a look that I suppose is reserved for friends. But I know we're more than that. I just don't know what.

It feels like I'm watching something that I shouldn't be, so I turn back around to Adina. "There are so many people here. Did most of you go to school together?"

"Oh God, tons of us! That group over there," she says, and points across the room to five or six people sitting on the couch. "We were all in the same class." One of the guys in the group she's referencing spots Adina, and she waves him to come over. "That's Ryan. He was our TA in first year." She nods toward the *beautiful* blond man with blue eyes.

If I didn't know any better, I would say he's a champion surfer who stumbled into the wrong apartment. He makes his way through the crowd, and I quickly flip my hair over my shoulder, fluffing it up.

"Hey, Dina, how are you?" He leans past me to give her a hug and then offers his hand out to mine. "Hi, I'm Ryan."

"June." I shake his hand. Firm grip noted.

"How do you know Chloe?" he asks, his eyes on mine, and they're *so* blue. Like he's a Siberian husky or something.

"We met in freshman year," I say. "What about you?" I ask, pretending I don't know.

"I was a TA in one of her classes."

"Oh wow." I smile. "So what do—"

"Hey!" Ryan calls out behind Adina and me, to a girl who looks like his female counterpart—blue eyes and blond hair. She walks toward us and gives Ryan a quick kiss. "Hey, baby," he says. "Dina, June, this is my fiancée, Crystal."

"Nice to meet you." Adina tips her drink.

"Of course it is." I smile and shake Crystal's hand.

"What's that?" She leans in closer to hear me better.

"Oh nothing, I just—I see Chloe calling me. Nice to meet you both."

I leave the three of them and push my way to the kitchen. There's a table set up as a drink station and the bottle of wine we brought sits in the pile of red Solo cups and beer. I pull it out of the group and tuck it away in the cupboard below, making a mental note to remind Chloe about it for a rainy day.

There are probably a good fifteen people over capacity and I can't even see Adam anymore, but I spot Chloe on the fire escape by herself and grab another beer.

"Hey." I crawl through the window and sit beside her. The night air is sticky and hot, but it still feels cooler than inside the apartment. "You okay?"

"Just needed some fresh air." She takes the other beer from my hand and places it on her neck.

"I didn't know you knew this many people."

"I couldn't tell you who half of these people are," Chloe says. We both stare out into the city and watch the symphony of light across Manhattan. She leans her head on my shoulder and sighs. "So, this is it, huh?"

"What is?" I ask.

"This chapter." She shrugs and then shifts to look at me. "I don't know . . . throwing parties and not knowing what we want to do with our lives."

I take a sip and nod. Maybe there's a difference between not knowing what we want to do and not being able to actually do it.

"But this next chapter is going to be pretty fucking great, Chloe," I say.

"Maybe . . . I mean, don't get me wrong," she says. "I'm *so* grateful I'm at this point in my career, but sometimes I wish I could have it all. Is that selfish?"

"What do you mean?"

"Love and shit," she sneers.

Chloe's never said she's wanted a relationship. She's dated *many* guys and I've never seen her shed a tear for any of them. I'm finding solace in knowing that she wants what all of us do.

"It's not selfish to want love," I say.

"I'm just tired. Tired of people finding their person and getting married, or engaged, and meanwhile I can't even get a text back for a second date."

If a beautiful woman like Chloe who's on the path to becoming a lawyer is having dating problems, I'm fearful for the rest of us.

"You are the most confident person I know, and if—"

"But I don't know if that's a good thing," she says, and opens her beer. "I'm learning men are afraid of a confident woman."

"Then you're dating the wrong men," I say.

"Men are the worst."

"What about Ethan?"

"Get fucking real." She makes a face of disgust. "You're lucky you have Adam."

"Adam?" I almost choke on my drink.

"Yeah," she says earnestly. "Do you know how hard it is to find that?"

Words escape me, because I'm not positive I know what Chloe's getting at, so I ask my next question carefully.

"You . . . want a guy *like* Adam? Or you . . . want Adam?"

A loud cackle comes out of her. "You're sick—he's like my brother. I mean what you and Adam *have.*"

"Chloe . . ." I groan, not wanting to have this conversation again.

"Okay, can you be real with me for a minute?" She takes a sip of her beer. "Do you seriously not see him that way?"

"No," I say for probably the hundredth time.

"So, you're not attracted to him?"

"Chloe—"

"No, seriously, just humor me for a minute here." She squares her hips to me. "You look at Adam and you're telling me you don't see an attractive man?"

Do I look at Adam and see a six-foot-three man with a head of dark wavy hair, broad shoulders, toned arms, deep hazel eyes with a slight freckle of green in the sun, and a smile that makes me go weak? Do I look at Adam and see a friend whom I trust with my life, someone who will do anything for me, protect me at all costs, and be a shoulder to cry on when I need it?

"Okay, fine, I do. But so what? He's an objectively good-looking person!"

"Then what's the problem, June?" Chloe's tone changes.

I stand up and lean against the edge of the fire escape watching the neon spectacle below. When we're down there the world feels so small, like all that matters is us. Up here, you realize how big the world is, how insignificant we really are.

"He's one of my *best friends,* Chloe," I say.

My memory flickers to that night in the kitchen like it was only yesterday. I can almost feel the heat that pooled within me all over again.

"Men don't act the way he does for their *friends.*" Chloe stands up and leans beside me. "Can I give you my honest opinion?"

"Haven't you been doing that this whole time?" I raise an eyebrow.

"I think the two of you would be really fucking great together." She points the top of her beer bottle to the party. "And I think *he* hasn't made a move because he doesn't know where you're at. Talk to him."

I shake my head. "I can't risk losing him."

She frowns. "I think trying to keep him might be the bigger risk."

For a few seconds, we both stay silent. Beneath us, the sounds of horns honking and music from clubs starting to open echo to our level. My eyes rise to the night sky—maybe because you can actually see stars tonight, or maybe because I don't want tears to fall down my cheeks.

"You know what I think?" I nudge my body against hers. "I

think that there's about seventy people in there who are all celebrating *you,* and you need to enjoy it."

"If I must," she says, rolling her eyes.

"And hey." I grab her hand. "I appreciate you."

A smile takes over her face. "I appreciate you."

The two of us crawl through the kitchen window back into the party, and Chloe immediately gets pulled into a conversation with a group of people I don't know.

The garbage can is already overflowing with red Solo cups and beer bottles, so I pull out the trash bag and replace it with a new one. Considering Chloe's apartment is the size of a shoebox, typical for New York, I make an effort to be the good friend and at least throw this down the chute.

While pushing my way through the front door, I see two people making out in the hallway. *Making out* is actually putting it loosely; the girl is pressed up against the wall, torso on display, with the guy's hand under her shirt. His lips are on her neck as she breathes out—

"Adam."

"Shit." An audible gasp escapes me as I drop the trash bag.

"June—" Adam immediately steps away from Michelle and wipes his palm over his mouth while she adjusts her top.

"I'm sorry, I—"

"Wait, June—"

"Sorry, I was just taking out the trash." I clutch the bag of garbage and rush past them to the end of the hall.

I try to erase the image of Adam in a feral state from my mind. He never shares details, but I know he's been with plenty of women, and to see it with my own eyes confirms all of my not-so-idle curiosity.

The only thing similar to this shock was two summers ago, when I saw Adam shirtless for the first time and I was quite taken aback by the sight, more intrigued than anything. What I'm feeling now is more . . . hurt. Like I've lost him. He was never mine to lose, but now knowing I *can* lose him, that's almost scarier.

After stuffing the trash down the chute, I turn around and catch Michelle going back into Chloe's apartment. But Adam hasn't moved from his spot. Instead, he's standing in place, waiting for me. He's over fifty feet away, yet I can see the flare of his nostrils.

"I'm sorry, I didn't want you to see that," he says, and walks toward me, the sound of the party muffled through the walls.

"See what?" I play it cool. Maybe almost too cool, because he raises an eyebrow. "I don't care."

"Yeah, but still." He runs a hand through his hair, and I catch a whiff of alcohol on him. "That's why I came out here."

"You didn't have to come out here for my benefit; you're an adult." I walk past him, but he grabs my arm and then immediately lets go.

"Look, I just feel shitty, okay?" he says. "So let me apologize."

"You have nothing to apologize for." I fake a laugh. "Would you care if I was out here making out with a random guy?"

"Yes." He says it almost too quickly, and I wonder if he heard me correctly.

"Well, *I* don't care, Adam," I continue, "so don't worry about it." I walk back to the party, unsure exactly why I can feel my eyes welling.

Chapter 14

THE ONLY TIME I'VE EVER BEEN TO CONNECTICUT WAS A FEW weeks after Chloe first got a job in Stamford. It never made a lasting impression. Now, driving into Fairfield, where she currently resides, I'm charmed by the idyllic coastal town. When Adam turns onto her street, it feels like we're entering a forest with at least a hundred feet in between each home. Between Manhattan and Los Angeles, I don't remember the last time I've seen so much foliage.

"You're heeere!" Chloe squeals as she swings her front door open.

"We're heeere!" I echo, getting out of the car.

This house is the complete opposite of Perry, from the white walls to the largely open ground-floor plan, vaulted wood ceilings, and tree-filled views. It's bright and minimalist.

"I should've known when Adam said y'all were bringing something, it would be a full-blown catered meal." Chloe takes the dish from my hand and the box of food from Adam's. "Harper, it smells delicious."

"All vegetarian," he says with a wink.

"You're the best." She gives him a quick kiss on the cheek. "Babe! Where are you?!" she shouts over her shoulder, and on cue, Chloe's wife, Lucia, comes down the stairs holding their son, Teddy, in her arms.

"Welcome!" she practically sings through her British accent. Her hair is big and curly and she's wearing a deep red sweater that matches her lipstick and contrasts with her olive skin. There's an effortlessly cool aura about her. She and Chloe never had an official wedding, so the only time I've met her was briefly over FaceTime. It's hard to believe she's even more beautiful in person. "God, June, I can't believe we're *finally* meeting!"

"I know, it's about time!" I press my cheek against hers and she gives me an air kiss, but my attention shifts over to Teddy, whom I've seen only in pictures and videos. "Are. You. Kidding?! He's perfect!"

"Thank you! I still cannot believe how lucky we are to have him." She bounces him on her waist, and he lets out a little giggle. "And you must be Adam." Lucia and Adam exchange kisses on both cheeks. Teddy immediately puts his arms out to Adam and starts opening and closing his fists. "Oh! Look at that, he likes you!" Lucia seamlessly hands Teddy to Adam, who starts playing with Teddy's fingers, which causes the toddler to squeal with excitement.

There are certain things that an average person knows about babies—support their necks and don't wake them while they're sleeping. But seeing the innate paternal instincts that Adam possesses conjures up a wave of emotions within me that makes it hard to stay reserved.

"Thanks for hosting us," Adam says, looking over at Lucia.

"Are you kidding? The pleasure is all ours! I've heard so much about the two of you. It's almost criminal that this hasn't happened sooner."

Adam and I exchange a look. It still throws me off being referred to as a duo of any kind.

"How old is he?" Adam asks, his focus on Teddy, and I'm not sure if he's purposely trying to change the subject.

"He's going to be two in February." Lucia places a cloth with ducks on Adam's shoulder. Maybe it's the sight of Adam holding a baby, or how effortlessly he and Lucia are hitting it off; it could also very well be the fact that my best friend has the cutest baby I've ever seen in my life. But there's something about tonight that makes me feel like the Grinch, whose heart is growing in size.

"Okay," Chloe says as she comes out of the kitchen. "Dinner is pretty much ready so I'm going to herd you all into the dining room." She motions us out of the front foyer. We all follow, and I catch Chloe elbowing Adam. "Not a bad look, Harper," she says, nodding to Teddy still in his arms.

He elbows her back and then places Teddy in his high chair beside Lucia, who starts to strap him in.

Chloe subtly pulls me into the kitchen and hands me a charcuterie board. "I read the terms."

My eyes go wide, and I lean in closer. "And?"

"It's all legit. House belongs to both of you after the paperwork goes through. I even had a colleague on our real estate team look it over."

"All right," I sigh, a slight wave of relief washing over me knowing that this is real. "Okay, wow. Well, thank you."

She grabs two bottles of wine, and we walk back into the dining room. "So, since *Chef Adam* here has decided to show us up with his five-course meal, I don't want anyone saying how good his food is compared to mine when you start eating," Chloe warns us.

"So, we should probably get all the praise out of the way now." Adam winks at her, and the mere gesture makes me look away.

"*Wow.*" Chloe playfully hits his arm. "Look who's all of a sudden hot shit now that he owns a Michelin-star restaurant."

"All of a sudden?" He raises an eyebrow.

"This guy." She rolls her eyes and takes a seat beside Teddy and Lucia while Adam and I sit across from them. Since day one, Chloe and Adam have had an effortless sibling dynamic. In a way, I'd say Chloe and Adam are soulmates, platonically, of course. They're two of the funniest, most caring, and smartest people I know, and I've never been able to keep up with their banter.

"Okay, everyone, dig in!" Lucia claps while Chloe scoops the macaroni and cheese onto a separate silicone plate for Teddy. Seeing Chloe now with her wife and her child, in their beautiful home, is a stark reminder of how much time has passed. How much I've missed and how much can change. I tried so hard to create a new life that I didn't realize there were parts of my old life I'd miss. Parts that I now regret leaving behind.

"*Adam,*" Lucia says after tasting the congee. "You are the real deal."

"Okay, easy," Chloe says. "He's a professional chef."

"What other talents do we get to witness tonight?" Lucia puts another spoonful in her mouth. "June, do we get a burlesque performance during dessert?"

"Is that an option?" Adam turns to me.

"You wish," I laugh.

Adam simply raises an eyebrow, and I bite my lip and look down at my food. If I didn't know any better, I'd almost say we were flirting. *Are we flirting?*

"But the pleasure is mine, really." Adam turns to Chloe and Lucia. "It's been a while since I've been able to cook for friends like this."

What does that mean? What does Adam's personal life look like? Who are his friends? Why wouldn't he cook for Kelsey? All details I've actively avoided knowing, but that now I feel I need to understand.

"Well, this was so kind. Thank you, Adam." Lucia tips her glass to him and he nods in return. "June, how's Los Angeles?"

"It's good," I say, because *good* is really all it is.

"How long have you lived there again?"

"About five years now." I find myself making a conscious effort to not look at Adam.

"And how are you liking it compared to New York? Do you miss it here?" Lucia scoops a spoonful of mushroom kale bread pudding onto her plate.

"I can't stand how nobody walks around there," Chloe says, eating a bite of mac and cheese. "I had to Uber everywhere—it was so weird."

"My brother just moved there last year," Lucia says. "And he was saying that working out is like a *thing*."

"Yeah, I mean it's LA. *Everyone's* working out," Chloe says.

"Yes, but because you don't get your normal steps in, you probably have to make a conscious effort to be in shape."

"Well then, it would be perfect for Adam," Chloe says, and he smirks to himself.

"I will say, if you're into hiking"—I look at Lucia—"there are some really nice trails."

"You know, babe." Lucia pats Chloe's leg. "We should really make a trip down there. It would be nice to see Gerardo too."

"Yeah, we're long overdue," Chloe says with a nod.

"So, how did the two of you meet?" Adam asks.

"Bumble," Chloe and Lucia say in unison, then Lucia adds, "Fun fact—she was my first match ever." She blushes.

"I didn't know that!" I raise my eyebrows.

"*I* was not so lucky." Chloe glares at Lucia with flared nostrils. "It was hard out there."

"That's because you were only dating men," Lucia says, and then her eyes cut across the table. "No offense, Adam."

"None taken," he says, holding a hand up.

"God, remember Ethan?" I make a face.

"Please, this dinner's too delicious to spoil my appetite," Chloe says, holding up a hand. "Harper, do you still talk to him?"

Adam shakes his head. "I think the last time I saw him was when you did. But I heard he's married with like four kids, moved back to Long Island. He apparently has a Nintendo podcast? I don't know."

"What, really?" I shoot Chloe a look and then turn back to Adam. "Is it doing well?"

"Okay, so I was curious and googled it one day, and it's not *bad,*" Adam says.

"But it's not *good,*" Chloe laughs.

"Wild. Okay, sorry, enough about Ethan," I say, and reach for the sweet potatoes. "Lucia, I want to hear about your first date with Chloe."

"Well," Lucia starts. "We started out with brunch in Brooklyn and then ended up taking a train to Montauk and spent the whole weekend there. I deleted the app once we got home." Lucia puts a hand on Chloe's back and starts rubbing. "We eloped a year later."

I watch the slight exchange of squeezing hands and looks of *I love you* in their eyes and feel nothing but utter happiness for Chloe. Pure joy that she has the life she deserves.

"You two are the rare instance of successful online dating." Adam tips his head toward them.

"How did you know she was the one?" I ask.

Chloe and Lucia look at each other. "We didn't have to try," Lucia says, and smiles.

"It was like hanging out with your best friend," Chloe agrees. "And the sex is really good, and then one day you're like *wait, I can have this my whole life?*"

I begin to feel hot underneath my sweater, and take a sip of water.

"What about you two?" Lucia holds her hands out to Adam and me. "How did you meet?" she asks as if our relationship equates to the story they just shared.

"Oh." I look at Adam. "Um, we used to be roommates."

"Chloe told me!" Lucia puts a spoonful of food in Teddy's mouth, or tries to. "How did that happen?"

Adam starts to rub the back of his neck, a signature giveaway that he feels uncomfortable. He looks at me and raises his eyebrows as if to ask *do you want me to tell her?* I slightly shrug.

"June begged him to move in with her," Chloe answers before either of us can say anything.

Lucia starts snapping her fingers. "Yes, June!"

"I did not!" I say, my cheeks becoming flush.

"Oh, come on!" Chloe laughs. "Adam, didn't she?"

"Define *beg*," Adam says.

"I hate you." I shake my head and then turn to Lucia. "In my defense, I asked him to move in for *practical* reasons."

"Yeah, like cooking you dinner every night and reaching for things on the top shelf," Chloe says, and Adam and Lucia laugh.

"No, June, you're smart," Lucia says. "A young woman in her early twenties living all by herself in New York? Having a male roommate probably felt like protection too."

"Thank you!" I hold my hand out to Lucia. "And splitting the cost of rent and utilities. *Practical reasons.*"

"But seriously," Chloe says. "I can't believe we never talked about this. Harper, why did you say yes?"

"Are you kidding? I'd have to be an idiot to turn down living with June." Adam shakes his head, then looks at me. "Even now."

Teddy starts fussing and the conversation quickly pivots to Lucia's job as a radiologist, but I'm still stuck on our last topic. It feels like the air supply has been cut off from my oxygen tank.

AFTER DINNER, ADAM and I clean up the kitchen while Lucia and Chloe debate who should bathe Teddy and put him to bed.

"Babe, it might be faster if we just both do it," Lucia suggests.

"Yeah, you're right." Chloe takes a final swig of her wine and looks at Adam and me. "You two can behave yourselves, right?"

"Yes, Mom." I give her an unimpressed look.

"Just checking," she says, holding up both hands, then heads up the stairs.

There's a jazz vinyl playing in the background and the faint sounds of the crackling fire in the living room. Tonight has been such a wonderful evening that I almost don't want to ever leave.

Adam places the caramel apple pie I got into the oven and pulls out a tray I never got to take a peek into earlier.

"What's that?" I ask.

"Chocolate bourbon chai latte cake with butter pecan frosting." Adam reveals the most beautiful circular cake with the creamiest-looking frosting and pecan drizzles on top.

"Adam." My eyes go wide. "This looks incredible."

"I hope it's good. It's my first time making it." He cuts a small slice and places it on a side plate.

"As if anything you make wouldn't be good," I say.

When he passes me the plate, our fingertips barely graze, yet I forget to breathe for a moment. I take a spoonful of the cake, and the sound that comes out of me is not in my control.

"Holy shit," I say, my mouth still full. "This tastes like heaven." When I look up at Adam, his focus is on me, like he's studying my every move. "What?"

"Nothing," he says softly. "It's just . . . nice to do this again."

"Yeah." I nod. "Although your taste tests have gotten *a lot* better in the past five years."

"Thank God," Adam says, cracking a smile. Then he gets more serious. "Not just that, though. Tonight's been nice. Hanging out with Chloe again."

Leading up to tonight, there was an uneasiness rooted in my insides. I was worried tonight would feel like an evening with strangers, people I don't know anymore. That couldn't have been further from the truth. These past few hours, I felt like a missing puzzle piece that was suddenly found and placed in its right spot. There's a hole in my heart I didn't know existed that's now becoming full.

"It really has been," I say.

"Lucia's great," Adam says, cutting another slice for himself.

"Right? She and Chloe are perfect for each other."

"And Teddy." He looks at me, eyes wide. "I mean, he's the cutest baby on the planet."

"I'm sure they would not put up a fight if you wanted to babysit," I say.

"I might take them up on that. Good to know I've got a little buddy now." He smiles, and for some reason the thought of Adam, Chloe, and Lucia hanging out makes me . . . sad. "When did you start wearing your hair natural?" he says from out of nowhere.

"What?"

"Your hair." He nods his chin toward me. "You always used to straighten it."

"Oh." I reach for the top of my head. "I think once I turned thirty, I stopped caring."

"It always felt like something forbidden," he says. His gaze is set on mine for what feels like too long before he continues. "I'd mostly only get to see it after you came out of the shower . . . I like it."

I do everything in my power to keep my composure. I want to tell him to not picture me after a shower, I want to stop myself from picturing *him* just out of the shower . . . but I also don't want any of this to stop.

Yes, I want things to be easier, but it's too easy to slip into our old routine. Maybe that's all this is: an old habit dying hard. Or maybe it's the feeling I keep trying to bury deeper and deeper, as if it's not the only thought eating away at me every single second. *I miss Adam.*

"Thanks," I finally say. "I mean, since we're talking about appearances, I feel like I need to state the obvious." He raises an eyebrow. "You have aged like a fine wine."

He lets out a genuine laugh. "What?"

"Come *on,*" I say. "Don't pretend like you don't know how good *you* look."

Adam smiles and then reaches over for the bottle of red behind me. I hold my breath as his chest hovers over mine. Our gaze meets, and for a brief moment I glance at his lips to catch him quickly licking them. I want to shut my eyes and let my body take control, but instead I stay strong and watch his every move.

"More wine?" he says softly.

I know the look on his face all too well right now. It's one that's bordering on dangerous territory. My chest rises with my next breath as I reach for my glass.

"I'd love some."

I stand corrected. Week two living with Adam might be a lot harder than week one.

Chapter 15

APRIL, 8 YEARS AGO

As I'M WALKING TOWARD THE HOUSE AFTER REHEARSAL FOR a new Off-Broadway show, I see Adam sitting on the stoop. His hands are fisted against his mouth, pale, and his hair is a mess. It's cold for April and he doesn't have a jacket on. My instinct is to run to him, and I run faster than I knew I was capable of. He lifts his eyes to mine and stands up, and I drop my purse onto the ground.

"Adam, what's wrong?

"My mom" is all he says.

Instinctively, I wrap my arms around him, and he buries his face into my neck. I feel tears on my skin and let out a breath. It's then I find out Adam's mom has cancer.

EVERYTHING THAT HAPPENS afterward is a blur. I'm positive I scold Adam for not calling me sooner and he makes some excuse about not wanting to bother me at rehearsal, because he thinks I would've dropped everything. He's right, but there's nothing I could've done anyway. There's nothing either of us can do.

"Take a shower and I'll take care of dinner," I tell him.

"I'm already feeling bad—you don't have to make my stomach upset too," he says.

I open my mouth and then close it again. He gives me a weak smile and it somehow feels like I haven't seen it in years.

"I'm ordering takeout," I say.

For the rest of the evening, he doesn't bring up his mom and I don't ask any questions. The only thing I want to do is be there for him, so I wait for him to tell me on his own time. We end up falling asleep on the couch, and when I wake up Adam's head is on my lap and Netflix is asking if we're still watching *Friends.* I turn off the TV and nudge him gently.

"Adam," I whisper.

He rubs his eyes and lifts himself so he's sitting next to me. "What time is it?"

"Almost three."

"Shit." He pinches the bridge of his nose. We sit there in complete silence for what feels like minutes. "It's lung cancer," he says softly. "She did chemo a few years ago and she fought it. But now it's back, stage four." He lets out a breathless laugh. "She doesn't even fucking smoke."

I can't see his face, only his silhouette from the moonlight outside. Maybe it's better this way.

"What can I do?" I reach for his hand.

"Nothing," he mumbles. He moves his hand to swipe at his eyes, then puts it back on mine. "There's nothing—"

"I want to do something."

His hand squeezes mine, and while I can't see it, I feel him staring intently at me. "This is enough."

The entire time I've known Adam he's been strong; he never lets anything break his cool. He's tall, stoic, soft-spoken, and intentional. Yet this man in front of me feels like a child. I want to tell him that everything is okay, but I don't know if it will be. I don't know what any of this means.

"We'll get through this," I say. It sounds like something you should tell someone in this situation, but I mean it. "Together."

"I just—I don't . . . I don't know what I'd do without you, June," he says softly.

While I can't quite grasp why, it feels like my world is changing just as much as his. "That's what friends are for." I lean my head on his shoulder.

We don't say anything else, but I have a moment of realization. I'll probably never feel closer to anyone else for the rest of my life than I do right now.

THE NEXT DAY Adam doesn't leave the house—he barely leaves his room. I swing his door open and enter without knocking.

"Okay," I huff. "You have to go home."

He's lying on his bed, and it looks like he hasn't moved all morning.

"Are you kicking me out?" He laughs.

"Adam."

"I'm not doing this," he says, then rolls back onto his side and pulls the covers up. I know he's not trying to be stubborn. I know he's scared.

"You need to see her," I say.

"June, please—"

"You're going to regret it if you don't."

The second the words come out of my mouth, *I* regret it.

He sits up and turns to me, his eyes red and hollow. It's clear he's been crying. "Close the door."

"Adam, I—"

"Close the door," he repeats. "*Please.*"

I close the door and go to rehearsal feeling worked up and frustrated. We have a little bit over a month before the show opens, and at the end of the day, Diane, our choreographer, pulls me aside and says today my pirouettes have never looked better. Whatever fire is inside of me, she tells me to keep it.

While heading home, I pick up some Thai food because I know there won't be anything to eat for dinner. Adam's sitting on the couch in the dark, but he's clearly showered and there's a packed duffel bag at the bottom of the stairs. Our eyes meet, and he looks more scared than I've ever seen him.

"Will you come with me?" His voice cracks.

I place my purse on the side table and sit beside him. He smooths his thumb over my knee, and I don't think about the show, my rehearsals, opening night, any of it.

"Of course."

WE CATCH A 6:45 A.M. train to Long Island and then a cab to Adam's parents' house. The car stops in front of a quaint home on a residential street. There's an overused basketball hoop above the driveway with the net missing, and I picture a young

Adam doing layups while his sister circles him on her bike. Never living anywhere for more than a year growing up, I've always wondered what it feels like to come home.

Adam passes the driver a fifty and I follow his lead before moving any farther. There's a cotton pink hue in the sky, the sound of birds chirping, and a brisk morning chill in the air. Until the sounds from the streets of Manhattan are no longer existent, you realize how silent the world actually is.

"Are you ready?" I ask.

He looks over at me, and everything in his eyes is telling me it's not supposed to be like this. Any of it. Aside from being with Chloe and her mom, I've never done the *family* thing before. I don't know how to act around one; I don't know how to be in one. But my nervousness is combated by my wanting to be there for Adam. My hand finds its way to his and I interlace our fingers, giving him a gentle confirmation that I'm here.

"Yeah," he says softly.

We start walking and Adam reaches for a key in his pocket. Once he opens the door, his dad is already making his way down the stairs.

"There he is!" Adam's dad says proudly. "I thought I heard a car outside." His dad gives him a big hug and a few pats on the back. He's a handsome man with a full head of white hair and a plaid shirt on. He's tall—not as tall as Adam, but I can see where Adam gets his height from.

"Hey, Dad."

"And who is this beautiful lady?" His dad looks at me in a way that shows he knows exactly who I am.

"Dad, this is June."

"Hi, Mr. Harper. It's so nice to finally meet you." I put my hand out, trying to be mindful of the current climate.

"Oh, none of that *Mr. Harper* bullshit—call me Ford." He ignores the gesture and pulls me into a hug. "We're so happy you're here."

The Harpers' house is exactly how I would've imagined it. Beige carpeting fills the interior and there's an endless collection of framed family photos all over the walls. A few snapshots of Adam as a child catch my eye, and I make a mental note to tease him later. The furniture consists of mismatched suede and leather couches and the television is on, playing reruns of *Cheers.* I love it already.

"Adam!" A doe-eyed fifteen-year-old with long dark hair emerges from the kitchen. Adam's sister is tall and lanky, with a timeless simplicity to her beauty. Given the right hair and attire, she could be plucked out of the fifties. With almost a decade between us, I remember this age like it was yesterday. She's on the cusp of blooming from adolescence into adulthood.

"Sarah, I want you to meet someone," Adam says.

"Hi, June!" Sarah immediately gives me a hug. I'm surprised at first by how comfortable she is with me, but I hug her right back. Everything about the Harpers feels like I've stumbled into a sitcom family, and I don't want to change the channel.

"Hi." I smile. "Sarah, I've heard so much about you."

"Uh-oh." She gives Adam a speculative look.

I laugh. "Only good things, I promise!"

"Well, I've heard a lot about *you.*" She raises an eyebrow.

Now it's my turn to give Adam a look. "Have you?"

"Only good things," he clarifies, and squeezes Sarah's shoulders.

I'm seeing Adam in a new light; this environment brings out slight facial expressions I've never noticed before and a sense of calmness I haven't felt in the three years of us living together.

A gentle voice to our right causes the three of us to turn. "Hi, kids."

"Mom," Adam says, and I can hear his voice quiver slightly.

"Well, are you just going to stand there or am I going to get a hug?" She laughs.

He wraps his arms around her, and she practically disappears into him. Adam's mom is beautiful, with piercing blue eyes. She wears a thick, white knit cardigan with two diamond earrings, and a lavender silk scarf is wrapped around her head.

"Mom, this is—" Adam steps aside and gestures to me.

"June," his mom breathes out, smiling. She looks fragile, but her spirit is strong. "Finally," she says, and pulls me into a hug, and it feels like a hug I've been waiting for my whole life. It's the kind of embrace I never received as a child, the kind that makes you feel loved and protected. I think of a toddler coming out of a pool and being wrapped in a towel by their mother, receiving a tenderness you would never know existed until you feel it for yourself.

It takes everything in me to not sob and fall apart in this moment, and I think she knows. I can't tell for sure, but I swear she whispers *don't cry* in my ear.

AFTER SPENDING AN hour in this house, it's clear that the Harpers are the typical family I thought existed only on Nick at Nite. Adam's childhood is so perfectly painted in front of me: When he and Sarah come home from school Ford and Audrey have meat loaf ready for them, and at the end of each day they teach their kids a new lesson, not because they have to but because they love them. Instead of feeling resentful toward the Harper kids for having had the kind of upbringing I never got to have, I want to soak up every moment of this and pretend like I have a family of my own.

Over coffee and lemon pound cake, Ford and Audrey pull out the old albums and share embarrassing baby photos of Adam and Sarah.

"*Adam.*" I bring a shot of Adam and Sarah dressed up as the Big Bad Wolf and Little Red Riding Hood closer. "How adorable is this?"

"Mom used to make our costumes." He smiles.

"You made this?!" I pass the photo to Audrey.

She nods. "Oh yeah, I used to love all those arts and crafts when they were growing up."

I flip the page and see an almost sepia-toned photograph of a young Audrey and Ford in a hammock. Ford looks the same age as Adam, probably twenty-five or twenty-six.

"How did the two of you meet?" I ask them.

They smile at the question like they've never been asked it before.

"There was a carnival over in Cold Spring Harbor . . . it was '79," Ford begins. "We didn't have much else to do on a Friday night back then."

"Are you kidding?" Sarah says, lifting her feet onto the chair underneath her. "I would love to go to a carnival with my friends. I wish they still had them every year."

"Ford was on a date with Nancy Harrison . . ." Audrey looks at me.

"I was with a group of friends," Ford corrects her, and she playfully rolls her eyes. "I saw Audrey and her group lining up for the Ferris wheel, so I followed. Then we got seated next to each other."

"What happened to Nancy?" I ask.

He shrugs. "I asked my friend Jim to keep her occupied for a bit."

"And Jim and Nancy have been happily married for about thirty years now," Audrey says.

I laugh. "What! That's crazy! Audrey, what did you think when Ford sat next to you?"

"Well." She smiles. "He was two years older than me, so I always saw him at school . . . thought he was cute." She nudges him.

Audrey and Ford have been married for twenty-seven years. They bicker like an old married couple and look at each other like teenagers in love. People like to use the word *soulmates* when describing people like the Harpers. Love like theirs was meant to be; they found their way to each other, and it just *works.*

For me, the idea of two people choosing to go through life side by side, to become one half of a whole, knowing one day you'll lose them . . . is brave.

While Adam and I are standing in the kitchen drying dishes, he nudges me. "Want to see my room?"

"Your *room*?" My eyes go wide. "With your parents home?"

"As long as you're quiet, they won't notice."

"*Adam.*" I throw the dish towel at him, and he laughs.

I follow him upstairs and he takes me down the hallway, where I see more framed photos of graduations and family. I've always wondered what kind of families took photos at the portrait studios in Walmart or Sears, and it turns out, the Harpers are it. It only makes me love them more.

He opens a door on the left and I see blue walls and *Star Wars* posters. My face breaks out into an uncontrollable grin as I walk over to the action figures on top of his dresser. Beside them is a framed photo of Adam, no older than five, and his mom at a park. There's another framed photo of Audrey and Sarah in a photo booth and Adam and Ford popping in last minute and making funny faces. A small laugh escapes me.

"So this is where the magic happens," I say, still analyzing every detail of his bedroom.

"Actually, aside from my mom, there's a strict no-girls-allowed policy," Adam says.

"Not even Sarah?" I say turning to him.

"*Especially* Sarah." He takes a seat on the bed and then looks at me. "They love you."

"Adam." I have that lump in my throat again. It's a combination of sorrow and pleasure that I can't shake. These past few hours have been so fulfilling and at the same time, heartbreaking.

"I'm happy you're here," he continues.

"Me too," I say. "Your family is . . ."

"A lot?" He laughs.

"Perfect," I say seriously.

Adam's studying my face, and I follow his eyes scanning every part of me—my cheeks, my nose, my lips. He lifts his hand up cautiously and then goes to tuck a piece of hair behind my ear.

I inch closer, because I want nothing more than to be near him, and he does the same, until our faces are close enough that we're breathing the same air. He puts his forehead on mine and his fingers are now grazing my chin, gently tipping my mouth to his. This is happening, this is going to happen right now . . . and then I remember he's vulnerable and he's not thinking clearly.

"We should go back downstairs," I say, pulling away, and abruptly stand up. As I'm walking back down the hall, I don't turn around to see if he's behind me.

FORD AND AUDREY ask us to stay for dinner, and neither Adam nor I put up a fight. Adam insists on cooking, so he and his parents go on a grocery store run while Sarah and I stay back and watch reruns of *The Golden Girls.* She asks me if I know how to do a French braid and when I tell her yes, she begs me to do her hair.

"I want to paint my room," Sarah says while handing me a comb.

"What color?"

"I don't know. It's this light pink right now. But I think I want something a little more neutral." She shrugs. "It's just a lot with my mom doing chemo right now."

Before arriving, I had a slight anxiousness at the thought of meeting Sarah. Being fifteen is hard enough, and now having to watch her mom battle cancer is unimaginable. She seems lonely, and I feel like I see myself in her, which evokes a big-sister protectiveness in me.

"Well, next time Adam and I are in town, we can help you."

I wonder if it's bold of me to assume I'll be back, but Sarah turns her head, a big smile on her face.

"Seriously?" she says. "You wouldn't mind?"

"Mind? Oh my God, I would love it. I always wanted to paint my room growing up." I sit us both down on the floor and start brushing her hair.

"Is your hair naturally curly?" she asks.

"Unfortunately." While I usually straighten it, I didn't have time this weekend.

"I love it. I wish I had hair like yours."

"I wish I had hair like *yours,*" I say. "I guess we're always wanting what we don't have."

"I guess so," she says, and then a beat later turns her head a little. "So, are you Adam's girlfriend?"

I will say, it's concerning how a fifteen-year-old asking a mere question is making me go beet red. Thankfully she's facing the other way.

"We're just friends," I say matter-of-factly, because as much as I appreciate her bluntness, I'm not about to have this conversation with a teenager.

"But you act like his girlfriend." She blinks.

I do?

"I do?"

"Yeah, you're always like smiling and touching each other." She leans her head back and gives me a look. "And I don't know why, but you find his jokes funny."

"They *are* funny!" I defend him.

"If you like dad jokes," she snorts, and it makes me laugh too. I place the brush down and run my fingers through her thick hair, parting it three ways.

"That's friend behavior." I shrug.

"Yeah but . . . I don't know, it's different with you," she says, and I swallow because it looks like I *am* in fact having this conversation with a teenager. A very intuitive one.

"How?" I try to sound casual.

"I don't know." She starts picking at a hole in her jeans. "Adam doesn't bring girls home," she says, and I don't know why her observation means so much to me. "What's wrong?" Sarah turns around, and I realize I've stopped braiding her hair.

"Oh nothing—here, all done." My voice comes out a little higher than I'd anticipated. I grab a hair tie off her wrist and finish the job.

Sarah reaches for the back of her head, and then her eyes go wide. "Oh my God, it's perfect! Thank you!" She gives me a hug, then runs over to the bathroom to look in the mirror. "None of my friends can do it like this—they all wind up weird at the top," she calls out, and then slowly emerges, playing with the bottom of her braid. "June?"

"Yeah?" I say.

"You know, I think it's actually good you're not Adam's girlfriend."

Oh. Ouch?

"Why's that?" I clear my throat.

"'Cause then you won't break up."

BEFORE STARTING DINNER, Adam tells his parents we're going for a quick drive. We get into his dad's pickup truck and I notice him picking at his thumbnail and chewing at his lip.

"We should invite Sarah over one of these days," I say. "Let her spend some time in the city."

He takes a deep breath as if woken up from a trance and looks at me.

"Yeah, she'd like that." He smiles.

He reaches over to squeeze my hand before turning on the radio. My head turns to the open window and I close my eyes, feeling the breeze on my face.

We pull up to a small establishment next to the Long Island General Store that says *Murphy's Ice Cream Parlor* on a pink neon sign. There are about five or six people inside, and based on the wear of the building, I can tell it's an older business, maybe family-owned.

"Ice cream?" I give him a confused smile as he parks.

"Not *just* ice cream. This is Murphy's," he says like that's supposed to mean something. "I used to work here in high school."

There's a jukebox off to the side playing Ella Fitzgerald's "It's a Lovely Day Today" and on the wall are retro photos of customers in this very building eating ice cream. The selection of flavors displayed behind the cool glass is simple, and there's something charming about seeing options like vanilla and rocky road. Adam gets a double chocolate cone while I order strawberry, and we end up eating our ice creams propped against the hood of Ford's truck.

"What were you like as a teenager?" I ask, watching a few teens enter the shop.

"Oh, you know . . ." Adam starts. "Charming, funny, witty, smart."

"You forgot humble," I say, and he reaches over and pinches my side. I think back to my time in high school. "I don't think we would've gotten along."

"What makes you say that?"

"I was awkward." I shrug. "You probably just wouldn't have noticed me."

He takes a lick of his cone and keeps his eye on the teens in front of us. "Not possible."

Up the street, a mom chases her toddler, who's wearing overalls with sunflowers all over them and a matching hat.

"Are you kidding me?" I squeeze Adam's arm. "How freaking cute is she?"

"Okay, that is a very adorable kid," he agrees. "Why don't they make those for adults?"

"The overalls or the hat?" I ask.

"Both," he says.

"You could pull it off." I nod. "I'd probably have to get a pair too."

"Very Mary-Kate and Ashley of us," he says, and I laugh. The little girl ends up falling, and while no harm was done, she lets out a terrible cry that makes me wince. The mom scoops her up and bounces her against her hip, trying to soothe her. "Do you want kids?" Adam asks.

As unbelievable as it may sound, the idea of having kids has never really crossed my mind. At least not seriously. Can I imagine having a child right now? Absolutely not. There's far too much I need to work on for myself before being capable of caring for another human. Could I imagine having a child with a partner and a home in the future? Possibly, but the image is fuzzy. Not because I don't want it, but because it's never felt like a possibility.

In kindergarten, there were girls who would play with their baby dolls and push a pretend stroller around at recess. That was never me. Some people are *born* to have kids. Have you ever met someone with a child and you think *wow, yup, they were meant to be a mom.* I'm not one of those people, and my own mom definitely isn't. People have children because they want a family, and what do I know about families?

"I don't think so," I say, and Adam lets out a noncommittal noise. "Is that bad?" I turn to him.

"No," he says as he raises his eyebrows. "Not at all."

"I mean, if I'm fortunate enough to have a baby one day, that would be incredible." I take a breath. "But I'm not worried about living an unfulfilled life without one."

He nods and takes a bite out of his ice-cream cone. In the time I've known Adam, we've never talked about this, and I'm painfully aware of the silence coming from his end.

"What about you?" I ask.

"I want kids," he says. "Christmas morning with the family, birthday parties, graduations—all of those things, you know?"

"Mhm," I say, but no, I *don't* know.

"I want what my parents have," he says.

We leave it at that.

AT ONE POINT after dinner, which consisted of barbecued ribs and chicken Alfredo, Ford refers to Audrey, Sarah, and myself as *the girls* and it feels good. We've been here only a day and I feel like I belong.

Ford and Adam plant themselves in the living room to watch a football game while Sarah does her homework at the kitchen table. Ford, an older version of Adam, is so calm, collected, and always wanting to make everyone feel at home. It would've been nice to grow up with him as a dad. Sarah, a younger version of Audrey, is whip-smart and confident. She has a lot of the characteristics I didn't have growing up.

Glancing out the window to the backyard, I see Audrey sitting under a maple tree with a cup of tea in hand. The fairy lights are on and she's wearing her large white cardigan from earlier. Our eyes meet through the glass, and she waves me to come outside.

"Did you get enough to eat?" she asks as I carefully open the back door.

"Oh yes, I'm stuffed." I take a seat beside her. "Thank you."

"And do you have rehearsals tomorrow morning?" Throughout the night she was asking all sorts of questions about the theater, more than my own mother ever has.

I shake my head. "I'm off for the next few days."

"Good, good." She pats my knee. "Are you nervous?"

Most people have asked me only if I'm *excited*, which of course I am. Nobody has ever asked me if I'm nervous.

"Terrified," I say honestly.

"Embrace that," she says with a finger pointed. "That's what it means to be human." She takes a sip of her tea. "Are your parents excited?"

"Oh." I shake my head. "M-My dad left when I was still a kid and . . . I'm not really close with my mom."

She gives me a new look, but I know it all too well, because it's the same look Adam gives me when he wants me to know that things are going to be okay.

"Well, that's their loss, isn't it," she says. "Adam and Sarah don't know this, because their grandpa passed away before they were born, but my father wasn't very nice. He never laid a hand on me, but my mother wasn't as lucky." She places her hand on my lap. "Blood doesn't mean you're family."

Maybe it's the night chill in the air, but a shiver runs through me. She'll never know what those words mean to me. "How are you feeling?" I squeeze her hand.

"Terrified." She smiles, and then shifts. "June, I'm really going to miss the two of you being here."

Today has been such an intimate experience, and I'm not ready to go back to reality either. For many reasons.

"I'm happy Adam invited me," I say, and she nods like she knows. "I'm sorry it took this long for me to come."

"You know, Adam is very special," she says. "Every mother says this of their children, but he really is."

"I know he is," I agree. In a way, it feels like I'm sharing one of my deepest secrets.

"He's lucky to have you."

"Oh no, Audrey." I shake my head. "I'm lucky to have *him.*"

Ford's at the window looking at us and Audrey waves to him, signaling we'll be inside soon.

"June . . ." She holds my hand, and her frail touch makes me start to tear up. I barely know this woman, yet she's somehow more of a mother to me than my own. "I hope you will come back again."

I place my other hand on top of hers and take in this moment, knowing it will be one I'll always look back on.

"Me too."

Chapter 16

22 DAYS UNTIL THE MEETING

I WAKE UP TO A TEXT FROM THEO.

> Heard from Dan's team. They want you to sing this week!

I sit up and read the text again, adrenaline coursing through my veins. My thumbs start typing then deleting, typing then deleting, until I decide to just call her.

"Hello?"

"Hey!" I breathe out. "Sorry to bother you."

"Oh my God, no worries," Theo says. "How's New York?"

"It's great," I answer honestly. "How are you? I got your text."

"Good, good," she says, the sound of children screaming bloody murder behind her. "So, I heard lunch went well. They want you to come in and do a song."

"Yeah, no problem. Ballad, I'm assuming?"

"Totally. I mean, between us, Dan absolutely loves you. There's just a few producers who need to sign off. It'll probably be tomorrow or Friday. I'll let you know ASAP."

"Sounds great. Thanks, Theo!" I allow myself to be excited.

"Of course," she says. "I actually— *BECKHAM! Give Stella back Squishy, now!* So, I'll be in New York on Friday for a gala. Will you be around?"

"Yeah, I'm here for another two weeks. What's the gala?"

"Manhattan for Theater. You know I— *Beckham! I'm not kidding—if you don't give Squishy back right now, we are not getting acai bowls,*" Theo says, and I hear the sound of Beckham's muffled crying in the background. In instances like this, I do wonder why parents bargain with their kids, but what do I know? "Okay, sorry," Theo says to me. "So it's Manhattan for Theater, the nonprofit. I'm working on getting you an invite. I think it's a good look if you attend."

"Sure, sounds good," I say. "What time?"

"Oh, how am I supposed to know? I'll email you— *STELLA! HE JUST GAVE YOU BACK SQUISHY, WHY WOULD YOU THROW IT OUT THE WINDOW?!*" Theo shrieks. "June, I gotta go."

"Oh God, okay, bye." My eyes go wide, and she hangs up.

My body falls back onto the bed, and I pull a pillow over my face to conceal my stupid smile. *Don't jinx it, don't jinx it, don't jinx it.*

To my surprise, I feel relieved when I see Adam downstairs. The past week he's always been out of the house by the time I wake up. Before I walk any farther, I take a mental snapshot of this moment—a view I never thought I would see again. He's leaning against the counter in a gray T-shirt, glasses, and flannel pajama pants. He has a cup of coffee in one hand while looking at his phone in the other.

I feel the looming cloud of tension over this house for the past week dissipate. Last night we passed a threshold, like we're *friends* again.

"Morning," I say softly.

Adam immediately looks up and puts his phone down. "Hey, coffee?"

"Please." I take a seat on the other side of the island. He pours me a cup, froths some oat milk, and adds a dash of nutmeg. When it comes to serving people, nothing is ever simple with this man. "Thanks." I take the mug and wrap my hands around the warmth of it.

"I would've made breakfast, but I just woke up like ten minutes ago." He runs his fingers through his hair, biceps fully on display. "What's your day looking like?"

"Doing absolutely nothing." I take a sip, excited to spend the day free as a bird. "Do you have work?"

"No, but I actually have to get some fresh produce for the restaurant." He takes a sip of coffee. "Would you want to come?"

"You buy the produce yourself?" I look up at him.

"Not every week, but now that it's autumn there are some things in peak harvest," he says. "I try to buy an assortment of things and come up with any seasonal menu items. If they're good, we'll make a deal with the local vendors."

"Wow." I raise my eyebrows, thoroughly impressed. "I'm in."

IT'S THE MOST perfectly crisp and clear October morning. As Adam and I walk toward the perimeter of the Union Square farmers market, I'm hit with the smell of maple and the warmth of sunshine on my face. Looking up, I see trees lined with golden leaves and a bright blue sky and ahead, a diverse crowd of people, all bundled in early fall attire.

Adam's hair blows in the wind, and he squints as he looks down the path. It's in moments like this when he's not paying attention that I allow myself to look at him. I notice subtle lines around his eyes that have developed in our years apart.

"Do you come here often?" I ask as we walk side by side. It takes no effort for our bodies to become tuned to each other's rhythm. We carefully observe the abundance of local vendors selling a variety of goods and produce.

"Probably once a month," he says.

"Where do you live?" I ask, realizing we haven't actually talked about this.

"Upper West Side."

"What, do you own a restaurant or something?" I tease, knowing very well that that part of town is hardly affordable.

"Something like that." He guides us to a vendor and starts looking at the purple cauliflower.

"I'm seeing Dan again this week," I say.

"Oh yeah?"

"I'm singing."

"How are you feeling?" he asks.

"Nervous," I admit, and it feels so freeing to say it. Part of me doesn't want Adam to know I'm scared. It's been five years, and I'm supposed to be better than this. I'm supposed to want to show him how much better off I am and how confident I've become. But he does this thing where he looks at me and doesn't judge me. Like my career isn't the one thing that defines me.

"You've got this." He's doing that thing that he always used to do. Making me feel like everything is going to be okay. "What'll happen if you get the part?"

I notice he doesn't ask what the play or the role is, like it doesn't matter. It never did for him. I could be playing Chorus Member 46 and he'd be just as excited for me.

"I guess I'd have to move back," I say for the first time out loud. Some Broadway revivals are a minimum of five hundred shows even if they're not successful.

I anticipate a response from Adam about how exciting that would be, but when I turn to look at him, there's another look on his face, almost pensive.

"Is that what you want?" He bags up cauliflower, collard greens, winter squash, and fennel.

"The work is more important than *where* I do it," I say.

Adam nods and we continue walking. We end up stopping at two more vendors for sweet potatoes and apples before I catch a glimpse of a booth that says *coffee* and instinctively take a step closer. We had a late night at Chloe's and I wouldn't hate having another fix of caffeine.

"Want some?" Adam asks over my shoulder.

"Please," I say, but lose focus when he places his hand on the small of my back and guides me to walk forward. You learn something new every day, and the lesson of the morning is I didn't know Adam Harper's hand still had the ability to affect my heart rate.

The smell of freshly ground arabica coffee beans snaps me back and I take an extra step to escape his touch.

"What are you thinking?" Adam asks.

Normally I would order my regular oat milk latte, but there's a seasonal menu framed to the side displaying concoctions like a rose cardamom latte and an autumn maple delight that pique my interest. I also notice that they have apple cider doughnuts and my mouth starts to salivate as I eye the little plump circles of dough sitting in cinnamon sugar.

"I think I'm feeling something with fall vibes," I say.

"I'll get something fun if you do," he says as he studies the menu. "Oh look, they have your favorite. Pumpkin spice latte."

"I don't have anything against pumpkins!" Then I add, acknowledging the added decor in front of Perry, "But you were right, they're a nice touch."

"Wow," he says. "I finally did something right."

I playfully nudge him with my arm, and even contact as innocent as that with our jackets on is enough to make my pulse flutter. Our eyes meet again, something that's been happening often since yesterday, and I blush. I am an adult woman, yet here I am, blushing.

Then, as quickly as those feelings rushed through me, I remember that there's a woman named Kelsey who exists somewhere in the city. Adam left to see her and didn't come back until the next day. I feel a tinge of jealousy, or perhaps even guilt, because there's definitely something happening here. I don't know what, but it's something.

My eyes shoot back to the menu. "I think I'm going to get the nog fog. *A unique combo of eggnog tea infused with clover, cardamom, nutmeg, and oolong with your choice of milk and cinnamon,*" I read. "What about you?"

"The hickory smoked s'mores latte," Adam says. "I'm not turning down the opportunity to try graham cracker milk."

"I didn't know you could make milk from graham crackers?"

"I think they just steep it in graham crackers," he says.

"Well, now you're just showing off," I say.

When we receive our orders, we step aside and find a spot underneath a maple tree.

"Moment of truth." Adam takes a sip of his drink. His eyebrows rise in approval, and he passes me his cup. "Want to try?"

The warmth of his cup feels different from mine, like knowing it belongs to him subconsciously alters my brain chemistry. His eyes follow as I bring the cup to my lips and the taste of espresso comes together with vanilla, dark chocolate, and hazelnut.

"Okay, that's *really* good." I hand his cup back and our fingertips slightly graze each other's. I pull off a piece of my apple cider doughnut and take a bite, my taste buds going wild with the warm nutmeg and cinnamon goodness. "Oh my God, now try this."

I pass the remaining piece to Adam, but instead of grabbing it, he lowers his head slightly and takes the pastry from me directly into his mouth.

My breath hitches at the sensation of his tongue swiping my skin and his lips around my fingers. For a moment his eyes lock onto mine, and I swear I stop breathing altogether. He gently pulls back, sucking the remaining sugar until I'm clean.

"Delicious," he says.

"Mhm." I swallow what little saliva is left and clear my throat.

As we continue to walk, I play what just happened in my

mind over and over again as if on film. It was no more than two people sharing a doughnut. Two *friends* sharing a doughnut. Friends who have taken *years* to get to this point and are not going to fuck it up again . . . especially when one friend is in a relationship, or a situationship, or whatever it is when someone tells you to come over because they're soaked.

"Hey, are you hungry?" Adam asks. It's a funny question considering we just ate a doughnut.

"You know what . . ." I look at my phone and see it's just past noon. "Starving."

WE END UP at this brunch spot in Williamsburg that I've never been to before. On the outside it looks like a hole-in-the-wall, but there's a line that would say quite the opposite. Based on the crowd of people, it'll probably take a while before I have something in my stomach. I'm hungry enough that I debate asking Adam if we should just grab bagels instead. But he doesn't get in line. Instead, he waits by the front door and pulls out his phone to text someone.

"I'm starving," he says, looking at me.

"Yeah, same—should we get in line?" I ask, but then I see a familiar face inside walking toward us. "Wait, is that—"

"Hey, man!" The guy approaching gives Adam a big hug and a hearty pat on the back.

"Hey, you remember June?" Adam gestures toward me.

"Hey, Robby." I smile, taking in his arms and hands, which are now almost completely covered with tattoos, and his mustache—which not a lot of people can pull off, but it is working for him.

"No fucking way," he says, then steps back for a second and looks at Adam wide-eyed. "June, how are you?!" He pulls me in for a hug.

"I can't complain." I laugh. It's really nice to see Robby again. "How are *you*?!"

"Oh, you know, hanging in there." He laughs, looking at the line behind us. "But, okay, let's get you two a table." He walks over to the hostess stand and steps behind it. For a few seconds, he and the woman, who's wearing red overalls and a striped blue knit top underneath, are pointing at the seating charts. She gives him a nod and he grabs two menus. "Follow me," he says, and he guides us inside.

It's absolutely packed. The walls are a forest green shiplap and the food is served on mismatched china. Similar to Alden, but there's something more raw and messy about this place, in the best way possible. There are old boxing-match posters on top of your grandma's favorite flowered wallpaper and four or five different chandeliers hanging from the ceiling.

"Here you go." He guides us to a corner table.

"Thanks, man," Adam says, and Robby gives him another pat on the back.

"I'll be back," he says, giving us a wink, and then heads to the kitchen.

I wait until Robby is out of sight before I kick Adam under the table. "Um, is this *his* restaurant?"

"He and two other guys opened it last year."

"I'm obsessed with the vibe." I look around.

"It's great. He has his dad's apple pie recipe on here too—it's delicious. And he still gets to cook and be in the nitty-gritty of it all, you know?"

"Why Alden?" I ask. The Adam I know would thrive in this environment. He never even wanted to eat at a Michelin-star restaurant, let alone own one. "Why not a place like this?"

"I don't know," he says, and frowns like nobody's ever asked him this before. "One thing kind of led to another . . . I'm grateful, but if I could go back, maybe I'd do things differently."

"I can't believe you have your own restaurant, Adam." I look at him sincerely. "*You did it.*"

He gives me a weak smile and then leans back. "I'm not the one who's a big film and TV star."

"I'm not either," I say, rolling my eyes. The idea of Adam following my career all these years makes me a little self-conscious.

"You were in a Brad Pitt movie," he says.

"I had *one* line and he wasn't even in the scene," I say with a laugh.

"Still." He shrugs. "It's pretty awesome."

But it doesn't feel awesome. When you're working in Hollywood, it never feels like booking a role is enough. People are working toward status, how many followers they have, how *big* a name they can be. Since leaving New York, the biggest acting role I've had is pretending that I'm happy with the choices I've made.

"Okay." Robby comes up to our table rubbing his hands. "What can I get you two?"

"I'll have the Mediterranean bowl." Adam hands his menu to Robby.

"And I'll have the short rib beef burger, please," I say wide-eyed and hand my menu over.

"Make that burger good," Adam warns.

"Yes, sir." Robby playfully salutes him.

"And fuck it," Adam says. "Add on the baklava banana bread too."

"I got you," Robby says, nodding. "So how are things? I've got to plan a basketball night or something."

"Same old," Adam says, and I sit straighter, enjoying this back-and-forth.

"Alden is no joke. Are you still opening another location?"

Adam looks at me for a second and rubs the side of his face. "Yeah, we're talking about it."

"Man." Robby shakes his head and looks at me. "Can you believe this guy? He doesn't stop."

"I don't have a line of people waiting around Alden right now," Adam says.

"Yeah, that's because your reservations are booked until January."

"You're only doing this to yourself by not accepting reservations." Adam gestures to the people standing outside the window.

"It adds to the appeal." Robby laughs. "All right—well, let me ring this in." He taps the table twice before disappearing.

"Baklava banana bread?" I raise an eyebrow at Adam.

"Don't tell me you're on some LA diet."

"Oh, hell no." I scrunch my face. "I was going to say, if you're lucky, I'll let you have a piece."

He nudges my foot under the table, and for a good ten seconds, I don't move and neither does he.

I'M ABSOLUTELY STUFFED after brunch, and it's at times like this that I'm thankful New York allows me to get my steps in.

"That was amazing," I say as we walk back through the streets of Brooklyn.

"Where to next?" Adam says.

I'm not ready to go back to the house. Ahead of me is a man pushing a baby stroller while simultaneously walking his dog. There's a woman wearing running shoes with her polished pantsuit, and two older men playing chess by a park with steaming cups of coffee at their side. I've missed this, and as cliché as it sounds, I want to do all the things New York has to offer.

"When's the last time you've been to Central Park?" I ask, and turn to him.

"For fun?" Adam raises an eyebrow. "You know, I can't say when."

"Would you want to go?" I ask in my most enticing voice.

"An autumn walk in Central Park," Adam says. "If I didn't know any better, I'd think you were a tourist," he says, walking toward the subway.

"And if *I* didn't know any better, I'd say you're taking New York for granted." I hurry to keep up with him.

Chapter 17

BACK IN THE DAY, WE USED TO GET OFF AT THE SUBWAY STOP closest to the reservoir and walk south through the park. Now I'm letting Adam lead the way, and once we get off at 96th Street, I know it's exactly where he's heading.

The fact that Central Park is actually man-made is something I think most people often forget. It's a park that puts most of the ones in Los Angeles to shame. Within it is a horizon full of skyscrapers and trees almost ninety feet tall displaying red, orange, and yellow leaves.

I would be lying to myself if I said this wasn't the most quintessential autumn afternoon in New York City. Kids are running around within feet of their parents, a couple jogs past us, and while there are plenty of people around, up ahead a vast field of grass makes you realize how big Manhattan really is.

It's not just the park that's making today feel special, it's being here with Adam. His head lifts to the sky, the cool wind gently brushing his hair, and there's a comfortable silence when we're like this. We're never trying, we just *are.*

"I forgot how beautiful Belvedere Castle is," I say. The structure sits tall in a sweeping view of the city.

People pull out their phones, snapping shots and selfies, and I see Adam unlock his. "Here, I'll take a photo of you."

"Of me?" I laugh. "I'm not a tourist."

"You kind of are," he says.

"Fine, but you have to be in it too." I turn so my back is facing the water, and he moves around to stand behind me, holding his phone out in front of us. "You take selfies without the front-facing camera?" I look up at him.

"It's too much pressure seeing myself," he says.

"A true twentieth-century man."

"Do *you* want to take the photo?" He looks down.

"No, you do it—your arms are longer," I say, and he positions himself behind me, slightly hunching so we're both in view, or at least so I assume we're both in view. In the time it takes for me to breathe, he's already moved away. "Wait, you did it already?"

"Mhm." He nods.

"How's it look?" I ask, mildly intrigued that he doesn't care how a photo of himself turned out.

He taps his screen and then shows me a selfie that honestly came out perfect. We're both in view while the castle is placed perfectly to the left of my head. The only detail that's concerning is how *good* we look together. Adam and I have had our fair share of photos with each other throughout the years—most of them from Chloe's digital camera that live on a private Facebook album. But as I look at his phone now, it's hard to deny we'd make a really attractive couple. "Oh," I say. "It looks good."

"Yeah." He nods.

"Do you mind sending that to me?"

There's a brief moment of hesitation, like that's the last thing he was expecting me to say. "Sure."

"Thanks," I say.

"Have you thought more about the house?" he asks as we walk along the water.

Oh right, that little detail.

"I haven't really," I answer honestly. "Been focused more on the audition . . . Have you?"

"A little," he says, and glances at the pond, the dark water rippling against the rocks.

"I've thought about what a difference it'll all make," I say. "Financially, you know?"

"Yeah." He nods.

"I mean, it's six million dollars. How crazy is that?" I laugh about the situation for the first time since hearing the news.

"Technically three," he corrects, throwing my line back at me.

"Right, right," I say. "Practically peanuts."

"Barely anything these days."

I smile at him, something I've been doing a lot today. But I can't help it when he's looking at me that way. Like he's the only person who can really see me.

"What are you going to do with it?" I ask.

"I was thinking about investing in another restaurant, but I don't know." He shrugs.

"What kind of restaurant would you open?"

"Everything Alden isn't," he says.

This whole time I've been focused on Adam's accomplishments and how well-off he must be. It didn't occur to me that this might not be it for him, that there's more he wants out of life. Maybe we've been going down the same path this whole time without realizing it.

"I don't think there's a polite way to say this . . ." I look down the leaf-covered path.

"Say it."

"But you own a restaurant," I say, stating the obvious. "A *good* restaurant. Will the money from the house really make a dent?"

Adam shoves his hands a little deeper into his coat pockets. "I paid off my parents' house, and Sarah's college tuition."

My chest tightens, and I tuck my memories far away.

"Oh," I say softly.

"But what about you?" He turns to me. "What would you do with the money?"

"Get my own place," I say almost too quickly.

"Oh?" Adam's eyebrows rise. "Where are you living now?"

"I *had* a place of my own, but last year I moved in with some friends while things were unpredictable with work."

"And are you . . ." Adam hesitates for a moment. "Seeing anyone?"

I don't know why the question makes me nervous. Like the secrecy of my relationship status was some kind of leverage I had over him. But then I think about Kelsey and how he's potentially in a relationship of his own.

"I was," I answer. My last serious relationship was three years ago, and I don't even want to think about the laundry list of deadbeats I've been on dates with since then.

Adam doesn't bother to ask for any details, he just nods as we continue to walk. Which I'm a little thankful for.

"Can I ask you a question?" I spin to face him. "Why were you okay with us living together?"

"Which time?"

"Seriously," I press as we continue to walk along the path. "You could have stayed at your own place. Was being in a brownstone that important?"

He takes a beat before answering and then looks at me. "It's different for me, June."

"What do you mean?" I ask.

"I mean, I don't hate you," he says.

Is that what he thinks? That I didn't want to do this because I *hate* him?

"Adam," I say. "I don't hate you."

"You literally ran away from me the day we met with Mara," he says.

I knew he was eventually going to throw that in my face.

"I didn't *run away*," I say, and he stops walking. "Okay, fine, I did run away . . . but that's not why."

"Then why?"

"I asked you first, Adam," I say. "Don't change the subject."

"I'm not." He exhales. "I just—"

"Then why did you want to stay at the house?" I press. "Was the commute really that bad? You didn't want to be comfortable in your own home?"

"Perry is home," Adam says intently, and it knocks the wind out of me. "And I've always been most comfortable with you. Maybe I thought you'd feel the same way."

He looks as gutted as I feel, and I know I've hurt him somehow. You can't spend six years with someone and not know these things. Maybe this is our chance to talk about the past. I've had endless nights to think about how this conversation could go. I've rehearsed dialogue in the shower, written unsent emails, but I'm still not sure how to do it. We could so easily open this door and air our dirty laundry, but I'm not ready for this conversation. Not yet.

"*Excuse me,*" a woman with a southern accent who's clearly a tourist (based on her backpack and *I♥NY* gift bag) interrupts us. "Would you mind taking a picture of us?" She points to her group of friends behind her, and three out of the five are wearing shirts that match the gift bag in her hand. My gaze quickly shifts back to Adam, who's going to have to wait for a proper response. *Thank God.*

"Yes, of course!" I say a little too brightly, taking a step closer. She hands me a phone and I follow her toward the group of women. They all huddle together and smile in front of the water. "Okay, everyone say *I LOVE NEW YORK*!"

"*I LOVE NEW YORK*!" they repeat, and start laughing.

I take about forty-five different photos from various angles. I ask them to pose, make funny faces, jump in the air—that one in particular takes a good three minutes—and they're ecstatic.

"Thank you so much!" says the woman who initially asked for the photo. "This is our first time in New York."

"No kidding!" I act surprised.

"I know! Can you believe it? We're having dinner in Times Square and seeing *The Lion King* tonight," she says, like she's just told me they have tickets to see the Beatles.

"Oh, wow! Have the best time," I call out to the group of women behind her, and hand back her phone.

"Thank you again," she says, and squeezes my hand. "What was your name, dear?"

"June," I say, smiling. "And you?"

"Susan," she says. "Well, June. Thank you, and you have yourself a good afternoon."

"No problem! Have a good rest of your trip, Susan," I say, and wave at her and the rest of the ladies as they leave. Turning around, I see Adam sitting on a bench a few feet away on his phone. "Okay, all done!"

"Do you think they have enough photos?" he asks, not trying to hide his sarcasm.

"Look, I just wanted those women to have memories from their trip!" I say. "Did you know this is Susan's first time in the city?"

"I don't know who Susan is," he says flatly.

"The one with the *New York* shirt." I look down at him and he just blinks. "Come on, let's keep walking."

"June, I know what you're doing."

"I'm not doing anything!" I say as innocently as I can.

"Does that voice really work on anyone?"

I turn to face him and start walking backward. "You tell me."

Adam lets out a big exhale and stands up.

"I MEAN, WE have to go on," Adam says.

We're standing in front of the famous carousel. It's that golden-hour time of day when the sunlight illuminates the red bricks surrounding the fixed attraction. Getting in line might be the cheesiest thing we do all day, but that bridge was crossed when we ordered seasonal drinks and decided to walk around Central Park.

"Obviously," I say.

We follow the formation, and there's a couple a few feet ahead of us who can't be older than nineteen, kissing . . . *really* kissing. I turn to Adam and give him my most uncomfortable face. He looks at me, confused, but then clocks the heavy make-out session happening a few feet away.

"God, to be young and horny," his says, his voice lowering. I smack his arm and hide my giggle. The couple doesn't hear us, but now the guy has his hands in the girl's jeans pockets and her head is resting on his chest while they sway back and forth in place to the organ music.

"I think we, as a society, have forgotten the true meaning of love," I say. "Cupping your girlfriend's ass and slow-dancing in line for a children's ride."

Adam barks out a laugh and grabs both of my shoulders, turning me around to keep walking. He lowers his head and whispers behind my left ear, "Don't shit on them—they only have another six months before they break up."

I laugh, but am almost entirely distracted by the feeling of Adam's hands. The sound of his voice vibrates through me and his breath on my neck gives me goose bumps. It's innocent, but I can't control the heat that's pooling within me. He finally lets go after what feel like the longest six seconds of my life, and I can think straight again. The couple begins to make out yet again, and I sigh.

"I wonder what it's like to be so enamored and completely unaware of your surroundings," I muse.

"Well . . ." Adam says.

"Well, what?"

"Have you forgotten about Nick?" he says.

My eyes go big because I, in fact, have forgotten about Nick. I don't know if I'm more thrown off by the thought of a guy I met at a bar almost ten years ago—whom I had no more than two dates with—or the fact that Adam remembers him.

"What about Nick?"

"Oh, come on," he says. "The two of you couldn't keep your hands off each other."

"What? When?!"

"Chloe's birthday," he says. "In Brooklyn."

I cover my face with my hands, remembering only snippets of that night because I was *very* drunk. "Oh my God, you're right . . ." The only recollection I have is of making out with Nick and throwing up on the sidewalk on my way home. "You saw all of that?" I ask, horrified.

"Unfortunately."

"In my defense, he was a model." I point a finger. "And what, like you were any better?"

"Me?" His eyebrows rise.

"At least that was only one night. I had to watch you being all lovey-dovey with Riley for months—" I immediately stop once I realize what I just said. Her name catches Adam off guard too, because he doesn't say anything. "Sorry, I—"

"It's okay," he says, brushing it off, and his gaze lifts toward the carousel.

I'm well aware Riley's a topic that's been avoided. When I saw Adam at Mara's office, the first thought I had was to wonder if he and Riley were still together. Unless I straight-up ask him, there's no way for me to know. It took only one post of the two of them together for me to unfollow Adam on every possible social media platform . . . and that was five years ago. But considering Adam hasn't brought Riley up and that he's receiving sexts from a random woman, the clues point to no. They're not together.

The grooves between Adam's brows tell me that maybe now isn't the best time to ask him what happened between him and Riley. Instead, I figure this is a better time than any to ask him a different uncomfortable question.

"Are you dating anyone?"

"No," he says almost immediately.

"Okay . . . are you sleeping with anyone?" I amend.

"Define *sleeping*."

"Penetration," I say.

"God, June." He looks around. "I was joking."

"What about Kelsey?" I ask, ignoring him. If Adam and I are going to really turn over a new leaf, I want us to be on the same page. No more walking around the house shirtless, picking me up to grab pots, or licking sugar off my fingers if there's potentially someone else in the picture.

"Kelsey?" Adam frowns.

"Yeah . . ."

"What about Kelsey?" he asks, confused.

I stretch my neck out, keeping my eyes locked on his. No reaction. Is he really going to make me say it? "I saw her text." I shift.

"What text?" he asks, and I really don't want to say it out loud. "June." Adam narrows in on me. "What text?"

"I don't want to repeat it, okay?" I whisper-shout, aware of the people around us.

"Great, then I guess this conversation is over."

"Okay." The look on his face is a mix of impatience and confusion. I move in closer to him and lower my voice. "It said *I'm soaked. Get over here.*"

Adam goes still. "Jesus Christ." He takes a step back. "She was talking about a pipe bursting at the restaurant."

My face simultaneously drops and turns bright red. "A pipe?!"

"Here." Adam pulls out his phone and shows me his conversation with Kelsey. Ten minutes prior to the text that I saw, there's a photo of a broken pipe in some back room of Alden, surrounded by water. "She's our GM."

"Fuck," I say. There's no possible way for this to get more embarrassing for me, although I guess if Adam actually laughed in my face that might be. "How was I supposed to know she was your general manager? What was I supposed to think?"

"*I'm soaked*?" Adam shoves his phone into his back pocket. "Who even says that?"

"I mean, I don't know! People that are horny?" I shrug, still mindful of our surroundings.

"So, you thought I literally dropped everything I was doing just to get laid? I'm not a seventeen-year-old."

"Okay, look." I hold my hands up. "She texted you that, and then you left and didn't come back until the next day. I clearly misunderstood."

"For what it's worth, Kelsey is happily married with three kids."

"Of course she is," I say, humiliated.

"So, this whole time you thought I was seeing someone?" he asks.

The line starts moving again and we find two horses. I gravitate toward a white one with gold and pink flowers while he chooses the black stallion with a royal blue sash beside me.

"Kind of," I say, but Adam just shakes his head. "Are you upset or something?"

"No, of course not," he says. "It's just . . . disappointing."

"Disappointing?" I frown. "How?"

"Nothing," he brushes it off, and then turns to me. "Just as long as you know now that I'm not dating anyone," he says, his eyes demanding my attention. "And I'm definitely not sleeping with anyone."

The music suddenly kicks in and we start moving. Amid the crowd of people, light bounces off colorful patterns in a kaleidoscope of emotions. My body starts going up and down, very similar to how my heart feels right now.

Chapter 18

Sometime between sunset and nightfall, we end up sitting on a bench overlooking the East River and a view of the Brooklyn Bridge that most people would kill for. Nights are colder now, so I pull my jacket collar around my neck and sit closer to Adam for what I tell myself is solely body heat.

"What time do you have to be at work tomorrow?" I ask.

"There's a private lunch for some Wall Street investors—they do it every month. I'll go in to help prep," he says, and I let out a little laugh. "What?"

"Nothing." I shake my head. "You're just—you're an *adult.*"

"Yeah, when the fuck did that happen?" He runs a hand through his hair. "Some days it feels like yesterday when I was still in school. Then I think of all the years of work and late nights and . . ." He looks at me, his eyes fixated like they see more than what's in front of him. "I mean, you were there."

I was. Every day we lived together, we were both working in tandem toward our dreams. Memories play like footage from an old home video in my mind—all of the monologues I performed in front of him, the songs I practiced and made him listen to, the nights he iced my back, my ankles, or my feet after rehearsals. Then another roll of film plays, one showing the recipes he asked me to try, the diners and food joints I would eat at just to get a glance of him in the kitchen. The nights we both swore we were giving up, and the pep talks we'd give each other saying *we'll get there someday*. And now we're here.

For the first time since reuniting, I'm *seeing* Adam. I didn't realize all those years ago, but he was just a boy. I was just a girl. We were kids in our twenties who felt like we knew everything, and somewhere along the way from then to now we grew up.

"I wish I could've been there," I say quietly. "When it all happened."

"Me too." He gently tips his chin to me, acknowledging my career. We watch as the NYC Ferry glides along the river toward Midtown, a neon spectacle as its backdrop.

"You know, when I was at Alden the other day"—I nudge him with my elbow—"I was very impressed."

"Oh yeah?" He nudges me back. "Does it get the June Wood stamp of approval?"

"It sure does," I say.

"You'd love the tagliatelle," he says.

"God, that sounds *so* good right now." I throw my head back.

"Do you want some?" he asks.

"Now?" I look at him, confused, because he says it like it's not almost midnight. "Isn't the restaurant closed?"

"Yes," he says. "But I *do* have a key."

I bite my lip. Pasta does sound good right now, and I'm not entirely ready for the night to be over.

"Let's do it."

THIS TIME, I'M entering Alden through a poorly lit back alley leading to the rear entrance.

"This kind of feels like the last place I'm going to see before I get thrown into a van," I say as I wait for Adam to unlock the door.

"Oh, were you not up for that?" he says.

"Not really feeling it tonight." I shrug.

He opens the door, and the lights are off. "One second—stay here."

He disappears to the right, and at the flick of a switch, I see I'm in a hallway leading to the kitchen. Thanks to Adam, I've seen a few different kitchens in my lifetime, but as we turn the corner, I'm in awe at how big the space is. *This* is a kitchen. When I was here with Dan, I remember being impressed looking through the glass window, but up close, I'm speechless.

"Whoa," I say, analyzing the stove ranges. There are endless shelves surrounding us full of wine bottles from floor to ceiling, something that Alden is famous for. It's no surprise people make reservations just to take photos of the interior.

"Still hungry?" Adam asks over his shoulder, going through the commercial fridge.

"If you are," I say, suddenly feeling small.

"Why don't you take a look around. I'll have this ready in fifteen." He starts putting some pans on the stove. "Pick a bottle of wine you want too."

"Sounds good," I say. "Where's the restroom?"

"Down that aisle there," Adam says, pointing. "And to the left."

I take my jacket off and place it on the first booth to my right, along with my purse. There's something intimate about having the whole restaurant to ourselves. The lightbulbs on drooping pendant wires cast a warm glow throughout the dining area. Meanwhile, brick walls, marble tables, aging mirrors, and blue-and-burnt-orange tilework on the ground are the perfect backdrop.

I attempt to make myself look a *little* more presentable after running around Manhattan for twelve hours. When I emerge from the ladies' room, a framed photo catches my eye.

Among more than fifty eccentric paintings and photographs, there's a black-and-white one, a little out of focus. It's a snapshot from a rainy night in front of the Imperial Theatre. At first glance, it looks like a beautiful homage to the Theater District, but looking closer, I see a woman with her back to the camera, gazing up at the marquee. A poster for *Rent.* The hairs on the back of my neck stand up as I reach out to touch the photo and outline the thick black frame. I remember this day exactly.

Adam's dad had given him a film camera earlier that month, but to my knowledge, he'd never gotten the film developed. In an instant, whatever walls I had up begin to shatter like waves crumbling a sandcastle. I didn't even know this photo existed, and now it's sitting here among artwork and memories in a place that is Adam personified.

When I reenter the kitchen, there's a mouthwatering smell filling the air. On top of the stainless-steel countertop are two bowls of pasta that put any meal I've ever looked at to shame.

"Black truffle tagliatelle." Adam gestures to a bowl, a symphony of herbs, salted butter, and caramelized mushrooms sitting on a bed of thick pasta.

"Wow . . . I didn't realize how hungry I am. Also, does this work?" I hold up a bottle with an intriguing coral label that I pulled from the wall.

"Perfect." He takes the wine from me and pours two glasses. "Do you want to sit down, or . . . ?"

"You know, I've always wanted to eat in the kitchen with the chef." I grin. "May I?" My eyes go to the countertop.

"Who am I to deprive you of your fantasies?" Adam says, and I hoist myself up to sit on the counter.

"Are you kidding me?" I say through a mouthful of pasta.

"It's one of the more popular dishes." He laughs, and leans against the counter with his bowl in hand. "I never get to make it for myself anymore, though, so thank you."

"Did you come up with the recipe?" I ask.

Adam nods. "Everything on the menu."

"Wow," I say, more to myself than him, not hiding the fact that I'm impressed. *Very* impressed. But not surprised.

"So." Adam twists his pasta onto his fork. "What happened with Liam?"

My ex-boyfriend's name is the last thing I expect to come out of his mouth, but I deserve this. It's clear we've opened an honest line of communication in the past twenty-four hours. I lower my bowl a little and breathe in.

"I, uh, was going through a little bit of a rough patch a few years ago," I say, feeling more vulnerable around him than I ever have before. "Couldn't eat, couldn't get out of bed, just not great all around . . . and he couldn't take it anymore."

What I don't share is that I wasn't going through depression; I was going through heartbreak.

"How are you now?" he asks, like the Liam part of the story doesn't even matter. Like my well-being is the only thing that he cares about.

"Better." I nod assuringly, because it's the truth. "I guess it was just hard, being in a new city, newish career, not knowing anyone. But therapy really helped."

"Therapy's been good for me too," he says, a look of relief on his face. "I'm sorry things didn't work out with Liam."

"Don't be." I shake my head and wave a hand. "That was doomed before it even started," I say, and Adam just nods, lost in thought.

"Look, earlier, about Riley—" Adam starts, but I don't want to talk about our exes. I don't want us to think about the past. All that matters to me is the here and now.

Interrupting him, I say, "Adam, it's okay. You don't have to explain anything. Whatever happened with you and Riley, with me and Liam, it doesn't matter anymore. It's done." I smile.

"Yeah." He nods thoughtfully. "Okay."

I lift my bowl back up and finish the rest of my pasta in an embarrassingly short amount of time. After placing it off to the side, I take a sip of my wine. "Oh wow, that's good too."

"It should be," he says. "That's one of our most expensive bottles."

My eyes widen. "Why didn't you say anything?"

"It's fine," he says with a laugh.

"How much is it? I'll pay you."

"June, stop."

"Just tell me!" I demand.

"One seventy," he finally says, and I pull my lips inside my mouth.

"Okay, how about I wash the dishes?" I offer.

"Deal—I think you'd look pretty sexy with those rubber gloves." He nods to the washing station. He's definitely flirting, and I don't hate it. I laugh and try to kick him from where I am on the counter even though I'm nowhere within reach.

"Hey, thanks for today," I say.

"Did you have fun?" he asks.

I nod. "Did you?"

"I'm still having fun," he says, and I catch his gaze quickly go from my eyes to my lips. I swallow. In this moment, there's nothing more I want right now than to be near him, to feel him.

Although we're completely alone, the four feet of space between us may as well be four miles. His forearm muscles slightly tense as he adjusts himself against the counter. There's no denying I'm still beyond attracted to Adam. It's an attraction where you just need someone with your entire body and soul. The physical exterior is only a bonus—I want his mind, his thoughtfulness, his protectiveness. I want all of him.

Adam takes a sip of his wine, then pushes himself off the counter and moves to stand in front of me. Something within me, the stimulated part, slightly inches my knees open. His eyes glance down, but he doesn't step in between them. Instead, he sets his glass to the side of me and lifts his hand, placing it behind my neck. Goose bumps cover my skin, and I feel like there isn't enough air in the world for me to catch my breath. Gently, his hand swipes my earlobe while the other touches my cheek. My breath deepens and my eyes close, because he may as well have reached over and put his hands down my jeans.

He lets go, and I suddenly feel cold. When my eyes flutter open, he's holding up an eyelash on his index finger.

He leans in close, dropping his voice to a whisper. "Make a wish." I lick my lips and look up at his hazel eyes, already fixed on mine. Somehow, after a full day out, the scent of his body-wash is still sticking to his shirt, and it's igniting my pheromones. Not looking away for a moment, I lean in and blow out.

"I was scared." I feel a release once I say it.

"Scared," he repeats, more like a statement than a question.

"When you asked me why I ran, the day of the meeting."

His jaw muscles tense. "Why were you scared?"

"You know why," I say, and take a sip of the wine still in my hand.

"I have a few ideas," he says, then carefully takes my glass and sets it down. "But I'd like to hear it from you."

I tremble a little. There's nothing between us anymore, literally and metaphorically. Nothing to hide behind. My blood pulses through my veins, knowing that the wall around myself and my heart is crumbling more and more with each second of this conversation.

"I was scared that if I got close to you again . . ." My voice cracks. "I wouldn't be strong enough to leave this time."

His chest moves up and down, his breaths deepening. "Are you still scared?"

"Terrified." I look up at him.

Adam steps back, squeezing the nape of his neck, and I don't know if this is on my account or if he's telling me that he doesn't want this. But I hook my heel around the back of his thigh, forcing him to move closer. I'm not letting this moment pass by me. Not again. It's frightening but electrifying, because I haven't felt this way in years—not since living with him—wanting someone as much as I do right now. And this time, I don't care about the consequences. I want to live in the moment.

"What are we doing?" he asks.

"We're about to kiss."

In one swift motion, his lips are on mine, and it's everything I could ever have wanted. There's a current in my blood, coursing through my veins as I become flush with heat. One of his hands is lost in my hair and the other is on my hip, pulling me to the edge of the counter, pressed up against him. There's a sense of urgency, want, need, as Adam takes the lead. Yet every movement is controlled.

My fingers grip his shirt, and I feel his tongue swirl inside my mouth. God, he feels better than I remember. It's a warm, messy feeling. It's like we're two kids again, who just want to feel each other, though the slightest contact is almost too much to handle.

When my touch moves to his neck, his hands move to the sides of my ass, and a deep hum vibrates against me. Despite me sitting, he's grabbing whatever he can, closing every inch of space.

"Adam," I breathe against his mouth.

Slowly, he trails his lips to my cheek, then my ear. I'm mistaken—nothing about this is messy. Adam moves with intention, knowing exactly what pulse points drive me wild. It's not even from memory—it's like he's a pianist tuning my body to create the perfect note. When I push my chest against his, I feel him smile as I let out an uncontrollable moan, the lower part of me pulsing.

Fisting his shirt, I pull him in closer, almost knocking the wine bottle over. "Shit." I catch it just in time.

"Here." Adam swiftly moves our bowls, glasses, and the bottle, making room on the workstation.

"Such a gentleman," I breathe out, watching his every move.

"Oh, I don't know about that," he huffs, and drags his palm through my hair while the other squeezes my waist. His tongue swipes just below my ear as heat flashes in my most sensitive areas. "The things I want to do right now are pretty ungentlemanly."

A shiver shoots up my spine as I think of all the possible things Adam could do right now. The things I want him to do. I want him to pull my jeans off, turn me over, and make me cry out his name in a way I never have before.

"That sounds . . ." I slowly exhale as he trails kisses down to my collarbone. "Yeah . . ."

I'm not making any sense. Nothing makes sense right now. My primal instincts are in control and all I can rationalize is how much I want this. Right now, I don't even remember the last time I've been touched this way. Probably never. As far as I'm concerned, no man on the planet exists aside from Adam Harper.

"Tell me to stop," he says against my skin, and that's actually the last fucking thing I'm going to do. He's not stopping, and no part of me wants him to. "June," he grunts, and I dig my nails into his back. "You either stop me right now"—he squeezes my ass and whispers into my ear—"or I'm pulling these jeans off and having a second meal."

My insides shudder and I crash my lips back onto his. I whimper against his mouth, not realizing dirty talk had this effect on me.

"Please," I beg. I can't get enough of Adam, and I want nothing more than to feel his lips on every inch of my skin. There's a buzz in the back of my brain and my cognitive senses become fuzzy. My physical intuition has completely taken over and what I want is for Adam to do all of the unspeakable things to me right here on top of his kitchen countertop.

The curve of his muscles tenses as I move my hand down from his shoulder to his chest to his stomach. Even through the fabric of his clothes I feel each chiseled angle. When I palm his growing erection I let out an audible gasp while he instinctively pushes in with a grunt.

"Fuck." He blows out a breath. Knowing I have the ability to make Adam waver turns me on even more. I want to learn what his desires are, what spots on his body spark a reaction, and how he feels inside of me.

With a flick of his thumb, he unbuttons my jeans and waits until I let out an approving nod before going any further.

"Sh-Shit!" I cry when I feel one of his fingers rub over my underwear.

"Now who's soaked?" he says into my ear.

I let out a laugh as my forehead falls onto his. "Shut up," I reach for the waist of his pants and start to undo the button.

"No." He stops me. "Not like this."

"Why can you do what you want, and I can't?" I ask, practically pouting.

"My kitchen, my rules." Adam nips the side of my neck that's most sensitive. "Do you think I can make you come like this?"

"Positive," I breathe out, and grind against him.

He removes his hand from my pants and I let out an embarrassing whine. His fingers travel under my sweater, and the sensation of his skin touching mine makes my head roll back. He moves his hand up slowly and begins to trace the outside of my breast. A slight grunt comes out of him when he realizes I'm wearing a lace bralette, leaving very little to the imagination.

"Fuck, June." He puts his forehead against mine, with a laugh of defeat.

"Hey, you're not supposed to be in—" A voice interrupts us, and we both look over Adam's shoulder. "Oh shit—Adam?"

I move faster than I ever have in my life and jump off the counter, almost spraining my ankle, and fix my sweater.

"Hey, Covey." Adam coughs. He runs a hand through his hair and subtly adjusts himself.

"Sorry, man, I was still in the area and saw the lights on." The man by the refrigerator puts his hands up in the air. "I didn't know you were here."

Adam takes a deep inhale and nods. "All good. Covey, this is June. June, this is Covey, our head chef."

"It's a pleasure to meet you." I give him an embarrassed wave.

He bows his head to me awkwardly. "Um, well, I'll get out of your way. Adam, see you tomorrow." He holds a hand up to both of us and disappears out the back. Adam and I turn to each other and burst into laughter.

"God, I'm so sorry," I say with my hands over my face.

"It's a good thing he didn't walk in on anything else," Adam says. "I would've had to fire him."

My face drops. "You would *fire* him?"

"June, I don't think you can come back from seeing your boss having sex on top of your workstation," he says while putting our bowls and wineglasses in the sink.

"*Adam!*" My blush intensifies. When he turns I can tell he's trying to conceal a smile. "What?" I sigh, worried that he's going to tell me my whole boob is out or something equally embarrassing.

"Nothing." He shrugs, a curve of his mouth revealing itself.

"Just say it."

"That was, um, not on my bingo card for tonight," he says, and the curve has turned into a full-blown smirk.

"And you think it was on *mine*?!" The two of us start laughing again. "We are not talking about this anymore. We're moving past it." I wave my hands out in front of me. "We're past it."

Adam nods. "We're past it."

"Past it," I repeat.

"Come on," he says and walks over to the booth to grab my jacket and purse. "Let's get out of here."

Chapter 19

JANUARY, 7 YEARS AGO

ADAM ENDS UP GETTING A JOB AT LUCA, A NEW PIZZA JOINT in Carroll Gardens, Brooklyn. Calling it a *joint* is actually doing it a disservice—it's not the type of place you wander in looking for a convenient $2 slice at 2 A.M. There's a large sidewalk patio where you can always find groups of people drinking natural wine, and its industrial interior is the ideal place for impressing out-of-towners. Although the menu is quite minimal, I've never passed by without seeing Luca packed to the brim. Even five months after its opening, the hype doesn't end.

It's a Tuesday afternoon, and while the line is moving fast, I've still waited approximately fourteen minutes before I finally get within view of the inside and catch a glimpse of Adam in the back. He's tossing a pizza with his hands, and I fight the urge to take out my phone and record him. I wave from where I'm standing but he doesn't notice me. I whisper-shout "Adam" as if that will help, and a guy working the register looks over and then calls back into the kitchen.

"Yo, Ad, some girl keeps calling you."

Adam frowns and looks over at the crowd. When he spots me waving, he wipes his hands on a towel, then points to the back entrance. It's a shame to leave my place in line, because there are only six people in front of me, and I am kind of hungry.

When I get to the back alley, he's already standing there, waiting.

"Are you okay?" he asks in a slight panic. "What's going on?!"

"I'm fine!" I laugh, feeling bad that I caused any sort of stress. "I tried calling and texting you."

"Shit, my phone's dead," he says. "What's happening?"

"Well," I say slowly. "I wanted to tell you in person that . . ." I take a deep breath and collect myself. "I got a part in the revival of *Chicago*!" I scream, and in one motion Adam's picking me up and swinging me around.

"What?! Holy shit, June! Oh my God!"

Since *The Mousetrap*, I've been fortunate to book back-to-back plays—all of them Off-Broadway and a handful of speaking roles. When I got the chance to audition for *Chicago*, the only person I told was Adam, because I didn't want to jinx it.

"I got the call like an hour ago, it hasn't even hit me—"

"You're going to be on Broadway, June." He says it in a way that makes this all very real. The look on his face alone sends me into tears of joy. He puts me down and tucks my hair behind my ear.

"It's in the chorus, *but* I get a solo part in the 'Cell Block Tango,'" I say like he has any idea what that means.

"Fuck yeah, you do." Adam is the only person who has never said they're proud of me, like being proud means he somehow doubted my achievements. It's one of the many things I appreciate about him.

"I just—I can't even process any of it right now," I say.

I'm going to be on *Broadway.* I remember the nights I spent as a child in bed praying that I could be there one day. The memory of my mother telling me it would never happen . . . and a part of me believed her. It feels like today is the beginning of the rest of my life.

"Well, we're watching the movie tonight to celebrate," he says like it's a given. "What did Chloe say?"

"I'm going to call her after," I say.

For a split second, his face is unreadable. Like he's almost surprised I told him first, but in fact I never thought twice about it. Adam was the first phone call I made after getting the news, and when he didn't answer I jumped on the subway straight to Luca. Looking back, I can't place exactly when the shift happened . . . when he became that person for me.

"Okay, well, tell her to come over tonight," he says. "I'll bring some pizza home."

"I will." I beam as he inches the door open to head back inside. But then it all happens so quickly. One minute he's a few feet away, about to return to work, and the next he's running back and I'm in his arms, my feet not touching the ground. He gives me another squeeze and kisses my cheek.

"This is just the beginning, June," he whispers, although nobody is around us. He puts me back down, and the only thought in my mind is how it feels *too* good being in his arms.

"CAN WE JUST take a minute to talk about how you're going to be doing *that*?" Chloe says through a mouthful of ricotta-and-prosciutto pizza as we watch Catherine Zeta-Jones belt out "All That Jazz."

"Except I won't be, because I'm not playing Velma Kelly," I say for the third time since the movie started. Which was only five minutes ago. "I'm just in the chorus."

Adam shifts on the couch to face me. "You are not *just in the chorus*."

"You are going to be on fucking *Broadway*, June!" Chloe grabs my arm and starts shaking me from the other side.

Since I'm sandwiched between my two biggest cheerleaders, I don't fight them, and I let it settle in that this is really happening.

"Do you ever think about where we're going to be ten years from now?" I ask, taking a bite of pizza.

"We'll be in our thirties." Chloe makes a face of disgust. "That's scary."

"You're going to be a successful criminal-defense lawyer living in a rooftop penthouse on the Upper West Side," Adam says.

"Harper." She puts a hand to her chest. "And a rich husband?"

"Obviously," he says, nodding.

"You know, sometimes I do think about moving somewhere warm, though," she says.

My eyes widen, because in all the years I've known Chloe, this has never come up. "You would move?! You love New York!"

"I don't know, maybe!" she says. "These winters are tough."

"At the rate of global warming, there might not be winters in ten years," Adam says with a shrug.

I look at Adam and shake my head. "I don't think I could ever leave New York."

"Well, what if you wanted to go into film or something?" Chloe asks.

A snort escapes me. "Yeah, right."

The odds of becoming a film or television actress are one in five billion. With the number of people in college who tried and are *still* trying to get an agent and land a role, I'd have a better chance at competing in the Olympics.

"It's a possibility!" Chloe says. "I mean, I'm sure *Chicago* is going to open some doors for you."

"Yeah, but *movies*? That's totally different." I shake my head. "Besides, I don't want people seeing my face that close up." I laugh.

"What are you talking about?" Adam frowns. "You're stunning—you'd be great for film."

Oh. I'm not quite prepared for my heart to skip a beat as a reaction to Adam calling me *stunning*. Especially so casually. He's occasionally told me I look good when I ask if he likes my outfit. He's mentioned that he prefers my hair when it's left in its natural state. But for some reason, this is different. It's a confirmation of something that has felt entirely one-sided for years.

"He's right," Chloe says, which completely takes me out of the moment, thank God.

"Let me just worry about not screwing up my Broadway debut first, please." I reach for another slice of pizza, this time the one with mushrooms and truffle oil.

"Ahh, I am so excited for you, June!" Chloe wraps her arms

around me again, pushing me into Adam, resulting in my head being buried in his chest. *Has he been working out more?* "Life as you know it will never be the same."

IN FEBRUARY, WE find out that Audrey is undergoing lung surgery. It's a point in her battle that nobody anticipates or knows how to handle. Through many conversations with the doctors that Adam insists on being present for, we prepare as best we can, and thankfully the surgery is a success. The cancerous tissue is removed with no complications and Audrey's new routine will consist of follow-up appointments every few months.

During Audrey's recovery time, Adam and I both take the week off and stay at the house with Ford and Sarah. Despite the circumstances, I've never felt closer to the Harpers. They exude love even in the darkest of times. On Thursday night, Adam and Ford meal prep while Sarah and I spend time at the hospital until visiting hours are over.

"Mom, what color do you want?" Sarah holds up two nail polish bottles, one containing a sparkly purple and the other a soft pink.

"Well, that one is really something, isn't it?" Audrey laughs, bringing the purple polish closer.

"It's fun!" Sarah says.

"And that's exactly why I'm choosing it." Audrey gives me a wink.

"Sarah was convinced you were going to choose the other one," I say.

"Well, there's enough nails to go around." Audrey unfolds the blanket lying on top of her, displaying her feet. "I've got ten fingers and ten toes."

I sit on the left side of Audrey with the pink bottle while Sarah crosses her legs on the foot of the bed with the purple. I brush the first layer of pink nail polish on Audrey's thumb, admiring the classic, delicate color. It's the perfect shade against her fair skin. Looking over to Sarah, I immediately notice the bright sparkles and think how it captures the light within Audrey.

"How's calculus, Sarah?" Audrey asks. Sarah started her junior year of high school in the fall and has opted in for all of the classes I would never have even entertained at her age.

"It's great," Sarah says.

"Great?" I raise my eyebrows in disbelief.

She immediately laughs. "Adam said the same thing."

"There's a reason why Adam went to culinary school and I majored in theater."

"Spoken like a true right-brain," she says.

"I'm with you, June," Audrey agrees. "She gets it from Ford."

"But you were a teacher!" I say.

"English teacher," she corrects. "Very different."

"Can confirm." Sarah points the nail polish lid in our direction. "She's not helpful at all when it comes to math or science homework."

"If I see numbers, I send her straight to her dad."

"Are your parents artistic?" Sarah asks me.

"Nooo," I scoff, and begin to paint Audrey's right hand. "My mom was never into any of the movies I liked, or cared about musicals, and I think my dad was in finance? Probably an accountant or something."

"Maybe you were adopted," she says.

"I think in order to be adopted, your parents have to actually want you," I say.

"We want you," Audrey says earnestly.

"No, seriously." Sarah looks up. "When you came to pick me up at school a few weeks ago, one of the girls thought you were my older sister. Honestly, I didn't correct her."

"It would be an honor to be your big sister," I say, feeling touched by the idea.

"I've always wanted a sister." Sarah looks at her mom. "No offense to Adam."

"Well, then let's make it official." Audrey squeezes my wrist with her free hand. "June, you are now adopted into the Harper family."

"Audrey!" I laugh.

"Oh my God. Wait, what a good idea!" Sarah says a little too loudly. She sits up and gestures for me to pass her the nail polish in my hand. I pass it over and she swipes the varnish over her pinky, coating it pink. Afterward, she takes my pinky and paints it. "There," she says, satisfied. "It's a pink-y promise . . . See what I did there?"

"Wow, maybe you're more right-brained than you thought," Audrey says.

Sarah proudly offers her pinky to Audrey and me. "We knight thee—"

"Knight?!" I laugh.

"Don't question it," Audrey whispers.

"We knight thee," Sarah continues, "June Wood-Harper. And this is a promise that we'll always be family no matter what happens."

Audrey links her pinky to Sarah's. "I think Harper-Wood is catchier for the stage. What do you think, June?"

There's a growing warmth in my chest and my mouth splits into the biggest smile. *Family.* It's a word that most people take for granted. To say you have a family is a privilege, a birthright. For the first time, I finally know what it feels like to be wanted, to be loved . . . and it's the best feeling in the world.

I bring my pinky up and link it so we're in a three-way promise. "June Harper-Wood it is."

ON MY NIGHT off from rehearsal, I end up meeting Adam and Robby at a bar in Chelsea. The Knicks are playing Golden State and apparently this is an important game. Chloe was supposed to come with me, but she's been working long nights for a new case she's on.

It's very crowded and the Top 40 playlist is louder than it needs to be. I unzip my jacket and spot Adam and Robby at a high-top table with half-empty beers and a plate of nachos.

"There she is!" Robby stands and gives me an affectionate hug. He's a big guy, as tall as Adam, but his physique is more lumberjack-esque and his light hair and blue eyes differ from Adam's dark features. "It's been a minute—how are you?"

"Oh, you know, same old." I take a seat in between him and Adam, facing away from the TV screens.

"Ad was telling me about *Chicago*," Robby says. "Congratulations."

Adam's focusing on the game, but when my eyes cut to him, he notices and gives me a subtle wink.

"Thanks, Robby." I smile. "I mean, it hasn't hit me yet. We open in a few weeks, and it's just been craziness."

"I bet," he says. "I've gotta get tickets. Ad, when are you going?"

Adam pulls his attention away from the screen. "Uh, I'm going with Chloe opening night, and then my family's coming down to watch at the end of April."

Robby flashes a smile. "Want to watch a third time?"

"Yeah." Adam nods. "Just let me know when."

"Adam, you don't have to watch it *three* times." I place my hand on his forearm.

"Are you kidding? I'd watch every night if I could," he says, popping a chip into his mouth.

"Hey, June, what do you want to drink?" Robby asks.

"Oh no, you stay here. I'll get it." I stand up and look for my wallet in my purse.

"Here." Adam pulls out a twenty and hands it across the table.

"Thanks." I grab it and head to the bar, which is only a few feet away.

I can hear Adam and Robby talking behind me. I catch my name, so I subtly turn my head to the side and pretend I'm watching the basketball game.

"June's really something," Robby says, trying to talk over the noise. "You're really not together?"

"No," Adam says, shaking his head.

"So . . . does that mean I can ask her out?"

Adam's beer bottle pauses against his parted lips. "No." He takes a sip.

My head whips around and I wave to the bartender, asking for a vodka soda with lime. As I wait for my drink, I start to feel warm. It's probably because the bar is well over capacity, but that doesn't explain why I'm blushing.

Once the Knicks lose, we call it a night and Adam and I walk home. He's had a couple of beers, nothing out of the ordinary, but he's quieter than usual.

"Sorry we lost," I say.

He shrugs. "This just means Robby now owes me fifty."

"So you were hoping we'd lose?!" I laugh.

"I was *hoping* I'd be proven wrong," he says. "But they haven't had the best season."

Even though it's cold, neither one of us seems to be rushing to get home. When I glance over, there's a warm amber glow on Adam as we walk under the streetlamps.

"Robby's fun," I say, not really knowing where I want this conversation to go. "I should hang out with you guys more."

"Yeah, he likes you," he says and then lets out a chuckle.

"What?" I ask.

"Nothing." He shakes his head.

"*Adam,*" I say impatiently.

"Robby said I was right," he says, and puts his hands in his pockets.

"Right about what?"

"You," he says, looking straight ahead.

"What about me?"

"That you're the coolest girl he's ever met," he says, like it's the most normal thing you could ever say about anyone.

"What?" I stop and give him an unconvinced look. "You did not say that."

He realizes I'm not beside him and turns around. "I did," he says defensively.

This isn't fair. We can't have this conversation so nonchalantly. What I'm worried about is him saying something he might regret . . . or maybe I'm just not ready to hear him say what he means.

"Well, thank you." I keep walking and move past him.

He follows, and it takes barely any effort for him to catch up. "You don't believe me."

"I didn't say I didn't," I say, brushing him and this whole conversation off.

"Okay, well, now it's your turn," he says.

"My turn for what?" I ask, annoyed.

"To say something nice about me," he says seriously.

"How many beers did you have?" I raise an eyebrow.

"Three and a half," he says. "I'm nowhere near drunk, June."

We stop and I stare at him, squinting. I lift my index finger in front of his face and move it back and forth for him to follow. He obliges and rolls his eyes.

"Okay, fine," I say. "You're very tall."

"That's not a compliment," he says flatly. "That's a fact."

"I don't know what to tell you." I start walking again.

"I'm only slightly offended that you can't think of something nice."

"You make the best lasagna I've ever tasted," I say. "Happy?"

"Really?" he asks.

"Really." I suppress a grin.

"Thanks." He nods to himself like he's making a mental note. "Robby asked if he could ask you out."

There it is. I was wondering if that conversation would ever come up or if Adam would keep it to himself.

"Oh?" I play dumb, and Adam nods. "Why didn't he?"

"Would you say yes?" he asks.

Robby's an attractive guy, funny, energetic. But the thing is, I wouldn't say yes and it's not because he's Adam's friend. For some reason, I wouldn't say yes to *anyone* right now.

I shake my head. "No, I don't think so."

"Good," he says. "You're too good for him."

I laugh. "He's like your best friend."

"No, *you're* my best friend." My throat pulses. I'm speechless. Adam's never said that, at least not to me.

"Hey." I link my arm to his. "You're my best friend too."

"Well, I better fucking be." He kisses the top of my head.

Chapter 20

21 DAYS UNTIL THE MEETING

KISSING ADAM LAST NIGHT WAS EITHER THE BEST DECISION I've ever made or the worst. In true gentlemanly fashion, Adam walked me to my room and kissed my forehead before heading to his room. All night I thought about our magically quintessential New York day, about the softness of Adam's lips, the firm grip of his hands around my waist, and the fact that his dance card is not in fact full. All factors that could completely change what happens at the end of the month.

Old June, and by that I mean yesterday's June, would panic and avoid the situation. Today's June doesn't care, and I decide to not let the unknown ruin the cloud I'm on.

When I head downstairs, I'm greeted with a large white paper bag sitting upright in the middle of the kitchen island. There's a handwritten note propped up beside it.

Thought you'd be hungry.

Cream cheese in the fridge.

I hold on to the scrap paper with a stupid smile on my face as if it's a goddamn valentine. Inside the paper bag is an assortment of New York bagels, still warm. The smell of sesame and yeast fills my senses as I look at a display of blistered beauties with a caramelized sheen. If anyone is still questioning it, the bagels in New York *are* indeed different from those anywhere else. I choose an everything bagel, slather scallion cream cheese on top, and curl up on the couch.

June

Okay, update.

I text Chloe and then see three dots in our chat less than fifteen seconds after.

Chloe

???

June

I was wrong and Adam doesn't have a girlfriend.

Chloe

So who was all wet waiting for him . . .

June

Long story, it was someone who works with him. He's single.

Chloe

I see . . .

June

DON'T start!

Chloe

Hahaha I didn't say anything!!

June

I'll tell you more next week. Love u

Chloe

Love YOU xx

I open up my inbox and see one unread email from Theo that says my audition is tomorrow at 11:45 A.M. at a studio on Forty-second. They'll want me to sing a couple of songs from *Les Mis,* but I should prepare an additional ballad just in case. I've learned through experience that having a slot before lunch is always a good thing, because it gives producers something to think about while they eat. She also attached an invite for a Manhattan for Theater Gala tomorrow night. I frown and scroll to her name on my phone. On the first ring, she answers.

"Hey, June!"

"That was quick." I let out a breathless laugh.

"I was already on my phone," she says.

"Of course," I say. "So, I got all the details for the audition. Anything else I need?"

"Nope, you're all set. Break a leg," she says comically. "Also, I'm flying in tomorrow afternoon. I'll meet you at the gala."

"I saw the attachment," I say. "I didn't know it was at the Plaza . . ."

"Yeah, wear something nice."

"I don't have anything nice," I say.

"*Buy* something nice. You'll be doing the step and repeat."

Step and repeats aren't unfamiliar to me. They're press walls that are really meant for bigger names in attendance, but sometimes Theo pulls off getting me on the list. Knowing that I'm intended to walk the carpet means this is not an event I can back out of.

"Okay, I'll find something," I say. "What time do you land tomorrow?"

"Like two-thirtyish. I have an afternoon meeting, but I'll see you there. Liz and Henry are also going."

It's no surprise that two of my former *Rent* costars will be in attendance. They started a podcast called *Showmance* a few years ago and have been attending every theater event since.

"Oh cool," I say. "It'll be nice to see them again."

"Totally. Okay, I need to run but good luck. I'll see you tomorrow!"

Great. I throw my head back. What every woman loves—finding the perfect outfit under pressure.

IT'S ALMOST SIX when I come back from a day of shopping. Finding a dress for a gala is not as easy, or as fun, as one would think. Thankfully, I found something that I absolutely love and didn't break the bank. Since Adam won't be home for a couple of hours, I decide to do something I never could back in Los Angeles—take a bubble bath.

In the upstairs bathroom, there's an ivory clawfoot tub with gold feet that wouldn't even fit in my tiny bathroom in LA. It's one of the post-renovation additions, and while I've been eyeing it, I never felt comfortable enough to use it. On the windowsill, there's a display of various essential oils and bath salts, something that previous Airbnb users never touched, based on the still-pristine packaging.

I draw the bath, light a few candles, and put an acoustic playlist on my phone. If I'm doing this, I'm doing it right.

The water is warm, and I breathe in a delicate, sweet smell as I tie my hair over my head. Once I sink into the tub, the heated water hugs every inch of my skin and I lie back on the rim, closing my eyes. My thoughts travel to the events of last night. What the fuck even happened? One minute it's too painful to look at Adam Harper, and the next I want him to rip my clothes off with his teeth.

I descend into the bubbles and can practically *feel* his hands gripped around my waist and hear his grunts if I focus hard enough. The feeling of his chest under my hands is a lucid memory, as are his smell of cedar and the sensation of his breath against my neck. No other person has ever been able to conjure this desire within me, the aching in my esophagus, the fear of what will happen if I never get to touch him again.

There's a weight I've been carrying for years that slowly starts to pour out of me, oozing like lava until I feel free. *I want Adam Harper.* I want him, all of him, and maybe I don't have to be afraid of that anymore. We used to be two halves of a whole. There was no June without Adam. No Adam without June. I want to get back to that.

"June?" Adam calls from downstairs, interrupting my thoughts. I cough and quickly adjust the bubbles around myself to make sure that nothing is showing.

"In here!" I call back. Moments later, there's a knock on the door and he carefully opens it.

"Oh," he says, caught off guard by the sight, I'm sure. "Wow."

"Hey." I sink a little deeper into the water. "How was work?"

"It was . . ." he says, not at all trying to hide his stare. "Good," he says, finally making eye contact with me. "How was your day?"

"Good," I say, copying him. "I have my audition with Dan tomorrow . . . and apparently a gala at night?"

He raises his eyebrows. "Manhattan for Theater?"

"Yeah, how'd you know?"

"I was invited too," he says. It had slipped my mind that Alden is a contributor to New York's theater initiatives, and I'm pleasantly surprised when I remember.

"Well, maybe I'll see you there." I smile.

He puts his hands in his pockets and leans against the doorframe. "It's a date." The words cause my cheeks to tinge pink, and it doesn't help that the only thing covering my entirely naked body is a thin layer of bubbles. "Did you have dinner?" he asks.

"Not yet," I say, shaking my head, but dinner is the last thing on my mind. Adam taking off his clothes and climbing on top of me, *that's* on my mind.

"I'll make something," he says.

"Do you need any help?" I ask.

"No, you relax. I'll let you know when it's ready." He winks and then walks away.

I'm left with a stupid, childish grin on my face. I close my eyes, submerging myself into the bath.

MY LAST AUDITION was a self-tape for a limited thriller series for streaming. I filmed a monologue in my living room that consisted of crying and screaming. And if you're wondering, I did not get the part.

I'm now headed to a very different audition on Forty-second and there's an energy pulsing through the chilly morning air that brings me back to my early days in theater. There's something about the adrenaline of walking into a room and turning the eight hundred square feet of space into your stage, picturing endless rows of people watching you, and giving them a performance you can't redo. There's no *cut* or *let's try that again.* Whatever you give them in that moment is what they're getting. It's terrifying but it makes you feel alive.

The building has a narrow hallway surrounded by brick—a tiny detail I forgot was specific to the East Coast. Everything from getting off the elevator and waiting to be brought inside the audition room is a blur. It isn't until I'm standing in front of Dan and four unfamiliar faces that I regain some sort of awareness.

"June," Dan says like he's excited for me to be there, and I find it comforting. "Nice to see you."

I smile. "Nice to see you too." I'm standing in the middle of a bright room with nothing but a piano and a fold-up table with three people sitting behind it. The space is large, with high ceilings that show industrial piping overhead. Rehearsals will probably take place here. "And so nice to meet everyone."

"June, this is Laura, our music director." Dan starts gesturing to the other people in the room. "John and Amy, our producers, and Holly, our choreographer." Everyone gives me a friendly wave and a *hello.* This is the team that's bringing one of the decade's most celebrated musicals back to Broadway . . . and they want to listen to *me.*

"Okay." Dan claps. "So, let's just dive into it. We're all familiar with your background, but of course it's been a few years since you've been on stage. We really just want to hear how your voice has developed. Whenever you're ready, we'd love to hear you start with 'On My Own,' then we can do 'I Dreamed a Dream.' Sound good?"

"Right, of course." I walk over to the side of the room where Laura is sitting behind the piano. I take a deep breath and give Laura a cue that I'm about to start.

The first chords are being drawn, with her foot lightly grazing the pedal. The notes follow in a slow but free pace and my voice accompanies the melody.

The lyrics flow out of me, filling the room with the sound of one of *Les Misérables*' most popular songs. I close my eyes and feel each and every word, allowing myself to give in to every emotion.

I'm transported to that night in front of the Imperial Theatre, a memory that sits on the walls of Alden.

It was the night I found out I'd landed my first lead role—Mimi in the Broadway revival of *Rent.* Just after midnight, Adam and I took a walk to the theater to celebrate. He was in a very brief photography phase, after being gifted a film camera. We both saw the marquee that read *Rent* and I became fixated with emotion, unable to look away. After what felt like minutes, he came up behind me and said *you did it.* There was an usher waiting by the door, a man in his late sixties who told us that he'd been working there for over forty years. Adam told him that he was looking at the new Mimi and before I knew it, the man said *call me Mort* and let us enter.

Once we were inside the theater and saw the rows and rows of velvet chairs and the stage, one bigger than I've ever performed on, Adam told me to go up there. *I can't do that* . . . I said, knowing the idea was ridiculous. He asked Mort for permission, and he gave us his blessing. I got up on stage and Adam sat smack-dab in the middle of the theater and I sang. I sang to nobody but him, but sang as if the world was watching me. I sang "On My Own," and have never performed that song since.

Now I belt out as loud as I can, and I hear the power of Laura on the piano, the room vibrating.

I didn't realize I wasn't, but I'm alive again.

Chapter 21

MAY, 7 YEARS AGO

TWO MONTHS INTO *CHICAGO*, I FIND OUT WE'RE BEING EXtended for another 250 shows. It's then I decide to quit my part-time job, a true sign that my career as a performer is *real.* I've been working at the Arcade Bookshop since I was nineteen and my manager, Dot, has never been more understanding. She tells me that I always have a job there if I need it but hopes that I never have to come back. I repay her by gifting her four complimentary tickets to the show, which she's more than grateful for.

On my first free afternoon in weeks, I celebrate by reading my last book purchase, which has taken me months to finish. Adam's fumbling in the kitchen, but I don't look up.

"Lunch is ready when you want it," he calls out.

"One second." I keep reading, determined to finish the last chapter. My eyes travel through the words of the last page. "Aaand . . . done!" I slam my book shut and place it on a shelf, displaying its bright red spine with gold embroidery.

On the table are two sandwiches wrapped in waxed paper and a grease-soaked bag of onion rings from our favorite local spot.

"Eggplant parmigiana is on the right," he calls over his shoulder while filling up two glasses of water.

"Have you talked to your mom since her check-in yesterday?" I take a bite into an onion ring.

"Yeah, I—" He stops. "Wait, how'd you know it got moved up?"

"She called me earlier this week," I say.

Adam sets the waters on the table and takes a seat. "You know, I feel like she calls you more than she calls me."

The past four months have been a whirlwind of early-morning rehearsals, late-night performances, and shifts at the bookshop. It's the busiest I've ever been in my life, and the sole thing that's been keeping me sane are weekly phone calls with Audrey. It happened almost immediately after I went with Adam to Long Island. What was a quick call between him and his mom turned into *put June on the line, I want to say hi.* Eventually, she started calling me directly and I would call her when I wanted to. It didn't take long to develop a similar relationship with Sarah by text.

"That's because we're besties." I smile.

"She's happier when she talks to you." Adam unwraps his sandwich. "What do you two even talk about?"

"This and that." I shrug.

"Do, uh, *I* ever come up?" he asks.

I give him a smug smile and take a giant bite of my sandwich. "Wouldn't you like to know?" My phone buzzes on the kitchen table and I flip it over. My eyebrows rise as *Audrey*

Harper flashes across the screen. "Speaking of . . ." I answer and put her on speakerphone. "Hi, Audrey, you're on with me and Adam!"

"Hi, Mom," Adam says through a mouthful of his sandwich.

"How's it going?" she asks, her voice sounding weaker than last time.

"All right," I say. "We're just eating lunch before Adam goes to work. How are you feeling?"

"You know, hanging in there," she says.

"Audrey, I just finished a book that I think you'll really like." I take another bite of an onion ring. "I'll have to bring it over next time I'm there. It's a thriller."

"Oh, I've been in need of a new one," she says. "Give me something with a good twist at the end."

"I'm not saying anything!" I hold my hands up. "You're going to have to just read it to find out."

"Fine, fine. How are things with Maya and Aaron, by the way?" she asks.

Adam makes a face, and I wave a hand dismissively at him. I'm positive he has no idea Maya and Aaron are two of my castmates who are secretly hooking up.

"I mean, she hasn't said anything to me, but apparently Jamie saw them at this piano bar, the Duplex, on Friday," I explain.

Adam yet again makes a face because he doesn't know who Jamie is either.

"Oh dear . . . Well, I'm rooting for them. They deserve to be happy," Audrey says.

"I know, and they're so perfect for each other. I'm hoping it all works out."

We end up chatting for another fifteen minutes before Adam

asks if he can hijack our call and talk to his dad. As I pass my phone over, I tell Audrey that I'll call her next week, and for a moment I think that this is what it must feel like to be friends with your mom.

A COUPLE OF weeks later, I'm dropping off our rent check to Stanley on the other side of town. Most months Stanley comes to our place to pick up rent, but since I have free time today I decide to drop it off in person and bring him a sweet treat.

Stanley lives in an average apartment on the Upper East Side that is absolutely dripping with drama and rich decor elements that aren't particularly easy on the eyes. There's chunky wood furniture from, I imagine, the eighties or nineties. He also has a borderline hoarding issue when it comes to photographs, books, and paperwork.

"How are you, dear?" Stanley looks up from his home office desk, which is full, of course, of more paperwork.

"I'm good! Just dropping off this month's rent." I place it in front of him along with a chocolate croissant. "Aaand a little something else."

He gives me an *I told you to stop getting me things* look, but takes the brown paper bag anyway. "How did you know my blood sugar was getting low?"

"Just a hunch." I wink. "How are you?"

"Tired," he says, and lets out a dramatic sigh. "But I guess once you reach my age that's nothing new."

"I don't know. That's not too normal for thirty-six," I say, and he barks out a laugh.

"How's the show? I told you I have tickets for the fifteenth, right?" He sits back in his dark brown office chair, which I'm convinced is a prop from *The Rockford Files.*

"Yeah, Adam told me. I'm going to meet you afterwards and show you backstage, okay?"

"You don't have to do that," he says.

"I *want* to!" I insist, and am already excited at the idea of showing him around. Among the many artifacts around his home are framed *Playbill*s, Broadway posters, and a collection of scripts from eBay any theater buff would be proud to own.

"Well, I'm excited. And how's Adam doing? His mom's out of the hospital now, right?"

I think I mishear him.

"Sorry?"

"The hospital. She's out now?" he repeats, but I don't say anything. I can feel the blood drain from my face. "I-I'm sorry . . . I thought you knew," Stanley says apologetically. "I stopped by the house a few days ago and Adam told—"

"A few *days*?" I feel a knot in my chest. I turn on my heels and I don't even know if I say anything else before I'm jumping on the subway.

The house is empty when I walk through the door, but I hear a noise above me. I don't take my jacket or shoes off and run up the stairs, then burst into Adam's room.

"Why didn't you tell me?!"

Adam turns around, dumbstruck. He's pulling a sweater over his head, and I can tell he's getting ready for work based on the old jeans he already has on. There's a quizzical look on his face and I think maybe I have the wrong information. That this is a mistake. Then he looks down.

"June, I'm sorry," he finally says.

I can feel my eyes welling up. This isn't a mistake. "You should have told me." My voice trembles.

"Yeah . . ." he says softly. "Fuck, I know."

That's all he can say? I want to ask why he would keep this from me and if he has any idea how embarrassing it is to find out from Stanley of all people.

Instead, I ask the only thing I really want to know.

"How is she?"

"Not good," he almost whispers.

I know it's stupid and selfish for me to be so upset that I found out like this. Because whatever I'm feeling, he's feeling one hundred times worse.

"I'm going there," I say. Audrey's the closest thing I have to a mother and I want to be with her.

"No, you're not," Adam says harshly. "This is why she didn't want you to know. You're not skipping any performances because of this," he demands, and I can feel tears falling down my cheeks. I can't hold it in any longer. "I'm sorry I didn't tell you." His voice cracks, and now I'm mad at myself because I'm responsible for the look on his face.

"Adam—"

"Just please don't do anything . . ." he pleads. "Not yet."

I don't push it. I know that he's telling me he's going to need me. Soon.

I'M STANDING IN an unfamiliar kitchen watching Adam from across the room. There are about fifteen people between him and me, and I don't know any of them. My eyes travel down, and I pick a piece of lint off my black dress. I despise this dress. It was bought with the intention of wearing it today and I'm going to throw it out after the end of the night.

My gaze lifts back up to Adam, and his shoulders are sloping beneath his dress shirt. He's hugging relatives and nodding at what they're saying but I know he's not listening. Chloe and Robby are sitting at the kitchen table with Sarah, eating some sort of egg or tuna salad. I wouldn't know, because I haven't had an appetite in two days. We all stayed at the Harpers' house last night, and Adam demanded that Chloe and I stay in his childhood room while he and Robby took the couches.

The last time I saw Sarah I remember thinking how mature she is, how she's whip-smart and has a sense of humor wise beyond her years. When I look at her now, she seems like a child. I shoot Robby an appreciative glance and he gives me a reassuring nod that almost makes me cry. Everything almost makes me cry.

In one of the armchairs, Ford sits silently, almost as if he is in a trance. The occasional person pats his shoulder or crouches down to comfort him, sharing the same sentiment over and over again, *I'm sorry for your loss.* He smiles at everyone and nods like he's hearing them. But there's a vacant look behind his eyes.

There's an ache deep in my chest that I can't soothe, the smell of freshly cooked pasta in large tin containers, and the sound of chatter from the many conversations happening. Despite the sea of black fabric, one would think this was a party, a celebration. Maybe it is. Maybe this is meant to be a celebration of Audrey's life, yet I can't make myself feel anything but heartache.

Through the window, I watch the swing set in the backyard

slightly swaying back and forth in the breeze. There's a royal blue slide and I wonder whose kids use it. There are only a small number of children here today, all of whom are running around and laughing, yet nobody is telling them to stop. There's a broken plank on the wood fence and I wonder if that was caused by one of the kids, or perhaps a dog. So many stupid thoughts enter my mind, and I welcome them. Let me think of anything other than what's happening today.

Adam approaches the kitchen, ruffles Sarah's hair, and then stands beside me.

"Hey," he says. We've barely exchanged words this morning. I held his hand throughout the entire funeral, yet no words were exchanged. Hearing his voice now unravels me.

"Hi," I say softly.

"Want to get out of here?" he asks, and I shake my head.

"There's still more food that needs to—"

"Please, I just need to get out of here," he says desperately.

"Okay," I say, because of course I'll do anything he wants right now.

Adam briefly talks to Robby and they give each other a hug, followed by one from Chloe. Then he takes my hand in one of his, grabs his jacket in the other, and pulls me out the back door of the house. We get into Ford's truck and sit in silence until we pull into his parents' driveway, which is no more than ten minutes away.

He starts up the stairs before I even have a chance to lock the door. I let in a breath and scan the empty house. The last time I was standing here, Audrey was hugging me, telling me to come back soon. She was fine—she was continuing her treatment, and she was going to be fine.

I slip off my heels to follow Adam and I catch a glimpse of a book with a red spine and gold embroidery on a side table by the couch. There's a receipt wedged in between the pages being used as a bookmark. She had only about forty pages left. Audrey never got to the plot twist, and right now, I wish more than anything I had told her what it was. But I guess life gives us twists of our own . . . and it doesn't wait until we get to the end.

When I get to Adam's room, he's already tugging at his tie, but having trouble. Days like this feel like they should be dark and dismal, but the sunlight filters through the shades, casting a pattern on Adam's chest. There's a look on his face that's been there for the past week, and I want more than anything to get rid of it. To do whatever it takes. I walk over, take the silk in my hands, and loosen the knot gently. I'm focused on the tie, but I can feel his gaze on mine, burning an imprint on the top of my head. I slide the fabric over his shirt and place it on the dresser next to the framed photo of Audrey and Sarah in the photo booth.

"Thanks," he says, but his mind is elsewhere.

The house is so silent I can hear the sound of kids walking outside. I'm not sure what time it is or even what day, but I imagine they're coming home from school.

Adam comes up behind me and I turn around, wrapping my arms around him tight. He buries his face in my hair, taking a deep breath in, and I'm getting used to this, how he holds me. He's been doing it a lot the past few days, and it feels like the most natural thing in the world. It almost feels unnatural when we aren't touching.

He pulls away after a moment and we lock eyes, his so dark and hollow that he almost looks like a different person.

"Can we just . . . lie down for a second?" he asks, but he's already walking toward the bed. I follow and we lie side by side, staring at the ceiling. "I don't know what I'd do without you, June."

I'm focused on the fan circling above and when I move my head, I see that Adam is asleep. As my eyes close, I have a frightening thought—I have no interest in lying next to someone who isn't him.

Chapter 22

20 DAYS UNTIL THE MEETING

SIX INCHES. THE DOOR'S CRACKED OPEN SIX INCHES, AND that's all I need for a clear view of Adam's bare back. He's shaving in front of the mirror, hair damp, pushed out of his face, and he's wearing a towel around his waist. *Holy hell.* This isn't like night one, when I was afraid the mere sight of him would blind me; this time I indulge, and can confirm he's even more in shape than he used to be. Through each stroke of his razor, back muscles twitch that I didn't even know existed on a human.

I fight the urge to open the door and pick up where we left off. It's been over twenty-four hours since our kitchen rendezvous, and subsequently, he's seen me half naked in the bathtub and I'm now being taunted by the flex of his torso.

We haven't discussed the other night, and it feels like we're playing a wicked game of cat and mouse. I'd be lying if I said Adam hasn't been in the back of my mind all day . . . or the past five years. But how does one enter the next phase of their relationship with their estranged best friend turned roommate and now co-homeowner?

"Hey, how did it go?" Adam's looking at me through the mirror, and I wonder how long I've been standing here. Surely over thirty seconds and yet, I still don't move.

"Oh, it was, um . . ." It seems like I've lost the ability to walk *and* speak. He turns around and pushes the door open a little bit, so I now see his whole body. I clear my throat, collecting myself. "It went well. A little surreal to be singing again, but now we wait."

"I wish I could've heard." He cleans the remaining shaving cream off his face and puts away his razor. I try not to analyze the ripple of every muscle on his body, how soft his skin looks, each freckle on his chest, and that damn V-line. "What song did you sing?"

"'On My Own,'" I say.

He smiles to himself while wiping off the counter. "You always killed that one."

It's actually comical how distracting he is, adjusting his towel and pushing his fingers through his hair.

"Were you done in here?" I ask. "I was going to take a shower before tonight."

"Yeah, just need to do one more thing." He fills the space between us and gently puts his hand on my jaw. Our eyes meet for a brief moment, like he's confirming this closeness is okay. He then tips my chin toward his and places his mouth on mine. It's soft and brief, unlike the other night. I surrender to his touch and that we're doing this. We're casually giving each other kisses in the bathroom.

"That was nice." I smile.

"It was."

"Missed you," I say, and my heart twists because he has no idea what those words mean to me, what it means for me to give him those words. I should be scared, terrified. But that shield of armor I had over my heart cracks and splinters more and more as each moment in this house passes. The words *moving too fast* cross my mind, yet how can this be too fast when it feels like we're just picking up from where we left off?

"Me too," he says softly. He gives me another kiss, a few seconds longer but just as gentle.

"How was work?" I ask.

"A little stressful. Just a lot going on."

"Anything I can do to help?" I offer.

"Have you ever worked prep?" he asks. "One of our guys is out sick this week."

"Anything *else* I can do to help?" I laugh.

"I'll think of something." He shifts, and I notice his aggressively defined abs.

"Are you excited for tonight?" I lean my head against the bathroom door, looking up at him. Adam's eyes have a few more lines around them, but they're still warm even after all these years. His hair is still that same dark shade of brown and his smile makes me feel like nothing else matters. Looking at Adam is like watching one of my favorite comfort movies—I already know every line like the back of my hand, so now I look for the smallest details I may have missed the first time around.

"I am," he says. His eyes travel down to the slit of skin in between my sweater and my jeans that he's grazing with his thumb. "Are you?"

Despite how our first week started off, I'm not a cold person. How I felt was unsettling, and nothing about how I acted made me feel good. But now, after these past couple of days, I feel like I'm able to let my guard down. I'm able to really see what's in front of me, and I'm starting to feel something new. I feel safe.

"I'm more excited for afterwards," I boldly say. It's new for me to be talking like this, especially to Adam, but it feels natural. I trace my finger along his collarbone, down to his chest.

"Oh yeah?" He raises an eyebrow. Adam has to stop by the restaurant again before the gala, and it makes me a little sad we can't arrive together.

"Maybe by then, you'll think of ways I can help relieve that stress." My finger moves lower. He lets in a sharp inhale, and his hand moves down to my ass. "In the meantime"—I stand on my toes and reach to bite his earlobe—"I need to take a shower."

Adam grips my hips and I let out an uncontrollable gasp. He lifts me and we switch spots, me now in the bathroom and him by the doorframe.

"It's all yours." He closes the door behind him with a wink. I'm left standing in the middle of the bathroom, wildly turned on and already counting down the hours until tonight.

SET UP ACROSS the entrance of the Plaza hotel is a step and repeat, with an already significant crowd taking photos and other actors doing press interviews. Manhattan for Theater is one of the biggest nonprofits dedicated to supporting the arts in North America, so tonight is a big deal for the Broadway community.

Someone opens the door of my Uber and I step out, smoothing my dress—it's a deep emerald green, floor-length, with one long sleeve and one side sleeveless. I flip my loose curls over my shoulder—the look took over an hour of blowing out to achieve, but thankfully was worth it. A group of people on the other side of the gate with *Playbill*s and printed headshots patiently wait for performers far more well-known than me to arrive.

"June!" My head turns, but I don't see anyone I know. Then I hear my name again. "June Wood!"

Behind the gate, a group of girls in their early twenties starts jumping and waving their hands when I notice them. As I walk over, they hold out their pamphlets and a pen. I'm floored to discover they all have *Playbill*s from my run in *Rent*.

"Wow, nice to meet everyone." I take the pen and start signing. It's hard for me to recall the last time I did this, probably at the stage door after one of the *Rent* performances.

"Would we be able to take a picture with you?" one of the girls asks.

Me? I want to say.

"Yes, of course!" I take her phone from her and pose in a selfie style with the four girls behind me. Everything happens so fast. If this were anywhere else, I'd want to talk to them, but I'm called to the carpet and before I know it, I'm posing in front of flashing lights.

I'm not, and never was, looking for fame. If that were the case, I would've taken Shivani's advice and started a TikTok account years ago. The validation of having those girls want to meet me isn't some satisfaction of being famous, it's knowing that I was really good at one point. I used to be really good at what I did, and I loved it.

After mindlessly posing, I'm ushered inside the hotel lobby, and I hear a familiar voice from across the way.

"June!"

Theo is in a killer black suit with a plunging neckline and nothing underneath. Her dark hair is pin-straight and tucked behind her ears. She's taking her time walking toward me, because Theo does not rush for anybody.

"Oh my God, fancy meeting you here!" I give her a hug. "You look so good."

"Are you fucking kidding me? Look how hot you are, June. What is happening?" She holds my arm up and steps back, eyeing me from head to toe.

"Ouch?"

"Oh shut up," she laughs. "You know you look good."

She *is* right. Not to toot my own horn, but when I took a final glance in the mirror, I was caught off guard by how the last-minute look had come together.

"How was your flight?" I ask.

"Awful," she says, and rolls her eyes. "I barely slept last night so I'm pretty much dying right now."

"But you look good doing it."

She takes an hors d'oeuvre from a server passing by while I politely decline. "How has New York been?" she asks. "I feel like it's been years since I've seen you."

"You know, I've really missed it," I say.

"I mean, you better get used to it because if all goes well—"

"Theodora!" I grab her arm. "Don't jinx it!"

She stops and looks at me, all joking aside. "You really want it, don't you."

"Why are you so surprised?"

She shrugs. "I've just never seen you *excited* about anything. Sometimes I've wondered if you even really want to be in TV or film."

Theo is not only my agent of five years, but my friend. She's the only person in the world who knows how hard working in LA has been and how many times I've had to hear rejection after rejection. So, she's not wrong. There *have* been times when I've wondered if I still want to be an actor.

"This is different," I say honestly. "I want this."

"Speaking of." She takes a bite of her crab cake. "I know who they cast as Valjean." My posture straightens and she nods in response. "Philip Summers."

"Philip Summers?!" I whisper. Philip Summers is a voice I'm no stranger to. He's a Broadway veteran who played Marius in the 1996 run of *Les Misérables* in London. "Are you serious?"

"He just signed the contract this afternoon," she says.

"Wow, okay." I take a deep breath in, trying to be as casual as possible. But for obvious reasons, I'm freaking out on the inside.

"Shit, I have to go say hi to a few people." Theo moves her head next to mine and gives me an air kiss. "I'll see you inside."

I make my way through the Palm Court and enter the Grand Ballroom. It's absolutely breathtaking. There are marble pillars and arches surrounding the space, as if we're in a historic theater without the rows of seats. There are dark burgundy velvet curtains with gold tassels and the live band is playing a jazz rendition of "On the Street Where You Live."

There are well over two hundred people at this event, and it's hard to find a familiar face. Except there's a silhouette that's almost too familiar to me in the distance. It's like being transported back to one of Chloe's many parties as I spot *him* in a sea of people, as if it was a skill. Adam's leaning against the bar, talking to two other men.

When we were roommates, there had never been an excuse for us to get all dressed up. I almost miss a step, because I've never seen Adam look like this in all the years I've known him. Wearing a black suit with a matching black shirt, he is the definition of tall, dark, and handsome. I now understand what the word *swoon* means. His hair is subtly pushed back, highlighting his freshly shaved face, and I have to literally bite my tongue right now to hold it together.

As if he has felt the same magnetic pull, he glances up at me, then back to his conversation, quickly followed by a double take. His posture straightens and I see him nod to one of the men and pat his arm before he starts walking toward me.

"Wow," he says, eyeing me from head to toe.

"You clean up good, Harper," I say as I walk toward him.

"You look—" he starts, and I turn around, showing him the full view of my dress from behind. "Jesus Christ."

"You like?"

"I don't think *like* is the right word," he says. The way Adam looks at me makes me feel like the sexiest woman alive. "Would you like a drink?" he asks.

"I'd love one." I smile, and he gestures for me to walk toward the bar.

"Hey, how's it going?" he asks the bartender. "I'll have a Macallan 12. Neat. And she'll have a . . ." He looks over at me and squints. "Vodka soda with lime."

"You got it." The bartender taps the wood and turns around.

"You remembered my drink," I say, amused.

"I have a good memory," he says.

I shouldn't open this door. I shouldn't go too far into the past, but I can't help it.

"What else do you remember?" I ask.

"Everything," he says, passing me my vodka soda when it appears and tossing a ten into the tip jar.

"Like?"

"Ask me something." He takes a sip as we start walking nowhere in particular.

"What's my favorite color?" I ask, and he coughs out a laugh. "What?"

"Nothing, I just didn't know we were in fifth grade."

"Hey, if you don't remember, then—"

"Purple growing up," he answers. "But in college, you changed it to forest green because you felt that was more *mature.*" He looks at me.

Okay, he gets that one.

"What was my first acting role?" I raise my eyebrow.

"The Christmas Nativity play," he says without missing a beat.

"What part?"

"The angel." He smiles.

"Fine." I narrow my eyes. "What's the first movie we ever watched together?"

"Sleepless in Seattle."

"Wrong." My lips curl into a devious smile. "*My Best Friend's Wedding.*"

"Trust me, it was *Sleepless in Seattle.*"

"Adam." I shake my head. "Remember that night you came home late, and I was like ten minutes into the movie—"

"Of course I remember," he says, deadpan. "What *you* clearly don't remember is the night you felt sick after we went to that baseball game . . . and watched *Sleepless in Seattle.*"

I shake my head. "That was way later!"

"No, it wasn't."

"Oh my God, Adam," I laugh, more amused by his stubbornness than anything else. "Just admit you're wrong!"

"June, that night you were wearing those pink shorts and said you wanted to watch something with Meg Ryan and Tom Hanks. I remember thinking *there's no way I can get through an entire movie without touching her.*"

I open my mouth and then close it, stunned.

"You thought that?" I say.

"Yeah." He takes a sip of his Macallaster 12 or whatever the hell it is—why is it so attractive that he ordered a drink I've never heard of? Why is it turning me on that this is a black-tie event and he's the only person *not* wearing a tie? Adam has the first button of his shirt undone and somehow looks like the most put-together person in the room. Why does this sliver of information—that he wanted me eleven years ago—make me replay our entire history together?

"June!" I feel Theo's hand on my arm. She's standing beside me, holding a champagne glass. "Sorry to interrupt," she says, and turns to Adam. "Hi, I'm Theo." She extends her hand out to him, and he shakes it.

"Theo, this is my . . . friend Adam." I hesitate on the word for a moment, but he doesn't seem fazed. "Adam, this is my agent, Theo."

"Very nice to meet you, Theo." He smiles.

"June." She pulls me in a little closer. "Would we be able to chat for a second?"

"I'll leave you ladies to it." Adam tips his glass to us and disappears into the crowd, but not before giving me a subtle wink. I want to tell him to wait, but Theo is holding on to my arm.

"Okay, he's hot as fuck." Theo's eyes follow Adam and then look back at me.

"Oh. Yeah, well—"

"June, Dan Sackler is here." She continues, "I think you should talk to him."

"I just saw him this morning," I say. "I don't want to bother him."

"Trust me, you're not," she says. "This will only help." She nods to the opposite side of the room. "Look, he's over there. Say hi."

Theo pretty much pushes me in that direction. When I turn to look back at her, she gives me a big thumbs-up. There is nothing subtle about Theo. She's a powerful woman in Hollywood and she knows it. She works her ass off and knows what's what, so when she says jump, I *will* ask how high.

Somehow, the crowd keeps growing and the music gets louder. Dan's about twenty feet away still but he catches my eye and waves me over. As I get closer, he steps aside from his group and gives me a big hug.

"June, oh my God," Dan breathes out. "You look absolutely stunning."

"Oh, thank you, you look incredible too!" I say, eyeing his full-blown tuxedo.

"Look, you did an amazing job today," he says. "We were all really speechless."

My cheeks become flush, not used to receiving this kind of praise after a performance. At least not in a very long time.

"Thank you, Dan," I say sincerely.

"I'm not sure if you know"—he leans in closer—"but we cast Philip Summers as our Valjean."

"I heard." My eyes widen. "Which is absolutely insane. I'm a big fan of his."

"This revival is going to be a big deal, June. It's been fourteen years since the last run and there's already Tony buzz." He narrows his eyes. "And it would be our pleasure if you join us on this journey as our Éponine."

I'm positive I haven't heard him correctly, because I have no immediate reaction. But he's staring back at me with a smile on his face, and I feel like a bottle of carbonated soda someone shook, a wave of euphoria bubbling up within me, about to explode.

"A-Are you serious?"

"Yes!" Dan laughs and pulls me into a hug. "Congratulations, June, and welcome back to Broadway!"

Chapter 23

One minute I'm hugging Dan, and the next Theo is handing me a glass of champagne. A few other people whom I don't know, although I'm sure someone introduced me in the middle of the chaos, tell me congratulations. The room is spinning, and between the band's playing, the alcohol, and the chatter in front of me, details become foggy. Theo and Dan are staring like they're waiting for an answer, and I shake my head and squint.

"Sorry, what did you say?"

"We're aiming for rehearsals to start in November," Dan says. "So that should give you plenty of time to relocate."

"Relocate," I repeat.

Everything is suddenly feeling all too real. The show will run for *at least* nine to twelve months, and unless you're someone like Philip Summers, productions rarely have the budget to put up their principal characters in any housing. This is something that's crossed my mind often the past two weeks, but it's now official. I'm really moving back to New York.

"We can talk about all these details next week." Theo waves her hand. "Now go celebrate! If I don't see you, let's do a call Monday morning." She pulls me in for another hug and whispers in my ear, "Congratu-fucking-lations!"

Dan holds his glass up and gives me a cheer. "We're so excited, June. We cannot wait to get the ball rolling!"

The room continues to spin, and I feel like I'm on a high. Theo's voice rings in my ears, *we can talk about all these details next week,* but I don't want to think about any logistics, what comes next, or where we go from here. In this moment, I'm proud of myself, I'm ecstatic, I'm processing that this is *actually* happening, and there's only one person I want to celebrate with.

I hurry through the crowd, looking every which way, and finally, I see him. Adam's facing me, but chatting with another man and woman. Seriously, how does this guy know everyone?

Placing my drink on the closest table, I wave for him to come over. A smile forms on Adam's face, but he's locked in conversation, trying his best not to be rude.

My eyes widen to try and relay the urgency, and he looks at me with confusion, but slight amusement. I'm motioning at him, mouthing *COME HERE,* but he just cocks his head to the side, and now I know he's messing with me.

I mouth *I'm going to kill you!* and that's when he finally says something to the couple and walks toward me.

"I was really wondering how far you were going to go there—" he says, but I shut him up with a kiss. Something I've wanted to do all night. He's caught off guard for a fraction of a second before his hands are on my waist, his fingertips grazing the bare skin on my back. When I pull away, he rubs his lips together. "If

I knew this was what you wanted, I wouldn't have kept you waiting."

"Do you want to get out of here?" I ask desperately.

No need to ask Adam twice, because he already has his hand in mine, leading me back toward the lobby. As we're halfway there, the music stops and a spotlight flashes on a middle-aged woman in front of the band.

"Shit." Adam stops, and we both turn to look, along with hundreds of other people in the room.

"Hello, everyone," the woman says into a microphone. "My name is Lesley Foster, and I want to thank you all for coming to the thirty-seventh annual Manhattan for Theater Gala." The audience begins to applaud, and Adam and I follow suit. "Manhattan for Theater is the philanthropic heart of Broadway. We believe in the transformative power of the arts as an agent in bringing significant change in the lives of youth. Your support provides a transformative and inclusive community that inspires young lives through the performing arts." She holds a hand to her heart and a projector slide begins to descend from the ceiling. "And before we get into our special performances, we'll be starting off with our live auction."

"Do we need to stay for this?" I lift my head up and whisper to Adam, who's directly behind me.

"We can't leave in the middle of a charity auction," he says, more like he's telling himself.

Well, I'm clearly a selfish asshole.

"You're right . . ." I've waited eleven years, for crying out loud. Surely another hour won't kill me.

A middle-aged man steps into the spotlight next to Lesley and takes the microphone from her.

"Good evening, ladies and gentlemen," he announces, sounding like a game show host. "My name is Mitch Alderton and it's my pleasure to be your auctioneer tonight for Manhattan for Theater. If you look on your tables, everyone will have paddles with numbers. Simply raise your paddle if you'd like to bid and the incredible team at MFT will be doing the rest."

He takes a step to the side and looks up at the screen behind him, which flashes an image of the New York Knicks. "All right, first up we have four VIP full-season ticket memberships. Don't miss a single game at the Garden during the upcoming season. It includes three preseason and forty-one regular-season games." Within a second, he switches into full-blown auctioneer mode and I can barely understand a word coming out of his mouth. "Bidding starts at ten thousand dollars—" Someone raises their paddle. "We have a ten-thousand-dollar bid, now eleven thousand, we have eleven, will ya give me twelve—" More paddles start going up. "Thirteen thousand, okay, we have thirteen, will ya give me fourteen? Fourteen thous—"

Not only do the man's words become a jumble, but also I can't even fathom the idea of spending this much money on anything, and when I look up at Adam he's paying close attention to the auction. His eyes are scanning each paddle and *of course* it's turning me on. Of course he's invested in this, because he's a capable adult man who cares about the future of our youth in the performing arts.

"Next, we have a Cabo getaway! Dramatic landscapes and tropical coastline await you and three guests with a four-night stay in one of three stylish apartments." The auctioneer continues, "Indulge in sun-kissed Cabo San Lucas with a stay in a contemporary, ocean-view apartment minutes from the beach.

Biddings starts at twelve thousand dollars—we have twelve, will ya give me thirteen? Okay, we have thirteen—"

The photo on the screen is a sun-soaked shoreline with golden sand and a breathtaking view of the ocean. My mind wanders to an image of Adam on the beach, tanned, wet, and that V protruding above the hem of his swimming trunks.

I take half a step back, subtly pressing my ass into him.

"June," he warns, a firm grasp on my arm.

I lean my head back slightly so it's resting against his chest. "What?" I ask innocently.

"You're killing me." His voice comes out low, lower than usual, which makes the hairs on the back of my neck stand up. My body shifts and he places his hand on my hip, close to where I desperately want him to be touching. If he's trying to tease me, it's working. My body presses a little closer and his grip tightens. I swear I hear him grunt. "Fuck it." He takes my hand and starts walking.

"Wait, really?" I whisper-shout. "We're leaving?"

"I'll write them a check," he says.

"Won't that be a lot?" Considering how much these auction items are going for, I'm wondering if that's the best idea.

He turns back to me, still walking. "I mean, we do own a six-million-dollar house."

We step outside the Plaza, behind the red velvet ropes. The streets are adorned with shimmering lights, and I'm reminded just how spectacular Manhattan is at night. Adam hails the first cab he sees, and we slide into the backseat. There's not a lot of space, but once we settle in, I wish we were closer.

"Hey, man, how's it going?" Adam says to the driver. "West Village, please, 74 Perry Street."

"You got it, boss." He taps the address on his phone and starts driving.

As I cross my legs, part of my dress falls to the side thanks to the dangerously high slit, revealing my exposed thigh. Of course I'm aware of how it looks, but I don't bother to cover myself up. This new territory is exciting, and I'm liking how confident Adam makes me feel. Adam's eyes cut to my skin and then he rolls his head to look out the window while he reaches his arm over me and places his hand on my lap. Instinctively, I uncross my legs to allow him better access, assuring that nothing is exposed that shouldn't be. While his hand inches closer and closer to my panties, the feeling of his fingers on my skin causes me to bite my lip. Subtly, his middle finger swipes the damp part of my underwear, and it makes me whimper. Thankfully I'm drowned out by the music. Adam just smiles to himself and moves his hand back up to my leg and keeps it there the rest of the ride.

When we finally get back home, I throw my clutch onto the side table while Adam locks the door behind us.

"That felt like the longest car ride in the history of car rides," I say and walk to the middle of the living room. "Was that just me?"

Adam doesn't say a word and just walks toward me, his eyes hungry. But he stops at the arch between the foyer and the living room and leans against the opening with his hands in his pockets.

"Did I ever tell you how beautiful you are?" he asks.

There's that blushing that I clearly can't control. "If I recall correctly, there was a lack of words."

He lets a laugh out under his breath. "Not just tonight. June, please tell me I've told you that."

There are things he's said to me through the years, *you look better without makeup, I love your laugh, you're not like other girls,* compliments that would make someone think twice. But until this moment, they all seemed like observations that a friend would say to another—or at least I've convinced myself of that.

"I think there are a lot of things we've each said that the other didn't really hear," I say.

He nods, knowing exactly what I mean. "How are you feeling?"

"Happy," I say honestly, but for some reason, I don't tell him the most recent news. Telling Adam about the show opens the door to a conversation I'm not ready to have, at least not tonight. Right now, I feel good because I'm with him, not because of the show, and I want to relish that feeling. "But I could be happier."

His eyebrows rise but he doesn't move from his spot. "How can I help?"

There are *a lot* of things I know about Adam Harper, and one thing I know for sure is that the man aims to please. I've witnessed him creating dishes with precision and attention to detail with each and every ingredient. He knows exactly which seasonings bring out certain flavors in different proteins and what wine pairs well with what dessert. Once, he told me that the curation of the perfect plate is not unlike lovemaking, at which I laughed but now I know what he meant. If tonight is going to be anything like the way he cooks, I already know how satisfied I'm going to be.

"Touching me would be a good start," I say.

I slowly walk over to him, my heels clicking with each step. Even in my shoes, Adam's still a good six inches taller than I am. My hands grab onto his lapels, and I run the fabric between my fingers while he starts tracing the skin from the top of my arm down to my elbow.

"Do you have any idea how crazy you've been driving me?" he says, his voice low.

"Oh?" I look up at him through my eyelashes. "Why's that?"

"Your skin." He slowly turns me, then carefully pulls my hair to the other side, exposing my bare back. "Your smell." He gives me a kiss on my neck that makes me shiver while he moves his finger down my spine. "Your taste."

His breath makes me arch my spine, resulting in my pushing up against him. He hisses and gently bites my shoulder while one hand wraps around me, touching just under my breast.

"Adam," I breathe out.

"What do you want, June?"

My thoughts are unclear. This isn't like the other night in the kitchen, urgency rushing through us. He's taking his time, soaking up every moment of this, and it's driving me crazy.

"I want . . ." I try my best to focus. "I want *you*." I look up at him, and I've said it. I've said the words that have always scared me . . . and we're going to do this. Finally.

His hands explore my body—my hips, my waist, my back, my shoulders—but never touch the areas I want him to. It's in this moment I learn how underrated foreplay really is. There are only thin layers of fabric between us, but I'm dying to rip them off. Well, I want *him* to rip them off.

Adam's pressed against my backside, and fully hard. I reach behind me and feel all of him, but he swiftly grabs my wrist and spins me around, so *I'm* now pinned against the wall.

"Just wait." He starts kissing my neck, and with every nip of my skin it's almost embarrassing how quickly I'm becoming undone. His hands travel from my waist down to cup my ass, and the way he's grabbing me is unlike any way I've ever been touched. Like I'm the most tempting thing he's ever laid his hands on.

"Upstairs . . ." I run my fingers through his hair and lean my head back against the wall.

"Not yet," he murmurs, and then his body starts to move lower, until he's on his knees. It's like he's hypnotized. My heels are still on, but he has a grasp on the backs of my ankles, and he moves his hands slowly up my calves to my thighs. I gasp more the higher he goes, as he feels every part of skin underneath my dress. Then he reaches for the sides of my thong, keeping his eyes on me as he takes his time pulling it down. I take a step out as he puts it in his back pocket, then watch him slightly push me apart and move his head forward.

"Adam, you don't have to—"

Suddenly, his tongue is on me, and it makes my eyes roll back. The feeling is something I could only have dreamed of . . . and believe me, I've dreamed of it. My balance is lost for a second but he grips me, holding me up. I move the side of my dress opposite the slit out of his face and stand there with my legs parted. We're placed perfectly in front of the mirror across the hall, and it's the most erotic image I've ever seen. He's kissing me down there the way he would my lips and I don't think I can handle it.

"So good," he says between my legs.

"Let's . . . have sex," I say. It comes out so naïve, but I can't think straight.

He looks up at me, still rubbing the backs of my legs. "You don't like this?"

What? "No, no, I do! I just, I want to make you feel good too."

He pushes his tongue back inside of me. "This is good," he says against my skin.

"But, Adam, I—" *Oh shit.* I lose my balance again and have to hold on to his shoulders. My eyes roll back and I'm certain if we keep this up any longer, I'm going to fall apart. "How are you . . ." The back of my head hits the wall, while one of my hands clutches his hair. ". . . so good at this?" He doesn't stop what he's doing—he's found a rhythm and I'm grinding myself onto him. "Right there," I breathe out, and I don't think I've ever talked this much during any type of sexual act.

"Mhm," he lets out, encouraging my movements.

"God, that feels so good," I moan, and I don't care how desperate I sound. His hands grip my thighs and spread me open a little bit more as his tongue finds its way deeper inside of me.

"How do you taste so good?" His voice is muffled.

"Fuck. Adam," I breathe. "I'm close."

He lets out a growl that vibrates throughout my body and I let ecstasy take over me. My eyes shut and I see nothing but white and feel Adam holding me up as I come undone. I focus on nothing but the pure pleasure throughout my body and trust he won't let me fall. When I finally regain awareness, Adam stands up and wipes his thumb over his mouth.

"Upstairs," he says.

There is nothing I want more than to rip his clothes off right here and now. I would happily have sex in the front foyer, but I nod and lead the way to his room.

There's a chill when we step inside the bedroom, and I rub my arms as he closes the door behind us, as if we could be interrupted. There's a soft light from his lamp and the smell of pine and laundry. As I approach the bed, he takes his suit jacket off and throws it onto a chair but doesn't walk any closer. Instead, he leans against the dresser and removes his cuff links, watching me like a lion watching its prey. I slip my heels off and sit on the foot of his bed, but he still doesn't move.

"Well?" I let out a laugh.

He puts his hands in his pockets and crosses an ankle over, which draws my eyes down to how hard he is.

"If I go over there"—he tips his chin in my direction—"there's no going back, June."

"I know." I swallow. I'm ready. I've *been* ready.

He pushes himself off the dresser and holds a hand out in front of me. I take it and he pulls me up and our lips crash into each other. I fist his shirt and quickly undo each button. There is no subtlety on my end, and I really don't care.

"Easy there," he laughs as I pull off the material and toss it onto the floor. My eyes go wide as I take in the exposed torso in front of me, each muscle prominent.

"Okay, seriously . . . what the hell?" I say. I don't think I'll ever get used to seeing someone as fit as Adam in real life, and I definitely haven't touched anyone as fit. My hands smooth over his biceps and I breathe out. "This isn't fair."

It looks like Adam *can* actually blush. He tries to conceal a smile, but his cheeks tinge a soft pink. I reach for his belt and before I undo it, I place my palm against him, which makes him hiss, "June, fuck."

"Yes, please." I unhook his buckle, stealing another kiss. Before I can pull his pants down, he grabs my wrist and turns me to face away from him, pushing himself against me again, just as we were downstairs.

"Wait." Adam lifts my left arm up and slowly pulls my zipper down, letting my dress fall off me. "I've wanted this . . . for so long. I want to savor it."

I turn around and for the first time in my entire life, I'm naked in front of Adam Harper. This isn't how I pictured it would happen. I would only *sometimes* allow my thoughts to wander here, being with Adam like this. In those fantasies we were much younger, less jaded, and my body would be a result of performing fully choreographed numbers six nights a week. But right now, being in front of him, nothing has felt more right. I'm in my truest form, and the way Adam's throat bobs at the sight of me makes me feel more attractive than I ever have.

"June . . ." His eyes travel across my body, lingering on my breasts. "You're perfect."

He had his face in between my legs just five minutes ago, yet somehow his words make me flush. "Thank you," I say softly.

He sits down on the bed and kisses my stomach. My eyes close as I enjoy the feeling of his hands palming my ass. "So fucking perfect," he says.

I push him farther back onto the bed and slowly crawl toward him, inch by inch. My fingers finally reach his pants and pull them off, revealing black boxer briefs and a substantial bulge leaning to one side. Slowly, I pull the briefs down too so there's nothing in between us. Despite the years of history, I've never seen *all* of Adam, and what's in front of me is perfect. My hands wrap around him and he lets out a pleasurable grunt. I go up and down and give him a kiss. He's warm and smooth, and when my lips meet his tip, I realize this is the first time I've ever enjoyed doing this.

He gently thrusts into it, holding the back of my head, but then pulls me up and sits up against the headboard as I readjust on my knees, straddling him. All I want is to relax myself into Adam, but he keeps us apart for now and starts kissing a trail to a breast, licking underneath and swirling his tongue around my nipple, teasing me. When he puts my breast into his mouth, I liquefy while he begins to slowly suck. It's gentle at first, but then he releases with a wet pop.

I reach my hand behind me, wrapping my fingers around him. "I can't wait, let's—"

"What do you want?" He moves on to my other breast.

"I want you i-inside me," I tell him, but dirty talk is unfamiliar territory, something I've never been good at.

He flips me over so I'm on my back and slowly slips a finger inside of me. I bite my lip and press myself into it. If just his finger feels this good, I can't wait to discover how good the rest of him feels.

"Is that what you want?" he asks gruff and low.

"More," I moan.

He smiles and slips another finger inside—there's no hiding how wet I am. He pumps his fingers and puts his lips back on my nipple, trying to fit more of me into his mouth.

"Adam, I think I'm going to . . ." *Holy shit.*

"If you don't think I'm going to keep making you come until you can't physically handle it, then you're in for a surprise," he says.

"O-Oh my God," I barely get out. His words alone undo

me—I'm falling apart on his hand. I've never had an orgasm twice in one night and all I want is a third.

"Condom," he says, my breast still in his mouth.

"I'm on the pill."

He looks at me. "I haven't been with anyone since . . . I'm clean."

"Me too," I say.

He sucks my nipple one more time and then guides himself inside of me. I squeeze his shoulders and let out an embarrassing moan, "Wait, go slow. I can't—"

He nods. "We'll go slow." It takes a few seconds, but as he keeps pushing himself inside, I feel myself opening up. It's a feeling unlike anything I've ever experienced. It's like his body was designed to fit perfectly into mine. "Jesus," he grunts.

"Fuck, Adam." I let my forehead rest on his. He waits for my okay to start moving and when he does, I wrap my legs around him and dig my nails into his back. More *fuck*s, *oh my God*s, *and Jesus Christ*s come out of both of us. "I-I've wanted this for so long," I say.

"How long?" He pushes deeper inside of me.

"So long," I say, not able to properly form any sentences.

"How long?" He stops, and I know he won't continue until I get specific.

"The beginning," I hear myself admitting.

"Liar," he challenges.

I push him onto his back and straddle him, carefully placing him back inside of me. I squeeze my eyes shut, taking in the new sensation of this position. It all feels too good. I start rolling my hips, wanting to feel everything. "Is this okay?" I breathe.

"You can use me however you want, June."

I feel empowered in a way I haven't felt during sex ever before. I steady myself, planting my hands on Adam's chest, and flip my hair, letting it fall over one of my shoulders. The way I'm moving is honestly surprising, but there's something within me taking over and, based on Adam's groan, he doesn't hate it.

"*Yes, chef,*" I say with a smile.

He raises an eyebrow. "Oh, is that what does it for you?"

"Maybe," I laugh. "All those times I saw you in the kitchen, in that chef's uniform . . . it was like *Magic Mike,* but with food."

"Shut up," he laughs, and slaps my ass.

"I'm serious." I grind against him. "There's something about seeing you in your element . . ."

He grabs my hips and flips me over, and I let out a squeal.

"I'm in my element now," he says, then leans in and nips my ear.

Fuck.

He thrusts against me, harder, and I have to grab the sheets around me.

"Tell me when you wanted me," I say.

"The moment I first saw you," he says, and I moan. "Every time you walked downstairs in sweatpants and a sweatshirt." He pushes in harder. "When you'd wear those yoga pants to rehearsal."

"Adam—"

"When you laughed at background extras in a movie," he says, and I can feel myself coming close again. "Your smell after coming out of the shower."

"I wanted you too." I shut my eyes, surrendering to the pleasure.

"Did you touch yourself thinking of me?"

I feel myself blush but answer anyway. "Yes."

"You know how many nights I thought about going down on you, June?" he asks, and his voice alone is giving me a visceral reaction.

"Adam—" I breathe out. "I'm close."

"Wondering what you tasted like."

"God, Adam—"

"The feeling of your legs around my head—"

"Adam."

I know we're finishing together; I can feel him pulsing in me as my eyes roll back in pure ecstasy. The room is suddenly silent with nothing but the sound of our heavy breathing. He gives me a gentle kiss on the lips and then one on my breast and I swat him away, laughing.

When he collapses beside me, I imagine we look like the end of a sex scene in a movie where the couple is panting and satisfied, except we don't have sheets wrapped around us.

So . . . this is what it's like to have sex with Adam Harper.

Chapter 24

SEPTEMBER, 6 YEARS AGO

AFTER *CHICAGO*, I LAND AN UNDERSTUDY ROLE AS MIMI IN *Rent.* While I figure the chances of actually playing Mimi are slim, I jump at the opportunity because I still get to be in the chorus every show. Then, two months after opening night, Cristina, whom I'm understudying, sprains her ankle and I take over. With four hours' notice before our matinee performance, both Adam and Chloe take the day off work and scalp tickets deep in the balcony. Yes, I do cry when they wait outside by the stage door afterward with a bouquet of flowers.

It all happens so quickly, but Cristina's three-week resting period becomes six and before we know it, she's off the show. I immediately cover for her until there's a solve, but one performance turns into two, then three, and suddenly the *Playbill* is being reprinted with my name in the role of Mimi Márquez.

There's a giant *CONGRATULATIONS* banner over the fireplace in the living room and a cake that I know for a fact is homemade sitting on the kitchen table when I get home.

"Adam?" I call out, taking off my shoes and jacket.

"How was it?" He comes running down the stairs wearing a hoodie and sweatpants. "I tried to get a ticket for tonight, but it was sold out."

My heart almost bursts at the effort he put in, the effort he continues to put in, because those tickets are *not* cheap.

"It was amazing, I still can't believe it. Also . . . you did not have to do all of this!" Eyeing the chocolate cake, I walk toward the table and point to the black line drawn in icing down the middle. "What's that?"

"Oh, that's a stripper pole," he says.

"Oh . . ." I laugh.

"We don't talk enough about how Mimi's a stripper."

Technically an exotic dancer, but I don't correct him. "What would you like to talk about?"

"It's hot." He shrugs a shoulder.

"Didn't know strippers were your thing." I scoop a bit of icing onto my finger and lick it.

"They're not." He walks to the cabinet and pulls out two plates and a knife. "*You* as a stripper . . . well, that's another story."

He cuts a piece of cake and gives me a kiss on the side of my head before cutting one for himself. It's been over a year since Audrey passed away, and neither of us has been on dates with anyone . . . but to say we're dating each other isn't exactly accurate. For the most part, our relationship has always been straightforward. We're roommates, or we're friends. But in the past few years, things haven't felt as black-and-white, and we're now in a foggy gray territory. We're *best* friends. We're best friends who live together. We're best friends who live together who have a suppressed physical attraction . . . but definitely aren't dating.

In all honesty, I don't really care. Things are good between us, we're happy, and there's no reason to have to put a label on anything.

Adam reaches for the remote, and when he asks if I'm too tired to watch something, I lie and say no. Within the first ten minutes I'll be passed out, but the couch and curling up next to him sound too tempting. He turns on an episode of *Cheers,* a favorite of ours, and when the title sequence comes on, I lean into his chest and he puts an arm around me.

"Thanks for the cake," I say.

"I'm sorry I couldn't be there," he says.

"This is better." I close my eyes.

"KNOCK, KNOCK." CHLOE leans against the doorframe of my dressing room. Her reflection stares back at me through the mirror as I put on my makeup.

"Hey, what are you doing here?!" I turn to her.

"I couldn't wait until later to tell you the news." She walks inside and closes the door. I sit up straight, worried because it's not like Chloe to be anything but cool about a situation.

"Are you pregnant?"

"Bitch, please," she scoffs.

"Just checking!" I laugh.

She leans against my dresser in front of me and bites her lip. "I got an associate job at one of my top firms."

"*Chloe!*" I shoot up from my seat and pull her into a hug that is so tight it even starts to hurt me. She reciprocates the embrace and we're holding each other in silence. "Chloe?! Congratulations!"

"Thank you!" she says, and when she pulls away, I see her eyes well up. "I can't believe it. It's just . . . *fuck,* it's been a journey, you know?"

"You deserve this." There's nobody I know more worthy of this next step in their career than Chloe. She's always been that person pulling all-nighters in the library, waking up at 5 A.M. to study, so she can have a social life after school. Chloe makes everything look so effortless, but I know exactly the hard work on her end that goes into it. "What's the law firm?"

She lets go of me.

"It's in Stamford."

"Stamford . . ." I repeat. "Connecticut?"

"The one and only." She gives a half smile. I didn't even know she'd applied to any law firms outside of Manhattan. "But it's only an hour-and-a-half train ride. An hour if you drive!"

"Yeah," I say with a nod. There's no way I'm going to rain on Chloe's parade. With the show and her work schedule, we've barely had any time to see each other anyway, and making the trip up to Connecticut is something fun Adam and I can make time for. A part of me mourns the twenty-minute walk from my place to hers, but this is the best news I could have hoped for her. "The train ride will give me time to read. This is a win-win."

"Okay, good." Her face lightens. "And I will be back down here every weekend."

"This changes nothing," I assure her.

"Promise?" she says.

"Pinky promise." I hug her again. "Chloe, I'm so happy for you."

"God, I love you, June."

"Love you more."

AFTER CHLOE'S CONGRATULATIONS-on-the-job but also goodbye-we'll-miss-you dinner, she, Robby, Adam, and I end up at Marie's Crisis Café. It's a belowground bar deep in the gay West Village. There's a piano at the center where musical theater lovers gather around the keys nightly to sing solo numbers. It's no surprise when we run into some of my castmates from the show. It's dark, dank, lit up by Christmas lights all year round, but sells the most affordable cocktails. We make our way past a group of people singing "I Got Rhythm" by the piano to find a booth in the back.

"Do you have a place to live yet?" Adam asks Chloe.

"Okay, so I have a two-bedroom apartment—*I know.*" She gives us an incredulous look because budget-wise it had been impossible for her to upgrade from her studio apartment in the East Village. "And rent is four hundred dollars less than what I pay now."

"*But* you're in Connecticut," he says.

"I swear, it's actually not that bad!" she says, somewhat convincingly. "It's cleaner, less traffic . . . I don't know, I kind of like it."

"You say that until you're craving a slice of pizza at four in the morning." Robby laughs.

"I don't eat pizza at four in the morning." She rolls her eyes and then takes a handful of nuts. "Did you know they invented the lollipop in Connecticut?"

"Is this your way of trying to convince us to move there?" Adam raises an eyebrow and Chloe throws a nut his way. It lands on his sweater, and he picks it off and eats it with a smug smile.

"Do we have any *Little Shop of Horrors* fans?" the man behind the piano asks into the microphone as he starts playing the opening notes of "Suddenly, Seymour." There are a few whispers at the bar, but nobody volunteers as tribute. "Come on, don't be shy, we need our Audrey!"

"Oh my God, June! GO!" Chloe grabs my arm, pushing me up. "As my going-away gift, please!"

Adam and Robby holler, clapping, and before I know it the group surrounding the piano starts cheering and brings me into the crowd. I am doing this *only* for Chloe.

Singing into a microphone on the opposite side of the piano is a man with green eyes and blond hair. He's wearing a gray T-shirt and I see a display of tattoos on one of his arms. This man looks like he could be a Hemsworth brother. The shorter one, but still. As he continues the opening verse, it's clear he has a decent voice. It's not Broadway material, but he would definitely make it past the first audition round of *American Idol.* The pianist passes me a second mic and when Fake Hemsworth notices I'll be singing the next part, his eyebrows rise into a smile, and he starts singing *to* me.

My lips move closer to the mic, and I turn to him, singing the next verse in my best New York accent. What feels like the entire bar starts cheering. Without having to look, I can *hear* Adam and Robby shouting while I spot Kate and Josh, two castmates from *Rent,* in the back applauding. Fake Hemsworth looks thoroughly impressed with my voice and starts clapping.

The two of us fall into harmony and there's something endearing about the way he's amping up the crowd. He's clearly having a blast, waving his hands around and putting on a dramatic stance when he directs his words to me. At the end of the song, the bar breaks out into more applause and he reaches over and gives me a high five. The moment is over instantly when the pianist begins playing "My Shot" from *Hamilton* and some other singers, already by the piano, start rapping.

Chloe, Robby, and Adam are still seated and whooing. When I walk back over, there are drinks at the table. Adam has his arm propped over the top of the booth and I reach to grab his hand. Our fingers intertwine in a little dance, not fully *holding* hands, but flirting with the idea.

"Aayyyy," Chloe says as she claps.

"I will never get over your voice, June." Robby tips his bottle of beer to me and Adam gives my hand a tight squeeze.

"Thanks, Robby." I smile.

Adam looks up at me. "What do you want to drink?"

I shake my head. "Stay here, I'll get it." My fingers unlock from his and I walk over to the bar. After ordering a vodka soda with lime, I feel someone shuffle in beside me. It's Fake Hemsworth.

"Hey!" He smiles, surprised to see me.

"Hey!" I say. "That was fun."

"You have a killer voice," he says. "You should do this for a living."

"I do." I nod, and he frowns.

"Wait, really?"

"Yeah," I say. "I'm in *Rent* right now."

"No way . . ." His face drops. "Okay, well now I feel like an asshole?"

"What? No! How would you have known?" I laugh.

"Okay, fair." He shrugs. "Let me start over. I'm Liam," he says. Oh, I guess the Hemsworth thing was actually spot-on. "Liam Dawson."

"June," I respond. "June Wood."

"Can I get you a—" He motions to the bartender.

"Oh, thanks." I shake my head. "I already ordered."

He sits down on the stool across from me and props his arm on the bar, making himself comfortable. "So what brings you here tonight?"

"It's my friend's going-away party," I say, and gesture to Chloe and our group.

"Nice. Where is she moving to?" he asks.

"Connecticut."

"I'm sorry." He makes a face.

I snort. "Hey, it's not so bad. Did you know they invented the lollipop?"

"You know, I can't say that I did."

The bartender passes me my drink and I take out a ten, but Liam stops me and hands him a twenty to cover us both.

"You didn't have to do that," I say.

He smiles. "I know, but I think my friends would never let me hear the end of it if I didn't at least try."

"Well, thank you," I say.

"It's my pleasure," he says, nodding.

"So, what brings *you* here tonight?" I ask in an attempt to be a social person and at least wait until he has his drink in hand, since he paid.

"A buddy's birthday." He looks back at the group by the piano, now jumping up and down to "My Shot."

"Fun group." I nod toward them.

"Yeah," he laughs. "Casey's in *Anything Goes* right now; the rest of us are just theater fans."

"I was going to say, I was impressed when you knew all the words to 'Suddenly, Seymour,' *and* the harmony."

He laughs. "That's only because I dabbled in musical theater in my youth."

Working in my field and living in New York, I've heard this before.

"What do you do now?" I ask.

The bartender passes Liam a pint of Guinness and he takes a quick sip. "I'm an actor too."

"Oh wow," I say. It's not actually hard to believe, considering how objectively attractive he is. "Are you in anything I might have seen?"

"Have you watched *Warriors*?" he asks.

"Uhh . . ." I don't tell him I haven't even *heard* of *Warriors.*

"That's okay if you haven't. But I'm on that show."

Oh, interesting. He's a TV actor.

"Well, I will be sure to add it to my watch list," I say. "Do they film in the city?"

"LA—but I'm here all the time," he quickly adds, and it feels intentional, like he wants me to know whatever this conversation is isn't necessarily short-term. "June, would I be able to ask for your number?"

Oh. You know, I hear about things like this happening with my friends, but having a cute guy at the bar ask for my number is not an average day for me.

"I—"

"You know what, I'm sorry," he says. "You probably have a boyfriend and I'm putting you in a really awkward situation. I'm just going to—"

"No, no, I don't have a boyfriend." I shake my head because, well, *I don't.*

"Thank God," he breathes out, putting a hand over his chest.

"Well, I *technically* don't have a boyfriend . . . I—" Over my shoulder, Adam and Chloe are laughing at something Robby's saying. There's nothing wrong with going on a date. Adam and I are not together. But then why do I feel like I'm betraying him somehow?

One of Liam's friends calls him over, saying they're going to request another *Hamilton* song.

"Hey, you know what. It's all good." Liam taps the bar and takes his beer. "It was really nice to meet you, June."

He's a nice guy and there really is no harm in continuing this conversation with this interesting, attractive man who wants to get to know me.

"Um, wait—" I say, knowing very well this is an impulsive act. "Let me give you my number."

"Okay, cool." Liam passes me his phone and I type it in. "I'll talk to you soon, June." He smiles, and then heads back to his group. I stay frozen at the bar, afraid to turn around, because all I can think about is if Adam saw any of that interaction.

Chapter 25

19 DAYS UNTIL THE MEETING

THE SUN HITS MY FACE, WAKING ME UP. INSTEAD OF THE DAZzling display of crimson leaves outside my window, I see a broad, bare back, wide shoulders, and a head of dark hair.

I haven't had this dream in *years,* except this isn't a dream. I'm in Adam's room and it's dawning on me that we really did have sex last night.

Sex is putting it lightly. It's like I've had a sexual awakening and all I want to do is see how many times I can orgasm, and how many ways I can make Adam breathe out my name. My eyes blissfully shut, thinking of last night. I didn't know it was possible—to make passionate love and at the same time have filthy, rough, erotic sex.

You would think something that's been building up for over a decade would cause some sort of shift in the universe, or even . . . be a letdown, but everything feels right. Seeing Adam peacefully inhaling and exhaling in front of me brings a smile to my face. Things are starting to make sense.

As I lean in to give Adam a kiss on the shoulder, he lets out a sleepy exhale.

"Mmm."

"Sorry, I didn't mean to wake you," I say with my lips against his skin.

"Never say sorry." He turns over to face me with his eyes still closed. I take in the small display of details in sunlight; every crease, the fullness of his lips, the way some of his hairs reflect into an almost auburn hue. He pulls me in closer, giving me a bear hug, and I get lost in his arms, not wanting to be found. "How'd you sleep?" He yawns.

"Never better," I say. For obvious reasons, I slept like a baby last night. "You?"

"You really tired me out," he says.

I laugh and then cuddle closer to him. "I can't believe we really did that . . ."

"You're telling me." Adam's body vibrates with a chuckle against me.

"Was it everything you imagined it would be?" I tease.

His body shifts and he looks down at me. "Better." He gives me a kiss.

I pull out of his embrace and slightly adjust. He's lying on his back, and as I throw one of my legs on top of him, the skin-on-skin contact reminds me that aside from the New York Rangers shirt of Adam's I'm wearing, we are both completely naked. My hands run over his chest and down his abs, and I scoot myself lower and lower until I'm sitting in between his knees and my hands are on an overwhelming display of morning wood. I feel like I'm seeing the world through new eyes, like the past five years were in black-and-white and now I'm finally seeing in color. I feel *alive,* and I want nothing more than to show Adam just *how* alive.

He hisses as I start to move both of my hands and lean down to give him a slow kiss.

"June." His head rolls back as I move my tongue from the base to the tip. When I put what I can of him in my mouth, he catches my arm. "Not yet."

"You don't want this?" I frown.

"Oh no, I want it." Adam groans, then sits up. "But let me cook you breakfast."

He gives me a kiss and lays me down on my stomach, gently massaging my shoulders. His hands move down to my back and I close my eyes, embracing this feeling. He takes a pillow and places it underneath my stomach and spreads my legs open a little bit, positioning his head in between them.

"Wait, what are you doing?" I look over my shoulder.

"I'm having *my* breakfast first."

IT TAKES A good forty-five minutes until we both take a shower, which takes another thirty. Somehow, we finally manage to get dressed. Adam's making shrimp tacos for us before heading to work while I sit at the kitchen island doing a *New York Times* crossword puzzle, and everything feels . . . easy. Like this is how it always should have been.

"What time is Chloe coming over?" Adam asks over his shoulder.

"One," I say, looking at the clock, which reads 12:46 P.M. We've been planning our famous Chloe and June Day, which entails doing nothing but watching movies, eating junk food, and pretending we have no responsibilities. My gaze falls to Adam chopping cilantro. While studying his precision, my stomach begins to tighten. "I was thinking . . . we don't need to tell her, do we?"

"Tell her . . . ?" he asks, still chopping.

"You know, that we slept together."

"I mean, I don't think we need to say *surprise, we had sex* the minute she walks through the door, no."

"*Adam,*" I laugh against my will. "Seriously."

"Do you *want* to tell her?" he asks.

"I don't know." I shrug. "But it's Chloe. She's going to find out eventually."

"Will she?" He walks over and places two fresh shrimp tacos with mango salsa in front of me.

"You know Chloe, she's perceptive . . . She's a lawyer." I take a bite, not waiting for it to cool down, because, well, a night full of sex builds up your appetite. "Oh my God," I say through a mouthful of spicy crema and slaw. "I just mean, we haven't had a chance to talk about this." I motion to the space between us. "And I'd rather figure out what this is first."

Not only are we sleeping together, but we now co-own a house. And while this is a better time than any, I still don't feel ready to share the news about *Les Misérables* until I know what exactly that means for us.

"Okay," he says, nodding. "Let's figure it out."

"What?" My eyes widen. "*Now?*"

"Yeah," he says, like it's that easy.

"We can't talk about this now," I say, and it comes out more nervous than I'd like. "She'll be here any minute."

He looks at the clock above the stove and squints. "Twelve minutes, actually, and knowing Chloe, probably sixteen."

He's not joking. He is very much ready to have this conversation. Figuring out what the hell a decade of built-up sexual tension with my best friend and a night of steamy lovemaking now means isn't something I was anticipating talking about before one in the afternoon.

"Okay . . ." My voice wobbles. "So . . . what are we doing?"

"Well." He leans back on the counter and rolls up his sleeves.

"I'm sorry." I shake my head. "Why do you always do that?"

"Do what?" he asks.

"Lean," I say.

"*Lean*?" he repeats.

"Yeah, you're always leaning on things, and it's hard to think because you look like you're posing for some fucking *GQ* article or something."

"Okay, I'm sorry. I'll stop leaning." He pushes himself off the counter and plants his forearms on the island between us. "Is that better?"

"You're still technically leaning, just forward now—"

"June," he warns.

"Sorry." I reach over and hold his hand.

He brings my hand to his lips and kisses my knuckle and gently places it back down. "Okay, let's talk."

Is there a world where Adam and I can *casually* be together these next couple of weeks? Is it possible to sign the papers, shake hands, and continue on with our lives? There are no excuses anymore. In my core, I know it's always been Adam. After last night, it always *will* be Adam. We have a connection that's lasted through many chapters of our lives, and if he's not my happily ever after, he's undoubtedly the one who will get away. But . . . does *he* feel the same way? That's an answer I'm afraid to find out.

As if on cue, the doorbell rings, and I jump off the barstool.

"That's Chloe," I say.

Adam smiles. "Saved by the bell."

Gripping my oversized cardigan, I run over to the front door and open it to Chloe, standing there with a pink box in her hand.

My eyes widen. "Are those from Moe's?!"

"I figured it's been a while since you've had these," she says.

"I love you." An assortment of twelve different doughnuts that smell unlike anything I ever had in Los Angeles looks back up at me as I open the box.

"I know." She takes off her shoes and throws her coat in the closet. "Is Adam here?"

"In the kitchen." I follow her.

"Chloe." Adam nods when she enters, and passes her a plate.

"See, Harper, this is why I miss you," she pouts. "I know I'll always be fed."

"I got you," he says with a wink.

I take a seat on the barstool and go back to my half-eaten taco. "Where's Lucia?"

"At work." Chloe takes a hearty bite of her taco. "But she wants me to tell you she is very jealous of Chloe and June Day."

"Chlo, how are things at work?" Adam asks, choosing to eat while standing.

"Brutal," she sighs. "There's this ongoing case I'm working on about this piece-of-shit religious couple that's been running a satanic cult."

"Fuck—"

"And it turns out the husband actually met his wife in high school, when *he* was a teacher. It just keeps getting worse," Chloe says. "But my clients are two of the girls who were inducted as teens. They've been with them for fifteen years."

Surprisingly, this is one of the lighter of Chloe's cases that I've heard about through the years.

"I don't know how you deal with this every day," I say.

"There's a deep satisfaction you get when putting horrible humans behind bars," she says with a smile. "Couldn't imagine doing anything else."

"Speaking of work . . ." Adam wipes his hands on one of the towels. "I'll let you two have your unproductive day of watching movies and eating refined sugar."

"Let us have this, Harper," Chloe says through a mouthful of shrimp. "How many parents with toddlers and full-time jobs get to watch double features?"

"I'm just jealous I can't join you," he says, then pops a tortilla chip into his mouth and looks over at me. His gaze lingers for a moment longer than usual, and it makes my heart thrum. "Okay, I'm off. I'll see you tonight." He winks.

Adam has been coming home every night, just as he's done for years before that, but now it's different. Now he's not just coming home. He's coming home to *me.*

I smile, tucking my hair behind my ear. "See you tonight."

Chloe looks at me, suspicion written all over her face. "What was that?"

I freeze, my eyes going big. "What was what?"

"*That*," she says, gesturing. "The look you just gave each other."

My eyes quickly flash to Adam in panic. "What are you talking about?" I turn to Chloe, shaking my head. Is this technically gaslighting?

"I know flirting when I see it." She squints as if she's being challenged.

"Flirting?" I scoff.

"Did something happen between y'all?" Chloe's eyes widen, darting back and forth between the two of us.

It would be great if Adam could help me here, but he's once again leaning and playing it very cool.

"No . . ." I say, knowing I could probably do a better job at being convincing.

"Holy. Fucking. Shit. Something *did* happen! I knew it!" Chloe points at me. "The sexual tension is off the charts."

"Off the charts?!" I laugh. "You're insane."

Okay, *now* this is technically gaslighting.

"Harper?" Chloe shifts her focus to Adam, who's frustratingly calm.

He shrugs. "I'm always flirty."

"Since when?! Y'all better tell me the truth, because if anyone deserves to know, it's *me*."

If I deny her claims right now, there's no coming back from this conversation. Avoiding is different from lying and I could never outright lie to Chloe.

"Fine," I groan, and turn to Adam, who slightly tips his head, showing that I have his blessing. "Something *may* have happened between us. But can we all move past it since we're adults?"

"*OH MY GOD*!" Chloe squeals, and bangs her hand on the kitchen island.

"At least I *thought* we were adults," I say, sighing.

"I knew it!" Chloe claps, way too excited about this. "The two of you keep staring at each other, and more than usual."

"I do not stare at Adam," I scoff.

"He stares at you," she says, raising an eyebrow.

Adam's still leaning against the counter, and merely shrugs.

I bring my hands together in a praying motion. "Okay, well, this was fun, let's just forget about—"

"No, wait, I have questions," Chloe says, wide-eyed. "When did it happen?"

This conversation simply cannot be happening right now. I crack my knuckles and Adam still continues to say *nothing*, which is his way of showing me that he will go along with whatever I want.

"Chlo . . ."

"Oh, *now* you two are being secretive, but when both of you got food poisoning on Fourth of July, you had no issue with me cleaning up your—"

"Okay, fine!" I sit up straight in disbelief that we are openly talking about this. "It happened last night."

"*Last night*?!" she repeats. "What does this mean? Are you two together?"

"We haven't talked about it yet," I say, looking at Adam.

She's nodding, and it's like I can see the wheels in her head spinning. Chloe's trying her best to keep quiet, but I know the minute we're alone I'm going to get harassed with questions.

"I respect that. But I'm not going to lie: I'm offended that the two of you were going to keep this from me."

"I was *eventually* going to tell you." I roll my eyes.

Adam lets out an uncomfortable cough and then pushes

himself off the counter. "All right, well, I'm going to head out," he says, and I internally panic as he walks toward me instead of the front door. "Have a good day." He gives me a soft kiss on the top of my head.

"You too." I blush, embarrassed by the public display of affection, but even more embarrassed by how much I love it.

"I ship it." Chloe takes a bite of her taco and is met with an eye roll from Adam before he leaves the kitchen. "That means I want y'all to be together."

"I know what it means." I shoot her an unimpressed look.

We both wait for the door to close, and once we hear the confirmation that Adam's gone, Chloe gives me a smug smile.

"What?" I ask, really not wanting to know.

"Don't *what* me, bitch. June Wood, you know damn well I've wanted you two to be together since day one. This is my good karma."

"Adam and I sleeping together is *your* good karma?" I say. "For what?"

"For all the assholes I dated. For living in Connecticut. For that time I worked overtime when Beyoncé had that surprise concert in Times Square."

I raise an eyebrow. "I thought you loved Connecticut."

"How did it happen?" she asks, changing the subject.

"I don't know." I shrug. "It just . . . happened."

"His penis just happened to go inside your vagina?" she asks.

"Yes," I say, nodding. "Exactly."

"This is huge, June," she says. "All the stars are aligning for you two to be together."

"Chloe . . ."

"I'm serious." She readjusts herself on the barstool and pulls herself a little closer to me. "Years have passed and here you both are, single, living in the same house again, which you now *own,* I might add. You both have your shit together and are clearly obsessed with one another. What's the problem?"

"Because it's not that simple." I sigh. "You weren't here; you don't get it."

"Okay, then tell me," she says, exasperated.

"Adam and I can't just *pick up* from where we left off," I say.

"June." Chloe frowns, her tone now completely serious. "What happened between you two?"

Chapter 26

NOVEMBER, 6 YEARS AGO

FOR THE PAST TWO YEARS, ADAM AND I HAVE ALWAYS GONE back to Long Island to celebrate his dad's birthday. Although Ford and I haven't bonded the same way Audrey and I did, we still have a special relationship that I'm very grateful for.

After we pick up the rental car, Adam clears his throat just as we get on the highway. "Robby's been talking about pulling together some people to open up their own restaurant."

"Oh . . . wow," I say, surprised at the idea and not entirely knowing what that would mean. Opening up a restaurant feels like one of those things you *hear* about people doing, but who actually knows anyone who's done it themselves? Adam's focus was always on what place in the city was hiring, what was the next position he could move up to. This is an entirely different conversation that I don't even think he's ever entertained. "Are you one of those people?"

"He brought it up to me, but I don't know . . ." He sighs. "It's a whole other side of the business I don't really know anything about."

"But you're thinking about it," I say, sensing his tone. When you spend every day with someone for as long as Adam and I have, it doesn't take much effort to read between the lines.

"I am," he says, and taps the steering wheel. "He wants to introduce me to a few investors, just to learn more and ask some questions."

"You should do it!" I shift in my seat to face him.

"Yeah?" he says.

"Yeah!" I encourage him. "I mean, it doesn't hurt to learn more. And regardless, even if nothing comes out of it, I'm sure knowing the ins and outs of the business can *always* help you in the long run."

A sincere smile takes over Adam's face and then he grabs my hand, giving it a gentle squeeze. "Okay, I'll do it."

"Can you imagine if you owned your own restaurant?" I throw my head back onto the seat. "That would be . . ."

"Fucking nuts?" he says.

"Fucking nuts!" I laugh. "What kind of restaurant would you open if you could?" I ask. It's actually something we haven't talked about, and I don't know the answer.

"I don't know." He shrugs. "I've always thought it would be cool to have a little hole-in-the-wall in Brooklyn or the East Village, something that only locals ever go to." He pauses for a moment, like he's about to say something he's never said out loud. "But it would be pretty crazy to have one of those places we could only dream of affording to eat at."

The concept feels strange. Talking about owning or investing in restaurants is something that adults do, and on some level, I still feel like Adam and I are kids and fresh out of school.

"You should go for the dream," I say.

"JUNE!" SARAH RUNS past Adam and almost knocks me off my feet with a hug. Her dark hair now cut to her shoulders with blunt bangs sweeping over her face makes her look five years older than she is. "Thank God you didn't have a show today. I feel like it's been years," she says.

"Yeah, if you didn't come, I don't think I'd be invited." Adam pinches my side.

"Have you gotten taller?!" I hold Sarah at arm's length and look at her from head to toe. She's got a good four inches on me. Although it's not a surprise considering the Harpers are all at least six feet. "It's only been like four months."

She shrugs. "Maybe you're getting shorter?"

"How much shorter can she get?" Adam says.

"I hate you both," I say, rolling my eyes.

"There they are!" Ford comes down the stairs, and it doesn't go unnoticed that he wraps his arms around me first, so I playfully stick my tongue out at Adam. "How are you, kiddo?"

"I'm good, I'm good!" I hand him a small gift bag. "Happy birthday!"

"Oh my—" He looks at Adam. "Did you put her up to this?"

"I had nothing to do with this." Adam puts his hands up. "And happy birthday, Dad," he says, and gives him a hug.

"June, how's the show going? You know, I was telling Ad I want to watch it again."

"You mean you tell me every other day." Adam takes off his jacket.

"It's great!" I say. "But not much has changed since the first time."

"You know, I didn't realize how much I love the theater," Ford says. "The singing, the dancing, the night out on the town. Sarah will be my date."

"What if I want to bring an *actual* date?" she says, and Adam shoots her the typical older-brother look. "What? I'm almost eighteen."

"No dating until you're at least twenty-five," he says, and she rolls her eyes.

"Ford, I think you're going to like your birthday present," I say.

He opens the gift bag and pulls out a red velvet box, inside of which are two black cuff links with gold trim and engraved music notes.

"This is . . ." The look on his face makes my heart burst. "You two, this is too much."

"Not at all," I say, shaking my head. "Now you have something to wear every time you come into the city."

"There's more." Adam nods toward the envelope inside the bag.

Ford sets the contents on the side table and opens the card, pulling out two vouchers. "What's this?"

"Two season packages for this year." I beam. "You get to see seven shows and bring any guest you want with you."

"Oh my . . ." he says, looking at the two vouchers in awe. "Thank you."

"It was all June," Adam says. "She got them months ago—I had to practically force her to wait to give them to you."

Ford gives me a big hug and whispers in my ear, "She would have loved this."

"I know," I whisper back.

Adam takes the keys to Ford's truck and says he'll be back in twenty minutes with the food, but I know he's also picking up a cake from Dortoni, the best bakery on Long Island. Sarah gets a call from someone she claims is a girlfriend, but I see the name *Justin* on her screen as she heads up to her room.

Ford and I end up sitting on the couch watching reruns of *Seinfeld,* and during commercial breaks, my eyes wander to the rest of the house. Everything looks exactly as it did the first moment I stepped inside. Not a picture has been moved from the walls, and while flowers have been swapped out through the years, the vases always keep their same spot on the tables.

When the episode ends, Ford walks over to the kitchen and comes back holding his laptop, with his glasses sitting on the tip of his nose. He asks if I can connect his Netflix account, which really means just signing in.

"Thanks, June, you know I know nothing about all of this." He falls onto the couch as if he's been running a marathon and passes me the laptop.

"Why didn't you ask Sarah?" I ask, pulling up his account.

"It's always a big deal for her. You know kids."

Maybe it's because I grew up without a father, or because Ford is one of my favorite people, but I never understood that sentiment. After logging in to Ford's account, bookmarking it, and clicking remember password, I hand the laptop back to him.

"There, all done," I say.

He adjusts his glasses. "I'll never understand any of this."

"And you'll never have to," I say. "That's what I'm here for."

"I'll also never understand why you and Adam aren't together." He looks at me.

I let out a little laugh under my breath. "Ford."

He's joked before about the idea of Adam and me dating, and it was always met with an eye roll on our end. The only difference now is that Adam isn't here, and it doesn't feel like Ford's joking.

"Just explain it to me again," he asks, like he's trying to understand a math problem.

I shake my head. "I don't think Adam would want me to—"

"Adam's not here." He waves a hand. "Think of it as my birthday gift."

"I already got you a birthday gift." I raise my eyebrow.

"Come on, and don't feel like you have to be nice just because I'm his dad. You're just as much family."

I smile, because hearing that is something I'll never take for granted. Maybe knowing I have a family now makes everything more complicated. "I don't know, Ford. Things are pretty good between Adam and me the way they are. Why ruin it?" I say, because it's the truth. Adam and I are *great* together, and neither one of us has plans of leaving, so why fix something that isn't broken?

"What would be ruined?" he asks.

"Adam's my best friend, there's so much history there . . ." I tuck a piece of hair behind my ear. "What if we broke up or something? I wouldn't want to lose that. *Or* you and Sarah."

He nods, processing what I'm saying. "Can I give you some unsolicited advice?"

"Always," I say with a smile.

"You're going to lose it either way." He looks at me with intent, and my skin prickles as if I'm full of tiny balloons that are being popped. "Either you or he is going to find someone else," he says like he's reading it from a crystal ball. "You'll go your separate ways, naturally, and you'll lose it. *Or* you both take a chance on this, you break up, and you lose it."

"Those don't sound like great options." I let out a breathless laugh.

"Option three is it works out and you get something so much better. All I'm saying is life is short." He places his hand over mine, and my throat begins to swell. "There's no way to preserve anything forever. Trust me, I know. You win, you lose . . . but you can't do either unless you take a chance."

MONDAY IS ONE of my favorite days of the week because we don't have any shows. It's the best time to do errands, make any doctor appointments, and relax at home while the rest of the world starts their nine-to-fives.

As I'm walking down Bleecker with a tote bag full of groceries, my phone starts ringing, and I dig to the bottom of my purse to see a 323 number I don't recall having saved.

"Hello?" I answer, anticipating a telemarketer on the other end.

"Hey, June?" the voice says back to me.

"Hi." I frown. "Yes . . . Sorry, who is this?"

"It's Liam, from Marie's Crisis Café."

I'm caught off guard, for two reasons. One being that it's

been two months since I gave him my number, and the second being that he's calling instead of texting.

"Oh, hey!" I stop walking, not really sure what to say. "How are you?"

"I've been good! I'm sorry it took me so long to reach out—I had some things come up—but I'll be back in the city this weekend. I was wondering if you wanted to grab some food?"

Liam's asking me to hang out is perfectly normal behavior considering I gave him my number. I'm conflicted, because while there's a tiny part of me that's intrigued by the idea of going out with someone who's interested in me, there's only one thing I can think of, and it's dark-haired, is six-foot-three, and can whip up a lasagna that makes me go weak in the knees.

"Um, you know . . . I would really love to, but the show is just crazy this week. I don't know if I'll have the time," I say.

"Oh, yeah, of course, that makes sense," he says. "I mean, I deserve that for taking this long to reach out. I'm sorry again, June."

"Oh no, please don't apologize, it's not your fault," I say, because he really didn't do anything wrong. My reason for saying no has nothing to do with *him*.

"Well, I'm there from Thursday to Sunday night, so if anything changes just let me know. I really enjoyed chatting with you."

"I did too." My voice goes higher than it needs to. "I'll for sure let you know if anything changes!"

"All right, have a good one, June."

"You too." I hang up with an unsettling feeling brewing within me.

The rest of the day I have trouble focusing on anything.

There's a feeling of guilt I can't shake. I don't know if I feel guilty that I turned down a date or guilty that I even had a date to turn down to begin with. The only thing I know is that there is absolutely zero reason why I should feel bad about Liam asking me out . . . right?

For the remainder of the evening, I end up waiting in the living room until Adam comes home. I feel like a parent waiting for their kid to come back from a party. Attempting to read a book is no use since I manage to get through only two pages in the span of three hours. When I hear the sound of the door unlocking, I shoot up from the couch, my hands immediately clammy.

"Hey, how was your day?" Adam throws his keys onto the side table.

"What do you mean?" I ask, and it comes out all breathy and defensive.

"What?" He frowns.

I shake my head, trying to calm myself. "Um, it was fine. Yours?"

"Work was madness." He walks over to the kitchen and pours himself a glass of water. "But we won."

"Oh, nice," I say, forgetting Mondays are his basketball nights.

"Maybe we can watch a movie tonight? Take it easy?" he says after chugging his water and using the back of his palm to wipe his mouth.

"Sure," I say, seated and staring ahead.

"Everything okay?" Adam makes his way toward the couch, taking a seat beside me. He smells clean, and the back of his hair is a little damp from the postgame shower. He moves his hand to hold mine and I take a sharp breath in. I don't remember the last time we touched, but it calms me. As I move my fingers to interlock with his, he pulls my hand up to his mouth and gives it a kiss.

My breathing slows down, and I look at him. "I missed you today," I say like it's a confession.

"I missed you too," he reciprocates, but his brow furrows. "What's going on?"

He's rubbing my knuckles with his thumb, and I inch a little closer so that our knees are touching. My gaze stays fixed on our hands, afraid to look up at him, scared to see what his eyes are revealing. His breaths deepen and I rest my forehead on his. His smell is intoxicating, something I could get drunk off of. There's an impulse in me I want to give in to. My hand moves to gently squeeze his forearm over his sweater, while he moves his to my thigh, and my breath hitches. This is new for us. We don't do this, yet nothing about it feels like we should stop. My heart begins to beat faster, louder; I can practically feel my pulse throughout my entire body. I'm almost embarrassed by the effect a sheer hand placement has on me.

Adam's touch slides up a little farther and then stops. I nod, giving him permission to explore my body. When his fingers trace the curve of my hip, I squeeze his biceps, letting out a slight whimper. Pushing him back onto the couch, I lift my leg up to straddle him and then suddenly both of Adam's hands are on my ass. This is new territory, on so many levels, and based on his firm grip he's enjoying this as much as I am.

As I remove my cardigan, exposing my tank top, he takes a deep breath in and hardens beneath me. I run my fingers through his hair and throw my head back in pleasure as he kisses my neck, careful not to touch my lips.

"June," he breathes against my skin.

"Kiss me," I order as I roll my hips into his. He groans and his lips crash into mine and it's everything I could ever have wanted, years of built-up tension finally leading to this moment. My tongue swirls in his mouth and neither of us stops for air. It's like we've been deprived of physical touch for years. Adam's fingers continue to dig into my hips, and I push my breasts into his chest. His hands move up my torso and cup one of my boobs and I let out an embarrassingly loud moan when he squeezes. He sucks on my earlobe and swipes his tongue over my ear, a move that I didn't know until this moment could undo me.

I reach for the button on his pants and undo it and he unhooks my bra from underneath my tank top and tosses it onto the floor, a skill that I assume must have taken practice, but it turns me on regardless.

"Is this what you want?" Adam breaks apart for a moment and I nod, kissing him deeper. I move my hand to squeeze him over his briefs. He shuts his eyes and rolls his head back. *"Fuck."*

"Yes, please." I kiss his neck.

"June." He pulls away, the look on his face bringing me back down to earth. "*Do you want this*?" he repeats, eyes darting back and forth to mine. "Because if we're doing this, there's no going back."

Hearing the question feels like someone cut my air supply from an oxygen tank. What is he really asking me? If I want to continue what we're doing right here, right now, or if I want the shift in our friendship that may result once we're done?

I've had so long to think about this. It's a question that's been looming over me for years before I even realized it. But right now, with Adam's hands on my body and knowing he might be there to catch me no matter what my answer is . . . I'm scared. I think of my conversation with Ford, and I worry that everything I know is slipping through my fingers before it's happened. What if years of history go down the drain for one night of giving in to my urges? What if I lose Adam?

"I . . ." I start, feeling overwhelmed. "I—I don't know."

His demeanor changes, as if he's been punched in the gut. "You don't know?" he asks, his body going limp. My lips are swollen, our clothes are a mess, he's still hard, and I don't know what's happening. "Is this something you're doing to just get it out of your system? Because I know what I want, June, and it's not to just have sex."

"No, of course not," I say defensively.

"Then what are we doing? Because the minute this happens, we're not going back to just being roommates. You don't come back from something like that."

"You don't think I know that?" I say, offended. "Adam, why do we have to talk about this right now? Why can't we just—"

"We can't *not* talk about this," he says.

"Adam, I don't want to ruin our friendship." I motion to what little space is between us.

"That's bullshit," he says under his breath.

"Excuse me?"

"That's bullshit, and you know it is." He adjusts our bodies so we're now sitting beside each other. "We fall asleep on the couch watching movies, we go grocery shopping together, you spend Christmas with my family . . ." He runs a hand through his hair, defeated. "You don't think it fucks with me when people ask *are you and June together? Why aren't you and June together?* And I have to say *you know . . . I don't know.*" His hand falls heavily onto his thigh.

His candidness is catching me off guard. In all the years we've known each other, he's never brought this up, and now he's throwing it back at me as if we've been going around in circles.

"Where is this coming from?"

"I've felt like this for a long time," he says. "I guess I just never said anything, because it was so clear where we were heading . . . But now, I don't know. I don't know what we're doing or what we are."

"We're best friends, Adam," I say, but after hearing it, I'm not really sure it means anything anymore.

He shakes his head like he's tired of hearing it.

"Don't tell me we're *friends,*" he throws the word back at me, and I can admit it doesn't feel great. "We crossed that line years ago. Five minutes ago, we were holding hands, making out, saying how much we missed each other." He wipes a palm over his face and takes a breath. "June, I don't have the desire to even look at another woman."

His words feel like arrows as I think about earlier today. Ever since I met Adam, I haven't wanted anyone else. It's a feeling I never really understood. I've never felt as safe or protected as I do when I'm with Adam. He's all I could ever ask for, and he's far more than I deserve. The life we built together, that bond of trust that takes years to form, and a place in his family that means more to me than anything.

I feel sick not only that I gave my number to someone else, but that I wanted to. I don't know why I did it. In a hundred lifetimes I would choose Adam over anyone else, but there's a tiny itch in my brain, an itch of curiosity that I wanted to scratch. An anchor of guilt pulls at me, getting heavier, and heavier, until I can't breathe, and the pressure suddenly feels like too much. I have to tell Adam. He deserves to know.

"I met someone," I whisper.

He shifts.

"You *met someone*?"

"Not recently—"

"The guy at the bar?" he asks. I didn't realize he had noticed, but I brush past it.

"His name is Liam and he's an actor too," I say, stating the only things I know about him. "But he called me today asking if we could go out this week—"

"That night was two months ago," he says like he's retracing his steps.

"I said no," I clarify, so he knows. "Even though he's a nice guy and we got along, I still said no," I press, hoping that he understands where I'm coming from. "Because of you," I say, my voice trembling.

I lift the side of my hand to wipe the tears pooling in the corner of my eye. There's tension in his jaw and a look on his face I can't read. I know every look of Adam's—the tired ones, the happy ones, the sad ones—but I can't read him right now.

"Hey, hey." Adam lifts a palm to my face and uses his thumb to wipe another tear. "Why are you crying?" he asks softly.

"I just feel guilty . . . I don't know why." I sniff.

"June, I don't want you to ever feel bad about anything because of me." I nod, but another tear falls, then another. Adam looks down and I can see his chest rise with a deep breath. "Did you want to say yes?"

The question throws me off. I don't want to tell him an answer I don't even know myself. I swallow, choosing my words carefully, but my silence is a loud enough response. His face drops, and I swear I can feel a chill come in between us.

Adam cracks a faint smile that's anything but happy. "I wouldn't want to get in the way of you sharing something special with someone."

"Adam," I say helplessly. "I thought about it, okay? Is that so wrong?" I tell him the truth, because I don't know how to be anything but honest with him.

"If there's a part of you that's curious, June, you owe it to yourself to see."

"That's not fair," I sniff, swiveling my body to face him. "We've never talked about this, and now you're blaming me for something that happened two months ago?"

"I'm not—" Adam runs a hand through his hair in frustration. "I'm not blaming you, June. I would never. But unless you can tell me that you're all in, then I don't want us to happen like this—" He gestures his hands to nothing in particular. "As a result of some heated argument? Our story deserves better than that."

"Adam . . ." My heart breaks into a million pieces because he's right, we do deserve better than that. Adam was raised on love—he's not afraid of it. I don't know how to be like that. "It's not . . . it's not that easy." My words come out broken.

"It *is* that easy." His voice softens, and when he stands up, I let go of his arm. I listen to the sound of his weight walking up the stairs and I sit still until I hear his bedroom door close.

Chapter 27

JANUARY, 5 YEARS AGO

EIGHT PERFORMANCES A WEEK ON BROADWAY WITHOUT TAKing any sick days is bound to catch up with you, especially in the winter. When I feel slightly under the weather, my director insists I take time off and let my understudy, Becca, fill in for the next two shows. Becca's never done a show as Mimi and missing *any* performance feels like failure on my part, but I swallow my pride and take the sick days.

"Why don't you heat up a can of soup?" Liam's voice echoes through my phone speaker while I forage the kitchen cabinets.

It's been almost three weeks since Adam and I had a real conversation. I would normally say it's just because work is busy for both of us, but there's no denying our lack of conversation, or *lack of trying to make conversation* when we're both home. Nights that would normally consist of us watching a movie on the couch have turned into him going out with Robby or me reading a book in my bedroom.

I wouldn't say Liam and I are *dating*, but I did end up going out with him when he came to the city. He took me to a Korean spot in Park Slope, and we've been in contact ever since. I don't see any future for the two of us, living on opposite ends of the country as we do, but right now, with Chloe focusing on work, it's nice to have someone to talk to.

"I'd much prefer a cheeseburger and fries," I say.

"Soup is good for you. Have the soup," he says.

There's a lonely can of some sort of chunky chicken noodle, and I guess it will do.

"Ugh, fine." I switch the stove on and pour the contents into a small pot. It takes all of five minutes before I have my dinner in a bowl.

"So, what do you have planned for tonight?" Liam asks.

"On the couch, watching *Sleepless in Seattle.* What about you?" I stick my tongue out to the spoon like a cat and taste the soup. It tastes like . . . canned soup.

"Still on set—it's probably going to be a late night," he says. Since our first date, I've watched a few episodes of *Warriors.* It's a period piece that has its own cult following, and is about, you guessed it, warriors. Liam plays the younger brother of the main character, and I've learned that he himself has a little group of fangirls online. "I actually should get back."

I pick my phone off the counter and take Liam off speaker. "Sounds good. Talk soon."

"Enjoy the movie," he says.

"If this medicine kicks in, I should be asleep in the next hour."

"Okay, I'll text you," he says. "Bye."

"Bye." I pull a blanket over myself, realizing I haven't had a night in alone in a while.

The soup is as good as canned soup can be. The chicken is very . . . chunky and very much tastes like not-real chicken. This is why you should always trust your gut and order the burger and fries. I push the bowl away from me and choose to starve.

Just as Tom Hanks' son is persuading him to go to Seattle, the front door opens behind me, and I hear Adam's voice. "You can wait here. I'll be a second."

I pause the movie and turn around to see Adam and, waiting at the door, a woman with long blond hair curled perfectly at the ends wearing a tight black turtleneck and jeans. The sight is a little jarring. The last time I saw Adam with another girl must have been well before his mom got sick.

"Oh, June . . ." he says, clearly not expecting me to be home.

Instinctively, I smooth over my stained sweatshirt and hair, which I currently wish wasn't in a very messy bun.

"Hey."

"Uh, Riley," Adam says, and I guess the blonde's name is Riley. "This is June." Adam gestures to me. "My roommate."

The word hits me like a punch to the gut. *Roommate.* It isn't until I hear it that I realize Adam's never referred to me as that before. I've always been *June,* no explanation, no reason to justify it.

"*Oh,*" Riley says, looking back and forth at Adam and me. I know that look all too well from experience—he didn't tell her he lives with a woman. "It's so nice to meet you." She walks toward me and puts her hand out.

"Actually, it's probably better if you stay over there." I cough. "Wouldn't want you to catch anything."

She takes a step back as if I've told her I'm the grim reaper, but Adam takes a step forward.

"Is that why you're not at the show?" He places a hand on my forehead. "Did you take anything?"

"It's fine—I think I'm just exhausted," I say. "Took some cold and flu medicine and made soup."

"You mean you *heated up* soup," he says, looking at the full bowl on the coffee table.

"Tom-a-to, to-mah-to." I shrug, and then Riley, who I forgot was standing by the door, quite literally clears her throat. I adjust myself and smile in the politest way I can. "Well, don't let me interrupt you two kids. I can go upstairs and—"

"No, no, stay where you are," Adam insists. "We were going out. I just need to change." He heads up the stairs and calls back to Riley, "I'll be one second."

He disappears, and I'm left awkwardly staring at her, or I guess she's left awkwardly staring at me. Or both.

If you were to look up *beautiful* in the dictionary, a photo of Riley would pop up. She has deep blue eyes, the kind of freckles that just graze her nose, and long, thick hair down to her waist that she could flip either way and it would still look effortlessly natural. Based on her appearance alone, I can tell we're cut from a different cloth.

"So," she says. "How long have you known Adam?"

"God, I guess six years now?" I say, surprising myself at how long it's actually been. "What about you?"

"Just a couple of weeks. We met at an art show . . . I saw him looking at one of my paintings and one thing led to another . . ." She laughs like I'm supposed to know what's funny. "Have you two been living together for a while?" she asks.

I'm no stranger to this question, and I know Adam's also used to being on the receiving end of it from my dates in the past.

"Yeah, but I promise it's not what you think." I shake my head. Since I can read between the lines and know what she's really asking, I try to make this easier for her, since she seems *very* uncomfortable. "I'm seeing someone."

"Oh!" She lets out an exhale as if she's been holding her breath this entire time. "That's not what I . . ." *Yes, it is.* "I mean, I didn't think . . ." *Yes, you did.* "That's great."

Adam comes down the stairs in a new outfit, a black shirt and denim jacket with a backward cap, which he likes to wear when he thinks his hair is getting too long. There's something effortlessly handsome about him, and I hate how the thought crosses my mind.

"June, are you sure you're okay?" Adam says. "I can make you something better than canned soup."

"Oh no, I'm fine," I say, shaking my head. "I promise."

"Okay, because Riley and I can always go out another day—"

"What about your boyfriend?" Riley asks me. My face becomes red, and it's not the sickness, although I do feel queasy. My eyes go to Adam's because I've never used the word *boyfriend.* Not to him, and not to Liam. In the entire time I've known Adam, I've never referred to anyone as my boyfriend.

"Liam?" is all he says, and I don't even know if he's talking to Riley or me.

More than anything I want to say *no, that's not what she means.* Or *Riley, shut the fuck up,* but in this particular moment, I have lost my voice.

"Yeah, June was telling me about him." She smiles.

"Oh," he says, and looks away, wipes a palm on his face, and then nods to Riley. "All right, you ready?"

"Yeah, let's do it." She smiles.

It's like I've disappeared from the room, my existence no longer acknowledged. I don't know what's happening, but whatever it is, it is happening far too quickly.

"Feel better," he says in my direction, but he doesn't look at me and walks out the door.

"Feel better, babe," she says genuinely, and then follows him out. I close my eyes and don't know why I start crying.

ADAM DIDN'T COME home that night. I know because I fell asleep on the couch waiting for him. He didn't come home the night after that, either, and eventually, another two weeks pass without Adam and me saying anything to each other. Between the show and what I figure are extra shifts of early mornings and late nights on his end, we haven't been in the same room for more than five minutes. While Chloe's been busy in her new role, I've continued to become closer with Liam, who checks all the boxes. I know Adam's been seeing Riley more, because I'll hear him on the phone in his room.

There's been a shift in our dynamic, and it's becoming almost unbearable. I want more than anything to get back to what Adam and I used to have, but with Riley and Liam it feels almost impossible. It's starting to dawn on me that it's not them, it's *us.* Adam and I are inevitably growing apart, and whether it's Riley and Liam or two other people a couple months from now, I don't know how to be friends with Adam while he has a girlfriend.

I often go back to that night on the couch, a true sliding-doors moment in our relationship. I wouldn't have done things differently, and I stand by my choices, but I never thought our dynamic would turn to *this* so quickly. New relationships, fractured conversations. I truly believed we would find our way back.

The stress has taken a toll on me. I'm rarely hungry and I haven't touched a book in over a month. I try to take walks in my spare time to let the fresh air motivate me, but all I want to do is curl up in bed.

After a Saturday-evening performance, Chris, my director, knocks on my dressing room door. I hardly notice it's been an hour since the show ended. Almost everyone's gone and I'm still in my costume, with a full face of makeup.

"Hey, June," he says, walking in carefully. "Do you have a second to talk?"

"Yes, of course. Is everything okay?"

"No, not really." He sighs. "These past few shows you haven't seemed like yourself." He leans against my dresser. "Choreography is a little sloppy and your voice sounds strained."

Constructive feedback is something I've always appreciated and there's never been a situation where I couldn't handle it, but right now, I feel like I'm in the principal's office and every single one of my flaws is being exposed. I'm overcome with embarrassment, knowing the entire company witnessed what Chris is telling me now. There's nothing I've worked harder at than my career, and I hate myself for letting my personal life get in the way.

"Chris, I'm so sorry," I say, my voice cracking. "I've just been going through some things at home. I promise I won't let it interfere anymore."

"I'm putting Becca on for Mimi for next week and you can swing," he says in a way that tells me this is nonnegotiable, and my whole world is turned upside down. I've *never* had an understudy take over my role for this reason, and it's not my pride that's making me feel nauseated. It's that the one thing I know is *mine,* the one thing I can control, is being taken away from me. That I wasn't good enough. *That I'm not good enough.* "It's only temporary, June, but we can't sacrifice the show."

"Of course." My voice cracks again. "I understand."

"Okay, thank you." He nods. "Is there anything I can do to help?"

I shake my head. "No."

"All right, I'll see you tomorrow," he says, and leaves my dressing room.

LATELY, IT FEELS like I've been walking around in a dream. I'm going through the motions, but rarely do they mean anything. Before shows I don't seem to remember how I got there. I now sing in the chorus every night, and don't feel the electricity I used to when I'm onstage. I go grocery shopping, and I can't make anything useful with the things in my cart. Tonight, I'm at a roller rink that just opened in Brooklyn Heights with Adam, Riley, and Liam, and I don't know how I got here.

Well, technically I remember how I got here. Riley briefly came over to the house last week to meet Adam and she suggested we go on a double date because Liam would be in town. That I remember vividly, because Adam didn't say a word and I pretty much had to go along with her suggestion like it was a great idea.

So now I'm sitting in a booth directly across from Adam, with Liam to my right. In any other circumstance I'd probably really enjoy this place—it's dark with pink, blue, green, and yellow fluorescent lighting everywhere and early-2000s hits playing on the speakers. It's pretty packed with a mix of couples, families, and teenagers on their skates and ordering food and drinks at the bar. I'm fixated on a family across from us with two children. I would give anything to be sitting at their table.

"So." Liam looks at Adam and Riley. "How did the two of you meet?"

It's beyond weird that this is the first time the four of us have been in the same vicinity. I'd barely call Riley more than an acquaintance, and this is the first time Adam's meeting Liam.

"Oh," Riley laughs, and loops her arm into Adam's. "Baby, do you want to tell it?"

I feel sick, for two reasons. One, that she just called him *baby*, and two, that it sounds like this is a question they get asked often.

"Uh, well, I was at an art show in Williamsburg . . ." he says, and I already feel like I've heard this story one too many times. "And she was one of the artists." He looks over at Riley and squeezes her hand. It's subtle, but I notice it.

"Okay, way to downplay it," she says, and playfully rolls her eyes. "He was looking at one of my pieces, so I went up to him and asked what he liked about it . . . He was singing my praises, and he didn't even know it was mine," she says.

"Well, clearly that's the takeaway here," Liam says playfully. "Riley is one of the most talented and innovative artists of our generation!"

"Oh, stop it, stop it," Riley pretends to object, but her hands wave toward herself in a *keep going, keep going* gesture.

"Did you study art in school?" Liam asks.

"No, actually! I have a business degree—would you believe it?" She laughs. "My dad's an investor and wanted me to follow in his footsteps . . . but painting is my first love."

"That's awesome." Liam nods encouragingly. "I think it's so admirable when people follow their dreams."

It takes every muscle in my body to actively keep myself from rolling my eyes.

Riley takes a sip of beer and then nods in Liam's direction. "So what do you like better, New York or LA?"

"That's everyone's favorite question, isn't it?" He looks at me, and I force a smile. "I mean, LA has the weather and the ocean . . . but New York has June."

"*Aww.*" Riley leans into Adam and puts her head on his shoulder.

The thing about Liam is that he's charismatic, the life of the party; in another life he could have run for Congress and gotten everyone's vote. While he means every word, he still knows exactly what to say in every situation. Seeing Adam and Riley together across from me, her arm looped around his, makes me realize that maybe I shouldn't take Liam for granted.

"Are you saying that I'm better than a morning surf session?" I try to quip.

"Well, now you're fishing." Liam nudges me.

"Have you ever been, June?" Riley asks. "To LA?"

"I haven't," I say, playing with the plastic straw in my vodka soda. "It's just hard with the show, but it's something we've talked about."

"I keep trying to convince June to move to LA and pursue film and TV," Liam says. "I have a screen test lined up for her at the studio—she just needs to get her ass over there." He playfully nudges me, and I let out an uncomfortable smile.

"Oh my God, why don't you?!" Riley sits up. "You have the perfect face for the big screen too. Doesn't she, baby?"

My eyes travel to Adam, who looks uncomfortable with this whole conversation. But I'm waiting for his answer with bated breath, because we haven't really spoken to each other in weeks. I'm desperate for any type of exchange with him.

Adam looks at me, *really* looks at me, probably for the first time in weeks, and for a split second, I forget where we are and whom we're with. I can't believe that a month ago we were so close to being something else and lately it's like we're strangers.

"You do," he says, and now it's even harder for me to breathe.

"Well." Liam stands, and the movement makes me flinch. "I think I'm going to try hitting the rink. Anyone else want to join?"

"Yeah, why not?" Adam moves past Riley and stands.

"I'm good for now." I lift my glass, still dizzy from the previous topic. "Going to finish my drink."

"I'll stay with you," Riley says, smiling, and then looks at Adam and Liam. "It'll give us time to talk about you both."

Perfect.

Adam's eyes cut to me, and he gives a tight-lipped smile. The two of them line up for their skates and I wonder what they could possibly be talking about. But I'm more curious if Adam is as uncomfortable being alone with Liam as I am with Riley.

"Sooo." Riley scoots over to where Adam was sitting. "How's the show going?"

"It's good," I say, and avoid saying much else. I'm still not back to playing the role of Mimi, and it doesn't look like that's changing anytime soon. I haven't told anyone about the new arrangement and even if I did, Riley is the last person I'd want to talk with about taking a mental health break.

"I'm definitely going to have to see a show sometime. I keep asking Adam but he's always busy. You know him," she laughs.

There's an unfamiliar, territorial feeling that comes over me. Why yes, I know Adam. I know what makes him tick, how he hates people who walk slow, his hopes and dreams, the pasta sauce recipe his grandmother passed down to him, how there's nobody harder on him than himself, that he thinks *The Godfather* is overrated, and how he keeps a photo of his mom and Sarah in his wallet. Yes, Riley, I know Adam.

"Yeah, those restaurant shifts are killer," I say.

"Ugh, brutal! Between that and all those business meetings."

My pride takes a jab when I don't know exactly what business meetings she's referring to. But I don't ask any further details, because the small, immature side of me doesn't want to give her the satisfaction.

I change the subject. "How are things with you?"

"Oh, you know an artist's life, waiting for my next painting to sell or the next art show to be booked." In that way we're similar, choosing unstable career paths because of our passion, and I commend her for it. "But the apartment hunting is going well."

"You're moving?" I ask.

"Yeah!" She nods. "Crazy, isn't it? I mean Adam's been at my place almost every night these past couple of weeks. And I've been meaning to find a bigger place anyway."

My head cocks to the side, not wanting to assume, but unsure of what she's telling me.

"Have you and Adam . . . are you thinking of . . ." I try to phrase my question. "Moving in together?"

"*Oh,* nothing is official yet." She blushes like I'm one of her girlfriends. "I mean, we've talked about it, but he's so focused on work right now it's hard for him to think about anything else."

They've talked about it.

They've talked about moving in together.

They've talked about a future.

They've fucking talked about it.

Suddenly it feels like the last six years are already a memory, a time that *was* and that I've already lost. On some level I thought this was temporary; I know how Adam feels about me and maybe he just needs to get this out of his system, the same way I do with Liam. I can't even be mad at Adam for wanting these things with Riley—she's beautiful, creative, fun—and I should be happy for him. I should be *so* happy for him. But why do I feel like this is something that deserves a June-and-Adam conversation? Adam's talking about making a life-changing decision with someone who isn't me, like I don't matter. Since when do I not matter to him? Instead of feeling upset that he wants to spend his next chapter with someone else, I'm hurt that he couldn't even tell me. That I'm no longer relevant in his life.

"Right," I say, and my mouth goes dry. I feel sick again.

"June?" Riley says. "Are you okay?"

"Oh yeah, I just"—I clear my throat—"need some water, something's stuck in my throat."

"Let me get you a glass. Stay here." She stands up and heads to the bar. My eyes follow her, and she walks up behind Adam, who's talking to Liam. Riley nods in my direction and Liam waves to the bartender, doing a drinking motion with his hands.

Riley's arm wraps around Adam's waist from behind and he looks down, pulling her in beside him. They look comfortable, like they belong together. I wince at the sight of it.

They've talked about it. I can't get the image out of my mind. They've talked about a future together. She's known him for a mere fraction of his life, and she was able to have that conversation with him. I've known him for six fucking years and I couldn't bring myself to tell him how I feel. How *do* I feel? I don't even know how I feel. I love Adam. Of course I do. I love him with every fiber of my being, and it *is* possible to love someone and be afraid of that.

Liam strides my way with water in hand. "Hey, here you go." He gives me the glass and I down almost the entire thing in one go. "All good?"

"Mhm, thank you." I wipe my knuckle across my mouth.

"You know"—Liam starts massaging one of my shoulders—"Adam and Riley are really great. I'm glad we did this."

When did Liam and I become *we*? When did *they* become Adam and Riley?

"Do you mind getting me another glass, please?" I look up at him.

"Yeah, of course," he says. "Are you sure you're okay?"

"Yeah." My head nods aggressively. "Just thirsty."

He spins on his heel and disappears back into the crowd. Adam and Riley are laughing about something; they're facing the counter to pick up skates but she's leaning into him and he's rubbing the small of her back. He looks *happy.* In all the years I've known Adam, I haven't seen him like this with anyone, and the sight of it sends my stomach into knots.

A little kid about four or five starts running toward them. I recognize him as one of the kids from the table across from us. He has a toy in his hand, some kind of action figure, and he starts waving it toward the bar, but only Adam and Riley notice him. His mom's in line a few people in front, calling him, but Riley raises her hand toward her, nodding that it's all good.

In an instant I'm transported to that day on Long Island, Adam and me eating our ice-cream cones, leaning against the hood of Ford's car, watching a little girl and her mom.

I narrow my eyes at the interaction. Riley crouches down to the child's level and starts playing with the toy, making him laugh. Adam follows and leans down next to them, his hand on Riley's shoulder, and they continue to make exaggerated gestures, causing the kid to stomp his feet with excitement.

Watching this makes my face go pale, the warmth inside of me gone as if someone has shut off my internal thermostat. This feels like a snapshot of something I shouldn't be watching, an intimate moment that suddenly makes me feel like I no longer have a place here. With him.

I want what my parents have. Adam's voice from that day rings in my ears.

It feels like the room is getting smaller and smaller, the ground beneath me breaking, each plank of wood being ripped out and crumbled. The child runs back to his mom and Riley stands up, wrapping her arms around Adam and giving him a kiss, and it all finally clicks. I'm not what Adam needs.

Liam starts walking back with another glass in hand. When I look at Liam I don't see a house, or kids, or even five years into the future. He's not my best friend who knows all the ins and outs of me . . . but I'm content. And maybe that's enough.

"Hey, I was thinking," I say when he takes a seat. "I want to go to LA. I want to do that screen test."

Liam's eyebrows rise. "Oh yeah? What changed?"

"Nothing. I just, I don't know—talking about it earlier made me realize that I should," I say. "I'm going to look at flights tonight, okay?'

He squeezes me and pulls me onto his lap. "I'm warning you, once you get there you may never want to come back."

As I watch Adam and Riley I feel my smile falling. "That's okay."

Chapter 28

"WELL, SHIT . . ." CHLOE STARES AT ME FROM THE OPPOSITE side of the couch. Sometime within forty minutes of me explaining what happened five years ago, we moved ourselves into the living room. "So, what did Adam say when you told him you were leaving?"

"Well . . ." I swallow. "I didn't."

"What do you mean you *didn't*?" She frowns. "You didn't what?"

"Tell him that I was leaving." I look down.

What was supposed to be a quick trip for a screen test was actually a one-way ticket with no intention of coming back. Getting it off my chest isn't necessarily freeing, it's bringing on a heavy weight of guilt and embarrassment that I've been suppressing for years.

"What are you talking about?" She looks at me incredulously, like she's still not understanding what I'm telling her. That there's no way it's true. Like I'm not capable of doing something so hurtful.

"I didn't tell Adam I was moving to LA," I say bluntly, because it's the only way she'll understand. "I told him exactly what I told you. That I was only going to visit for a week, and to attend some auditions."

"Yeah, and then you got a part on that show," Chloe says, nodding. "And decided staying there was the best decision for your career."

That's the thing with white lies. They become full-blown lies, and then if you say it enough, it becomes the truth. Or you can at least tell yourself it's the truth.

"I never had any intention of coming back, Chloe," I say regretfully. "I was just lucky I got that role. If I didn't, I probably would've made up some excuse to stay . . . I bought a one-way ticket."

Chloe's face collapses. "I don't understand. Why didn't you tell me?"

"I don't know . . . Because I was scared, I was embarrassed . . . I should've told you." I shake my head like it's the most pathetic excuse. Because it is. I feel my eyes well up. I remember how alone I felt, so unsure. It was one of the biggest decisions I've made and I didn't confide in my best friend. "You should've been the first person I told."

"How did Adam take it?" she asks, still trying to understand. "He wouldn't make it that easy for you."

I rub my forehead, revisiting a painful chapter in my memory. I let out a long breath and sit back, staring at the fireplace. My eyes go to that chipped spot on the mantel.

"When I didn't come back the next week, he was texting me, calling me, making sure I was okay." My voice cracks. "He left me endless voicemails that I never listened to, because it was too hard to hear his voice. Chloe, I knew the minute I heard him I would cave. So I sent him a text . . . and told him I was staying." I close my eyes and push through the rest of the details. "I told him, sent him the money for the remaining month of our lease, hired movers to pack the rest of my stuff, and then I cut ties. I blocked him and unfollowed him . . . I erased him."

Now there's a look of horror on her face. It's not the kind of face you make when you tell someone that their boss is sleeping with their secretary, or when your favorite celebrity couple announces they're getting a divorce. It's a face that tells me she's looking at someone she thought she knew . . . but who is now a stranger.

"No." Chloe shakes her head. "No way. I saw him after. I asked him how he was doing. He said he was good. He said he was happy for you, that it'd been a few weeks since you talked because you were both busy . . . but you guys were good," she rambles, her words spilling out of her as she remembers every detail. "We talked about it and he didn't mention any of this."

My stomach twists at the thought of that conversation. A part of me had wondered if Adam would confide in Chloe, but another part knew he wouldn't. Because that's Adam. He would never put Chloe in the middle of us.

"What happened with *Rent*?" Chloe asks.

"I told them I had a family emergency and needed to be on the West Coast," I say, and she nods, filling in the missing gaps. "I'm not proud of any of it." I lean in, hoping she believes me.

"How could you do it?" she says, and it's not a rhetorical question. "Adam really cared about you. Whatever you told yourself to sleep at night, June, that's still six years of friendship."

When your lives are intertwined the way mine and Adam's were, you don't simply stop caring about the other person. Most people would see our relationship as suffocating. Living under the same roof for years, knowing the ins and outs of each other's days, our thoughts, our mannerisms. But what happens is after that first night, that first week apart, you learn you actually don't know how to breathe without the other. I never stopped caring about Adam. In fact, I spent more time convincing myself I didn't care . . . and there was only one way to really make myself believe it.

"He had Riley," I say softly. Chloe just looks at me. Her eyes travel from mine to my nose, ears, shoulders, torso, analyzing the person in front of her. I have no idea what she's thinking. "Please say something," I beg. Chloe has something to say, always. Her silence is deafening.

"You just left," she says in a way that hurts. I think she wants it to. "Just like that." She snaps her fingers.

"I know." I bring my palm to my jawline, wiping away the pool of tears. "Chloe, I should've told you," I say again. "And I wish I could say I thought about coming clean every single day, but the truth is I didn't," I admit. "I didn't want to tell you about Riley and I didn't want to tell you why I left . . . and it wasn't you. I didn't want to talk about it with anyone, because I was in so much pain."

"June," she breathes out.

"You got your dream job, you started a new life, and I was so fucking happy for you," I continue. "I would never want to take any of those things away . . . but you were also gone. And texting or talking on the phone wasn't the same as you being here. It was different. And I don't know, maybe I was sad you left, and I was sad Adam found Riley, and maybe I should've told you, or I should've told him, or I should've stayed on Broadway. I should've done a lot of things differently . . . but I did the only thing I could've done in the moment. It was run. Run and forget about all of it. And I know it's fucked up and I know it's immature—"

"And selfish, and cruel, and fucked up," she says.

"I already said that." I sniff.

"Well, I'm saying it again because it's extra fucked up." We stare at each other, and I'm ready for her to get up and walk out of the house. Ready for the reaction I should have gotten years ago. "And I'm sorry you had to deal with it alone."

My face drops. "What?"

"I had literally no idea any of this was happening, and I don't know, I just wish you could've let me be there for you. We could have figured it out," she says.

"Chloe, you just got a job at the firm. You were in such a good place in your career," I remind her. "I was not going to be the reason you were distracted from your new life. None of this was important compared to that."

"June, you're my best friend. When it comes to our feelings, it's always important," she says. "You're not the only person who missed the way it used to be. I was in butt fuck nowhere Connecticut, in a stuffy office, scared shitless, slammed with work . . . and I missed my best friend."

"Chloe . . ." My voice cracks. I had no idea she felt this way.

"June, just because I left New York doesn't mean I left you."

Her words lodge deep into my gut and stay there.

"And I didn't just miss you back then," she continues. "I miss you now. I hate how life got in the way and we only talk once every few months, and I hate how Teddy can't grow up with his badass aunt June, and I hate how you're going to be leaving soon, because I know it won't be the same once you're gone." Now she's the one who's wiping away a tear, something I've only ever seen maybe twice in our entire friendship.

"I've missed you too," I say earnestly. Not the way we text it to each other and not in the same upbeat way we end our phone calls. But in a way that tells her I don't just miss her, I miss us. "And I hate all of those things too," I cry.

Chloe reaches over and squeezes my hand. It's a simple gesture that confirms she's here for me, and always has been. "Don't move to another city and lie about why you're moving again, okay?"

"I promise." I wipe a tear from my cheek. "Chloe, I don't deserve you."

"See, that's your problem, June," Chloe says. "You deserve to have people care about you."

My eyes cut to her. "I got the part in *Les Mis,*" I say, and it feels more like a confession than anything.

"You got— Wait, what?!"

"The revival." I nod. "Rehearsals start next month."

"What?! June! Congratulations!" She reaches over and gives me a hug. When she pulls away, her face drops. "Why aren't you happy?"

"Because it's real now, you know?" My voice quakes. "Being here in New York, going back on Broadway, fucking living in this house? And last time—"

"It's different this time," she says.

"I just . . ." I look up. "I don't know what to do."

"What do you *want* to do?" she asks.

"I don't know," I say.

"Yes, you do," she says firmly. "You've always known."

The words absolutely terrify me, but I allow myself to finally say them out loud.

"I love him."

Chloe gives me a smile. "Then love him."

It feels like we're two kids back on the fire escape, looking over New York. The concept of love and happiness is something that would solve everything. Here we are, almost a decade later, and that sentiment still rings true.

"Chlo, it's been hard . . ." I turn to her, and she frowns, not understanding. "I've worked so hard at my career and it's not even a good one . . . but it's all I have. I'm not like you, I don't have a partner or kids. Now I'm so close to finally being happy again, having my dream, and I can't risk losing that."

"What are you worried about?" she asks.

"That I can't have it all," I admit.

Chloe shifts so we're sitting side by side and I loop my arm into hers, resting my head on her shoulder. "You don't have to choose, June."

I take a deep inhale and wonder if she's right.

We lean our heads back and look up at the ceiling, listening to the whispers of the city's hustle and bustle outside. For the next few seconds, we're silent, and the weight on my chest slowly lifts.

"So can I ask you a question?" Chloe's tone has changed, and I nod. "How was it?"

My brows furrow. "How was what?"

"*It.*" She sits up straight and looks down at me. "I always pictured the two of you being wild, like dirty talk and shit."

"You've pictured us having sex?" I make a face.

"Are you really going to judge me right now?"

I roll my eyes and let her have this. "For what it's worth, I've never had sex and then wanted to do it again immediately after."

"Oh my God, June!" she screams, and I cover my face with my hands, trying not to blush. "Y'all are freaks."

"You're the one who asked!"

AFTER WATCHING THE entire *Star Wars* trilogy and debating whether or not we, as a society, have taken Luke and Leia's kissing too lightly, Chloe heads home and I'm left to clean up our mess of pizza boxes. As I'm wiping down the kitchen counter, I hear my phone ring and rush to the living room to answer it. The name *Theo* takes up my screen.

"Hey," I answer.

"Hi!" she says. "It's not too late, is it?"

"No, I'm free!" I hold my phone out and quickly look at the time: 8:06 P.M. "What's up?"

"So, I just got some news," she says. "Remember that self-tape you did earlier this year for that drama?"

My brain scans the *many* self-tapes I've shot over the course of the past nine months. "Which one?"

"The limited series about the woman who's somehow tied to all the murders happening in her small town?"

"Oh my God, of course," I say, remembering. I was heartbroken to find out I didn't get the part, but when it was announced that the role went to an A-list actress, it was just an honor to even be considered.

"Long story short, the casting director kept your tape and A24 wants you for a film they're adapting next year."

Each individual hair on my arms raises. "Wait, what?! Seriously?"

"Yes!" Theo says brightly. "They're working out terms and are going to send over an offer before next week. But I wouldn't call you if I didn't get the verbal confirmation."

"W-What's the role?"

"One second, let me pull up the logline . . ." she says, and I hear some mouse-clicking on her end. "Okay, I'll send you the script too but . . . 'A woman who gets a face reconfiguration quickly becomes obsessed with her past life when she meets someone with the identity she lost.' "

"Oh my God." I sit down on one of the barstools.

"I know, it's wild."

"Wait," I say. "What about *Les Mis*?"

"That's the thing. Production would start within the first three opening months," she says. "You wouldn't be able to do both."

"Oh." My breath dips.

"I know it's a lot to process. But what you need to do, June, is think about what you want—*really think.* Both of these are game-changing roles. I'm telling you, the minute it's announced you're in this film, you'll have your second and third production already booked before you start filming."

What I should be thinking about is my career, the opportunities to come, yet I see the choices weighed out on a scale and they're not this film versus Broadway. Or even New York versus LA. It's Adam versus no Adam.

"I'm emailing you the script now," Theo continues. "Read it and we can connect next week."

"Okay," I say.

"This is not a bad thing, June," she says in the most optimistic voice she's had this entire phone call. "Enjoy this."

I should be happy. I should be thrilled.

"Amazing" is all I'm able to say. "I'll keep an eye out. Thanks, Theo."

After taking a hot shower and making myself a decaf chai, I pull out my laptop and read the script labeled *Me and You.* The story is *The Twilight Zone* meets *Past Lives,* and I'm utterly captivated. The role of Isabelle is complex and gritty, allowing me to tap into emotions I never had to in any other production I've been in.

Once I moved to Los Angeles, my career veered from what I'd learned in acting school. Scripts like *Me and You* are the reason I wanted to pursue TV and film in the first place. On the other hand, musicals like *Les Misérables* are the foundation for my overall desire to be an actress.

The whole "deciding what you want to do with your life" thing turns out to be more tiring than I'd thought, because next thing I know, I wake up to Adam crouched down in front of me, rubbing my arm.

"Mm, what time is it?" I ask sleepily.

"It's almost midnight," he whispers. He gently closes my laptop and sets it on the coffee table. "I debated letting you sleep down here but wanted you to be in bed."

"With you?" I close my eyes again.

"Yes," he says with a little laugh. "Just let me take a shower first."

After turning off the only lamp in the living room, he effortlessly scoops me up and brings me upstairs. He doesn't really need to be carrying me, but I'm tired and selfishly enjoy being wrapped in his arms. Carefully, he places me in my bed and tucks in the sheets like I'm a child. My eyes close and in what could be ten minutes or an hour later, I feel Adam curling up behind me. There's a fresh scent of cedar bodywash, and I move myself closer to him.

"How was work?" I mumble.

"Fine. Wished I were here instead." He rubs my shoulder. "How's Chloe?"

"Really good." I yawn.

"Good." He gives me a kiss on my ear and squeezes me a little tighter. "Night, June."

"Night, Adam."

The possibility of having this every night lingers in the final moments of my consciousness.

ADAM TAKES THE week off work, and it gives me a taste of what life could be like—what life *is* like. We wake up and have morning sex, which I used to avoid at all costs. The days consist of afternoon, evening, and shower sex. When we engage in domestic activities like grocery shopping, cooking, or walking around the city, it feels a lot like our old life, but better. Now I'm able to act on my impulse to touch him, hug him, kiss him, and it's *fun*.

He's sitting at the kitchen table with his laptop one evening, the light from the screen glowing onto his glasses while I'm on the couch reading a book. His facial hair has grown back a little bit and he's wearing a white Henley with his sleeves rolled up and gray sweatpants. His guard is completely and utterly down, and there's something so attractive about Adam just *being Adam* in my presence.

"How are you so handsome?" I ask from across the room.

Adam's gaze lifts from his screen and he *hmm*s because he genuinely didn't hear me.

Setting my book down, I sit up straight, then lift my sweatshirt over my head, tossing it onto the ground. I pull my sweatpants and socks off and throw them in a pile, leaving only my pink underwear on.

Adam's eyebrows rise as he stares at my exposed skin. I pull my hair out from a bun and let it fall over my shoulders and down my back, and relax into the couch, smiling at the sight of his jaw muscles working overtime.

"I'm awfully lonely over here." I let out an exaggerated sigh.

He closes his laptop, remaining seated. "What would you do if I wasn't home?"

"I guess I'd have to satisfy myself." I shrug.

"Show me" is all he says.

Perking up a little, I bite my lip. My fingers travel to the hem of my underwear and hesitate for a moment before going any farther. I've never done this in front of someone before, but with Adam here, watching me, it's incredibly arousing. It's challenging me in a way I have never been before, not unlike the feeling of performing a monologue. I've done this countless times within the privacy of my own walls, but now there's an audience.

My eyes close as my fingers travel underneath the fabric, feeling how wet I already am. I gently rub myself the way I normally would and let my legs spread across the coffee table.

"Look at me," Adam says, and my eyes open.

He's still sitting, his glasses now off, and there's something about the look in his eyes, the way his throat bobs when I move my hand a little faster. The urge to show him what I do when I think of him, what I've done for the years we've been apart, feels almost more intimate than sex itself.

A slight moan on my end is all it takes for Adam to stand up, and I hear the sound of the chair squeaking against the floor beneath him. He's walking toward me, but I don't stop moving my fingers. He steps in between my legs and kneels down, pulling my panties off. He's not subtle about anything, and once I'm fully exposed, he buries his face into me and I throw my head back in pleasure.

"Holy fuck," I cry, as the flat of his tongue swipes my most sensitive areas.

He enters me, and I can't help but grip his hair in my hands.

"I said *look at me,*" he almost demands, and a grin slowly emerges on my face. I didn't realize they were closed, but I open my eyes and look. The sight of his head greedily moving up and down and the sound of his grunts instantly makes me come.

"Adam." I pull his head in closer to me, grinding my hips, and have one of the best orgasms I've ever had.

"I DIDN'T REALIZE our meeting with Mara is next week." Adam pours me a cup of coffee and then begins frothing milk for us.

It's his last day off work; I can't believe how fast the time went. Some days it feels like I've never left, that this is simply how life would have been if the past five years had never happened. Other days, it's hard to swallow that it's been almost three weeks.

"I've been having trouble with the concept of time lately," I say.

"How are you feeling about it all?" he asks.

Theo hasn't called me back since our chat last week. So while that's been in the back of my mind, I'm trying to not let those logistics get in the way of what Adam and I are rebuilding.

"You mean the house?" I ask.

"Yeah." He pours milk into my mug, allowing the froth to create a heart shape.

"I think . . ." I smile. "I'd like to own this house together."

"I'd like that too." Adam passes me my mug and leans in to give me a kiss. It's gentle, yet lasts longer than a peck. When we part, there's a brief moment when we smile at each other. Almost like there's this unspoken sentiment, like neither of us quite believes the universe has brought us back together.

"So, we'd rent it out?" I take a sip of coffee, the hints of cinnamon and nutmeg soothing. "Like we'd be landlords?" I chuckle at the sound of it.

Adam sits down at the dining table, and even though there are three extra chairs, I follow and sit on his lap.

"I mean, that could be one option." He wraps an arm around my waist. "Or we *don't* let other people live here."

The plan was always to either rent the house and use it as an investment or sell it. Now it's beginning to feel like Adam's asking me something else.

"Are you suggesting what I think you're suggesting?" I say.

"We're already living here." Adam takes a sip of his coffee. "And it's been nice."

"It has been nice." I wrap my arms around his shoulders. "Plus, it *would* be weird to have other people live here."

"So weird," he echoes.

"I got the part in *Les Mis,*" I say softly.

"Y-You did?" He smiles.

I nod. "Éponine."

"June . . ." He sets his coffee on the table and pulls me into a hug. His hands cup my cheeks, and he gives me a kiss, a kiss I don't want to end. "Congratulations. *Fucking Les Misérables.*"

"I know." I close my eyes.

He pulls away to look at me. "How do you feel?"

"Mixed emotions," I say.

"I can imagine," he says gently.

I adjust myself in his lap and take a deep breath. "I also got an offer for a movie . . ." I look up at him, and his eyebrows are now raised. "If I do it, I can't do *Les Mis.*"

"Oh wow." He lets out an exhale. "But, June, that's amazing news too." He grabs my hand, genuinely happy for me. "This is not a bad problem to have."

"I don't know what to do," I say, and I hold my breath waiting for his answer. Expecting him to say *stay here, choose me.*

"You'll make the right decision for you." He looks at me, his eyes warm. "And I'll support you either way."

There's a piece of lint on his sweater that I pick off and rub in between my fingers.

"How are Ford and Sarah?" I ask, looking at the small ball of cotton I made.

He drags a breath in, like my asking is the most intimate thing we've done all week. In a way, it is. His family is a topic I've intentionally avoided this entire time, but something I've been wondering about all these years.

"They're good," he says, and I'm relieved. "Dad's the same and Sarah's in med school."

Though it's nobody's fault but my own, it hurts to think of a whole chapter of her life finished that I wasn't around for. "Oh my God, med school? For what?"

"To be a radiologist," he says like he can't believe it. "It scares me how smart she is."

"Wow . . . Adam, that's amazing." I look at him and know how proud he must be. "You know, I'm not surprised. She was always smarter than all of us."

"Oh, definitely," he chuckles, and then his fingers lazily draw circles on my thigh. "They've missed you."

My heart drops. Ford never tried reaching out, and while I stayed in touch with Sarah for the first few years, we naturally drifted apart, being on opposite sides of the country. Phone calls about her dates and the stress of school turned into texts, then the occasional *Happy Birthday* text. Running away from Adam meant losing every part of him, even the parts I could hardly live without.

"I've missed them too." I squeeze his arm, making sure he knows. "Can I tell you something?"

"Always."

"Sometimes when I'm scared, or sad, or . . . just feeling lonely, I think of your mom," I say softly. "Like she's watching over me or something."

I'm not a religious person, but there's a part of me that likes to think Audrey is with me, giving me the strength to get through the things that are challenging.

"I do the same." A somber smile fills Adam's face.

"I think she'd be happy for us." I give him a little nudge.

"Oh, are you kidding?" Adam throws his head back. "She'd be ecstatic. She loved you, June. I wish I could tell her it all worked out."

There's a tight feeling in my throat I try to push down, while at the same time I hold back the tears forming in the corners of my eyes.

"I think she knows," I say. There's a spot between the crook of Adam's neck and shoulder that I bury my face into, and he kisses the side of my head. I swallow and feel Adam's hand gently squeeze my hip.

"June," Adam says softly. "You know I love you, right?"

My head lifts up to meet his gaze. He's staring back intently, eyes bigger than I've ever seen them before. Years of memories play across his face as he waits for me to answer. It's suddenly eleven years ago, and he's teaching me how to poach an egg. It's ten years ago, and he's giving me the only seat on the subway while he stands. It's eight years ago, and I'm ironing his pants before an interview. It's seven years ago, and he's crying into my shoulder as we pick Audrey's dress for the funeral. It's six years ago, and I spot him in the audience, cheering during my curtain call.

There are many things I could do or say in this moment, but I simply nod and move one of the hands wrapped around his neck down to his heart.

"I love you too, Adam."

It's not anything flashy or performative, because it's not a confession. It's not a declaration. We're simply saying out loud what we've both always known. What we've been showing each other for years.

I don't hold my tears back anymore and I place my head back in that crook, knowing it's *mine.* I can't help but think of all the years we spent apart, how during all that time we could have had *this.* I want to ask him if it was all worth it, but it's more of a question for myself. A question I'll never have the answer to, no matter how many years go by.

Maybe that's how life is—we do things because it's the best decision we can make in the moment, and there's no way of knowing if we made the right choice. There's no way to gauge if all of it's for nothing, or if it's so we can have everything.

Chapter 29

MARCH, 5 YEARS AGO

I'VE NEVER TAKEN THE LONG ISLAND RAIL ROAD BY MYSELF, but I guess it's time I start learning how to do things on my own.

When my cab pulls up in front of Adam's childhood home, there's an ache in my chest. Before I even get to the front steps, the door swings wide open and Sarah greets me with a big smile on her face. I swear she's getting taller and more beautiful by the day.

"Hi! I heard the car," she says.

"How's it going?" I hug her back and her long arms wrap around me. "How was school?"

"Aced my chemistry test."

"Hell yeah you did." I give her a high five as I step inside. "What about that history paper?"

"B-plus." She shrugs.

"Sarah, that's still great. You're too hard on yourself," I say. I know neither Ford nor Adam puts any pressure on her. Sarah's just naturally a star student.

"I know, I just don't want to screw up my chances of getting into Yale or Harvard." She sighs.

"The fact that those schools are even a possibility for you is a huge deal in itself." I take my coat off and sit at the kitchen table. "Also, where's your dad?"

"He's got his bowling league tonight." Sarah sits across from me. "He should be home in a few hours."

"Oh, that's okay, I can't stay long," I say, shaking my head. "I just wanted to make sure I see you before Wednesday."

"What's happening on Wednesday?" she asks.

"Well . . ." I conceal a smile. "I got a small part in a TV show . . . so I'm going to LA to film."

"*What?!*" Sarah's eyes widen. "June!"

"I know," I say. "It's *crazy,* but I wanted to let you know."

"That's so badass!" Sarah reaches over to give another hug. "What's the part?"

"It's for this really small part in *Warriors,*" I say. "It's only like two lines. Not a big deal."

"That's the show your boyfriend's on, right?" Sarah asks.

"Yeah," I say with a nod. I'm not going to pretend that Liam *isn't* the reason I got this opportunity.

"Wouldn't it be crazy if you became like a *Hollywood* actress?" Sarah's eyes widen. "Like how wild would *that* be?"

Here it is. The point in the conversation I've been anticipating. The reason why I came out here *without* Adam. Stabilizing myself, I take a deep breath in.

"Well, that's sort of what I wanted to talk to you about," I start. "I have other things lined up when I'm there, so I might be gone longer than I anticipate." It's not the entire truth. I don't have other things lined up, but that doesn't mean I won't try.

"Like how long?" Sarah asks.

"I don't know," I answer honestly. "But I want you to know that no matter what happens, I love you. I really do, and I'm so excited to see what you do with your life, because you're incredibly smart, passionate, and beautiful on the inside and out."

"June, you're talking like we'll never see each other again." Sarah frowns. I don't acknowledge her remark and look out the window to the maple tree in the backyard.

"Did you know I grew up never feeling like I had a family?" I ask, knowing I've never told Sarah any of this. "My dad left when I was a child, and my mom . . . well, she never wanted to be a mom. I have no siblings and my grandparents passed away before I graduated high school. It wasn't until I met you, and your parents, and Adam that I finally knew what it felt like to be a part of a family. And for that, I'll forever be grateful."

"June . . ." Sarah hesitates. "You're not coming back, are you?"

"I don't know." I wipe a tear in the corner of my eye. I know I shouldn't be unloading all of this on Sarah, but she's always been far more mature and intuitive than the average person her age. "But I need to see what else is out there," I say.

Sarah nods, and reaches for my hand. For a split second it's reminiscent of how Audrey would always take my hand and reassure me.

"Adam doesn't know, does he?" Sarah says. There's no hiding my tears anymore. The question alone causes me to break. I simply shake my head, not wanting to say the words out loud.

"June . . ."

"He'll be okay." I sniff, and nod reassuringly. "He'll be okay."

"And *you'll* be okay too, right?" Sarah says.

"We'll see." I let out a weak laugh.

"You will be," she says matter-of-factly. "If there's one thing my mom taught me, it's that we're only given what we can handle . . . and if we *can't* handle it, then . . ." Sarah's smile falters. "I would want nothing more than for you to marry my brother and stay here with us forever. But no matter what happens, June, you will *always* be family."

Chapter 30

8 DAYS UNTIL THE MEETING

In the eleven years I've known Adam Harper, I have prepared dinner for him approximately once. At some point, before I ever landed *The Mousetrap* and he got a decent-paying job, I was craving a box of Kraft mac and cheese. Adam offered to make some elaborate four-cheese concoction from scratch, and I insisted whatever came from the box would be better. We ate in silence and once we were done, all he said was that cooking it with milk instead of water would make it creamier and to maybe use the stove instead of a microwave. I never attempted to impress him with dinner again.

Luckily, I'm proud to share that I've learned a thing or two since then, like how to read a recipe. Today, I plan on spending the afternoon preparing him a meal he won't forget. I've found the perfect ravioli recipe online that I feel somewhat confident about executing.

I make a quick trip to the grocery store, though it looks like we have the majority of the ingredients already at the house. This should be easy, except for a small detail. I pull out my phone while studying the laptop screen in front of me. I skip over the story about the woman whose ex-husband ran away with her sister, which sparked the recipe for Rebecca's runaway ravioli.

After four rings, Adam answers.

"Hey, what's up?" I hear the clinking sound of plates and glasses and people talking behind him.

"Question: Do you have a pasta maker?"

"Like, personally?" he says.

"Yes." I scroll down the recipe, making sure there's nothing else I need.

"Why?" he asks skeptically.

"Because I need one—do you have one or not?"

"Of course I have one. Are you making dinner?" He sounds more surprised than I anticipated, which is only more motivation for me to do this.

"Well, I'm not using it to wring out my stockings," I say.

"Ew," he says. "Is that a thing?"

"I hope not." I close my laptop. "Okay, where is it?"

"It's at my place," he says.

"Oh." Right. *His place.* He has a place. I don't know why I haven't put much thought into it until now. Almost like outside of our bubble, he doesn't exist.

"I can get it on my way back—"

"No, I can't wait until then." I look at the clock. There's probably another four hours until he comes home, and that would defeat my surprise of having dinner on the table once he walks in. "Can I get it? Where do you live again?"

"If you don't mind going to the Upper West Side," he says. "Off 85th. Come over here and I'll give you the keys."

"Okay, see you soon." I smile like an idiot and hang up the phone.

EVEN THOUGH IT's freezing, Adam meets me outside Alden wearing only a dress shirt with the sleeves rolled up.

"Hi," he says, leaning in to give me a kiss. I forget we're in public, and I wrap my arms around his waist, pulling him closer to me.

"Hi," I mumble against his lips.

He slips his hands underneath my coat and squeezes my waist, a gesture fairly innocent on his end, but which nonetheless arouses me.

"Here you go." He hands me a single gold key. "I let the front desk know you're coming."

"Fancy." I take the key and put it in my pocket. "Is there anything else you need while I'm there?"

"I'm okay." He nods. "Take whatever you want."

"I'll see you tonight." I stand on my toes and give him another kiss.

He keeps a hand on my elbow. "Is it safe to say we're eating pasta?"

"Can you at least *pretend* you're surprised tonight?" I say.

"You're cooking dinner," he says. "Trust me, I'm surprised."

"Wooow," I say, and he pulls me back in for a kiss, laughing against my lips.

Adam's not one to give away laughs so freely, but when he

does, knowing you're the reason is one of the best feelings in the world. As I take a final look at him, he gives a wink, then heads back inside. For what feels like the first time in a long time, everything is how it should be.

I GET OFF the C train and walk to a gorgeous luxury condo just on the edge of Central Park West. It has the charm of an old New York apartment with the brown brick and a vintage exterior trim, but the details feel sleek and modern. It's a little weird seeing where Adam's spent his time in between then and now and the kind of life he's built for himself, a part of him that has nothing to do with me.

An older man wearing a dark suit greets me from behind the desk. "Good afternoon, can I help you with anything?" He smiles.

"Hi, I'm here for Adam Harper, apartment 1606," I say, pulling out the gold key in my pocket.

"Oh yes." He looks down at his pad of paper. "Ms. Wood. Right this way." He guides me to an elevator and then scans his key card.

I smile. "Thank you."

When I reach the sixteenth floor, I'm a little disoriented to discover this is a private elevator to Adam's suite. I use the key on the door directly in front of me and open it to his apartment.

"Damn," I say to myself.

Stepping out, I'm in a little entryway that tells me this place is bigger than I'd thought. I place the key on a table to my side and turn the corner. On my left are those floor-to-ceiling windows, opposite a view of the Manhattan skyline with Central Park below it. There's a kitchen that's so legit I know it's probably the sole reason Adam wanted this place, and to my right is one of those white Cloud couches in front of a mounted television.

Even though I'm the only person in the apartment, I say "*Hello?*" to nobody and walk down the hallway. The entire unit has a minimalist style, and in his room a king-size bed sits against the wall with a navy blue linen duvet. His bathroom is impressively clean, with matching navy hand towels folded over the rack.

Adam clearly has his shit together, but considering he had no idea I'd be coming over, the apartment is in pristine condition. I walk back into the kitchen and go through a few cupboards, scanning the collection of cookbooks he has along the backsplash before I see the pasta maker.

"There you are." I grab it and carry it back to the entryway. It's a lot heavier than I'd thought and I debate whether I should take the subway or grab a cab.

As I make my way to the front door, I catch an open box containing some random items in the corner of the living room. My curiosity gets the best of me, and I adjust the pasta maker over my hip as if it was a baby and walk toward the box.

From where I'm standing, I see a framed newspaper clipping from *The New York Times* with a review of Alden. Placing the pasta maker on the ground, I kneel, pulling out another framed photo. My fingers gently run along bronzed wood and I smile at an image of an Adam no older than eighteen, with Sarah and Audrey in front of the Brooklyn Bridge. My eyes begin to well up, because it feels almost like one of my own memories. I wipe a tear at the corner of my eye, knowing that Audrey would be more than ecstatic seeing Adam and me finally together, the way we should always have been.

When I place the frame back in the box, I catch a glimpse of another photo, one that makes it feel like the floor has fallen beneath me. My hands tremble as I pick up a silver frame with a Polaroid picture in it.

Smiling back at me through the glass is Riley in front of the Eiffel Tower, her hair blowing in the wind and Adam behind her, arms wrapped around her waist as he kisses her cheek. One of her hands grips his, while the left one is held up to the camera . . . with a diamond ring.

My lips go numb, and my heart starts to race. I don't know what part of me is processing this faster, my mind or my body. The minute a question forms in my mind, another one takes over until the *whos, whats, wheres, whens,* and *whys* have run through my head like a slot machine.

I didn't expect Adam to tell me every detail about his relationship with Riley. That's between the two of them and whatever happened is over and has nothing to do with me. But *this* . . . this is something big, something that I can't ignore. While there's no reason that this should change anything, I can't unsee it, nor can I control the churning in my stomach.

Suddenly I'm transported back to that day at the roller rink watching Adam and Riley being effortlessly happy. The part of me that wanted to leave was right. The part of me that thought I should stay was wrong. It feels as if the last few weeks have been a lie. I really believed the entire time we were apart that Adam and I were living similar lives, threaded through the same needle. *Swindlers* is nowhere near comparable to Adam's success with Alden, but on paper, we checked the box on our dreams. On the surface, we got what we wanted, but something was missing for both of us. *Each other.* Now, knowing that once I left, Adam's happily ever after was just beginning tells me we are actually much more different than I'd thought.

Their faces are beaming back at me, and I take deep breaths to keep my nausea at bay. I picture Adam asking Robby for help in buying the perfect ring for Riley, planning the quintessential Paris trip, getting down on one knee in front of the Eiffel Tower to profess his love, and the two of them coming back home to celebrate with Ford and Sarah. Them being happy that Adam *finally* found someone he can spend the rest of his life with instead of playing house with June.

June, who was never good enough to maintain a career on Broadway, never good enough to be in a long-term relationship, never good enough for her own parents, never good enough to land a role on a show that isn't canceled after one season. June, who was never good enough for Adam.

Chapter 31

AT 6:02 P.M., ADAM WALKS THROUGH THE FRONT DOOR.

"Don't come over here, it's not ready yet!" I shout over the sound of the range hood, my mushrooms and onions sizzling in a pool of garlic butter.

"I'm going to take a shower," he calls back from the front foyer. "Be down in fifteen."

Okay, I can do this. Fifteen more minutes is all I need to complete the finishing touches. Fifteen more minutes will also help me prepare for this conversation.

By 6:27 P.M., I'm carefully pouring my sauce over the thick pillows of ravioli and sprinkling a dash of parsley on top for color. I've never been prouder of anything I've cooked.

"It smells delicious." Adam leans over my shoulder to see what I'm doing. "It *looks* delicious." He gives me a kiss on the cheek, and I close my eyes because it feels too good. His lips, him coming *home* to me, all of it. This is all I've ever wanted, and I know I shouldn't pop this bubble. "You didn't have to do this," he says.

"I wanted to." I turn, slinging my arms around his neck to see that his hair is still a little damp, the whiff of his shampoo overpowering the smell of the food. He gives me a tender kiss and his hands touch the skin underneath my shirt. I let out a laugh as he travels close to the hem of my bra. "Stop! Sit down and wait to be served."

"Yes, ma'am." He squeezes my waist and sits at the table. "Were you able to find the pasta maker okay?"

I hesitate for a moment, like the question was accusatory.

"Mhm, it was under the cupboard like you said." I bring over two plates, setting one in front of him and the other on my side of the table, then take a seat.

He takes a bite of the ravioli, and his eyes go wide. "June, this is delicious."

"Really?" I smile.

"Really," he says, nodding enthusiastically. "The oregano is a great touch."

I'll never know how he can taste even a dash of oregano.

"Good, I'm glad you like it." I cut one of my raviolis in half and it's perfect, if I do say so myself. The cheese fills the pocket to the brim and the sauce is glistening. My eyes focus on the tiny swirls of steam ascending.

"So, how was your day?" he asks.

"Oh, fine." I nod. "How was yours?"

He places one of his elbows on the table. "Hey, are you okay?"

I play with my fork, moving it through the sauce, and then set it down against the shallow bowl. I'm not able to hold it in any longer. I take a deep breath and feel like water in a kettle about to reach its boiling point.

"What happened with Riley?" I ask.

Adam's brows furrow. "What do you want to know?"

"You were *engaged,* Adam," I say, like this is new information for him. For a brief moment, his eyes close, my reaction making sense now. "I saw a photo in your apartment . . . I'm sorry, I didn't mean to pry, but I saw it and—"

"I don't care that you saw it," he says gently.

"How could you not tell me something like that?" It comes out more hostile than intended, but I don't take it back. Adam wanted to spend the rest of his life with her—maybe he still wants to. A part of me, the part that can't help my insecurities, because I'm only human, now wonders if when he looks at me, he wants to be looking at her.

He stares at me, stunned. "I don't know, because yeah, we got engaged, but we didn't get married. I would've told you, June. We would've gotten there."

I stand my ground. "That's something you should have told me."

"I tried," Adam says, regretfully.

"When?" I shake my head.

"That night at Alden," he says. "But you didn't want to talk about our exes and—"

I gape. "You're putting this on me?"

"No," Adam says firmly. "No."

"What happened between you two?" I ask, knowing it's probably not my business.

"What happens in any relationship," he says. "It just didn't work out."

I let out a doubtful laugh. "That's it?"

"What are you getting at?" Adam frowns. "June, we don't talk anymore. I promise."

"That's beside the point," I fire back. "This is a whole part of your life you kept from me, Adam."

"There was never the right opportunity to tell you," he says.

"I think when she first came up would've been a great time." I counter.

He grabs the back of his neck and squeezes it. "I told you it *ended*—that is the only part that matters, June. We were *just* starting to open up to each other. I wasn't going to air all my dirty laundry, and I wouldn't think you'd expect me to."

"But that's the thing, Adam, I'm not some stranger that you open up to after five or six dates. It's *me*. You should've been honest with me." He lets out a scoff and shakes his head.

"What?" I say.

"I would *love* to be honest, June." His gaze burns into mine. "Why did you leave?"

His question causes my stomach to lodge painfully into my lower abdomen. The minute I agreed to this deal to live together, I knew deep down this conversation would happen, that it would be impossible for us not to have it.

"Does that even matter right now?" I ask defensively.

"I think I deserve to know, June," he says.

I look away from him, because it's too painful to see the look on his face. "I left for my career." In hindsight, that *is* a big reason I left. "It wasn't working out on Broadway, and I had that screen test lined up. I needed to do what was best for me."

"What do you mean it wasn't working out on Broadway?" He frowns. "What about *Rent*?"

"I got taken off and they gave the role to my understudy," I say, and look away, still humiliated all these years later.

"I-I didn't know that . . ." Adam says.

"How would you? I never said anything."

"Why didn't you tell me?" He sounds hurt. "You could've told me."

"It doesn't matter anymore." I shake my head, not wanting to relive that pain. "Besides, I'm sure you were busy ring shopping," I say, and it sounds immature and spiteful, but I don't care.

"I jumped into that relationship *because* of you," he snaps back, turning the tables. "Besides, you're the one who didn't even want to be in a relationship, remember? And then out of nowhere, you and Liam were together."

"That has nothing to do with this—"

"It has everything to do with this because *you fucking left, June,*" he says with more emotion than I can handle. "You didn't even have a conversation with me. What was I supposed to do?"

"So, your failed engagement is *my* fault?" I say.

"No, that's completely on me," he says. "But I'm talking about the choices *you* made."

Our words are coming out fast and furious; I guess that makes sense after years of built-up tension. My heart and mind are racing—I want to make sure Adam knows how I really feel.

"Look, Adam, I'm sorry," I say for the first time. "If I could do things over, I would."

He waits a beat and then gives an exasperated laugh. "You're sorry? After all of these years, that's all you can say?"

"I made an irresponsible decision, and I should've handled it better," I say. "I should've given you a heads-up or time to plan or sent Chloe to help—"

"This isn't about the logistics, June." He shakes his head and pinches the bridge of his nose. "I've replayed the last *decade* over and over in my head, and there are things both of us could have done differently. I don't know where or when it went wrong, but I know you were more than a roommate and you were more than my best friend. You can sit there and deny it all of these years later, but I know you felt the same. And one day, you just *left.* You left this, you left *us,* like it was so easy. Like none of this mattered."

"Of course it mattered!" A pain stabs through my chest, making it hard to breathe. "But what do you care? You seemed to move on pretty quickly," I say, knowing that while I was gone, he just continued on with his life and didn't bat an eye.

"Do you know what it was like to receive a goddamn *text message* from you saying that you weren't coming back? To call you over and over again for months knowing damn well you blocked my number but hoping *maybe today is the day she comes around—*"

"You were happy with her, Adam, I saw it with my own eyes." I fight back tears. "Our time had run out."

"That is *not* true, June."

"It is." I say to him what I've always told myself. "Me staying wouldn't have changed that."

"Do you know I lived in this house for five months after you left because I was stupid enough to think you'd come back?" he tells me. "Do you know how hard that was?"

"Yeah, well, I'm sure opening up your own restaurant, getting engaged, and finding a penthouse overlooking Central Park probably helped," I say.

His eyes lock onto mine. "Did you know?"

"Did I know what?"

"That you weren't coming back—"

"Adam—"

"Did you know you weren't coming back when we stood in that very spot," he says, pointing to the bottom of the stairs. "We said our goodbyes before your flight. Did you know you weren't coming back?"

I remember that day vividly. My stuff was in the taxi and Adam was on his way to a shift at Luca. There was nothing special about our conversation. He said good luck and I said thanks. We didn't hug and I tried not to look him in the eyes. I clutched the one-way ticket in my pocket knowing it might be the last time we saw each other. It was the toughest performance of my life.

There are a few seconds of silence. I can practically hear my heartbeat interlaced with the sound of Adam's breathing.

"Yes," I say, and Adam looks away, breaking our eye contact like he was hoping my answer would be different. I wish it was. We sit in silence as I look down at the pasta that I used as a coping mechanism all day, now practically untouched, my appetite gone. I break the silence with the one question I've been wondering about all day. The one question that I'm terrified to know the answer to. "Who ended it?"

"What?" He looks up.

"The engagement," I clarify. "Who ended it?"

Adam averts his gaze to his feet, as if he doesn't want to see my reaction. "She did."

And now it finally feels like the bubble has popped. Fragments of my and Adam's story floating around us as tiny droplets only to shrink, flatten, then disappear. In what felt like a love story between the two of us, it is now revealed that I am in fact the supporting character, the second choice, the afterthought. The two of us were brought together not by some act of fate, but because of a clause on a sheet on paper.

There's no doubt in my mind that Adam loves me—there's no faking what we share. What hurts is that it wasn't enough. *I* wasn't enough until I was the only option.

"I think I'm going to head to bed early," I tell him, because there's not much else to say.

"Yeah." Adam stands up and nods, like he's finally getting something that he didn't before. "It's probably better if I just . . . go home."

"Okay," I say softly, not stopping him.

Unlike last time, I'm able to step back from this moment and see what's happening. Adam and I had our second chance, and we lost it. We tried, *really* tried, and it didn't work.

After a few minutes, Adam comes downstairs with his luggage in hand. He grabs his coat from the closet and the gold key I left on the counter. When I hear the front door close, I know he's not coming back.

Chapter 32

DAY OF THE MEETING

After zipping up my suitcase, I sit on the edge of my bed, pulling up my flight information. I'm catching the red-eye after our meeting with Mara today and then just like that, heading back to my life. Like the past four weeks never happened.

Adam and I haven't spoken since our fight. I thought about calling him, but at this point, there's not much left to be said. There's no use in reaching back out to him unless we have a future together, and we don't. At least, not in the way I thought.

Upon leaving, I do my due diligence and make sure everything is back to its original placement, everything's unplugged, and the trash is taken out. Before hailing a cab, I take a final look at 74 Perry, and a weak smile escapes me. It's the end of October, and there's a beautiful display of pumpkins placed in front of all the brownstones, including ours.

It feels like a lifetime has passed since being at the skyscraper in Tribeca almost a month ago. I repeat the same motions as before—head up the elevator, sit in the waiting room—except this time, I'm eagerly anticipating Adam walking through the doors.

My time alone left me with a lot of thoughts. Maybe all Adam and I were ever meant to be were roommates, or friends, or even investment partners, whatever bullshit term you want to slap on. I don't care, as long as we're *something*. I'd rather be something and have it kill me, than nothing.

"June?" Mara turns the corner, wearing a new pair of thick-rimmed glasses and a black muumuu. I follow her down the hall into her office and take a seat across from her. "How have you been?"

"Fine," I lie. "How have you been?"

"Oh, good—my granddaughter came here last week. She's studying in London!"

"Wow," I say, trying to sound as impressed as I can be. She types a few more things on her keyboard and pulls out some documents.

"Sorry, just give me one more minute," she says. "I'm pulling up your files."

I smile. "Take your time." I glance behind me, keeping a lookout for Adam, the anticipation killing me. I smooth out my sweater and tuck my hair behind my ear.

"So what did you think of Perry? The renovations are great, aren't they?"

"Oh my God, yes," I agree. "It's really beautiful. I almost can't believe it's the same place."

"Mm." Mara lets out a noncommittal noise. "All right, here we go." She starts printing papers and grabs them from the printer behind her. "Thank you for reviewing everything last week. Makes this process a lot easier . . . I just need you to sign here and here, and the house is all yours." She slides over two stacks of paper with an X marked on two different spots.

"I'm sorry," I say. "Shouldn't we wait for Adam?"

"Mr. Harper? Oh no." She shakes her head. "He signed everything yesterday."

"Yesterday?" I frown. "I could have sworn our appointment was today."

"It is," she says with a smile. "But he's not needed anymore, now that he's forfeited ownership. So it's just your signature we need."

"*Forfeited ownership*?" I repeat.

"Yes." Now Mara seems like the confused one.

"What . . ." I start. "What does that mean?"

"It means he's not coming." She lets out a little laugh. "His forfeiting ownership means that *you* are now the sole owner." She nudges the pen a little closer to me. "Congratulations."

Everything from that moment on feels like a blur, like I'm in slow motion while the world continues to move around me. Mara's in front of me and I know she's talking, but it's like I'm stuck in quicksand, as if I'm slowly falling into a dark hole and nothing else matters. There's movement coming from her end, like she's waving her hand for my attention, and I bring myself to focus on her.

"Ms. Wood? Are you okay?"

I swallow and shake my head. "I'm sorry. I just . . ."

Mara looks concerned. "Did you not know this was going to happen?"

"No. I mean, I just . . . I forgot the process." I let out an awkward laugh. "Sorry."

"Right," she says skeptically. She then slides in my direction a file organizer full of papers. "Well, how about you spend some time looking over these again. I can also email you the forms and you can send them back with an e-signature by tomorrow end of day."

"That would be . . ." Words continue to escape me. "Great. Thank you."

"Not a problem. I just do want to remind you that if we don't get the documents back by tomorrow, the property will be absorbed by the bank."

"What about Adam?" I ask.

"Ms. Wood." Mara's tone sounds a little impatient. "Aside from full ownership, the terms of this agreement have not changed since we spoke four weeks ago. If you don't make your decision in the next twenty-four hours, neither you nor Mr. Harper will own this home, and the six-point-two million will be absorbed by the bank."

I know I'm not in the right headspace, but there's no way I can let this past month be for nothing.

"Actually." I sit up straight and take the pen sitting on the desk. "No need to send them. I'll sign now."

"HOW COULD HE do this?!" The blood rushes to my cheeks and I pace outside of Mara's office building. "It's always been the plan to own the house together."

"So, it's official? You actually *own* Perry?" Chloe's voice combats the sound of street traffic in my ear.

"Yeah." I let out an incredulous laugh. "I signed the paperwork and everything. It's official."

"Okay, well, this is not a bad thing!" Chloe says, and I grip my phone, dying to see how she'll spin this. "It's stressful owning property, but I will help you through it. You just focus on catching your flight and thinking about whether you want to sell it or keep it and—"

"Sell it," I say without missing a beat.

"Are you sure?" she says.

It was hard enough having to stay there all week by myself, and now, after everything, there's no way I can be in that house and not think of Adam. I need a clean break.

"I can't, Chloe. I can't keep that place, it's too hard." I shake my head and clutch the folder of documents against my chest.

"Okay." She takes a beat. "But don't sell now. The market is terrible—wait until after the holidays."

That's sound advice. I know the basics when it comes to real estate, but I certainly don't keep up with the market, considering I was never close to buying property of my own.

"Right. Okay." I switch my phone to the other ear. "I just, I can't believe he just didn't show up. No warning. Isn't that fucked up?" I say, but I'm met with silence on the other end. "Chlo?"

"Look, I'm always Team June," she says, and I feel like I'm about to get served a *but* sandwich. "But, isn't this what *you* did to *him*?"

"Well . . ." I let out a pathetic breath. "*Shit.* I guess but I don't know. Two wrongs don't make a right."

"No, but you're missing the whole point in all of this. You think Adam did this as a big fuck-you? From where I'm standing, he just gave you six million dollars."

AS EXPECTED, LOS Angeles greets me with sunshine and its staple seventy-degree weather. That feeling of cozy warmth, vibrant colors on the trees, the scent of pumpkin and nutmeg, and crisp air that can be described only as the perfect autumn afternoon is long gone.

On my first night back, Shivani, Zach, and I order sushi and I half pay attention to the reruns of *The Real Housewives* they want to watch. I decide to not tell them about Perry Street, *Les Misérables,* or the upcoming film until I decide what my next move is.

"So, how was New York?" Shivani reaches for a piece of sashimi.

"Did you change your mind about hating it?" Zach asks.

"The verdict is in." I nod. "I can confidently say I do *not* hate New York City."

"Ayy." Zach starts snapping his fingers.

"Did work put you up in a nice place?" Shivani asks. "Last time I was there I stayed at this really cute spot in Chelsea."

"Oh, no." I shake my head. "I just stayed with a friend."

"A *friend*?" Shivani raises her eyebrows.

"It's not like that—he's an old friend." I take an eel tempura roll and dip it in soy sauce.

"*He*?" Zach repeats.

Shivani turns to Zach. "I have been trying to set June up with someone for almost six months and she insists she isn't looking for anything. Now I know it's because she's got some *friend* back in New York. I get it."

Why I continue to talk escapes me. Maybe it's to prove a point, but I don't know if it's to myself or someone else across the country. "Set me up with Brad," I say to Shivani.

"Ben?" she asks.

"Yeah, set me up with Ben."

"Are you sure your *friend* won't get mad?" Zach asks, then takes a sip of his miso soup.

"Yes, I'm sure." I roll my eyes and turn to Shivani. "Can you remind me how you know him again?"

"He's a regular at the Pilates studio . . . natural supplement company . . . He's also a real estate agent . . ." Shivani says like she's trying to jog my memory. "I haven't hung out with him in a social setting, but he's nice and he's hot. I'm not saying marry him, but have fun, see where it goes."

In two weeks' time, I'm on a date with Ben-not-Brad. A relationship isn't something I'm looking for right now, but dating is a nice distraction. We meet at this New American spot in Venice that feels far too pretentious and I'm instantly annoyed at having to circle the block four or five times to find a parking spot.

The restaurant is fine, really leaning into the minimalist beach vibe. Ben's already sitting at a table toward the back. Shivani was right—he's a good-looking guy, with light brown hair in a very specific cut. I'm wearing jeans with a white cashmere sweater; his style is leaning on the athleisure side with an eccentric pair of Jordans.

"Hey, June." He stands up and gives me a kiss on the cheek. He places his hand on the small of my back and guides me to sit down.

"Hey, *Ben,*" I say his name, proud of myself. "Nice to finally meet. Shivani only has wonderful things to say." I take a seat.

"Likewise. I'm happy we were able to get together." He takes a seat across from me and doesn't touch his menu. "So, I hear you're an actress. Have you been in anything I may have seen?"

"I've been in a few things here and there," I say with a shrug. "Have you sold any houses I may have driven by?"

He really gets a kick out of that and laughs louder than I expect. "You're funny."

The waiter appears and pours us both glasses of water.

"I'm good if you are." I look to Ben and he nods. Turning to the waiter, I hand him my menu. "I'll have the chicken parmigiana, please."

"And I'll do the steak frites." Ben passes off his menu. "Oh, and two glasses of your best Pinot Noir."

"Actually," I jump in, "can I do a vodka soda with lime, please?"

"Perfect," our server says, nodding. He turns to Ben. "And how would you like your steak cooked?"

"Well-done," Ben says. "Thank you."

"Well-done, huh?" I say as the waiter leaves.

"I know they say medium-rare is the best way to eat it, but I can't deal with all that blood," he says, shaking his head. "I like my meat cooked."

"I just always feel like you can better appreciate the texture and the taste when it's medium-rare," I say.

"Oh, no way, it's too gummy," he says. "The meat needs to be properly cooked to appreciate it."

I shrug. "To each their own."

"Should we have the cook come out here and settle it for us?" He raises an eyebrow.

"Chef," I say.

"Pardon?"

"You mean have the *chef* come out here," I say as politely as I can.

"What's the difference?" Ben says.

I know I shouldn't be judging this man by his ignorance in ordering a steak and his inability to know the difference between a cook and a chef.

"A cook is someone who can follow a recipe," I say. "A chef is someone who creates it."

He blinks. "But the chef is also cooking . . ."

It takes almost everything in me to not ask if this man is for real right now.

"Correct." I smile. He's lucky I'm too defeated to retaliate. Our server comes back with my drink and pours Ben a sample of red. Ben swirls it and gives an approving nod after tasting.

"So, June," Ben says. "Where are you from?"

"I'm originally from Toronto, but I used to live in New York."

"Oh nice, I love New York. I'm from Boston." He takes a sip of his wine. "What brought you there?"

"I went to Columbia, studied theater," I say.

"Right on," he says, and I think I actually hate how he just said that. "My sister's obsessed with musicals, and it sort of rubbed off on me."

"Oh yeah?" I raise my eyebrows. "What's your favorite musical?"

"*Wicked,*" he says. A classic answer for anyone who says they love musicals but doesn't actually know any musicals. "I know, I know, typical. But it's really fucking good."

"I'm not knocking you," I say with a laugh. "I love *Wicked.*"

"What's yours?" he asks.

"*Les Misérables.*" I force a smile. "It's what got me into acting."

He nods. "Nice," he says. "Well, June, here's to hoping you get to be in *Les Mis* one day." He holds up his wineglass.

I raise my glass and clink his. "Here's hoping."

THEO AND I have our monthly lunch, and this time we go to Terra in Century City because it's across the street from the agency.

"How was that date you went on last week?" she asks as we take our seats.

Despite it being November, it's seventy-three degrees, so we get patio seats on the rooftop. There's not a cloud in the sky, so naturally Theo keeps her sunglasses on.

"Fine." I shrug, then glance at the menu, knowing already I'm going to get the little gem salad.

"That doesn't sound good," she says, eyes glued to her phone as she furiously types.

"There wasn't really anything wrong with him," I say. "Just . . . I don't know, didn't click."

"Fair," she says, still focused on her screen, which isn't unlike Theo. I'm used to it. After a few moments, she inhales, then places her phone face down on the table. "*So,*" she says, and takes off her glasses. "Have you been able to think about what you want to do? We've got to give an answer to A24 and let Dan know if you're passing."

"Yeah." I play with one of the rings on my middle finger. "I want to do *Les Mis.*"

"Okay," Theo says skeptically. "Did you read the script?"

"I did and it was *incredible,* Theo, it really was. It's a dream role but . . . I've been thinking about this a lot. I know I said I didn't want to go back to theater, but I *have* to do this. It was one of the hardest decisions I've had to make, but I'll regret it for the rest of my life if I don't."

"June," she says, and leans in closer, placing both of her forearms on the table. "My job is to get you the best opportunities possible for the career that *you* want. I am your cheerleader, and I will pave the way for you to shine. If you want to do *Les Mis,* then you're going to fucking do *Les Mis.*" She smiles and then sits back. "The only thing is, the show isn't covering relocation, so we need to talk about that." She takes a sip of her drink. "Any chance you have a place to stay in New York?"

Chapter 33

THE LAST TIME I LANDED AT JFK, MY HEART WAS RACING. I was scared for what was to come. This time, my heart is still racing, but I'm now exhilarated. This is a new chapter of my life and one where I don't know the ending.

With my three pieces of luggage at my side, I hail a cab, and the driver helps me put my things in the trunk.

"Okay, ma'am, where to?" he says in a thick Bronx accent.

"74 Perry Street, please," I say. "In the West Village."

"You got it." He plugs the address into his phone and starts driving. "So, are you visiting or are you home?"

Past the windshield ahead is a painting of the skyline, the sunset kissing the tops of skyscrapers and billboards. It's a stark difference from the hills and palm trees back in Los Angeles. The move is bittersweet. I owe a lot to LA and the person I've become in my time there. Maybe one day I'll be back but right now, I don't miss the city I spent the past five years in.

"I'm home," I say.

The brownstone looks exactly as it did when I left, except the two pumpkins set out front are the only ones left on Perry. I pick them up and toss them into the trash bin on the street and open the door. There's a comforting feeling when I enter the home, knowing that in fact it *is* home. *My home.* And I have no intention of selling it anymore. Both times I left this house I had no plans of coming back, and now it'll be waiting for me at the end of every day. It's a new beginning.

The sky is now dark, with fluffy clouds drifting past the window. While I'm grateful that a place so special to me is now mine, I'm overwhelmed by a pang of loss. Like something is missing. Someone is missing.

Mara let me know that all furniture is included except for a few art pieces that were on the wall that are now gone. Aside from that, everything looks the same as I left it. I take a quick glance at the kitchen, and the hairs on my arms stand when I clock the pasta maker sitting in the middle of the island, untouched. I place it deep in the cabinet below and start bringing my luggage up to my room.

The door to Adam's room is halfway open, and a teeny tiny part of my brain pictures the impossible. For a moment I hesitate, but then cautiously reach for the doorknob. Slowly, I open the door, hoping to see something I know isn't on the other side. The room feels cold, colder than the rest of the house. There's no trace of the person who used to call this room his. I close the door behind me with no intention of stepping back in there for a while.

THE PRESS FOR *Les Misérables* has been unlike anything I've ever seen. This much marketing for a Broadway show comes once in a blue moon. The billboards around the city are no joke, and our first month is sold out before we've even started rehearsals. It's mostly because of Philip Summers coming back to Broadway, but this is the first time *Les Mis* has been in New York in over a decade.

Four weeks before opening night, the cast and chorus come together for a table read. Since the show is a singing-only musical, it's expected that we all know our parts, and the table read is really us singing through the entire show.

It's nice seeing a familiar face in Dan as our director, and the principal cast is absolutely incredible. Philip Summers is just as kind as he is talented, and Anthony Batiste, who just came off *The King and I,* is playing opposite me as Marius. Tony Award winner Samantha Gates is Cosette, and Jon Dhingra is our Javert, whose voice is as powerful as ever.

After our run-through, Dan asks the chorus and principal cast to stay a few extra minutes. We sit in the empty rehearsal space, the very room I auditioned in. The bleak white walls and floors surround us, and Dan turns his chair around, hanging his arms over the back to face us.

"Everyone sounded incredible. I hope you all felt the energy today, because I know I did," he says, and the rest of us nod and agree. "I don't think I told any of you this, but *Les Misérables* is not only one of the most acclaimed musicals in history, but it's important to me for personal reasons. After coming out, things weren't easy. My family wasn't supportive, and it left me in a really, really dark place. I discovered *Les Mis* around this time and thought *how the hell can there be a musical where every single character is going through trauma?* It's heartbreaking, but it's beautiful.

"The music, this story, and the characters are more to me than just notes on a page. They're real, and it saved me. I want to do my very best to bring this musical back to life. Each person coming into that theater every night, I want to save them too."

Within moments, Philip starts clapping, and then Samantha, and then the rest of us join. Hearing the sounds of whistles and encouraging words, I feel like I'm finally where I need to be.

For the rest of the day, Dan's speech plays on repeat in my mind, leaving me to reflect on my career journey and how I've come full circle. Once I get home, I pull out my phone and scroll through my list of contacts.

Mom.

My thumb trembles, hovering over the call button, but I press it and hold my breath as I wait.

"Hello?" I hear my mom's voice on the other end, and it makes me instantly tear up. I don't remember the last time I spoke to her; it must have been years ago.

"Hey," I say, unable to actually call her *Mom.* "It's June."

"I saw," she says, not sounding particularly fazed that we're having a conversation. I can hear shuffling and cupboards opening and closing. I assume she's making dinner.

"Um, how are you?" I ask.

"Just home from work. A little tired," she says, the sound of the television now in the background.

"Are you still at the same place?" I ask, wondering if she's still working at the call center.

"Yeah," she says.

"Well, that's good," I say. "How's Ted?"

"Who?" she asks.

"Your boyfriend?" I say, praying that was his name.

"Oh . . . uh, who knows. I'm with John," she says. "We met in Vegas—good guy. He owns his own business."

"Oh," I say, not sure if she's wanting a congratulations.

"He's taking me to Mexico next month," she adds.

"Nice," I say, not knowing how to react to that. "I, uh, wanted to let you know I'm going to be in the *Les Misérables* revival. It opens a week before Christmas . . ." I wait for her to react, but I hear only more background noise from the TV. "I was wondering if you'd want to come?"

"Isn't that what you used to listen to all the time?"

"Yeah." I smile, surprised that she still remembers. "That's the one."

"Well, how about that? One of those chorus roles?" she asks.

My nostrils flare. "No, it's one of the leads. Éponine."

"Wow, well, congratulations." She sounds genuinely surprised, and the fact that she is only bothers me. "That must pay a lot."

I ignore her remark. "Do you want me to reserve you a ticket? You can stay at my place . . . I have a house now," I add, hoping maybe that will impress her.

"That's okay. I wouldn't be able to get time off work."

I crack the tops of my knuckles. "The show will be running for a while, you don't have to come now. It can be in a few months."

"June," she says, exasperated. "You're a grown woman now. You don't need your mom at your plays, do you?"

If ever my mom was going to give me words of encouragement, this was the opportunity.

"No, I guess not," I say. This is the part where I hang up,

where I get mad at myself for calling her. But instead, I smile. I smile because I know that I've gotten everything I can from this woman, and that's okay. "Thanks, Mom."

"Good luck to you, June," she says.

"You too."

ONE OF THE things I love about New York is how easy it is to find Chinese takeout. Back in LA, unless you're actually in Chinatown or ready to pay top dollar for Din Tai Fung, it's quite a challenge to order intoxicatingly delicious dan dan noodles and pork soup dumplings the minute you want them.

My favorite spot from when I used to live here is only a few blocks away from Perry and it's, thankfully, still open. After ordering, I take a seat off to the side at one of the empty tables by the door when I hear my name.

"June?"

A woman with blond hair under a bright red beanie, jeans, and a long navy wool coat is standing a few feet away from me. She's effortlessly New York stylish and striking with not an ounce of makeup, only the autumn night chill giving a slight pink glow to her cheeks. It takes me a moment longer than it should to realize who's in front of me.

Oh shit.

"Riley?"

"Oh my God! What are the chances?!" She opens her arms to me, and I stand up to give her a hug. "How are you?!"

"I'm good, I'm good." My voice comes out louder and higher than I've ever heard it. "How are *you*?"

"Oh, you know, same old." She waves a hand, her free-spirit energy still intact after all these years.

"Are you still painting?"

"Not exactly," she says, and tilts her head. "I opened up an art gallery with a friend of mine. I guess I put that business degree to use," she adds, laughing.

"Wow, that's amazing. Congratulations, Riley."

"How's LA? Are you still there?"

I shake my head. "No, actually I just moved back here a few weeks ago."

"No way! God, it's been so long. Well, New York is happy to have you back." She adjusts her tote bag. "I'm sure you've missed the two-dollar pork buns." She nods to the wall of mismatched photos of food and prices written in pink and blue highlighter.

"Oh, they're literally the only thing I've been eating this week."

Riley was always someone I never felt like I could be friends with. Our interactions could be only surface level, because it was, frankly, too painful for me. Now, as I strip away whatever insecurities got the best of me, she's someone whose energy is quite contagious.

"I heard you're in a new show too. Congrats!" She beams. "It's on my list but it's been so hard for me to watch any TV—you know how it is."

"Oh please, don't watch on my behalf." I shake my head. "Besides, it got canceled."

"Oh no—"

"It's fine, really," I say. "I'm coming back to Broadway actually, so it all worked out!"

"Oh, get out! What show? I'll have to make sure to get tickets," she says like she will genuinely be purchasing tickets.

"Les Misérables."

Her eyes widen. "Seriously?"

"Yeah, why?"

She shakes her head like she shouldn't have said anything. "No, it's just, that was Adam's favorite." She lets out a tired laugh.

For a brief moment, I'd allowed myself to separate her from him, so much so that hearing his name now feels like the wind being knocked out of me.

"Riley, I'm . . . I'm sorry about what happened," I tell her, because it feels like the right thing to say. If this were a friend, maybe I would ask why she ended things with Adam, but it actually doesn't matter anymore.

"Oh." She looks down and I know I hit a nerve. There's a manufactured smile plastered on her face when she finally looks up. "Yeah . . . well . . ."

"Are you okay?" I ask, hoping it comes out as genuinely as I mean it.

"Sorry." She shakes her head. "Yeah, I'm fine. It's just, um, seeing you again, talking about Adam . . . it's kind of all coming back. I know that sounds silly—"

"No," I say, realizing the irony. "I actually know exactly what you mean." The two of us stand in an awkward silence, and I know we're both thinking of the same person.

"I just wanted us both to be happy," she says sincerely. "And it turns out we couldn't be with each other."

Standing here with her, it's become apparent that I've been

looking at Riley as a woman who took something away from me, as someone who has something I never will. But the two of us are more similar than I thought. She's the same as me, as Chloe, as Lucia, as my mom . . . as Adam. We're all just people looking for love and doing the best we can.

That woman who was staring back at me in the photo, beaming in front of the Eiffel Tower, who thought her whole life would take a different trajectory, is now in the same Chinese restaurant as I am. After almost six years of harboring resentment toward a woman I barely know, I'm finally past it.

"I should've known after LA," she continues, and then quickly grabs my hand. "But, June, I hope you know I don't have any hard feelings."

I squint, trying to understand. "I'm sorry, LA?"

"When Adam went to LA," she clarifies, but I'm still confused.

"When did he go to LA?" I ask.

Riley frowns. "Did he not tell you?"

I look at her intently. "Tell me what?"

Her mouth opens and then closes; she looks just as disoriented as I feel.

"It was like, I don't know, three years ago?" She sits down at an empty table and I slowly follow. "We were in the thick of wedding planning and he said he needed to see you." Her eyes lock on mine, and I feel like the room is spinning. That would have been two years after I left. Two years since we last spoke. Years after I blocked his number, he still wanted to talk? She waits for me to say something, but I don't have anything in me. "He was never really the same after you left, so obviously, I told him of course. I thought he wanted to invite you in person or something . . . I didn't ask. He was gone for a couple of days and never told me how it went."

I interrupt her. "I never saw him, Riley."

She frowns, like this information is a missing piece in the story that either completes it or throws a wrench in it.

"He was distant when he came back. More than usual," she adds. "I mean, it's not like he did in the first place, but he *really* stopped caring about wedding details after that trip. Then six months before the wedding, I confronted him. All the signs pointed to him cheating on me or something."

"Was he?" I ask, afraid to find out the answer.

"I mean, not physically . . ." she says, her gaze fixed on me. She leans back in her chair and takes a deep breath. "Lesson learned. Never accept a proposal from a man when you know he's in love with someone else."

"He was . . ." I try to continue, but it feels like I have a golf ball in my throat, like my insides have been tied and I'm gasping for breath. "In love with someone else?" I ask, and she just nods. "Who?"

"Order for June!" one of the waiters calls out.

"Who do you think?" she says, but there's not an ounce of resentment.

I wave to the cashier. He brings me a white plastic bag filled with two Styrofoam takeout boxes.

"Riley, do you want this?" I inch the boxes closer to her. "There's something I have to do."

Chapter 34

I've never done track and field, or been one for jogging, so I can confidently say I'm running faster than I ever have in my life.

The closest subway stop is four blocks away and I just keep running. Running past all of the people, down the stairs, through the gate, and onto the train. I don't even sit down; I don't even know if I'm actually on the right line. Was it the C or the F train I needed to get on? It's not until we reach 86th that I know I'm good.

Once I emerge onto the busy streets of the Upper West Side, the sky is a deep pink, the sun starting to set. I continue to run down the block until I see Adam's condo and fly through the glass doors, which causes the security guard at the front desk to stand up.

"Hi, ma'am," he says cautiously. "Everything okay?"

"Yes," I say, gasping for air. I clutch my chest and take a few breaths in. Jesus Christ, my esophagus feels like it's literally on fire. It's burning. "I, um . . . need to go to, uh . . ." I try to remember Adam's unit number. "Um, Harper," I breathe out. "Adam Harper."

"Oh, Adam, of course. Are you on the list?" the man asks. *List? What list?* "What's your name, ma'am?"

"June Wood," I say. I'm seeing bright spots everywhere, which can't be a good sign.

He starts scrolling through his computer, frowns, and then flips through a notebook to his right.

"I'm sorry, I don't see your name here," he says. "I'll need confirmation from Mr. Harper before allowing you upstairs. Let me give him a call."

"Um . . . sure." I sigh and sit down on the bench across from him while he makes the phone call. The next fifteen seconds feel like fifteen minutes.

"Hey, Adam, it's Don. Are you home? Oh, sorry to bother you at work," he says, and I stand up. "We have a woman here . . . Sorry, ma'am, what's your name?"

"Actually, you know what?" I start making my way toward the doors. "That's okay. Thank you for your help!" I call over my shoulder.

It takes me twenty-six minutes to get to SoHo, and in that time, I sit on the subway with different scenarios weaving through my mind. What if Riley got it all wrong and Adam never went to LA? What if he did go but it wasn't to see me? What if he's not even at work anymore? What if he never wants to talk to me again? All highly feasible options.

When I get to Alden, there's a pretty decent crowd waiting by the door. An instrumental version "All I Want for Christmas Is You" plays on the speakers and there's a subtle display of garland wrapped around the edges of the hostess stand. I push through about five or six people, and the hostess, who isn't the same person who was here last time, gives me a smile.

"I'm sorry, ma'am, you're just going to have to wait a second," the hostess says.

"Oh no, I'm sorry," I breathe out. "I don't want a table."

"You're still going to have to wait a second—"

"No, look, I'm here for Adam Harper," I say. "He's the owner."

"Yes, I'm aware of Adam Harper. If you could just wait one moment, please." She pulls out two menus and hands them to another hostess. "These two will be going to table fifty-four." She gestures to a couple behind me, who does not look impressed.

The other hostess brings them into the restaurant, and then a man wearing a suit and tie strides toward me. He looks like he's in his mid-forties, bald, only slightly intimidating. I'm assuming he's the manager.

"Hi there." He smiles in a somewhat condescending way. "Is there something I can help you with?"

"Hi, yes, I'm looking for Adam Harper," I say for what feels like the fiftieth time today.

"He's occupied at the moment. Is he expecting you?" the man asks.

"Well, no, not exactly," I say. "But if you could just tell him that June is here—"

"We can let him know, but unfortunately, we can't guarantee when he'll be able to come out. We're going to have to ask you to step outside."

"Step outside?" I scrunch my face. "Are you kicking me out?"

"Ma'am, we just kindly ask—"

"Okay, seriously, *why* does everyone keep calling me *ma'am*?" I say loud enough that some people in the restaurant turn their heads.

"*Miss,*" the man says.

"Look, I'm cold, I'm tired, I didn't eat my dinner, and I'm sweaty as fuck, and I just need to talk to Adam for five minutes!" I shriek.

"Just calm down, please," he says.

"I'm calm!" I say in a way that absolutely negates my point. "I just don't understand what the problem is—he's not the president. It's not like I'm some Alden groupie who wants to take a photo with him. I just have a mild emergency, and I need to speak with Adam."

"Okay, you're going to need to step outside," he says, gesturing to the front doors.

Then a familiar silhouette in the distance starts walking toward the kitchen across a sea of people. It's him. A head of dark hair and broad shoulders. My heart is thundering in my chest, faster and faster until I feel every pulse throughout my body.

"Adam!" I call out over the music, over the bald man in front of me, over the crowd, over the clanking of pots and pans in the kitchen.

My eyes are only on him, so that I don't realize until I *feel it* that someone's hand is around my arm and guiding me backward toward the door. As I'm being ushered out, Adam's head turns in our direction, and it takes almost a fraction of a second before he's rushing toward us.

"Hey, *whoa, whoa.* Colin, what's going on?" he says to the manager, whom I guess I can now call Colin.

"Apologies for the scene—we were just sorting this out." Colin continues to guide me toward the door, and I'm too stunned to say anything.

"No, that's not necessary. And please, you can let go." He motions to my arm. Colin immediately releases his grip and gives him a concerned look, and after a reassuring nod from Adam he heads back toward the hostess stand. Before I know it, everyone goes back to business as usual. "I'm sorry about that," Adam says to me.

"It's fine." I adjust my coat.

"Is everything okay?" he asks with a genuine look of concern on his face.

"Yeah." I nod. Finally, I have Adam to myself. I've been chasing him down for what feels like half the day and now he's in front of me and I don't know what to say. "Sorry, I didn't mean to scare you or anything, but I was in the neighborhood and . . . thought I would say hi."

"Right." Adam gives me a half smile. "Well, it's a little busy so I should probably get back. Thanks for stopping by." He turns.

"Why didn't you tell me you came to LA?" I say, and when he stops I know he heard me.

He turns around. "How did you know about that?"

"Does it matter?" I say.

He stares at me, struggling to read between the lines. He furrows his brow and sighs. "Why are you here, June?"

"If you were there for some other reason and I'm misunderstanding everything, then that's fine. I'll leave it."

"I came to see you," he says.

I take a step toward him. "Why?"

"Look, can we—" He moves aside to let some people enter. "Can we do this outside?"

Fine—I guess having this conversation at the front of his restaurant probably isn't the best look. I nod and watch as he walks down the hallway past the kitchen, disappearing behind a back door. For a *brief* moment, I wonder if he's abandoned me, but then catch my breath when he emerges with a jacket on.

We start walking east. It's dark and freezing outside so I reach into my bag and put my hat back on while Adam wraps his scarf tighter around his neck. The streets of SoHo are adorned with shimmering lights, the air filled with the smell of cinnamon from somewhere far off.

"Why did you come to LA?" I ask him again.

"I never wanted to marry Riley," he says, his words heavy. "We were looking at venues and guest lists and it was becoming too real. I needed to see you. I just . . . I couldn't go through with something like that without seeing you again. I know you told me to leave you alone, but I needed to know if . . ." He shakes his head. "So, I asked Chloe where you were staying . . . I didn't tell her I was going, just said I needed to send you some stuff as a surprise and I lost your address." He continues breathlessly, "I was outside your building, debating whether or not I should knock on the door, which was so fucking stupid, because I flew all the way there and planned it.

"Anyway, I saw the two of you—you and Liam—going inside. You were coming out of the car, carrying groceries. That was really it. You didn't do anything out of the ordinary, but just seeing you with someone else, happy, living your new life . . . I don't know, I didn't want to ruin that."

Riley was right. He looked for me.

"And then what?" I ask.

"When I came back, Riley said I was being distant . . . different," he says like he's trying to remember the words she used. "All I kept telling myself was *if June can be happy with someone else, so can I.* But she saw through it . . . That's why she ended it."

"I wasn't happy, Adam," I say, all the pieces starting to fall into place and my throat tightening. It's like it was yesterday—I can remember the endless nights of tears from missing him, from running away, from losing my life.

"Then why didn't you come back?" he asks again, like he knows my career wasn't the only reason.

"I didn't think there was anything to come back to," I say. "I didn't know you wanted me too."

"God, June, *of course* I did. You broke my fucking heart." His voice cracks. "I was trying to give you your space, let you figure out what you needed to. I didn't want to push you, and then before I knew it, we were with other people and I thought you were happy . . . that you'd moved on. That it was done."

"Is that why you proposed?" I say.

He nods, like he's afraid of what I might think of him if I knew the truth.

"Why didn't you tell me all of this?" I move closer to him.

"Because I was a coward," he says. "I stayed in a relationship for years that I didn't want to be in and wasted her time . . . and I fucking hate that I did that. I'm not proud of it, and I didn't want you to see me that way."

"Adam, relationships end, and that doesn't mean they wasted anyone's time." We continue walking, with no destination in mind.

"No, I did," he says like he's already had this argument many times before. "Because I knew I loved someone else and did it anyway."

He says it like it's already passed. Like he's made his peace with the fact that it's gone. *Loved.*

"Adam . . ."

"I answered your questions, June." He turns to me. "You go to my apartment, come to my work . . . Was this all about Riley?"

"No," I say, and shake my head. "It was never about her. It was about me and my insecurities and my fears and not knowing how to deal with that. That's why I left."

He looks at me intently. "What were you scared of?"

"That I wasn't good enough for you," I say.

We turn the corner onto one of the empty residential streets. It's quieter, but with all the Christmas lights, there's a hazy glow behind Adam.

"How do you know what I want? What's good enough for me?" he asks.

"You want what your parents had," I say, throwing his own words back at him. Words I never forgot. "You want a family and a marriage and things that I couldn't give you."

He looks at me in disbelief. "You really don't get it, do you? I want *you,*" he says. "The years I spent with you were the happiest I've ever been. I chased that feeling and I couldn't find it. So no, I don't care about a family and a marriage, or any of those things I thought were important. I care about being with someone who makes me happy. In whatever way they want to be with me."

I'm shivering and my fingers feel numb, but there's a warmth pooling inside of me. I stop walking and turn to face him.

"The last time I told you how I felt, it ruined everything," he continues, and I think about that night on the couch. I think about that night often. "Seeing you in Mara's office, I wanted so badly to just tell you all of this, lay everything out there, but you were *here.*" He looks at me like he can't believe I'm even standing in front of him. "You were *back,* and *we* were back. There was a chance to do this all over again, and I didn't want to fuck it up. I didn't want to let you go. I didn't want you to leave."

"Why were you so certain I was going to leave?" I ask helplessly.

"History?" He shrugs slightly.

There's a pain deep in my core that spreads throughout my body. It hits my hands and my feet, and finally lodges itself in my throat. The realization is too much to bear. I did to Adam what people did to me my entire life.

Years of chasing approval from my mother, figuring out why my father didn't stay; it always felt like it was because I wasn't good enough. I now see that it was never about *me.* It was about *them. Their* insecurities, *their* fears, and *their* reasons were out of my control. It feels as if I'm looking into a mirror and seeing the same look on Adam's face that I'm so familiar with in myself.

I never want Adam to feel like he's not good enough.

"After I left New York I felt different . . . unhappy. I never knew why." I tremble. "I was convinced it was because I hated LA or maybe I just wasn't cut out to be an actress. Now I have my dream role and my dream house in my favorite city in the world and I'm *still* unhappy." My voice cracks, and the view of him blurs through my tears. "Adam, I've loved you for eleven years and I'm positive I'm going to love you for the next eleven after that, and after that. My whole life I've been afraid of losing what I love . . . and that's why I left. Because maybe if I left first it would be easier. I was trying to protect myself, and instead everything I was afraid of happening to me, I did to you."

I bring my palm to wipe at the sheen of wetness on my cheeks. "You are my person, Adam, my *home,* and I know I fucked this up. I didn't deserve a second chance, and I definitely don't deserve a third one. I'm not asking you to forgive me. I just want you to know that I'm sorry. I'm so sorry."

He frowns, and I'm bracing myself for him to say it's too late, that I've broken his heart too many times and that we're better off as friends. I couldn't blame him.

"Adam?" I plead, hoping he'll say something.

"June . . ." There's a groove in between his brows and his eyes are darting back and forth between mine. "Don't you know by now that it's *you*? It will *always* be you."

A smile flickers on my face and a sound of disbelief leaps out of me. I cover my mouth in embarrassment. Maybe everything happened the way it was supposed to. Maybe the things worth having in life *aren't* supposed to come easy. Despite the years apart, Adam and I have found our way back. We *want* to love each other and now we can.

The way we deserve to be loved.

"I guess I owe you an apology too," he says.

"For what?" I sniff.

"I was afraid too." He holds my hands, and the feeling melts me. "I always knew how I felt, yet I was afraid to tell you."

"And how is that again?" I ask, because I need to hear Adam say it. I need to know this isn't a dream.

"That I love you, June." He holds my face. "And no matter how hard I try, I'm not capable of loving anyone else the same way."

My hands reach for Adam's coat, and I pull myself closer into him, letting the warmth of his body move into mine. His arms wrap around me, and when we kiss, everything is worth it. All the nights we went into our respective bedrooms, watching each other go on dates with other people, denying our feelings, and all the years apart. It was worth it.

"You gave up the house," I say softly.

"It was never about the money, June."

"It wasn't?"

"I mean, *a little.*" He lets out a small chuckle. "But I would've done it for free."

Another laugh escapes, and I pull Adam into another kiss. A kiss that, more than anything else, feels like home.

"I have a proposition." I smile, and he raises his eyebrow. "What if we live together?"

Chapter 35

After three demanding, challenging, and incredibly rewarding weeks of rehearsal, it's opening night. My dressing room is shared with Samantha, who plays Cosette, and Dhruva, who plays Fantine. While we get into costume, you can hear vibrations of aahhhs and various vocal warm-ups from the rest of the cast throughout backstage.

"Is everyone ready?" Dhruva asks while Sam zips up her dress. "My heart's racing. Twenty years doing this, and opening night never gets easier."

"We got this!" Sam grabs her arms and gives her a playful shake. "What about you, June? How are the nerves, being in front of an audience again?"

"I'm actually excited." I look at them both in the mirror while powdering my face. "It's the only thing I actually *haven't* been nervous about in a long time."

Dhruva pulls us all into a group hug and we set our heads together, making sure not to move the microphones taped to our foreheads. "Here's to a killer opening night, and the longest run on Broadway!"

"Dhru!" Sam gasps. "Don't jinx it!"

"I'm not jinxing!" She laughs. "I'm manifesting!"

Max, our stage manager, quickly knocks on our open door, clipboard in hand and headset on.

"Ten minutes to curtain."

Sam decides to stay behind and continue getting ready, but I walk over to the wings to watch the opening number. There are murmurs of *break a leg* and *good luck* rippling through the hallways and the wings. I find a spot off to the side and once the orchestra starts playing that first note, there's a chill throughout my body. Hearing the set of chords that I used to listen to almost every night in my childhood bedroom feels blissfully overwhelming. The curtains finally rise and we're in it. We're on a three-hour adventure, and it's riveting.

Peering into the audience, I analyze each person's face, each person who paid an arm and a leg for these tickets a week before Christmas. Every person is here hoping to escape to a different world for one night, a world that we're going to bring to life for them.

There's an older couple, smartly dressed in the front row, who I have a feeling live in the wealthy part of Manhattan and have Broadway season passes. Then a family with two young kids who look about thirteen and seventeen. I assume they're from out of town visiting New York for the holidays. In a row behind them, a group of women in their mid-thirties. And in the middle section, a head of dark hair and hazel eyes.

Adam is staring intently at the stage, and to his left are Sarah and Ford, and to his right, Chloe and Lucia. I wipe a tear pooling in the corner of my eye as I study each of their faces. *This is my family.*

Matt, one of the ensemble cast, elbows me after the first song is over. "Hey, you good?"

"I'm great." I sniff. "Break a leg," I whisper, and hurry backstage.

For the rest of the show, I'm able to completely immerse myself in my character, putting anyone who's watching out of my mind. At the top of the second act is my time to sing "On My Own." I walk to center stage, the spotlight follows me, and the beginning notes from the piano below echo throughout the entire theater.

The words and the music fill me. I feel like a candle that's never been lit until this very moment. I stand in place the entire song, my voice carrying the melody, and the audience watches me light up. When the orchestra stops, I allow myself to look at Adam for an instant.

In this moment, there's nobody else in the theater except the two of us.

The final curtain is called, and it's almost like a wedding. Months of buildup and work toward one event and it's suddenly over in the blink of an eye. Except I'm lucky that I get to do it over and over again.

We all celebrate with a toast backstage, and some of the cast leave through the stage door and meet the fans who are patiently waiting to take pictures. After removing my makeup and changing into an oversized knit cardigan and jeans, I walk out to the theater lobby with the remaining cast to greet our family and friends.

My group is standing off to the left, chatting and laughing. I wish I could take a snapshot of this moment.

As I hurry down the stairs, Chloe is the first one who spots me.

"Juuuuune!" she sings, holding her arms open for me to jump into. My body collides into hers and she squeezes me. We're acting like two teenagers and I really don't care. "YOU. WERE. INCREDIBLE."

Lucia hugs me next, with a big smile. "June, I cannot believe how amazing the show was—everyone was absolutely brilliant. I actually started to tear up during 'A Little Fall of Rain.'"

"Lucia, thank you so much." I squeeze her hand and then lock eyes with Ford.

"Whad'ya think, Ford?"

"I think I'm going to have to ask for your autograph," he says. "And walk over to the box office and get myself another ticket. Holy hell, I cannot wait to watch it again."

"Really?" My eyes light up.

"I swear. You killed it, kid." He pulls me in for another hug and gives me a kiss on top of my head. He's wearing a cashmere sweater with a dress shirt underneath, and I spot two tiny black cuff links with gold trim and engraved music notes.

"Congratulations, June!" Sarah wraps her arms around me—she's far taller than I am now and I almost can't believe how grown-up she looks. She has dark, wavy brown hair and bangs and possesses an effortless beauty. She looks just like her mom. "The show is amazing!"

"You really liked it?" I ask.

"Obviously I liked it! Also"—she leans in closer—"there's someone in the chorus and I'm dying to know if he's single . . ."

"Who?" My eyes widen. She pulls open her *Playbill* and points to Matt. "Yes. We'll talk." I squeeze her elbow and then lock eyes with Adam.

"Hi," he says.

"Hi," I say.

"Did I ever tell you how much I love you?" He wraps his arms around my waist as I loop mine around his neck.

I shake my head. "I don't think you did today."

"I love you and you are fucking amazing." He gives me a kiss. "Congratulations, babe."

"I love you," I say, knowing I will never get tired of the words and all the different ways it can come out of my mouth.

Chloe squeezes my arm. "Sorry, lovebirds, we've got to head back to Teddy."

"Give him a hug for us," Adam says.

"Congratulations again, June," Lucia says, and gives me another hug. "Seriously, I cannot believe we were able to watch this on opening night. It's going to be the biggest show of the season."

Sarah nudges Adam with her body. "We should probably get going too. We'll see you all at New Year's, right?"

"Yes! See you there." Chloe gives her a kiss on the cheek and points a finger at Ford. "Ford, you better not skip out," Chloe warns. "You are staying awake until the ball drops."

"Don't you worry, Teddy and I will both be up past our bedtimes." He laughs.

It'll be our first New Year's Eve all together in Connecticut, and nothing could make me happier than seeing Ford on babysitting duty.

"Sarah, are you driving?" Adam asks as he helps Ford put on his coat.

"Yeah," she nods.

"Okay, get home safe." He gives Sarah and Ford a kiss, and I do the same. "We'll see you on Christmas."

Once everyone leaves, I hear my name being called behind me and Adam and I turn around.

"June!" Dan waves. He's been giving everyone congratulatory words all evening, but this is the first time we're face-to-face. "'On My Own' was heart-wrenching," He gives me a hug and then shakes Adam's hand. "Nice to see you again, Adam. How'd you like it?"

"It was phenomenal, Dan," Adam says. "Huge congratulations. You outdid yourself."

"Seriously," I say, smiling at Dan. "None of this would be possible without you."

"Well, that's not entirely true." Dan turns to Adam. "I feel like I owe you a little thank-you."

Adam raises an eyebrow. "For what?"

"Do you remember when I was at Alden last year for that dinner with Maureen and Scott?"

Adam frowns for a moment and then nods, remembering. "Oh yeah, yeah."

"So, you briefly mentioned the *Rent* revival." Dan looks at me. "I swear, it was the quickest mention . . . and how you were a fan of June's performance. I totally forgot about her until you brought her up." He waves a hand. "Anyway, I kept your name in the back of my mind for a rainy day . . . or for a little fall of rain." He winks, very proud of himself for the *Les Mis* pun.

My head turns to Adam, mouth open. "You said that?"

"I was a big fan." He shrugs. "Still am."

Someone across the way calls out to Dan and he holds up a finger to them and squeezes my arm. "June, you need to get some rest. Or celebrate. Whatever you need to do. But I'll see you here at noon tomorrow. Congratulations again." He presses his cheek against mine in an air kiss.

"See you tomorrow," I say.

Through the crowd of people, Theo emerges, a huge smile plastered on her face. "There she is!"

"Theo." I give her the tightest hug I can. "I'm so happy you were able to make it out."

"Are you kidding?" she says. "I wouldn't miss this for the world. Plus, I will take any opportunity I can get for my husband to watch the kids."

I motion to Adam beside me. "And I'm not sure if you remember Adam?"

"Of course—Manhattan for Theater Gala." She goes up on her toes to give him a hug. "How are you?"

"I'm great. Nice to see you again, Theo," he says.

"I hope you're taking care of June. LA misses her."

"He is," I interject before he can say anything, and he just gently rubs my back.

"*So.*" Theo takes a deep breath in and gives me a *let's talk business for a second* look. "I have an update on *Me and You.*"

"Oh." I raise my eyebrows. "Okay . . ."

"The director's deal fell through," she says.

"Wow, that's—"

She nods to tell me she's not finished. "Script problems, budget started going over, execs were shuffled around." She takes a breath. "The whole thing fell apart."

"Shit . . ." I look up at Adam and then back to Theo.

"You made the right choice." She shrugs a shoulder.

"God, Theo." I shake my head in disbelief. "Thank you for everything."

"You make my job easy," she says, squeezing my hand. "Now enjoy your night, celebrate all the things. I'm on a 5 A.M. flight tomorrow, so I will email you next week, okay?"

"Yes, perfect. Thank you again."

"Nice seeing you again, Theo." Adam gives her a hug before she disappears back into the crowd, and then turns to me. "Wow, okay. How are you feeling?"

This is probably the biggest high I've ever been on in my entire life. I jump into Adam's arms. Thankfully he has good reflexes and catches me, and we stand there for a few seconds just hugging. Lately it's hard to list what I'm even thankful for—it would be a laundry list. But mostly, I'm grateful for this whole, incredible new chapter of my life.

"I'm feeling really good." I start to tear up.

"Do you want to celebrate?" he asks. "Or do you want to sleep?"

"I want a cheeseburger with onion rings," I say.

"Then a cheeseburger and onion rings you shall get." He carefully sets me down. "Also I meant to tell you: Mara called me earlier."

"Oh yeah?" I zip up my coat and put my hat on.

"The new paperwork is all finalized." He opens the door for me, and we walk into the chilly December air.

A huge smile takes over my face. "Really?"

He nods and holds my hand. "*We* are officially homeowners."

I stop in front of him and stand on my toes to give him a kiss. "You know what I'm thinking?" I say against his lips.

"Mhm?"

"I think we should go home and celebrate."

Chapter 36

6 YEARS LATER

THERE ARE SMALL MARKINGS INSIDE ONE OF THE UPSTAIRS closets that catch my eye. Not marked with a pen or pencil, but scratched in. Each a few inches apart.

"I've never noticed this before," I call out over my shoulder, and Adam crouches down beside me to get a better view.

"They look like growth markings," he says.

"Interesting." I run my fingers gently over the indents as if they are braille.

"Do you think they're from the little girl ghost who lived here before us?" he asks.

"*Adam.*" I hit his leg, and he laughs. "It's weird to think of anyone else living here."

He stands and pulls me up with him. "You okay?"

My eyes scan the empty bedroom—the coat of paint on the wall from four years ago, the discolored patch on the floor from a wine spill fourteen years ago. Without all of the furniture, everything feels a lot smaller. The last time I saw the place like this, I was a girl in my early twenties just trying to find a roof over my head.

I nod yes. "Are you?"

"Yeah." He puts his arm around me and kisses the top of my head. "Are you hungry?"

"Always."

"Dinner's almost ready." He gives my waist a gentle squeeze and heads down the stairs.

I'm left by myself and walk over to the window, the same window I'm used to looking at every morning when I wake up. The leaves are a deep red and orange right now, and I see our neighbors across the street bundled up in their jackets, putting out their pumpkins and Halloween decorations.

Stepping out to the hallway, I peek inside the second bedroom, which is also empty aside from a few boxes full of books and a single desk. Although it's been our office for years, it will always be Adam's room to me.

I graze the banister as I head down the stairs. The dark oak under my fingertips. It's crazy to think this wood will be here a lifetime after us. I'm starting to appreciate little details I've never noticed before.

All that's left in the living room are our couch and TV, still mounted because Adam and I agreed those aren't being moved until the last possible moment. There's an open box on top of the bay window seat and I check it to see if it's packed up enough to be sealed. Inside sits a framed Polaroid photo that Ford took on our wedding day.

We woke up on a Tuesday morning, I turned to Adam, still

half asleep, and he said *I want to marry you.* He had a ring ready and once I said *me too* neither of us could wait for a wedding. That Friday, we called Ford, Sarah, Chloe, Lucia, and Robby and told them to come to City Hall, and they dropped everything to attend. Afterward, we sent a group text to our other friends, sharing that we'd just gotten married and inviting whoever was free to come celebrate with us at our favorite bar on Bleecker.

Adam and I are shoving two white cupcakes in each other's faces and laughing. To this day, it's my favorite photo. Behind it are a few other framed snapshots, Adam's ticket to the opening night of *Les Misérables,* the selfie we took at Central Park, and a group photo of everyone at Audrey's, the restaurant Adam opened last year in East LA. It's no Alden by any means; at capacity it holds only fifty people. It's the hole-in-the-wall spot only locals know of, but it turns out that was the dream all along.

Carefully, I place the contents back in the box next to my Bubble Wrapped Tony Award for best actress in a musical. Something I will never get over.

Adam emerges, holding a black file box under his arm. "Babe, let's add this to the stuff in the office. It was with the donation pile."

"What is that?" I take it from him and sit on the couch.

"For the house," he says. "We have all the digital copies, but just in case."

Adam is still a true twentieth-century man.

"Oh jeez." A puff of air bursts out of me as I see the very folder Mara handed to me the day ownership was transferred.

"This feels like a lifetime ago . . . Remember when you forfeited ownership and didn't tell me?"

"Mmm." Adam nods. "Remember when you moved to another state and didn't tell me?"

I tuck away a smile and swat his leg.

"Wait, what's this?" I pull out a small white envelope with *Adam and June* handwritten on the front.

Adam frowns. "I've never seen that."

Flipping the envelope over, I open it and give Adam a tentative look when I pull out what's inside.

Adam and June,

Last month I received my official diagnosis that I have Alzheimer's. Please don't feel sorry for me. By the time you read this, it will be long past the point of condolences.

The reason I'm writing you this is because I forgot how I celebrated my 30th birthday. I've been searching my brain and I can't remember. I don't remember the name of my high school English teacher, and I don't remember what my grandmother looks like. The memories are lost.

What's not lost is my memory of the two of you. I remember the lasagna Adam would make me. I also remember watching June singing onstage. I remember how you treated me. These memories are few and far between, but they're what are important to me right now. It's been some years since I've seen you both, and while I don't know what you're doing now, I don't doubt you're doing all the things you wanted.

I'm told I need to make a plan for 74 Perry Street. I have no more family, no children, no next of kin, no friends younger than retirement . . . I promise it's not as depressing as it sounds . . . I'm leaving it to the two of you. You two loved that house as much as I and the generations before me did. It's safe to say you're the rightful owners. I don't expect you to pass it down, but I trust you'll care for it and one day find the right people to live within those walls.

Thank you for your kindness and showing me that there's love out there in this world. I hope you cherish it and continue to make memories that I no longer can.

Stanley

My throat tightens and I wipe the tears on my cheeks with the back of my hand. Adam pulls me in close as I bury my face into his chest.

"You okay?" he asks.

I nod and sniff. "I can't believe we never saw this."

"It's a beautiful letter." Adam rubs his thumb over my shoulder as we sit in silence. The sound of the oven timer goes off and the two of us adjust. "You sure you're okay?"

"Yeah," I say, and Adam nods and heads back into the kitchen. "I'll keep this in a special place." I pick up the file box and place it with our belongings under the fireplace and tuck Stanley's letter in with our wedding photo.

Adam returns, holding two plates of lasagna. The smell of garlic and beef fills up the room.

"Want to watch a movie?" he asks.

"Yes, please." I fall onto the couch and grab the plates from him. I gesture to a giant throw blanket in a box. "Can you pass me the blanket over there? It's freezing."

"Want me to turn on the heat?" He tosses it over to me.

"No, I'm good." I shiver and lay out the blanket on the couch. "I should take advantage of being cold before we move. I can't believe it's three days away."

"Are you nervous?"

It's been six years since I've been in a television show, and I'm at the point in my life when I know I can go back to the theater if I want. But now I want to try the things that scare me. I'm ready to go back to TV.

"I think I'm more excited than anything." I cut into my lasagna and let the steam air out. I turn on the TV and the first thing that's served to us is *My Best Friend's Wedding*. "Oh my God, when was the last time you watched this?"

His eyes go wide like he's thinking and he pushes his glasses up. "Man, I don't know. I think when *we* watched it? I just remember Julia Roberts is the villain."

"She's not the villain," I say through a mouthful of pasta. "She's just in love with her best friend and she doesn't tell him until it's too late." He turns to me, and I see the corner of his mouth curve up. "Shut up." I nudge him and press play.

If you were to see a snapshot of this moment, you might be able to guess what's happening. Us eating lasagna while watching a rom-com. Me reciting my lines in my head while Adam thinks of a new dish for his restaurant. A brownstone sitting in the middle of the West Village on a crisp autumn evening. It's a moment in time that looks just like one from years before, but it's not. It's different this time.

Acknowledgments

THIS IS THE FIRST BOOK I'VE EVER WRITTEN, AND IT WOULD simply not exist without the support of many, many people.

To my husband, Jeff Richard, thank you. Thank you for (1) choosing me to spend every day by your side and (2) reading drafts upon drafts . . . upon drafts and listening to me talk about June and Adam for months upon months. Thank you for every note, every encouraging word, putting up with me writing in our kitchen every morning at 5 A.M., and telling me I'm a writer when I didn't believe it. Thank you for supporting me through truly every single thing I do. I love you.

To my agent and a dream of a human being, Samantha Fabien. You read this story when it was much different and still saw the potential. Your notes gave June and Adam their best chance and made me a stronger writer. For that, I am forever grateful. Thank you for trusting me and my brain. I am utterly grateful that you see me worthy of being part of your talented roster. You are the Theo to my June, and I'm so incredibly excited for this journey we're about to go on together.

To my editor, Alicia Clancy. Thank you, thank you, thank you. Thank you for seeing something in this story, for being as obsessed with June and Adam as I am. Thank you for believing in my abilities as a writer, and for trusting that I could get this book where it needed to be within the timeline we had. Your notes were a game changer—you forced me to tap into emotions and creativity in ways I could never have done on my own. Thank you for shaping me into a writer I didn't know I was capable of being.

To the entire Penguin Random House and Bantam Dell team: Deborah Sun de la Cruz, Marion Garner, Jean Slaughter, Catherine Knowles, Emma Ingram, Emily Siegmund, Taylor Noel, Kimberly Hovey, Emily Isayeff, Hope Hathcock, Caitlin Van Dusen, Jenny Abella, and Megan Whalen. Thank you for all that you do for the writing community and thank you for publishing this book. To the Root Literary team, Holly Root and Taylor Haggerty, thank you for bringing me into the family. It's an honor to take a position alongside some of my favorite titles and authors.

Melinda Rosenberg, the journey from the inception of this story to completing my first draft was a very special time in my life; thank you for being a part of it, and for everything. Olga Khaminwa, you read a very early draft of this and gave me nothing but game-changing notes. Thank you. Thank you for the car rides (which I believe were true moments of manifestation) and for that safe space. Rachel Kitch, oh Lord, you have kept me sane through all of it. For that, I owe you so much. Jackie Garcia, you have changed my life in *so* many ways. Above all, I'm thankful for your friendship and constant support in all I do. Traci Doromal, thank you for reading literally anything I write (even the questionable Bennifer fanfics). Jen Nugent, Bela Sullivan, and Steph Sagala, I guess this all really started with my self-insert Julie fanfic in eighth grade. Thank you for being my first-ever readers. Marilee Devries, Cassandra Juradinho, and Teri Hart, thank you for being you. Without your friendship I wouldn't be able to do half of the things I do.

To Irene Bischofberger, Amy Yasbeck, Saakshi Dhingra, Shelby Calvert, Leonor Castro, Bridget FitzGibbons, Candice Heath, Sarah Sather, Kathryn Flaschner, Miriam Salamah, Bronwen Keyes-Bevan, Natalie Sue, Kayla Olson, Ande Pliego, Yolanda Chow, Gretchen Schreiber, Naina Kumar, Elissa Sussman, Katharine Johnson, Alexa D'Ambrosio, Gabriella Gamez, Micky Garcia, Sarah Chung, Camille Duet, Sarah Adams, Toni Francis, Kristen Berry, Amy Lea, Karina Evans, and Jessica Joyce . . . each of you in your own way has contributed to my writing journey, whether through reading this book when it was barely a story, or through your support, inspiration, or words of encouragement. Thank you.

To my mom, Sylvia, and my dad, Joe, and Essie and Murray. Thank you for always supporting me, especially when I told you from out of nowhere, "I wrote a book," and you all had no idea I even liked writing. Mom, I could not do half the things I do without you. I love you so incredibly much, and I don't tell you that every day, but I hope writing it in this book for the world to see makes up for it. Kenickie, I can't believe we're here. To Tita Susan, Tita Sonia, Tito Jay Arr, Alex, Anjelica, Steph, Jen, Andrew, John, and the rest of my incredibly supportive family (I'm Filipino, so you know there are too many to mention), thank you.

To my community theater family from the days of my youth (especially the *Les Mis* company), who clearly made an impact on me, to the TC Discord (Ashlee, Ruby, Kandace, Monica,

Chelsea, and Gio), who know very well what this story means to me and to all of us, to anyone who's ever read and left lovely reviews on my incredibly niche fanfics, to John and Joyce, and to anyone else I may have missed, thank you.

Also, Annie. I love you more than anything. Thank you for keeping my lap warm.

Lastly, to YOU, the reader. Thank you not only for reading this entire story, but for taking the extra time to read these acknowledgments. I appreciate you so very much for deciding to start this book and staying with it until the very end. I'm excited to share more beautiful love stories with you.

Joss Richard (she/her) is an editorial and social director who's worked at companies such as Hello Sunshine and Reese's Book Club, the Walt Disney Company, *The Ellen DeGeneres Show,* Netflix, and Paramount. She's also the creator and host of *Three's Company, Too: A Rewatch Podcast,* and has been formally recognized with a Daytime Emmy Award. Born in Toronto, Ontario, to Filipino immigrant parents, Richard currently lives and works in Los Angeles, California.

jossrichard.com
Instagram: @joss.richard

About the Type

This book was set in Caslon, a typeface first designed in 1722 by William Caslon (1692–1766). Its widespread use by most English printers in the early eighteenth century soon supplanted the Dutch typefaces that had formerly prevailed. The roman is considered a "workhorse" typeface due to its pleasant, open appearance, while the italic is exceedingly decorative.